GW00384107

# FLOREAT LUX

Robert Brace

This is a work of fiction. All of the characters, organizations, and events portrayed in this novel are either the products of the author's imagination or are used fictitiously.



Front cover photograph: Odalisque © Robert Brace
Back cover photograph: River Windrush, upstream of Bourton-on-the-Water © Robert Brace

Cover design by the author.

First Edition: September 2021

Library of Congress Control Number: 2021910705

ISBN 978-1-7373192-0-7

Privately published, September 2021, New York.

www.RobertBraceAuthor.com

# FLOREAT
# LUX

*And to the woman were gyven two wynges of a great egle, that she myght flee into the wyldernes, in to her place, where she is nourysshed for a tyme, tymes, and halfe a tyme, from the presence of the serpent.*

—Revelation 12:14 (Taverner's 1539 Version)

*I hope to paint something that will ruin the appetite of every son of a bitch who ever eats in that room.*

—Mark Rothko

# I

A WOMAN STANDS with a letter in her hand. She stares ahead with an expression of mild discontent: whatever she has just read did not please her. An exhalation of frustration or annoyance, and her breath mists: it is a cold room.

She puts aside the letter and takes up the envelope.

The stamp is printed without a country of origin, a philatelic peculiarity that identifies it as British. On the lower left is a dark blue 'Royal Mail' sticker, declaring that the envelope is to be delivered *par avion*. No return address, like the letter. The stamp has been franked, and she can make out the words *Marylebone, London* forming an arc across the top, but the date below is blurred. Her name and address are written in the same ragged hand as the note—whatever reason the author chose to use old-fashioned nib and ink, it was not to display penmanship. On the back are the remains of a wax seal, bright vermillion, and she wishes now that she had photographed the impression before breaking it.

A beast of some sort, she thinks. Horned.

The paper matches that of the letter, high quality, heavy stock, and the interior is lined with an overlay of gold foil. She wonders if the wax seal and foil lining are just affectations, or whether they were chosen because the combination ensures that no one can access the envelope's contents without leaving undisguisable evidence of having done so.

She puts down the envelope and takes up the letter, reading it more slowly this time.

*Dear Madam,*

*Your recent enquiry regarding my client, Mr. Bronaryre, Esq., has been directed to my attention.*

*I hope you will appreciate that in these uncertain times it is imprudent to pursue delicate matters in any form of written record (so often subpoenaed) or electronic communication (so often compromised), and therefore under the present circumstances I regret that I am unable to offer you any assistance. However, should you happen to find it convenient, I would be entirely willing to discuss the matter with you privately and in person.*

*It is my habit to attend Evensong of a Wednesday at Temple Church (extra-parochial), located between the City and Saint Clement Danes. I usually take a pew at the back, by William the Marshal.*

*I have the honour to be, madam, your faithful and obedient servant,*

The signature is illegible—presumably deliberately so, given the absence of either letterhead or return address: the author of this note did not intend that she could respond. The first name is short, perhaps *Ross*. The surname is longer and might begin with a *P* or a *D*, but the rest is just scrawl. However, there are two postnominal initials that are clear enough: *QC*.

She looks it up: *Queen's Counsel*—an honorific title given to distinguished barristers in Britain and, in the ceremonious ways of the class-conscious English, includes the privilege of wearing distinctive silk robes while in court. Not that she has any doubt as to the Englishness of the author—*enquiry* with an *e* and *honour* with a *u*, referring to London's financial district as *the City*, the appellative *esquire*, and the elaborately flowery valediction all point to it.

She wonders who William the Marshal might be. The addition of the unnecessary and somewhat fussy *extra-parochial* suggests a punctilious author, a person concerned with the minutiae of ecclesiastical status. Perhaps the lawyer has a secular role in the church that he suggested as a meeting place, and maybe a marshal is a sort of church lay person, like a sexton or a verger, with whom he is on friendly terms.

The idea of going to London is ridiculous, she thinks, doubly so now that her dissertation is complete: even if something new should emerge there would be insufficient time to incorporate it before the submission deadline. Plus the cost; her room is cold because she has turned off the heat to save money, and instead works in the free warmth of the reading room at the public library up in Bryant Park—crossing the Atlantic would subtract a large sum from her carefully conserved scholarship funds. But the letter is intriguing, and if she were not to go she would always wonder what might have come of it.

She opens her laptop and starts searching for the cheapest airfare from New York to London.

# II

LONDON IS TEN DEGREES of latitude higher than New York, and consequently winter light fades much faster there, something the woman failed to take into account when setting out for the church. The Temple is London's legal district, a complex congeries of ancient structures accumulated over many centuries, not always easy to navigate, much like the law itself. She discovers that the Inner Temple is a warren of serpentine footpaths and narrow passageways, something that would have been difficult enough to negotiate by day, but which in the dark is an impenetrable maze.

Soon, she is lost.

She checks the time: it is already six P.M. and Evensong would be starting. There is no one to ask for directions. The only sign of life is an occasional yellow-lit window high up in one of the many old buildings crowding in upon themselves, or sometimes the sound of footsteps echoing like hers upon the flagstones, the direction indecipherable in the labyrinth, there and then gone as their unseen source hurries away.

Suddenly, she is enveloped in mist. Her plan had been to match a street sign with the map—a map that she has come to realize is insufficiently detailed and poorly labeled. In this fog it will no longer be possible: she cannot see the street signs. She continues as best she can, hoping to happen upon something useful, or perhaps to hear the sound of the service, now that Evensong must be underway.

She comes to a small square, black railings and fog-dampened paths separating little patches of greenery: a pocket-sized park. Someone stands nearby, but when she approaches to ask for directions it turns out to be a statue, mute bronze resting upon a stone pedestal. By crouching close and using her phone as a lamp the woman can read the inscription: the statue is of John Stuart Mill, the philosopher. The map that the hotel concierge gave her, essentially a tourist pamphlet, has the various sights denominated by numbers and listed in a key. Among them, she finds the John Stuart Mill statue.

She is at the far side of the Middle Temple, having somehow completely traversed both Inner and Middle Temples, and missing the church along the way. The Thames is just ahead of her, silent and unseen; the sudden fog is explained.

She reorients herself and, with a better sense of scale now, heads back the way she came, but further east, downriver, a route that she calculates cannot fail to find Temple Church. Eventually, she emerges through a narrow cloister into an open space. To her left is the church, the soft murmur of the liturgy audible in the cold night air, pointed Gothic windows glowing warm and inviting. The main portal is located on the side rather than at the end, meaning that latecomers must enter in view of those who managed to make it on time.

The congregation rises to its feet as the woman steps inside, and she briefly has the alarming impression of having been the cause. All except one, an elderly round-faced gentleman with abundant gray curls sitting alone in a pew at the back of the church. Unlike the others, the man faces not the celebrant but her, as if having expected her arrival. He smiles in welcome and signals with three raised fingers, like an aged Boy Scout.

In the middle of the chancel is a choir wearing white surplices over scarlet cassocks, a mixture of men and boys. A few determined organ notes sound and then the choir begins a hymn. She makes her way around the perimeter to the back of the church.

The gray-curled man stands as she joins him, and offers a pudgy hand in welcome. He only comes to her shoulder, although she is not wearing heels, but he has compensated for height with girth.

"Thomas Ravenscroft," he whispers as they shake hands. "Delighted to meet you, Miss Lancaster."

The *Ross* was *Thos*, she realizes, an English written contraction of his first name.

"Sabrina Lancaster," she offers in return, although it is obviously unnecessary. "How did you know what I looked like?"

"I am familiar with the congregation. A stranger, especially a young woman alone, is quite unusual here, I can assure you. And so American; my, how differently our cousins hold themselves, and how differently they gaze out upon the world. Who could it be but you?" This declaration leaves him breathless. "Shall we sit?"

They sit.

"I'm afraid that you've missed the prelude," he says. "Charles H. H. Parry, laudably rendered. Both the *Magnificat* and *Nunc Dimittis* will be Stanford, a real treat, but for which we now pay with Bairstow's rather ponderous Psalm 48." He offers her a small printed program, and points to the current line: *Walk about Zion, and go around about her: tell the towers thereof.*

"Where's William?" she asks.

"Who?"

"William the Marshal."

"Ah, Pembroke. He's over there." Ravenscroft nods toward the rear of the church. It is not a vestibule or portal, as might be expected in a traditional church, but instead a strange circular extension, as if having been tacked on as an architectural afterthought. It is empty of people, but what appear to be several half-sunken sarcophagi occupy the floor, their occupants' effigies rendered in high relief upon the lids. "He's on the left, surrounded by his sons," Ravenscroft continues. "William the Marshal is the only man ever to have unhorsed Richard Coeur de Lion. He spared Richard but slew his horse. It gives me great comfort to sit by a man capable of dislodging kings."

The psalm concludes, and they sit for the lesson. Ravenscroft talks no more and shows every appearance of listening attentively, even enjoying it. Sabrina takes the opportunity to inspect the church's interior: smooth stone soaring in a mixture of pointed windows and vaulted arches, the pulpit perched precariously upon a single slender pillar, the wood of the intricately carved reredos darkened near ebony with age, richly ornamented sacerdotal vessels and vestments, the air cool and still and heavy with collective superstition. A calming place, she thinks—notwithstanding the nearby presence of a dead horse slayer—somewhere designed to soothe the spirit into at least a temporary suspension of disbelief.

The service proceeds with a series of sittings and standings, a kneeling at what the program identifies as 'The Collect,' winding through hymns and anthems and the two Stanfords: fine enough, but Sabrina felt a greater profundity in the Bairstow, notwithstanding Ravenscroft's dismissal of it. The congregation remains standing after the final hymn, the minister offers a concluding benediction, and then the choir and clergy proceed in dignified procession down the aisle and out of the church. The organist begins anew and Ravenscroft briefly cocks an ear.

"Gigout," he says, satisfied in successfully identifying the composer, despite having surrendered his program. "An excellent choice for the Voluntary."

"You know your music, Mr. Ravenscroft."

"They say that knowledge is power, Miss Lancaster, but if so I confess that I have found no evidence of it in the ability to distinguish a toccata from a fugue. But here I am talking about power when we have the real thing right by us." He stands. "Shall we pay our respects?"

While the congregants quietly file out the side door, Ravenscroft leads Sabrina to the back of the church, with the effigies.

"This was the original church," he says, in full voice now, no longer constrained to the hushed tones he used during the service. "The circular construction seems unusual to us, accustomed as we are to basilican rectilinearity, but this church was, of course, the London headquarters of the Knights Templar—before their suppression—and Templar churches were commonly round." So it is not this part that is the architectural afterthought, Sabrina realizes, it is the rest of the church. "According to the official account, the round design was modeled on the Church of the Holy Sepulchre, in Jerusalem." Ravenscroft leans closer and lowers his voice. "Actually, it was intended to recall the Dome of the Rock, what they called the *Templum Domini*—that building is technically octagonal rather than circular, although its dome *is* circular, and the seals of Templar Grand Masters depict the *Templum Domini* as entirely circular, dome and walls, notwithstanding the architectural facts. But I choose not to pursue these finer points with our clerical brethren." He stands up straight and resumes his normal voice. "Are you familiar with the Templars?"

"Not at all."

"They were a military order that arose during the Crusades, based in Jerusalem, which had been taken in 1099. The *temple* part comes from the Temple of Solomon, on whose site they had their headquarters. Their mission was to protect Christians, especially pilgrims traveling to the Holy Land. It was as an adjunct to this latter obligation that they devised a system whereby the traveler could deposit valuables with local Templars before setting out on his pilgrimage, and then redeem funds against them from the Templars in Jerusalem, and so was born a financial system using letters of credit—the Templars, in addition to being a military order, became bankers. Thus they possessed two of the three paths to power: money and might.

"As the Crusades crumbled the Templars gradually retreated westward, first to Acre, then Cyprus, eventually back into Europe, and the monarchs suddenly found that this once small order pledged to poverty and pilgrims in faraway Jerusalem had transformed into a large, rich, and powerful force in the middle of their own realms. King John discovered this to his disadvantage: it was William the Marshal who negotiated the signing of the Magna Carta—he was a man capable of dislodging kings in more ways than one, you perceive? Come, let me introduce you."

He takes her to an effigy in the central group.

"This is he," Ravenscroft says. "These two by him are his sons."

It has the appearance of a tomb sunk partially into the stone floor, with only the carved lid standing proud. The effigy depicts William the Marshal in full medieval military regalia, a long shield held at the ready to his left, and on the other side a stout fist clenching the hilt of his unsheathed sword, as if ready to continue dethroning in the afterlife if things were not to his satisfaction. His head is wrapped in chain mail, and the face it surrounds is stern and determined, as hard as the stone from which it is carved. William was not a man much given to humor or fancy, Sabrina thinks.

"In unhorsing Richard, William merely taught the young man a lesson," Ravenscroft says, after having allowed her to contemplate the tomb for a while in silence. "But John's wings he clipped rather more severely, and in a way which was to reverberate throughout history, an act that we still feel the echoes of today. Strange to say, John held no ill will toward him; in fact, he was grateful to William for having engineered an end to the conflict with the barons. This church even became the state treasury under John, with the Templars taking charge of the royal funds. It was John who appointed William as Earl of Pembroke, and on John's death he, Pembroke, became regent to the then nine-year-old Henry III—that is, he became the ruler of England. Not bad for a man born with neither land nor fortune. The Archbishop of Canterbury called him the best knight that ever lived, but I would rather call him the most effective."

Sabrina looks around the room. The walls are bare stone here, the windows narrow, but with the lack of furnishing and low tombs it feels spacious. There are grotesque heads carved into the tracery, leering or screaming—one fellow is having his ear bitten off by what looks to be an enraged ferret. Some of the effigies strike strange poses, lying with their legs oddly crossed, or standing upon animals. The room is part dungeon, part armory, part fortification, part crypt.

"What a strange place this is," Sabrina says. "How different it feels from the other side."

"High Church," Ravenscroft says, cocking his head toward the chancel and reverting to a whisper, "which is to say, Anglican never having quite reconciled itself to the Reformation. They still lament the liturgical lapse from Latin into the vulgar tongue, and basically never progressed beyond the King James Bible and 1662 Book of Common Prayer. But here in the Round—well, this may be the oldest part of the church, but in a sense it is the most modern: there is no sacerdotal pedantry in this room, just the will to power."

She follows his gaze back down to William the Marshal, and they contemplate him in renewed silence.

"What do you see?" he asks after a while.

"Determination."

"Self-satisfaction?"

"No, none."

"Quite so," Ravenscroft says. "Like Alexander, or Caesar, or Napoleon: never done and self-satisfied, but always doing and looking forward."

There is a meaningful throat-clearing from the chancel and looking up they see that the line of people leaving has dwindled to the last talkative stragglers. They walk over and join it. Sabrina opens her bag but Ravenscroft halts her with a hand on her arm.

"Quite unnecessary, I assure you. I am generous enough for two." He extracts a long coat wallet and pulls from it an ochre-colored banknote: fifty pounds. "Why don't you read it?"

He hands her the banknote. There is a flamboyant *Bank of England* etched beside a portrait of the reigning monarch, evidently from her younger days.

"Other side."

She turns it over. The portraits here are of two men—James Watt and Matthew Boulton, as serious and determined as William the Marshal. There is a large steam engine between them: Watt's invention, Sabrina knows, and she assumes that Matthew Boulton must have been a collaborator. Then she sees what Ravenscroft evidently meant for her to see: a quotation: *I sell here, Sir, what all the world desires to have – POWER.*

Ravenscroft leans in close as he plucks the bill from her hand and says *sotto voce*, "I keep leaving them these little hints, but they never seem to catch on."

He drops the bill into the basket; mostly it has coins, and the few banknotes are far smaller in denomination.

The minister has not missed this generosity and smiles warmly as he shakes Ravenscroft's hand. Ravenscroft compliments him on the sermon, and then they spend a moment tut-tutting about the weather before Ravenscroft moves on.

It comes to Sabrina's turn, and the cleric inspects her unapologetically as he shakes her hand, but asks no questions. Sabrina has the sense that she is not the first curious stranger to have shown up at his church in Ravenscroft's company, but that he has learned to keep his inquisitiveness in check.

Sabrina and Ravenscroft step out into the courtyard. The fog has expanded from the riverbank, and they are enveloped in mist. It is cold but not unpleasant after being inside, and Sabrina takes a deep breath of sharp briny air.

"What's the third?" she asks.

"Third what?"

"You said there are three paths to power. The two the Templars possessed were money and might. What's the third?"

"Ah, the third is the trickiest: it is men's minds. Difficult, but very effective; worth trying if you can pull it off. Take this edifice, a magnificent building on priceless land, but maintained how? We have just witnessed it, have we not, a line of people putting money into a basket as they file out the door. But purchasing what? Absolution? A place in the afterlife? Or perhaps just peace of mind?"

She realizes why Ravenscroft was paying such attention to the lesson: it was not the content that interested him, it was the technique.

"What happened to the Templars?"

"They were suppressed. Phillip IV of France learned the lesson of Runnymede better than his English contemporaries: he closed the order, burned their leaders at the stake, put recalcitrants to the sword, and of course took possession of their wealth—or at least that part of their wealth that he could lay his hands on, property mainly."

"And the rest?"

"Gold. Jewels, a common form of portable wealth back then. Silver plate, too. Most of that slipped away."

"Where?"

"Ah, as the Bard said, thereby hangs a tale." He rubs his hands. "Come, let us repair to my chambers and fortify ourselves against this climate in the English manner."

"How's that?"

"With a good cup of tea."

# III

RAVENSCROFT IS surprisingly fast for a short man of broad girth, scurrying along the mist-shrouded paths with a confidence born of familiarity. He leads Sabrina swiftly through the Inner Temple, a convoluted web of winding alleyways and narrow cobbled lanes that in the nebulous darkness feels to her like a catacomb. The fog makes identification difficult: she sees only passing glimpses of things that briefly emerge and then quickly disappear: a low stone arch that she must duck to negotiate; a boot-scrape projecting from the pavement, threatening to trip passers-by; an iron gate with hinges that squeak as if to raise the dead; a set of steps whose stone is scalloped with centuries of feet having trod upon them. With all the twisting and turning she has soon lost her sense of direction, and this is deliberate, she realizes: he is purposely leading her on this merry scramble to disorient her.

At last, they arrive at an anonymous portal set into a nondescript brick building. The door is painted glossy black, with an elegant fanlight above. There is no polished brass plaque, such as a prosperous barrister might be expected to display, nor even the buzzer with a handwritten label of someone less thriving. There is no identification at all, not even a street number.

Ravenscroft unlocks the door and they step inside. The place smells musty and old. He closes the door behind them and switches on the light, revealing not a professional premise's entrance lobby or reception area, but instead just a small vestibule, uncarpeted, with a door to the left, a narrow staircase to the right, and between them a little hallway leading to the back. It has an air of abandonment, or at least of little use, and she wonders how a lawyer whose chambers are in such a place can afford to leave £50 banknotes in church collection baskets. They take the stairs up, arriving at a passageway corresponding to the hall below, again with a single door leading off it. Ravenscroft opens the door, finds the light switch, and invites Sabrina into his chambers.

The room is large, or would once have been so, but much of the available space has been reduced by an accumulation of bookcases and cupboards and shelves, all of them seemingly overflowing with paperwork. There is a lone window, but the lawyer's heavy carved desk is by the opposite wall, near the fireplace: perhaps the little natural light that would seep in through the narrow alley was insufficient to justify positioning the desk away from what is apparently the room's sole source of heat.

There is no monitor on the desk, just a blotter, a tarnished silver inkstand, a brass desk lamp with a green glass shade, a letter rack with an opener lying beside it, and on the far side a cluster of items—a stumpy candle attached to a broad base, a tapering rough-cast metal cylinder employed as a paperweight, and a cigar-sized roll from which the covering paper has been torn, revealing a bright red interior, like a fat crayon. She stares at them in momentary puzzlement until realizing that this is where his letter to her must have been sealed.

Part of one wall has been fitted with pigeon holes from which protrude papers in great variety: bound and unbound; folio and quarto and foolscap; some in folders made of stiff cloth-covered board and others in long rolls secured with ribbons of scarlet or black satin.

Not everything is paper: a decapitated brass artillery shell, standing by the door, performs the duty of umbrella stand; a gilt clock sits atop the mantle, its ticking the loudest thing in the room; and on top of a corner cupboard is an owl, large and horned, that some taxidermist contrived to configure with wings spread, as if about to launch upon an unlucky vole.

When all the wall space was taken up Ravenscroft took to using freestanding furniture: the floor is cluttered with chests and cabinets, but even these were inadequate, for loose paperwork occupies almost all the available horizontal surfaces, often in teetering piles threatening to collapse. One of these is on the only spare chair, an old leather-upholstered wingback by the other side of the fire, and Ravenscroft's first action is to hastily remove the documents from it and then with an open palm offer her a seat.

Sabrina accepts, looking around at the paperwork-strewn room in wonderment.

"You must have a great many clients, Mr. Ravenscroft."

"I have only the one client—that same gentleman whom you came to discuss. However, he does keep me busy."

Ravenscroft moves to a side table on which sits a tea set, and a kettle upon a hob. He plugs in the hob and switches it on. The kettle makes a low noise as the water begins to heat, and Ravenscroft looks at it admiringly.

"Isn't electricity wonderful, Miss Lancaster? We take it so much for granted, but when you stop to consider, such an amazing thing."

"I was just thinking that you seem to take very little advantage of electricity, Mr. Ravenscroft." There is no evidence of a computer, or a printer, or a photocopier. There is a telephone on a stand by the desk, a big black Bakelite device with a rotary dial, a type of telephone that Sabrina has only ever seen in old black-and-white movies.

"One doesn't like to become a slave to anything, does one? Even to something as singular as electricity. I find that I get by with what I have. I must say that I sometimes look with pity upon those unfortunate creatures who seem unable to proceed along a footpath without their heads buried in a small screen, and wonder if they are not rather like zombies. However, I must confess to being a slave to one thing."

"What's that, Mr. Ravenscroft?"

"Earl Grey." He opens a tin by the kettle and proffers it for Sabrina's inspection. She leans forward. Inside, there is tea. "Please, take a sniff." Sabrina leans closer and inhales. Besides the sharp tannic smell of the tea, there is something else: a pungent underlying bittersweetness, something lush and exotic.

"What's it flavored with?"

"Oil of bergamot, a type of Asian citrus fruit." He continues talking while spooning some into a teapot. "Legend has it that the mixture was given to Earl Grey by a Chinese Mandarin in gratitude for the earl's people having rescued his son from drowning."

"Was he a sea-faring man?"

"No. Charles Grey, who became the second Earl Grey, was a Prime Minister of England. It was under him that slavery was abolished in the British Empire, and he was the author of the Reform Bill of 1832, a document which—representing as it were a completion of the process that was begun with the Magna Carta—is to the British constitution what certain amendments are to the American constitution. Thus it is that tonight, Miss Lancaster, we have had the opportunity to pay our respects to both the start and end points of a six-hundred-year process dedicated to delivering humankind from tyranny."

He turns back to the table, busying himself with tea preparations, and she wonders what the purpose is behind the history lesson, elliptically delivered with English indirectness. Her eyes return to the desk.

"May I look at the seal?"

"Certainly."

She takes it from the desk, as hefty as a cudgel, and inspects the underside.

"What is it?"

"Rosicrucian." The kettle boils, and he continues to talk while filling the pot. "That is, representing the Order of the Rosy Cross, and so I use red wax to continue the tradition, so to speak. Now, we'll give you a moment to draw." This last comment is apparently addressed to the teapot.

Ravenscroft places two cups and saucers on the desk, pours the tea through a strainer, and then adds milk and sugar. He stirs briefly before drinking appreciatively. Sabrina stirs and sips in turn, then replaces her cup. "Thank you, but I hope that I didn't come all this way just for tea."

"Ah, yes, the time has indeed come to discuss the reason for your visit." Ravenscroft takes his seat at the desk. He opens a drawer and pulls from it a piece of paper she recognizes as the photocopy of the letter that she had enclosed with her own. "I wonder if you would be kind enough to tell me the circumstances by which you came into possession of the document in question."

"Well, as I explained, I'm a postgrad at NYU. I've been lucky enough to work with Justice Scaglietti—I mean to say, I *was* working with Justice Scaglietti."

"Yes, a great loss. A fine legal mind, admired on both sides of the Atlantic, one that will be sorely missed. And also no doubt something that on a personal level has profoundly impacted your studies."

"Not really. I had already finished the bulk of my work with him at the end of last summer. The Supreme Court term runs from October to June, during which he is mostly in D.C., and in any case he would have no time for someone like me when court is in term—the only people with access to him then are the other Justices and his clerks."

"Nevertheless he made time for you when term was over. A very generous thing to do."

"He lived alone."

"But had many friends."

"Many admirers. He was not a man for friends."

"And yet for a Supreme Court Justice to essentially give up his free time to help a student—but then I understand that the subject matter was an analysis of his opinions, and perhaps it is not unknown for a man to be willing to expound his opinions, legal or otherwise, should he find a willing ear. Especially if that willing ear were young and female—I believe the late Justice had something of a reputation in these areas."

It was true, but she had never felt the least hint of it from him, even when he had invited her to stay overnight, alone after the staff went home, just the two of them at Netherly, his great pile on the Hudson. But he had female companions, more than one, notwithstanding the conservative Catholicism: she had seen the evidence of it in one of the bedrooms.

"I think that Justice Scaglietti was under the impression that the dissertation might, in future, expand into a book."

Ravenscroft smiles with understanding. "Ah, yes, I quite see now." His eyes fall to the desktop, and he taps the photocopy lying flat upon it. "But you have still not told me how this letter came into your possession. Not the sort of thing he would have shown you himself, surely?"

"No, I came across it after he died."

"You still have access to his papers?"

"I did. A week after the funeral I received a call from his sister, Marianne Channing. They were twins: Mariano and Marianne. She invited me to lunch at the Palm Court. I thought it would be to ask about her brother, her brother late in life, that is—they were not exactly estranged, but I gathered that, although they were close as children, there had been a falling out at some point—and I assumed that after having lost her brother so suddenly and unexpectedly she now wanted some closure. I dreaded going, but how can a person say no in such circumstances?

"I showed up, wearing my Sunday best. What I found was not a grieving sister but a perfectly composed and dry-eyed woman who, apart from the expected preliminaries, showed not the least interest in her brother's last months. Instead, she showed a great interest in me."

"In you?"

"I was surprised that she had even heard of me—the funeral was a private affair, and certainly I had not been invited. She evaded when I first asked, but after I pressed she admitted that she had gotten my name from having quizzed the staff at her brother's estate. That's how she put it: *Of course, it was necessary to quiz the Netherly staff, and your name came up*. It made me wonder why it was necessary to quiz the staff in the first place. We ordered, and all through the meal we talked about me. She asked about my studies, how the scholarship funding worked, what my supervisor was like, what progress I had made with the dissertation, when I expected to submit it. For a moment I thought that she might actually ask to read it. But then it finally became clear why we were there. *Riano's papers are still at Netherly*, she said."

"Riano?"

"The Justice. In public life, he was always Justice Mariano Scaglietti and was never referred to with a diminutive. But she called him Riano, probably had done since childhood."

"I see. Please, what happened next?"

"She told me that she had ordered the staff to leave all his papers untouched, and had both the library and the study locked. *They'll need to be gone through*, she said, *cataloged and whatnot, which will require someone with suitable training*. Then I understood: she wanted me to sort through his papers. *It occurs to me that you are a person with the appropriate training*, she said, *and no doubt you already have familiarity with many of the papers in question, as well as a sense of what my brother kept where, and so forth. Plus, with your dissertation near completion, perhaps you will have time, and my brother's estate would naturally compensate you—quite handsomely, in fact.* I had not anticipated this and didn't immediately respond. *Of course, it would require a certain delicacy*, she suggested, *a keen personal understanding of my brother in order to correctly separate from his legal papers those items of a more private nature*. She let that hang there a while, and I realized that what I was being asked to do was not merely catalog the papers, but also to make sure that anything embarrassing or compromising would never come out. I think she had assumed that because I was studying her brother's opinions that I was therefore an admirer of them, and their author, and so could be relied upon. Oh—"

A shadow suddenly darts across the room to her left.

The lawyer holds up a halting hand. "Please don't be alarmed." He removes his cup from its saucer, fills the latter with the remaining milk, and then gently places it on the floor by his feet. "Come, Madame Defarge. Come, come."

A cat emerges from behind a bookcase, coal-black apart from the eyes, which are a startlingly bright yellow, and which never leave Sabrina, even while it sups from the saucer.

"You will understand that in a building of this age, mice are a given, and a threat to my records. Madame Defarge keeps them at bay."

The interruption gives Sabrina time to consider how long she has been talking, which is far longer than was necessary to answer

Ravenscroft's question. She realizes that he has quietly lulled her into revealing her position without himself having given anything away, and decides that, appearances aside, this little gray-curled man is a shrewd lawyer.

Ravenscroft looks up from the cat back to Sabrina.

"And so you accepted?"

"I did."

"How did it proceed?"

"We made arrangements to meet at Netherly, on the following Sunday. I wondered if this was because there would be no staff there on a Sunday. I took the train and walked from the station, something that I was used to. When I got there the main gates had been left open, something that the late Justice—who detested anyone arriving unannounced at his house—would never have done. At the end of the drive was an old black Mercedes that I recognized, and leaning upon it was Marianne Channing, casually smoking and apparently content to gaze over the grounds, presumably taking in what was now hers. I would have expected at least Mr. Channing and a bevy of relatives helping to sort the contents of the house, if not workers and moving vans, but she was alone.

"*I'm keeping this*, she said, patting the fender. *It's all I want*. I asked if she would not keep the house, too. *He left it to the Jesuits*, she said. *The Jesuits*… From the way she said it, I felt that I could now guess the underlying cause of their falling out. We went inside and she unlocked the library and the study, two rooms with which I was already familiar. She wanted all the Justice's paperwork—books, documents, letters, files, everything—to be sorted into four categories: an archive suitable for donation to a university, cataloged; professional papers not appropriate for the archive, also cataloged; personal papers to be retained by the family; and then the rest."

"The rest?"

"I took this as a euphemism for 'to be destroyed.'"

"What about computers and the like?"

"I asked that myself. She said that two of her brother's computers were Supreme Court property, and the Justice Department had already sent technicians to reclaim them. The third was a personal computer, a laptop, but no one knew how to unlock it and so she had the hard disc destroyed. There was probably little on it: in all the time I was with the Justice I never once saw him use a computer, and he had a reputation for disliking them: his clerks were required to submit in print and use colored pencils for markups, although software designed for the purpose would have been much more convenient. He liked hard copy and loved books, a man at his happiest searching through endless volumes of case law to find just the right precedent; he was a paper kind of guy."

"As indeed am I," Ravenscroft says. "Probably he and I are of the last generation that will not consider such devices indispensable. I wonder, did Mrs. Channing happen to mention to which university the archive will be donated?"

"She did: Loyola."

"Ah, and perhaps there we have a reason why she was so concerned that no materials of an unsuitable nature would be among the donation—one wouldn't wish to disturb the good Jesuit fathers. And so tell me, where did you find this letter, which Mrs. Channing would no doubt have wished for the burn pile?"

"In Blackstone, oddly enough. Originally I assigned the Justice's copy of Blackstone to the second category: professional rather than personal, although too common to warrant inclusion in the archive, but then it occurred to me that he might have made annotations, in which case they would be of scholastic interest. I began leafing through them and, sure enough, found many instances of marginalia. The letter was in Volume Four, and the rest I think you know."

Ravenscroft leans back in a pose of consideration, contemplating not the letter on his desk but the woman sitting opposite him.

"So you were not an admirer of the Justice after all." It is a statement, not a question.

"Mrs. Channing invited me to make research use of the materials that I was cataloging."

"Even so, an admirer would have destroyed this letter, research or not."

His eyes never leave her during the long silence that follows this pronouncement, judging her, and she has the sense of suddenly being at a crux, one of those capricious but supremely important moments whose effects will resonate throughout the rest of one's life.

"No," she admits, "I am not. That is not to say that I did not respect Justice Scaglietti: he had an incisive intellect and a brilliant grasp of jurisprudence. Nor did I personally dislike him; just the opposite—he was excellent company: billowing with good humor when out of the public eye, never quite easygoing but always entertaining, and certainly never trivial. Never boring. Zero small talk, and of course famously acerbic, but I didn't resent his unguarded candor, as so many did—I found it refreshing in an age where every statement is endlessly hedged so as to offend no one. And boundless curiosity, legal and otherwise. These were all qualities to be admired."

"But?"

"But he lacked that one essential quality of a first-rate jurist: he could not bring himself to be at a remove from the matter at hand. He lacked balance. For him, every case was a battle, something to be won or lost rather than rationally and objectively decided. And the closer the matter was to his personal beliefs, the more obdurate he became. One of the weapons he used was a rigorous interpretation of language, a punctiliousness that bordered on the ridiculous. He justified this as strict constructionism. He wrote a dissent in *United States versus Miraclear Corp.*, arguing that the prefixes *cipher-* and *crypto-* are not synonymous. He wrote the minority on *Greene versus Alta County School System* that sought to strike down a lower court ruling because the Latin abbreviation *et al.* could refer not only to the usual gender-neutral *et alia* but also to the gender-specific *et alii* or *et aliae*. And it was his vote that overturned *Compton versus Landon*, in part on the placement of a comma. All of these were major cases—is there such a thing as a minor case that comes before the Supreme Court?—being decided on the basis of tortured semantics. Imagine the wanton recklessness of it: overturning a major precedent on the positioning of a punctuation mark."

Another long silence follows, which the lawyer eventually breaks.

"I think that perhaps when he suddenly died your feelings were not unmixed," he says. "There was a measure of relief, was there not, because now he would never ask to read your dissertation?"

"I see that the late Justice was not the only man with an incisive mind," she says. "Yes, I've felt guilty about it ever since he died, although it's obviously irrational."

"Yes, perfectly irrational. We have absolutely no obligation to the dead, and to believe otherwise is a biological absurdity," he says. "By contrast, our obligations to those not yet living are quite immeasurable." He finishes his tea, offers a refill to Sabrina, and then stands to pour a second cup for himself. She takes the opportunity to get to the point.

"And so to Mr. Bronaryre."

"It's Bron-a-RIRE," he says, correcting her pronunciation while pouring the tea. "It's Welsh, you know. It literally means breast of gold, but in this case the *breast* is metaphorical, signifying a hill—so, *golden hill.* I find these Welsh words so very difficult to pronounce, the only way to remember them is to make up a rhyme. Brynn Mawr rhyming with 'tin star,' for example." He puts down the teapot. "I believe that you went to Brynn Mawr at one time, did you not?"

Sabrina does not respond, since it is clear that he already knows the answer—the comment was just Ravenscroft's way of conveying that he has done his homework.

"What rhyme would you use for your client's name?"

"'World-a-fire,'" he says, resuming his seat. "Has such a nice apocalyptic ring to it, don't you think?" He stirs his cup thoughtfully before continuing. "And so, Miss Lancaster, perhaps you will tell me exactly what it is that you would like from my client?"

"I should have thought that obvious, Mr. Ravenscroft. What was the nature of Mr. Bronaryre's relationship with Justice Scaglietti? What were the circumstances that led to its abrupt termination? What was the *greatest possible abomination before the eyes of God and man* that the Justice referred to?"

"Goodness gracious, did he really put it that way?" Ravenscroft picks up the letter and reads through it out loud, not in the tone of someone reviewing a document in intimate conference, but with a sonorous declamation that recalls the reading of the lesson at Temple church.

> *Mr. Aneurin Bronaryre,*
> *Sir,*
>
> *I regret that, upon the deepest reflection following our last meeting, your motives and intentions—once seemingly honorable and laudable—have become all too clear to me.*
>
> *The corrupt logic that has led to this degradation is beyond me—perhaps it was always there, a small cancer of malignancy, long dormant, but now having metastasized into a hideous tumor of horrendous proportion. Whatever the cause, I perceive now a perversion of a most foul and depraved nature. Your plan, Sir—and what would have made you believe that I would ever countenance such a scheme I cannot imagine—is nothing other than the greatest possible abomination before the eyes of God and man.*
>
> *You will thereby understand that, from this moment forward, you must number me among you enemies, never to meet again in amity.*
>
> *Yours not in Christ, as of course I would never have saluted you, nor in Reason, as once to my shame I did, but with the utmost ill will,*

"It's not signed," Ravenscroft says. "What makes you sure that he was the author?"

"Who but Justice Scaglietti would write so emphatically, so Old Testament? And clearly an author with legal training: the many doublets, for example, like *motives and intentions*, *honorable and laudable*, *foul and depraved*—these echo the doublets of classic legal syntax, like *terms and conditions*, *null and void*, *cease and desist*."

"Perhaps it was planted. Left there for you to find?"

"There is the handwriting for a start, which I am familiar enough with to recognize. And also the original, which you have not had the opportunity to see, is written in purple ink."

"Is that significant?"

"Yes, it's a well-known quirk of the Justice. He used a particular shade, called Violette Pensée, manufactured by the French company J. Herbin. As a boy, Scaglietti was educated for two years in France at a Catholic boarding school. It used to be that a J. Herbin pen-and-ink set was issued to all French school children, and apparently his Jesuit teachers continued the practice."

"Then a clever forgery, perhaps?"

"Down to the nib? I know that pen, Mr. Ravenscroft, a vintage Montblanc that the Justice used for making fair copy of what he considered to be his most important opinions."

The lawyer reflects on this for a moment, then nods in acceptance while replacing the letter on his desk.

"Then let us stipulate, for the moment at least, that Justice Scaglietti was indeed the author. Now, please forgive me, Miss Lancaster, but I am obliged to ask you this question: what business is it of yours? I trust you understand that I am speaking as the Devil's advocate."

"Without knowing exactly what the letter is about it is hard to say. But the date is a little over a year ago. At the time, oral arguments in *Compton versus Landon* had just concluded, and the court was in recess to consider what was to be the most important and divisive Supreme Court case of his generation. As I'm sure you know, it was decided five-to-four, with Scaglietti writing the opinion for the majority. That opinion is one of several that I analyze in my dissertation, and certainly the most significant. It would be of great value to understand the Justice's state of mind on the eve of writing it."

"But I think, madam, that you have made a fundamental error."

"An error?"

"Certainly. Consider again the circumstances of its discovery."

"In Blackstone's *Commentaries*?"

"Not in Blackstone in particular. But in a book, in the Justice's *own* library."

She sees where the lawyer is driving. "You mean, the letter was never delivered."

"Precisely."

"But presumably it was just a copy. Or a draft."

"In longhand? And in a favorite pen, reserved, as you said, for special occasions? Would Justice Scaglietti really have done that?"

"Do you have a better explanation, Mr. Ravenscroft?"

"Indeed, I do. Occam's razor: the best explanation is the simplest: Scaglietti made an error."

"Are you proposing to assert that the Justice, after writing such a letter, would suddenly have had second thoughts about your client, and decided that it was all just a misunderstanding?"

"A much simpler mistake, Miss Lancaster. He got the date wrong."

"The date?"

"Wrong year, to be precise. Who of us has not made the same error of a January, when dating a letter or a check or some such, to have accidentally written last year's date? And this, naturally, explains why it was never sent."

She realizes how logical this sounds. "But then that would mean it was actually written *this* year."

"Yes, it would. January the third, presumably."

"Just a week before he died."

"Yes, again."

She feels in his answer that subtle Englishness again, the ability to convey meaning beneath the words with the faintest change of intonation or emphasis, the product of an upbringing in which to be imperturbable is the measure of a man, and only the vulgar demonstrate.

"You are intimating, I think, that the fact of this letter and the fact of the Justice's death a week later are unlikely to be a coincidence."

"Some might suggest that; it is of course not for me to say."

Which, she understands, is an English circumlocution for *Yes, obviously.*

"Then why in Blackstone? Why not just throw it away, or better still burn it?—certain Netherly had enough fireplaces going in January."

"Perhaps he placed it there temporarily while considering how best to dispose of it, or maybe there is an even simpler explanation: someone suddenly coming into the library, say, and the Justice quickly hiding the thing inside whatever was at hand, which happened to be Blackstone."

Not possible, Sabrina thinks, no one was allowed into Justice Scaglietti's library uninvited, but then she realizes that that is not quite true. The exception was herself: she was given free rein there—it was the room in which she worked when visiting. And then, feeling the cold prickling of an unwanted realization, she considers again the revised date and reviews her own activity at that time.

New Year's Eve spent alone but not unenjoyably, in bed to stay warm while reading a novel happily unrelated to her studies; the long New Year's Day with the public library closed; gratefully back at work the next day; and then the train up to Netherly the following morning, watching through the window snow falling on the Hudson. The Third.

The large iron gates that guard the entrance to Netherly had been open that day, unusually so, given that Justice Scaglietti was not a man to invite unexpected visitors, but then as she approached she saw why: a big black sedan coming down the drive. It had swung out of the estate and turned left, toward her. She had watched its passage, curious as to who else might be calling on the Justice today, but the windows in the back were too dark, and all she caught was a glimpse of a liveried chauffeur.

She took advantage of the open gates to pass into the estate, glad during a snowstorm to avoid the usual wait by the intercom.

That snow had softened her tread as she walked up the long drive to the mansion. At the house she had removed her boots and put on the ballet slippers she always took in her bag when visiting Netherly, not to be noiseless but to avoid marking the polished wooden parquetry of the floor. She had gone straight to the library, as usual. He had been in there. She cannot say that she recalls him being unduly surprised, nor what books he had at hand at the time, but nevertheless she knows now with an instinctive certainty how the letter came to be in the Blackstone: he was hiding it from her.

Ravenscroft interrupts her thoughts, and she hopes that her expression has given no hint of a sudden revelation. "I note that there is no address on the letter," he says. "I wonder how you came to address your enquiry to my client."

"I looked it up."

"Looked it up where?"

"On the internet."

"My client has no presence on the internet, Miss Lancaster. He does not hold so-called social media in very high regard."

"But he is the principal of a Cayman Islands-registered company: Pendle Hill Investments."

"A company that has no website."

"But which is required, if engaging in transactions in the United States, to register a Form 13-F with the Securities and Exchange Commission. The New York Public Library makes various databases available to research scholars free of charge. The only one that came back with a hit was the SEC's, EDGAR. That filing includes the U.S. address: in this case just a post office box number, but that's enough. I assumed that there would unlikely be two Aneurin Bronaryres in the world."

The lawyer huffs a little. "The internet. Such a dreadful thing."

Sabrina cannot help smiling: this is the first of their exchanges in which she has bettered him.

"Please tell me about your client, Mr. Ravenscroft."

"What would you like to know?"

"Is he English? American? Where does he live? What does he do for a living?"

"As to nationality, Mr. Bronaryre is the holder of several passports, including instances issued by the two countries you mentioned. He owns a number of properties in various countries, and travels between them, and elsewhere, as his interests dictate. As to what he does for a living, well, I suppose I would categorize him as an investor, as of course you are already aware from the 13-F filing, but perhaps scholar-adventurer would be a better characterization."

"Did he get the letter?"

"You are in possession of the letter, madam—it was never sent, and so never received."

"The Justice would have written another copy," she says. "This time with the correct date. Did your client receive such a letter, Mr. Ravenscroft?"

The lawyer does not immediately answer, instead sitting back and considering the question, the fingers of the hands resting on his fat belly forming a little steeple. He remains in the pose, staring down at his shoes and apparently lost in thought. Eventually, Sabrina feels the need to prompt him.

"What was your client's relationship with the Justice? What was the disagreement about? What is the plan that Scaglietti referred to?"

The lawyer seems momentarily at a loss, as if having forgotten her presence, but he quickly collects himself.

"I am afraid that our meeting must now end," he says at last. "It has been a very great pleasure to meet you, Miss Lancaster."

"End? Are you telling me that I've traveled all the way across the Atlantic for nothing?"

"Certainly not."

"But you haven't answered my questions."

"Oh, as to your questions, they will be answered—not tonight, but soon enough. My client will do that himself, I imagine." He stands, still in good humor, evidently believing this to be a perfectly reasonable position, and that polite goodbyes are now in order.

Sabrina remains seated. "Mr. Ravenscroft, that is very far from a satisfactory response."

He spends a moment in thought, perhaps considering how best to remove her from his chambers without a scene. "Very well," he says, "then please allow me to offer you a surety of good faith."

He steps around the desk and moves to a small console by Sabrina. He opens the top drawer and then the one below, apparently without finding what he is looking for. He rummages through a third drawer, first taking from it a cricket ball, as red as a cherry and as shiny, too, which he places on the top where it rolls around precariously while he continues searching. Next to emerge is what appears to be a small rodent, not stuffed into a stiff pose like the owl, but supple, like a scientific specimen. Madame Defarge looks at it with great interest, the first time the cat has taken her feline gaze from Sabrina. When Ravenscroft places it on top of the console Sabrina sees that it has wings, distinctively webbed and scalloped, and wonders if this is English humor, a parody of a pub name perhaps—Ye Olde Bat & Ball. Last to come out is a wooden box, a few inches square, bearing a smooth satin finish.

He offers it to Sabrina. "The surety."

She accepts the box and opens it. Inside, wrapped in a soft cloth, is a medallion, struck in silver and tarnished with age. She takes the thing in hand and inspects it more closely. It is not a medallion, she realizes, but a coin, an inordinately large one: about two inches in diameter, and hefty. The obverse depicts a knight mounted, sword drawn and brandished, above a medieval towered city. There is a Latin inscription around the circumference. On the reverse is more Latin, and a date: 1644.

She looks back up at the lawyer, but instead of providing an explanation he asks, "Beneath the *cheval passant*—do you recognize the city?"

"Should I?"

"It has hardly changed these past four hundred years."

Sabrina looks again at the obverse. The knight is not a knight but a sovereign of some kind: he wears a crown. She studies the depiction of the city beneath his striding horse. There is no evidence of a canal or a gondola, items that would have signified the only city in the Latinized world she can immediately think of that has remained unchanged in four centuries.

"I do not."

"There are many spires, are there not?"

"Yes."

"Matthew Arnold once called it *the city of dreaming spires*."

The line is familiar, and thinking about it she realizes that there is another city not much changed from medieval times, one that is not far away.

"Oxford," she says.

"Indeed, Oxford. The tower to the left is Magdalen College." He pronounces it in the Oxonian fashion: *maudlin*. "The spire directly below the horse is Saint Mary's, with Lincoln College to the right of that. The Bodleian is beneath the stirrup."

Sabrina looks from the coin to the lawyer, who is beaming with delight. "You know, I myself was at Magdalen when I was up," he says.

"And I once climbed that very tower, late at night, without permission, and while exceedingly tight. I was almost sent down because of that little foray."

Sabrina cannot help returning to good humor: the thought of the little lawyer having once been a carousing student fills her with an urge to laugh out loud, and she looks back down at the coin.

"So this is what you might call a monetary surety in the most literal sense?"

"Well, yes, the coin certainly has value, but it is not as something with an objective worth that I entrust it to you. You see, this particular coin, this exact one, holds great sentimental value for my client. He has been after me for many years to find the means of acquiring it, and it just so happens that I was recently able to do so. Now that this coin is in your possession he will surely seek you out, and for as long as you retain it I would say that you have the fellow over a barrel, so to speak. He will have no option but to answer your questions to your full satisfaction, after which you may simply give him the coin. A wonderful arrangement, in which everyone benefits—such a rare thing in jurisprudence; the thought of it quite fills me with joy, like an early spring. I am all aquiver with delight."

"But, as Mr. Bronaryre's legal representative, would you wish to put him in such a position?"

"Ah, but I am my client's counsel, am I not? And it is part of an attorney's duties and obligations to deliver that counsel without fear or favor, even if one is perfectly well aware that one's client does not wish to hear it." He leans down close and drops to a whisper, although there is none but the cat to hear. "What I'm saying is: it will do the fellow good to squirm a little." He stands back upright and resumes his normal voice. "And now, on the subject of advice, I hope that you will not be offended if I offer some to you."

"Please go ahead."

"Firstly, the coin is more than just a surety, it is also a lure. As with any lure, one must exercise patience. Be prepared to wait. Secondly, keep the coin on your person at all times. Even when bathing, you should keep the coin with you."

"You think that your client might attempt a burglary?"

"No, although he is perfectly capable of it. The thing is that he might approach at any time, and you should always be prepared."

"Even while bathing?"

"Even then. My client has no interest in the social norms or the niceties of polite society. If he chooses to make his appearance when you are in the tub and dressed as nature presented you, then I'm afraid that appear he will do. And now a third and final piece of advice: when Mr. Bronaryre finally rises to the bait, you must be very careful."

"Careful in what way? Are you saying that I should be armed?

"Oh, goodness me, no. I don't mean anything to do with physical security. I am talking here at the psychological level. My client is a clever man and can be very persuasive. That doesn't mean that you should automatically gainsay whatever he may choose to assert; indeed, you need not do anything at all. What I really mean is that he possesses an uncanny sense of other people's vulnerabilities, and is not above exploiting them to his advantage. In short, he manipulates people."

"You make your client sound like quite an ogre, Mr. Ravenscroft, but perhaps I'm not as vulnerable as you think."

"I don't think you're vulnerable at all. I wouldn't have suggested any of this had I thought otherwise."

# IV

ON THE AIRPLANE heading back home, while glancing through a copy of the *Telegraph* that the flight attendant offered, Sabrina pauses at a headline.

***Priceless Coin Stolen from the Ashmolean***

At the bottom of the page is a photograph of the stolen object, and the instinctive sense of foreboding she felt when the article first caught her eye is immediately confirmed: it is the same coin that is currently sitting in her pocket. She reads the accompanying story.

> *OXFORD—One of the most revered treasures in the collection of the University of Oxford's Ashmolean Museum, a Seventeenth-Century coin known as the Oxford Crown, has been stolen, museum officials confirmed today. At a news conference held this afternoon, the Director of Communications for the museum, Denise Ashford, said that it was unclear precisely when the coin went missing, as the thief or thieves had left in the empty display case an official-looking notice stating that the item had been temporarily removed for cleaning and preservation, but that the theft could not have occurred earlier than last Monday morning, when a museum tour guide specifically remembers the coin being in place. Ms. Ashford*

*revealed that this sign had even fooled the gallery staff responsible for inventorying items at the end of each day.*

*When asked to appraise the value of the coin, the Head of Philately and Numismatics at Christie's auction house in London, Reginald Weatherstone-Smith, said today that the coin was so rare that no value could be placed upon it, but also so rare that no legitimate buyer would ever purchase it, given that it could only be the stolen item. "Quite ironic, really," he said. "The Oxford Crown is at once both priceless and worthless, as it can never be replaced and also can never be sold." He suspected that an obsessive private collector must have been behind the burglary, someone who knew that it was unsellable, and wanted not the money but the object itself.*

*The coin was struck by Thomas Rawlins in 1644 in Oxford, at a time when England was embroiled in the Civil War. London sided with Parliament, and so the King, Charles I, moved his capital to Oxford. His court was established at Christ Church, with the queen occupying Merton College and the King's parliament, sitting in rivalry to the Westminster legislature with which he was at war, meeting in the Bodleian Library's Convocation House. The coin bears the King's equestrian portrait on one side, and on the other his war aims, inscribed in abbreviated Latin. The mint was set up at the present site of St. Peter's College, and much of the coinage was struck from melted university silverware. The mint was closed in 1646 with the fall of Oxford to parliamentary forces. The coins are exceedingly rare: it is thought that just a hundred of them were ever minted. Only a handful survive today, but none in such fine condition as that of the Ashmolean's.*

*Thames Valley Police are scheduled to hold a press briefing tomorrow morning.*

Sabrina puts the newspaper aside and briefly wonders if she is being used as a convenient mule for the movement of stolen goods across international borders. But it seems unlikely: a criminal gang would use one of their own people for such a task, not a stranger who, if becoming aware of the robbery, could be counted on to go straight to the authorities. Besides, when checking in at Heathrow for the return flight she discovered that her ticket had been upgraded to first class, without charge to her—what criminals would pay to upgrade a mule? And as Mr. Reginald Weatherstone-Smith of Christie's had so ably articulated, as a criminal undertaking the theft of the Oxford Crown made no sense: it would be stealing something that could never be sold. There is some other game being played here, she decides, but what it is she has no idea.

Nevertheless, she is in possession of stolen property, leaving her with no option after landing at JFK but to approach the first customs officer she finds and state the facts plainly. Sabrina wishes that she had not read the newspaper, which would have left her in blissful ignorance, and she finds herself irrationally annoyed with the flight attendant for having offered it to her.

AT JFK, SABRINA does not approach a customs officer; instead, she just walks out the gate and into the arrival hall without hesitation or hindrance, and takes a bus back into Manhattan. She could always plead ignorance, Sabrina reasons, although she knows that she has little capacity for dissimulation, and under questioning would no doubt spill out everything right away. The truth is that she is curious to unravel this little mystery, and the coin is apparently the key to doing so—after which, she reasons, she can simply mail it back to the Ashmolean anonymously.

AFTER SABRINA'S return to New York, the days turn into weeks, and then the weeks into months. Finalizing the dissertation and preparing for its upcoming defense fully occupy her. She barely eats and bathes, and puts off considering what best to do with the Oxford Crown, although the incriminating coin remains at the back of her conscience; it is in her pocket every day and under her pillow every night. She begins to vaguely resent the weight of the thing, literal and metaphorical, its awkward size and unjustifiable possession becoming ever more burdensome with the passage of time.

The day for her defense arrives. It takes place in Vanderbilt Hall. Defenses are all *vive voce* and open to the public, but normally attended only by the three-person dissertation committee, plus a handful of faculty members interested in the subject. Sabrina enters the auditorium to find that there are far more people than usual, forty or fifty in total, many of whom she does not recognize—they have come because of the link to Scaglietti, she realizes; even deceased, the Justice is a celebrity.

She does not allow the presence of the unexpected auditors to distract her, makes her arguments more or less cogently, and survives the questioning which, to her surprise during the second round, the chairman opens to the audience. The questions are generally predictable, and she fields most of them with ease, all but the last. It is asked by a man sitting alone in the back row—rangy, thirties, slightly disheveled, rather shy. The chairman has requested that all questioners first stand and introduce themselves and their affiliation. The man rises hesitantly to his feet.

"Wilkins, Sancta Civitas," he says. "I wonder if you would care to comment on Justice Scaglietti's consideration of the Doctrine of Necessity in deciding *Compton versus Landon*."

"As far as I'm aware," Sabrina responds, "he did not consider it at all. There is no reference to the Doctrine of Necessity in his decision, nor in the drafts of that decision, nor in his own trial notes, and certainly the Justice never alluded to it in any of my discussions with him, whether in *Compton* or any other case. I would also say that, despite his reputation, the Justice had an abiding respect for *stare decisis*, even if sometimes honored in the breach." This remark evokes smiles from the audience, for Scaglietti had a fearsome reputation for riding roughshod over precedent. "Cases invoking the Doctrine of Necessity are rare. In the centuries since its articulation there are few enough precedents in English and International law; none, so far as I know, in American law. He would have been loath to raise it, even though in *Compton* it clearly would have suited his position."

Such a negative answer is an invitation to rebuttal, for surely the man would not have asked so pointed a question without something up his sleeve, but he only smiles politely and resumes his seat, apparently satisfied with Sabrina's response.

The second round of questions ends, and with it Sabrina's defense of her dissertation. From the smiles and handshakes at its conclusion she knows that it was successful, and she will soon be *Doctor* Lancaster.

Her immediate instinct is to return to her apartment and celebrate, but before leaving Sabrina decides to make a detour downstairs, to the law library that connects Vanderbilt Hall with Furman Hall.

Any law library can be counted on to have a copy of Blackstone's *Commentaries on the Laws of England*, and NYU's has several editions. Sabrina soon locates the same version as Justice Scaglietti's, recognizable by the russet leather binding. When cataloging Scaglietti's Blackstone for the Justice's sister, Sabrina had laboriously noted each instance of marginalia, by volume and page number, determined to thoroughly catalog the materials, however dull the work. She does not recall the subject matter at the place where she found Scaglietti's date-errored letter, but there had been a note scribbled in the margin, and the fact that she found the letter there made that particular location stick in her mind: Volume IV, page 30.

She takes from the shelf the fourth volume, opens it to page thirty, and finds the following passage:

> *Another species of compulsion or necessity is what our law calls duress* per minas*; or threats and menaces which induce a fear of death or other bodily harm, and which take away for that reason the guilt of many crimes and misdemeanours; at least before the human tribunal...This however seems only, or at least principally, to hold to positive crimes, so created by the laws of society; and which therefore society may excuse; but not as to natural offences, so declared by the law of God, wherein human magistrates are only the executioners of the divine punishment, and therefore, though a man be violently assaulted, and hath no other possible means of escaping death, but by the killing of an innocent person: this fear and force shall not acquit him of murder: for he aught rather to die himself than escape by the murder of an innocent. But in such a case he is permitted to kill the assailant.*

So the Doctrine of Necessity question had not been random after all: it had been on Justice Scaglietti's mind, and the man in the back row somehow knew it. If Sabrina's assumptions about how the letter came to be in his Blackstone are correct, then the Justice had been considering the Doctrine of Necessity on that same January 3rd when, quietly slippered, she had come upon him in the library.

Perhaps the man's question had been intended to prod Sabrina. She races back to the auditorium, hoping to catch him before he leaves, but when she arrives the hall is empty.

Sabrina returns to the library, and this time instead of Blackstone she locates a global register of universities and colleges—she might have lost her interrogator, but in academia it is usually possible to track someone down through their institutional affiliation. She tries looking up Sancta Civitas, the name of the college to which the man had professed to be associated, but finds no such entry. She tries online instead, but 'Sancta Civitas' returns nothing associated with academia, nor the various research institutions and foundations and think tanks that, although facilitating scholarship, are themselves non-teaching.

Most of the search returns refer to a musical work of the same title, an oratorio by the English composer Ralph Vaughn Williams, composed in the early Twentieth Century. The libretto was taken from the Book of Revelation, some from the authorized King James Version, but much of it from Taverner's earlier 1539 translation. She is unfamiliar with the oratorio, but reading through the article she can tell that it was a major work, requiring not just a full orchestra and chorus, but also a second 'distant' chorus. Obviously somber in tone, echoing the Great War that had not long ended, or perhaps instead the proletarian near-revolution known to history as the General Strike, an event that had accompanied its 1926 premier.

That premier, she notes, took place in Oxford, at the Sheldonian, Christopher Wren's great theater, and at the mention of the city she cannot help feeling for the coin in her pocket.

It reminds Sabrina that her excuse for not dealing with the Oxford Crown earlier—the need to prepare for the upcoming defense of her dissertation—has now expired. The time has come to return the coin to its rightful owners.

THE DAYS THAT FOLLOW Sabrina's defense are mostly occupied with filling out applications for postdoctoral fellowships. Her colleagues at NYU have hinted that they would be receptive to her remaining with the university, but after years at the same institution Sabrina feels the need for a change: Boston, perhaps, or sunny California.

In between postdoctoral applications, Sabrina prepares to return the Oxford Crown, an undertaking that she plans with the precision of a bank heist. She purchases a padded envelope with which to anonymously mail the coin back to the Ashmolean, plus a book of stamps whose postage would be more than adequate to convey it across the Atlantic, both bought while the weather is still cold enough to warrant the wearing of gloves when conducting the transaction, leaving no chance of fingerprints, and both paid for with cash rather than risking the inerasable electronic record of a credit card. But her sentiments toward the coin are not unmixed: at night she often enjoys in brief sleeping wakefulness putting her hand under the pillow and feeling there the crown's comforting heft, gently rubbing the surface, recognizing the spires by feel alone now, and which become dreams. It makes her sleep better, she imagines, and by day she realizes that familiarity is giving birth to affection—the reason that the padded envelope remains unused in the drawer.

Sabrina decides that she will mail it without fail after receiving formal notification that the defense of her dissertation was successful and that she is to be awarded her J.S.D., the last hurdle in her studies, a suitable day for fresh beginnings.

Meanwhile, she has a final piece of research to do.

AT ONE TIME the New York Public Library on 42nd Street had contemplated moving the stacks from their location directly underground, beneath the main building, out to distant New Jersey, but the scholarly outcry against the ensuing waiting period had led to a reversal, and so Sabrina's filling out of stack requests from the catalog and handing them in at the readers' services desk is followed as usual by the particular pleasure of seeing them rolled up into capsules that are then slotted into pneumatic brass tubes and whisked away below. She imagines a legion of subterranean workers somewhere deep beneath them, dwarf-sized creatures operating by gaslight alone, dutifully receiving the requests and retrieving the volumes for return to the light-filled world above.

Soon she is sitting at her usual spot in the reading room, beneath the soaring windows of the western side, with Thorne's translation of Henry de Bracton's *De Legibus et Consuetudinibus Angliae* open before her. Bracton, she has discovered, was the first to articulate the Doctrine of Necessity in English law, preceding Blackstone by five centuries, and her purpose today is to find out exactly what it was that he had to say. She has also learned that Bracton was an important member of the *coram rege*—essentially a privy council—advising that same Henry III for whom William the Marshal had been regent. Bracton was still a youth when the latter died, but as she reads through his commentary, emphasizing that the monarch is monarch only if obtaining and exercising his power in accordance with law, she wonders how much Bracton's ideas had been influenced by that king-dislodging knight into whose granite face she had stared at Temple Church—certainly Ravenscroft would have been pleased with the arguments.

Bracton's efforts may be said to have culminated in the first English parliament, alarmingly known as the Mad Parliament. That historic legislature, she is surprised to learn, sat not in London nor Westminster, as might have been expected, but in Oxford—Sabrina wonders at how that city seems to keep coming up lately.

Finally, she locates what she sought, eloquently summed up in just a single unequivocal sentence: *That which is otherwise not lawful is made lawful by necessity*, as clear, succinct and uncompromising an articulation of the Doctrine of Necessity as could be stated.

Sabrina steps away from the desk and out of the library, wanting to stretch her legs. She buys a bratwurst from a street vendor and takes a seat in Bryant Park to consume it while considering what she has discovered. That the Doctrine of Necessity was on Justice Scaglietti's mind is beyond doubt: the fact of the note on the page at which the letter was found means that he had not opened the Blackstone at random: it had already been open there, and he had been studying it closely enough to have written in the margin that short, cryptic comment: *All of them?* Presumably he was referring to the 'crimes and misdemeanours' part of *which take away for that reason the guilt of many crimes and misdemeanours*—Scaglietti had been wondering if the Doctrine of Necessity could be applied to any crime, not just 'many,' perhaps even a crime as great as that undefined *perversion of the most foul and depraved nature* he had referred to in the letter to Bronaryre.

Sabrina finishes her lunch and goes back into the library. She left the Bracton open when she stepped out, a way of signaling to library staff that her absence was temporary and so the volume should not be returned to the stacks, but when she arrives at the desk she finds that it has been closed.

Whoever closed it inserted a bookmark to keep her spot.

The bookmark is an envelope. No stamp or franking or Royal Mail sticker this time, just her name typewritten by a genuine typewriter: she can see the impressions left by the keys. The paper is plain, standard stock. Inside is a printed card, an invitation to a cocktail party taking place this evening. The venue is the Museum of Modern Art. The cocktail party, which is really a fundraiser, includes a private viewing of a new exhibition there.

Nothing else. No note.

She looks up and tries to catch the eye of anyone who might have been seeking a reaction, but no one is looking at her. She returns to the invitation, reading it more carefully now, even the fine print on the back, listing the donors. There she learns that the exhibition was made possible with the generous support of, among others, Pendle Hill Investments.

Sabrina had given up on this Bronaryre person ever showing himself, but now she realizes that his lawyer's assertion had not been disingenuous after all—as Ravenscroft had warned, if she was patient then his client would eventually contact her, although an anonymous invitation seems a very roundabout way of doing so.

She is suddenly grateful for having been so tardy in returning the Oxford Crown.

# V

THE MUSEUM OF MODERN ART has closed to the public for the day, but Sabrina is admitted after showing her invitation at the door. She is directed to a wide staircase leading up to an atrium, where the cocktail party is underway.

There is a good-sized crowd, a hundred people at least, perhaps twice that. No university grunge tonight; these people are dressed in a way which, whether meant consciously or not, is a subtle assertion of wealth and position: the donor class, she thinks of them. There are waiters with trays of food, a table with drinks, the quiet murmur of hushed conversation.

She fetches a glass of champagne and surveys her surroundings. Much of the atrium is open to the hall below, giving the sense of standing on a large platform hovering inside a vast interior space. High above rise the floors of the museum, and through the windows she catches glimpses of what lies within: a wiry Miró; a Mondrian of doleful Dutch regularity; a Matisse vibrant with lush Provençal light. One of the white expanses of wall on the enclosed sides bears a long panel of Monet's endless water lilies, the other holds a pair of flamboyant de Koonings. She wonders how the museum selected them for this prime position—the beginning and end of modernism maybe: the cautious subjugation of form in Monet to its raucous abandonment by de Kooning; or perhaps a second polarity:

the migration of the center of the art world from Paris to New York that is represented by these paintings.

She takes a seat on a bench by the de Koonings and waits for whoever invited her to come and show himself.

No one does so. After twenty minutes and a second glass of champagne, the only people to have approached her are waiters with trays of hors d'oeuvres. One of them comes by with little tuna tartares that Sabrina politely declines, but the waiter insists.

"I was asked to deliver this to you," he says, proffering a paper napkin.

She accepts it and asks, "By whom?" but the waiter has already moved on.

Sabrina examines the napkin. There is nothing on either side, but when she unfolds it she finds a message written within.

EXIT THE MUSEUM AT 8:00 P.M. VIA THE 'A' FIRE ESCAPE
A CAR WILL BE WAITING OUTSIDE

She does not bother trying to catch someone looking for a reaction this time, and instead calmly refolds the napkin and puts it into her evening purse. The note, and its strange method of delivery, does nothing to relieve the persistent feeling of vague paranoia from her continued possession of the Oxford Crown.

Sabrina finishes the champagne and heads upstairs to the exhibition.

The subject matter is a peculiar one for an art institution: "Is Art Dead?" The question is treated as a debate, in which various paintings and sculptures and installations are presented as arguments, both for and against. Oldenburgs and Warhols and a Jasper Johns serve as introductory statements, assertions that art was unquestionably still vibrant and alive into the 1970s, but a series of later works seems mostly intended to show a sudden decline in the decades that followed—vacuity of purpose expressed without virtue of technique, as one placard states. Jeff Koons is quoted by both sides; Damien Hirst by the Yeas alone, along with the critic Robert Hughes's caustic characterization of such works as *the tedious spectacle of ineptitude*. Two large buttons are situated at the exit, marked *Yea* and *Nay*, an invitation to register a verdict. Sabrina ignores them and instead locates the 'A' fire escape in an alcove by the bathrooms. At eight o'clock precisely she takes it and goes down the stairs as fast as her high heels will allow. At the bottom is a door with a large sign warning that an alarm will sound if it is opened. She disregards the sign and pushes the handle.

There is no alarm. She wonders whether this is because the thing only sounds at a security desk, or if someone deliberately disabled it for her to exit quietly.

Sabrina emerges onto a darkened 54th Street, the other side of the block from the museum's brightly lit main entrance, and now she understands the purpose of the note: it was to direct her out the back way, a means of ensuring that she is not followed. This section of the street is a no-stopping zone but nevertheless there is a lone car parked there. Standing by it is a woman, who from the uniform is apparently the chauffeur. She wears a peaked cap and double-breasted gray jacket, unbuttoned despite the cold, matching jodhpurs tucked into brightly polished brown boots, and beneath the jacket a white collared shirt with a gray silk tie. She stands with one gloved hand on a door handle and the other on her hip, a slightly exaggerated posture, as if a model posing for a photo shoot.

Sabrina approaches. It is a large vehicle, black paintwork shining under the streetlights, the chrome glistening, a car that has somehow avoided the crust of salt and sand that coats most vehicles in Manhattan this winter. The windows in the back are blacked out, and Sabrina suddenly realizes that she recognizes this car: it is the same vehicle she witnessed coming down the drive at Netherly, that last time she had called on Justice Scaglietti, a week before he died.

She comes to a halt in front of the woman.

"I've seen this car before," she says.

"And also the chauffeur," the woman responds. She removes her hat, releasing a thick mane of tightly curled blond hair that had been bunched up beneath it, a distinctive feature that Sabrina does indeed recognize.

"You were in the seat behind me on the flight from Heathrow," she says.

The woman nods affirmatively, removes her glove, and holds out a hand. "My name is Hippolyte," she says, pronouncing her name in the French manner, with a silent *h* and the *i* as a long *e*. When Sabrina takes her hand the woman leans forward and kisses her on each cheek, in the way that Continentals do. She releases Sabrina and opens a rear door. "It is necessary that we leave now."

Sabrina gets into the car. Hippolyte closes the door, takes her position behind the wheel, and starts the engine. There is no vibration or sound, just a flick of the gauges coming to life, the only indication that the motor is running. The driver turns to face Sabrina.

"My name means unleasher of horses, and so you see it is appropriate that I should be the driver." She pats the steering wheel with a gloved hand. "I shall unleash these horses now."

She leaves the curb and proceeds down the street. Sabrina examines her surroundings. The interior is sumptuously upholstered in soft leather and paneled in polished walnut. But what most strikes her is the smell: rich warm tones of wood and hide, but something else, too: an exotic scent lying beneath the others, pungent and hard to define.

They come to a halt at the red light on Fifth Avenue.

"What sort of car is this?" Sabrina asks.

"A Bentley."

"It's beautiful."

"And safe," Hippolyte replies. "The tires are run-flats, the body is armor-plated, the glass is bulletproof."

"All this for me?"

"For my master."

Sabrina wonders if *master*, like the osculatory greeting, is one of those things that would seem less jarring if she were French, too.

# VI

THE BENTLEY TURNS right onto Fifth Avenue, heading downtown. Soon it has entered the labyrinth of lower Manhattan, a warren of crooked streets, cobbled pavement, and cast-iron buildings with broad plate-glass windows.

Sabrina sits back in the soft leather and takes in the passing streetscape. This is prerevolutionary Manhattan, she thinks, the Manhattan of the Dutch and the English—a baroque confusion of streets with strange names like Gansevoort and Nassau and the Bowery—a contrast to the orderly grid of numbered thoroughfares above Fourteenth Street that is the Manhattan of Americans, a city laid out with the deliberate rationality of a new and enlightened republic.

The black car glides along. It seems darker down here, Sabrina thinks, as if the power grid petered out as it came south, leaving streetlights only half glowing, dull incandescent bulbs insufficient to illuminate the shadows beneath. People become few and then none as they reach the Financial District, a buzzing hive by weekday, but mostly deserted at night.

The Bentley comes to a silent stop.

"In there," Hippolyte says, pointing to the building across the street. "Take the last elevator."

"You're not coming?"

"No."

Sabrina gets out, emerging from the warmth of the car into air that is sharp and frigid and still. The street is really just a lane, narrow and devoid of traffic. She closes the door and watches the vehicle pull away until it disappears from view.

She is alone. This is the city post-Apocalypse, she thinks: intact but empty, silent and cold, something that a future explorer might discover and wonder at what became of the people who built it, like the conquistadors hacking through jungle and suddenly stumbling upon the deserted Tikal. The only movement is steam spewing from a street vent, a common sight in New York as if there were a second civilization beneath the city, an underground industrial-aged society whose existence was sometimes revealed by these strange outpourings of steam from beneath the earth, or the steel-shrieking squeal of a subway train rising through a sidewalk grating, a civilization whose only communication with the world above was via pneumatic tube at the New York Public Library.

Sabrina stares across the street. It is not a residential building but an office building, a tall tower topped with an elegant spire with large metal gargoyles protruding from the corners, something which would be a distinct part of the skyline in any other city, and was perhaps once so in New York, for it looks very old, built in the ziggurat-like step-back design of Manhattan's prewar skyscrapers. The facade is composed of limestone panels carved in low relief—flowing and streamlined in Jazz Age style—and which frame a revolving door flanked by two normal doors. They are glass-paneled, and on the other side Sabrina can see the interior of the lobby, gleaming stone and polished metal, an oasis of light against the darkened city, an Edward Hopper come to life.

She crosses the street. The revolving door is locked, but Sabrina finds one of the side doors open and enters. When it swings shut behind her she hears the sound of the bolt closing: the door has relocked itself. Maybe Hippolyte unlocked it remotely from the car, or perhaps there is a surveillance system somewhere, and whoever is at the other end of it recognized the Bentley.

It occurs to Sabrina that she is now locked inside this building until someone chooses to let her out.

There is a reception desk, but it is unattended. Despite the apparent lack of twenty-four-hour security, which suggests a building on the financial skids, the lobby is well maintained: marble floors and walls brought to a high shine and punctuated with brightly polished brass registers from which the deep bass rumbling of a distant boiler is vaguely audible.

She crosses the lobby to the elevators, high heels echoing on the polished marble. There are three alcoves with elevators, the first to floors 2-29, the second to floors 30-59, and the third containing just a single car with only one destination: the 60th floor.

Sabrina presses the call button. A small panel in the wall next to it slides open, revealing a black glass surface with the outline of a hand etched upon it, and four short pegs sticking up at the points between the fingers. There is a text screen above, bearing the instruction *Please place your right hand on the glass panel*. Next to it is a red light.

Sabrina places her hand on the panel and pushes the webbing firmly against the pegs. There is no further sound, but the red light turns green and the text changes to a simple *Thank you*. Sabrina removes her hand, the panel slides shut, and the doors to the elevator car open.

She gets inside, wondering what sort of person it is taking her to meet, who requires a hand print before admitting guests.

There are only three buttons in the car, one for the lobby, one for the basement, and one for the 60th floor, the last of which is already lit. The doors slam shut, and the elevator begins to ascend with a loud mechanical whine. There is no floor counter. The elevator feels slow, but at least there is no elevator music or television monitor, just the myriad rasps and clangs of heavy equipment in motion. Eventually, it arrives at the destination. The car comes to a shuddering halt, and the doors slide open.

Sabrina steps into the passageway. The doors close behind her and she hears the elevator begin its descent back down to the lobby. The passageway is short and uncarpeted, the walls painted an institutional beige. Fluorescent lights overhead; one of the tubes blinks and fizzes.

There is the hum of machinery nearby, and Sabrina realizes that she has been delivered to the utility area that tops every tall building. There are doors at either end of the passageway, both of which are large and made of metal: the one on the left is unmarked except for some greasy handprints, presumably those of maintenance workers; the other bears a warning sign: *Danger–High Voltage*.

Sabrina thinks that she must have misinterpreted Hippolyte's instructions, for this cannot be the correct place, but then she hears the sound of a latch unlocking behind the door on her right, the one with the warning sign. She stares at the door, waiting for whoever turned the lock to open it, but nothing further happens.

She steps forward and cautiously taps with the back of her hand, as if the *High Voltage* warning might apply even to the door itself. There is no response from within. She listens a moment, then tries the handle.

The door is unlocked. She opens it but does not yet cross the threshold, instead electing to stand in place and inspect the scene thus revealed.

On the other side is not the confusion of gray enamel cabinets and thick wiring harness that the *High Voltage* sign had suggested. Instead, it is a parquetry-floored gallery twenty feet in length, and at the end of which, beneath an archway on the left, are broad stairs leading down into a room that she cannot see, but whose light floods into the hall.

There are three coat hooks to her immediate right, two of which are occupied, one by a furled black umbrella, the other by a raincoat whose interior is lined in tartan. Opposite them is a small console supporting a shallow silver dish, evidently antique and probably originally intended for calling cards, perhaps now used for house keys, but currently empty. Several framed photographs line the wall, and at the end is a niche with a Grecian urn, red-figure, subtly lit by recessed lighting.

This is not an equipment room atop an office tower, Sabrina thinks, it is the entrance foyer to an apartment of the type found in the classic prewar buildings of Park Avenue, up in the high Seventies and low Eighties.

Sabrina wonders if she should call out but then decides against it: she is clearly expected, and all this furtive museum exiting and mysterious door unlocking is some kind of theater—a performance put on for her alone, although she cannot imagine why. She steps forward and cautiously enters the apartment but leaves the door open, unwilling to allow it to relock itself like the one in the lobby.

The first thing to strike her is the change in the atmosphere, not just figuratively but literally, too: the air itself is different, no longer the skin-parching air of New York in winter—already wrung dry by the exterior cold and then brought to even lower humidity by central heating—but instead in here the air is soft and moist, almost luxuriant. More than just moist: it feels vibrant—vital, in the core sense of that word: full of life, as if the oxygen level had somehow been raised, sharpening the senses. Sabrina takes a deep breath. This is not the harsh air of hibernal Manhattan, she thinks; it is the ozone-laden atmosphere of a South Sea island on the verge of a thunderstorm, bursting with energy and expectation.

She pauses as she passes the coat hooks and, sharpened senses already at work, detects a familiar scent. She gathers the raincoat to her face and inhales deeply. It smells like a wet field after a passing shower, she imagines, but there is something else too: that same odor as in the back of the Bentley: it is lush and tropical and slightly decadent, the way an alley in Mandalay might have smelled a hundred years ago, back in the days of sampans and rickshaws, of warehouses filled with spices in calico sacks and camphor-wood chests, of red-lanterned gambling houses and shadowy opium dens.

Sabrina releases the raincoat and continues cautiously down the corridor. The door suddenly swings shut behind her, followed by the sound of the bolt locking. She looks down and sees a matchbox-sized wall-mounted device, apparently some sort of electronic sensor, that must have triggered it as she passed by. She continues moving slowly down the gallery, trying not to dwell on the fact of now being doubly locked in.

The frames hanging on the wall turn out to contain not photographs but works on paper, although with no obvious connection between them: the first is a music score done by hand, even to the staff, with thick hashes instead of ovals for notes, and signed at the bottom; the second is a penned sketch in black ink, now turned sepia, hastily but expertly executed, depicting a woman in an attitude of repose—it too is signed, this time legibly: a Modigliani, presumably a copy; and lastly a sheet of calligraphy richly illuminated in gold and lapis lazuli, probably Islamic, strikingly ornate in comparison to the pair that preceded it.

Sabrina comes to the end of the entrance hall. To the left is the archway with several broad steps beneath it, leading into what she sees is a sunken living room. She takes the steps down and, with her view upward now unimpeded, gazes above in astonishment.

Although the floor area is not especially large the ceiling is wondrously high, higher than the room is wide, as high as Grand Central, soaring forty or fifty feet above the floor. Sabrina realizes that she must be inside the spire: the walls narrow as they rise, replicating the spire's tapering shape, and are pierced by slender windows formed by the glazed gaps between the vertical strakes that adorn the exterior. The structure is floodlit from outside, and high up through the windows is visible the shining and shadowed underside of one of the metal gargoyles, thrusting out from the building, half-bird and half-reptile, poised with wings unfolding as if about to take flight.

In the middle of the room is a broad square column forming what must be the central spine of the building. On one of the two sides visible to her hangs a large Pollock print from his Jack-the-Dripper period, but the wall is otherwise an unadorned stark white; the other side has been paneled in satinwood for the bottom ten feet or so, and contains a small door with mirrors on either side. Above that are a series of three narrow mezzanines giving access to bookshelves built into the wall. They are connected at the corner by a spiral staircase of black-painted metal, and so form a sort of vertical library, a clever use of space inside a spire.

The sunken part that she is in is the main area, furnished with a few stylish pieces in Art Deco or perhaps Art Moderne, and occupies most of the floor area.

A man's dinner jacket lies tossed across the back of the sofa.

There is a cut-crystal vase full of red roses on the table, a feminine touch strangely incongruent in this masculine space, and she wonders if they are here on her account. Steps on the far side lead up to another room, not very large, probably a bedroom. No kitchen that she can see, although there is a substantial bar. Apart from a small washroom to her left, tiled like a subway station, there is nothing else.

It is, she decides, very likely the world's most spectacular *pied-à-terre*.

It is also apparently unoccupied. But then the small door in the paneled part of the central spine opens.

# VII

ANY SPACE ENCASED by the skyscraper's central spine would have to be small, and from the appearance of the man who emerges, Sabrina suspects that it must be used as a dressing room. He is wearing a dinner suit but not quite: no jacket; the shirt cuffs are unfolded and unfastened; a bow tie hangs undone around his neck.

He spies Sabrina and steps forward with an arm extended but not, she soon discovers, in greeting.

"Here, would you mind?" He opens his hand, revealing two cuff links held in the palm. "My valet died."

She accepts the cuff links, and he assumes a posture of the crucified Christ.

"Dexter first, then sinister."

Sabrina begins on the outstretched right arm, neatly folding back the crisp French cuff and inserting the link. It has an unusual pattern: a pair of triangles, one inverted on top of the other, their bases bent in the middle and meeting in a cinquefoil. It strikes her as esoteric, vaguely occult.

"Rosicrucian?" she asks, recalling Ravenscroft's seal.

He looks at her with a raised eyebrow. "No, it is not."

The accent is difficult to place precisely: certainly Received Pronunciation at core—*valet* had included the *t*, and *here* had been pronounced with a diphthong distinct enough to have suggested that it was a two-syllable word—but there is none of the singsong rhythm and rising inflection usual in the English dialect: his manner of speech is even and direct: he must have lived much of his life in America. There is also a suggestion of an underlying Gaelic burr, perhaps a faint trace of the Welsh ancestry that had given him his strange surname.

She would have expected the same odor as with the raincoat, but detects nothing. Perhaps there is a second person in the apartment whose garment it is, or maybe with the sudden loss of the valet he has simply misplaced his aftershave.

Sabrina finishes with the right cuff and continues to the left. He wears a wristwatch on this side, an old Breguet bearing the marks of many years of use, and it takes her longer this time to get the cuff correctly folded. Bronaryre (for she assumes it is he) remains silent throughout this procedure, not looking at her nor even particularly aware of her, as if preoccupied with other thoughts. She had not known what to expect, but certainly not someone so unforthcoming. She decides to provoke him.

"How did he die?"

"Who?"

"Your valet."

"Jenkins? I don't know. In terror, I expect."

Sabrina completes the second cuff. He proceeds immediately to the bar, leaving her standing in the middle of the room—a man who is in no way discomfited by silences, she perceives; indeed, he seems to prefer them. She decides to match his reserve and says nothing while he mixes, a time-consuming process that involves ice, liquor, olives, and a few carefully applied drops of a mysterious liquid drawn from a small apothecary's bottle. He eventually returns with two cocktail glasses whose contents are cold enough to have made them frost in this tropical subclimate atop a winter-borne skyscraper.

"Dry Martini," he states, offering a glass.

"I'll take this one," she says, reaching for the glass he had intended for himself. "What was in the small bottle?"

"Extract of cassia. Fascinating how a little tree bark can so enliven a cocktail, like angostura in a Manhattan, or quinine in a gin and tonic." He allows her to take the glass without objection, and then raises his own.

"To a bloody war and a sickly season," he says, and then, responding to her look of puzzlement, "It is the traditional naval officers' toast for today, Thursdays, war and sickness being the two ways of culling the Navy List of competition for advancement, and thus increasing one's own chances of promotion."

They drink. She agrees that the addition of a little tree bark has resulted in an excellent Martini.

"Were you a naval officer?" she asks, a question that causes him to regard her with bemusement.

"You *are* Lancaster, are you not?"

"I am."

"The same one my solicitor Ravenscroft met with in London?"

"The same."

He puts down his glass and goes to a mirror to work on the bow tie. "Well, Lancaster, perhaps you had better recount what that miserable wretch told you about me."

"He said very little about you."

"Nothing… startling?"

"Startling? No, not especially. All he said was that you were a scholar-adventurer, and that you were a citizen of both the U.K. and the U.S."

He turns to face her, apparently expecting more, but when she adds nothing he says, "It appears that my lawyer is sporting with me," and returns his attention to the bow tie.

Sabrina takes a seat on the sofa and reviews the conversation with Ravenscroft, but there was very little detail in what the lawyer had told her about his client. She sits back and sips the Martini thoughtfully. With Bronaryre now facing the mirror and herself out of his reflected gaze, Sabrina takes the opportunity to examine her host more carefully.

His age is difficult to determine: he retains the physical sharpness of youth, but carries himself with the confidence of an older and more experienced man—mid-thirties, she guesses, and most of those years lived fully. Perhaps that accounts for the lack of BBC plumminess in the Received Pronunciation accent: it must have been knocked out of him by life. Middle height and build; no fat. At ease in a dinner suit. Well groomed; a man incapable of being slovenly, she thinks, no matter what the clothing. Not of any obvious type: someone uncongenial to easy categorization—in contrast to most men in her experience, usually just minor variations on a few well-worn themes. Clearly intelligent, and self-contained to a high degree; the type of person who when walking into a room subtly changes the atmosphere, someone whose presence injects a certain *frisson*. Above all, she decides, he is a man around whom no one would ever be quite comfortable.

These surroundings suit him, she thinks: singular and strange.

"Mr. Ravenscroft also mentioned that you have several residences, although he gave no hint that any of them was like this."

"I suppose it must seem unusual," he says, "but I'm surprised there aren't more of them. The spires of these prewar skyscrapers had a practical function: they were used to conceal utility equipment, particularly the three essentials always located on the roof: the water tank, the elevator motors, and the air-conditioning plant. But these days water tanks are no longer necessary—modern pumps are sufficiently powerful and reliable to keep the plumbing pressurized—plus elevator motors and air conditioners are far more compact today than their industrial-age forebears. So, when it came time for this building to modernize, I offered to fund the refurbishment of these items myself, in return for which the space in the spire thus opened up would be made available for my private use."

"You don't find it a little isolated, alone atop an office tower down here in Wall Street?"

"I like the isolation: it suits me not to have anyone around to pry into my business." He finishes the bow tie, puts on his jacket, and then turns to face her. "But you haven't seen the best part yet. Bring your glass."

He picks up his own and leads Sabrina to the same door in the spine from which he had emerged. She glances at the Pollock in passing and sees brush strokes—more precisely, drip marks—it is not a print, as she had first imagined, it is an original.

Bronaryre opens the door. It reveals not a dressing room but an elevator, far smaller than the one she rode up in, and which obviously does not go down to the lobby, since there was no hint of its existence on the first floor. Instead of the usual sliding doors this elevator has a small gate, just knee high, which he opens for her to enter, although she could have just as easily stepped over it.

It is a little jewel box of a thing, plushly carpeted and ornamented: wood paneling smelling of the years of furniture oil that must have gone into its maintenance, a fold-down seat upholstered in plump velvet, little gilded mirrors so that passengers can make a last-minute check of the angle of a hat or the fall of a cravat. There is a lever made of brightly polished brass with an ebony handle, which can be swung from an arrow pointing down to an arrow pointing up. It is currently on the arrow pointing down: the sixtieth floor is not the top story in this building after all. Bronaryre pulls the lever across to the up-arrow. There is a little mechanical whir as the elevator thinks about it, then at last a gentle shunt as it begins the ascent.

Sabrina catches herself in a mirror. The face she sees there does not reveal the unease that she feels, the slightly anxious sense that she has had since entering this intimidating building of concealed panels and concealed apartments and concealed elevators, and which has been compounded since meeting this brooding man, equally concealed and equally intimidating. It is a feeling not quite of dread, more a suspicion that whatever is to follow will not turn out in the way that she expected.

But then the evening becomes dreamlike. The second elevator ride ends not in the traditional manner, with doors sliding open, but instead with the entire elevator car emerging through the floor. It comes to a halt. Bronaryre opens the little gate, and they exit. When he closes the gate behind them the elevator once again whirs into action, and the whole contraption gently descends whence it came. The two sections of floor that had opened to accommodate its arrival now close back over its departure—a ship sinking under the surface of the sea, as if it had never been.

Sabrina gazes about her in wonderment. The room they have entered is not large, but it occupies the entire floor. All four walls are composed of floor-to-ceiling windows framed in polished nickel, and beyond which is arrayed New York City by night. She is in a glass box suspended high over the city.

"It's beautiful," she says.

"We're at the top of the spire, with just the pinnacle above us," Bronaryre explains, "thus the special elevator. It's cranked up by pinion gear, not hauled on cables in the normal way."

He turns on the interior light—a wide polygonal fixture of streamlined metal and milky glass mounted in the center of the ceiling—revealing the room's only two furnishings: a dining table in the middle, laid with ten places, and beside it a serving table on top of which sits a silver-domed platter and several brightly polished chafing dishes with little flames beneath them—the evening attire is explained: Bronaryre is hosting a dinner party.

Sabrina silently chides herself for having supposed that the roses were because of her.

He dims the light so that there is just enough illumination to walk around, allowing for the best appreciation of the view outside. It is a magnificent panorama, a sea of light. The marble floor is figured as a compass rose. Sabrina finds north and gazes out the northern windows at the vast sweep of Manhattan: darkened skyscrapers looming eerily nearby, topping out a little lower than this one, then the wash of brownstones and tenements until midtown, where the city swells once again, a monumental wave of buildings dominated by the *yin* and *yang* of Manhattan architecture: to the left, the masculine strength of the Empire State Building, dignified and reserved, and to the right the Chrysler Building, slender and beautiful, the woman in the room on whom everyone's eyes fall.

Apart from the disappearing elevator, there is no visible exit from the room. There are four small balconies, one at each corner, tiny platforms atop the necks of the gargoyles Sabrina had seen from below. Floodlit from beneath, they look like something William Blake might have imagined: great metallic dragons gazing malevolently down upon the city far below, searching for prey, poised for flight, ready to pounce. This is Gotham at its most Gothic, she thinks, a city of soaring heights and lurking terror, and with the elevator gone she is effectively imprisoned in this room, imprisoned not in a dungeon but an antidungeon, imprisoned in a glass cell in the sky.

She takes a stroll around the perimeter. The East River is below, a long dark passage festooned with the lights of the many crossings: the Brooklyn Bridge with its flamboyant cat's cradle of cables directly below; the more sober Manhattan Bridge abutting it; the Williamsburg a little further upstream; ungainly Queensboro at midtown; and, in distant Harlem, the noble Triborough. To the south is the harbor, the Statue of Liberty looking surprisingly small and fragile from this height, and beyond it the blue-gray Verrazano-Narrows Bridge spanning the entrance, the lights along the catenary curves of its suspension cables glowing like pearls on a string. Then the west: the remainder of the Financial District, skyscrapers old and new crowding in on one another, as if to form a protective ring around their queen bee: the New York Stock Exchange.

"Thank you for showing it to me," she says. "So much light."

"Ayn Rand says that when the lights go out in New York City, civilization will be at an end."

"There was a black hole over there, before they rebuilt the World Trade Center."

"And which proves her point, I think."

They stand in silence for several minutes. Sabrina is not yet at ease, but she is less uncomfortable than previously.

"Who is following me?" she asks.

"Following you?"

"The clandestine exit from MoMA…"

"Ah, that: a precaution only, to ensure that you did not inadvertently lead anyone to me."

"Who?"

"My enemies. They are not a threat to you."

"Do you have many enemies?"

"Countless."

"Was Justice Scaglietti among them?"

But instead of answering, Bronaryre checks his Breguet. "I'm late. I regret that it's not possible for me to answer any more of your questions tonight." He walks over to a sliver of wall between the windows, where an embossed escutcheon plate with a black button is located. On pressing it, the floor reopens.

"You may keep my coin for the present," he says.

"The Oxford Crown? I mailed it back to the Ashmolean."

"No, you didn't. It's in your left pocket right now."

"How could you possibly know that?"

"I can see its outline."

She carries a small evening purse but, wanting to keep the Oxford Crown upon her person rather than chance losing it to a mugger—she is in New York City after all, where mugging is so characteristic as to be almost a tourist attraction—she decided to put the coin in the pocket of the dress she had selected for tonight, her only cocktail outfit. She looks down. The dress is cut tight but not excessively so, and it must have taken a keen eye to spot the coin.

"Nevertheless, I'm returning it," she says.

"Why would you do that?"

"Because it's stolen."

"Indeed it is," he says. "Stolen from me."

Before she can respond the elevator arrives, and they begin the descent.

"I have something for you," Bronaryre says after they reenter the apartment. He climbs the spiral staircase to the second of the mezzanines, where he searches the shelves. He soon extracts a volume and comes back down.

"Here," he says, offering it to her, "you may take this as evidence in support of my claim."

Sabrina accepts it. It is not a book but a periodical titled *The Numismatic Chronicle and Journal of the Numismatic Society*, published by the British Numismatic Society, designated as Volume 17 and dated April 1854 to January 1855. The cover is stiff paper, probably once cream but now dun-colored. She looks up at the man who gave it to her.

"How could something dated 1854 be relevant?"

"Provenance," he replies, escorting her toward the door. "The only way to demonstrate legitimate ownership of an object is to establish an uninterrupted history of its disposition, is it not?"

They come to the front door, and a simple way of determining if the raincoat belongs to someone else suddenly occurs to her.

"What an interesting lining," she says. "What sort of tartan is it?"

"Black Watch," he replies, without hesitation: the raincoat is his. "I served in the Black Watch at one time."

"Iraq or Afghanistan?"

"Passchendaele." He holds up a halting hand. "No more questions for now. If you choose to return the Oxford Crown to the Ashmolean then you must do so, but I ask that you first consider what I have told you. Meanwhile, I have something very important to accomplish."

"What's that?"

"Find out what my lawyer is up to."

He opens the front door. A man is standing there, hand raised to knock, and looking momentarily startled by the door having opened just as he was about to do so. His eyes go from Bronaryre to Sabrina, and his expression melts into one of genial good humor.

"My dear," he says, doffing a wide-brimmed hat and bowing gracefully. "I do hope that you will be joining us."

He is apparently one of the dinner guests. He is very strangely dressed: long vest and coat with a rough black woolen mantle or cloak over it, something that she had first mistaken for an academic gown. His shoes are buckled. He is not a young man but wears his hair long and this last, along with a certain vague familiarity of his features, makes Sabrina wonder if he is an aging rock star. Bronaryre speaks up before Sabrina can reply.

"Miss Lancaster regrets that she is unable to do so," he says. "Perhaps another time."

"Lancaster you say? Well, how very appropriate, for I see that any rose other than red would blush in your presence, madam."

Sabrina laughs—he was obviously a charmer in his day. "I seem to be encountering red roses in the strangest of circumstances lately," she says. "I'm wondering if it's a coincidence."

"Beware of coincidences," the man cautions, waving a finger in mock seriousness. "They are like the sons of York, not to be trusted."

Bronaryre hustles his guest inside, and she gets the impression that he would have preferred them not to have met. "Hippolyte is waiting downstairs," he says. "She will drive you home." He closes the door without waiting for a reply.

It is not until Sabrina is again in the back of the Bentley, reflecting upon the evening while heading uptown, that she realizes why the man on Bronaryre's threshold had seemed familiar. She takes out her phone and soon finds an image that confirms her guess, although what she has discovered is clearly impossible.

When she returns to her apartment, Sabrina's first action is to begin a journal. It will not be a diary—something she thinks of as a conceited inversion chronicling the dull minutiae of existence for the doubtful enlightenment of a disinterested posterity—but simply a record to contemporaneously log events and observations, a device with which to order the mind. She pulls a new notebook from the shelf—grid-lined and with plain brown cardboard covering, string-bound instead of the more usual staples or, worse, those spring-like metal spirals—and makes her first entry.

*I have met the recipient of Scaglietti's scathing letter, at last.*

*Younger than I expected; younger than the Justice by more than a generation, and it is hard to imagine what might have brought them together. A shared sense of asceticism, perhaps. Scaglietti certainly had it: his refusal to avail himself of the usual conveniences of modern life; his dogged dedication to pen & ink; to printed case records; to a sixty-year-old Mercedes with cracked leather seats and a gear shift on the steering column. Plus his Catholicism: in his case not something sourced from a deep sense of faith (he openly flouted all ten commandments—even the Fifth, given that he was such an uncompromising defender of the death penalty) but instead from a simple need for serenity—for the form of the mass, not its substance.*

*I had the same sense from Bronaryre: the disdain for small talk and social graces; his simple delight in tree bark and apparently an old coin; and anyone else living in such a place would surely have adorned one of those inner walls with an enormous flat-screen television, not rows of books and an original Jackson Pollock.*

*Asceticism, but a luxuriant asceticism—in both cases: Netherly was no monk's cell, and Bronaryre's* pied-à-terre *is more a* pied-à-ciel. *But neither needs luxury in the traditional sense (I slip into the present tense despite the Justice's death; he is still present in my mind). No need for display, to be obsequiously indulged or pandered to (indeed, they both prefer their own company). But they do need beauty: Scaglietti needed it in his surroundings (hence Netherly); in music, certainly; in language; in women (I always dressed well when calling on him, out of respect, of course, but also because I was conscious of that underlying need).*

*Bronaryre needs it, too: the Breguet; the sky-cell; the Modigliani.*

*But this is just speculation, and I am no closer to discovering what was behind Scaglietti's letter. No answers, just more questions:*

*—Who are these faceless enemies who might have followed me to find him?*

*—What is it that the 'miserable wretch' of a lawyer failed to reveal?*

*—What is so particular about the coin?*

*—And what was Benjamin Franklin doing on Aneurin Bronaryre's doorstep?*

# VIII

I SAW BENJAMIN FRANKLIN the other day," Sabrina says. "He was from Philadelphia, wasn't he?"

Ravenscroft is too engrossed in his cheesesteak to reply. Eventually, he swallows and washes it down with a hefty draft of ale. When meeting this time he had immediately declared that his digestion was too delicate for airline food and, given that he had not eaten since a light breakfast consumed twelve hours and five time zones ago, he proposed that they postpone further discussion until after lunch. The tavern is noisy, and she can tell that he is considering using this as an excuse to ignore her question, for he clearly wants to continue his demolition of the hoagie. Her own lies half-eaten and discarded on her plate; she would have preferred a salad. Hunger wins out, and the lawyer takes another ravenous mouthful. He does not give the impression of being a man with a delicate digestion, especially as the cheesesteak was preceded by a dozen Blue Points, slurped straight from the half-shell in rapid succession.

"I saw him at your client's apartment," she persists. "Don't you think it strange that I should have seen a man who has been dead for two hundred years at your client's apartment?"

"Boston," he mumbles.

"Boston?"

"He was born in Boston."

"Your client?"

"No, Franklin. You asked where he was from: he was from Boston. He moved to Philadelphia as a young man." He swallows in hasty frustration and takes another swig of ale. "Why you should choose to incommode an elderly gentleman of dyspeptic persuasion, one who has for the first time just endured the horrors of transatlantic air travel, I cannot imagine."

"The first time? You mean you've never been to the U.S. before?"

"Many times, but always by Cunard."

"Ah."

He does look put out and so she takes pity and allows him to finish his meal in peace. They occupy a nook by a bow window giving onto a streetscape of historical Philadelphia, probably not all that much changed since Franklin's time. The weather outside is blustery and sharp, a good day for such a spot, snug in a cozy room by a blazing fire. The tavern is genuinely from Franklin's day, the floor planks broad and uneven, the ceiling low and beamed, the windows small and mullioned—in tourist season it would no doubt be crowded, but at this time of year it is just well enough patronized to make it pleasantly convivial. He finally finishes the cheesesteak, drains his glass, and sits back with the satisfaction of a man who has narrowly averted disaster.

"Americans avow the hamburger as being their great contribution to global cuisine," he says, "but to my sense, it is the humble cheesesteak that deserves that high honor. I think the reason that the cheesesteak has not achieved world fame is because it doesn't travel well: for some reason they never seem quite right unless one is in Philadelphia; perhaps it's the nature of the griddle, bringing the onions to such unctuous sublimity, or maybe it's more basic than that: the brand of cheese, say, or the bun itself. I suppose it's like ful, which can be immensely enjoyable when floating down the Nile but is something that one would never order outside of Egypt." He signals to the bartender, who has been lingering at the end of the counter nearest them, apparently to better observe this strange specimen sitting opposite Sabrina.

"I say, do you have Navy Rum?"

"I do."

"Two, please. Rather a large one for me, plus the bill." He turns back to Sabrina. "Settles the stomach, you know."

"I'm being followed," she says.

"What makes you say that?"

"There was a man in my carriage on the train. When the conductor came through he bought his ticket, which is unusual because it's more expensive than buying it from the ticket office before boarding. It occurred to me that perhaps he had been following me since I left the apartment this morning, but didn't overhear the destination when I bought the ticket at Penn Station, and so had no option but to follow me onto whichever train I boarded."

"And because he bought his ticket on board you think he was following you?"

"That, plus the fact that he's outside right now, watching the tavern. He's huddled by a doorway across the street, trying to keep warm."

Ravenscroft turns to look and soon locates him. He spends a long moment studying the man before speaking.

"Looks like he's just waiting to meet someone."

"Maybe, but your client put on a great show of ensuring that I wasn't followed before I met him. That, coupled with the surety you gave me being stolen property, has left me on guard."

"Poor chap does look chilly," Ravenscroft says, unperturbed. "Hope he doesn't catch a cold."

"It doesn't worry you that I might have been followed?"

"Not really," he says. "It is to be expected."

Before she can ask why, the glasses of rum arrive: small for her but a double for Ravenscroft. To her surprise he immediately adds sugar, stirring it in with the unused oyster fork. He raises his glass.

"To the success of your dissertation," he says. "I must say that I enjoyed it very much."

"You've read my dissertation?"

"Yes, of course."

"But how could that be?"

"Quite simple: like all doctoral candidates, you were required to submit copies to the university library. I obtained a facsimile of one of those copies. It is in connection with your thesis that I wished to meet with you today." He tries his rum and smiles with pleasure. "Ah, nectar—won't you join me?"

Sabrina picks up her glass and takes a small sip. She imagines that jet fuel must taste much the same way.

"Mr. Ravenscroft, I don't believe that you 'endured the horrors of transatlantic air travel' just to discuss my dissertation."

"Well, of course I do have other matters to attend to, as you are about to see." He takes out a pair of spectacles and uses them to inspect the check, then extracts the long coat wallet she remembers from Temple Church and removes from it a wad of notes. He carefully picks out the correct bills, unused to banknotes that are all the same size and color. From the fatness of the wallet, Sabrina concludes that Ravenscroft habitually pays for things the old-fashioned way: with cash—she wonders if this is because he, like her when purchasing the return envelope for the Oxford Crown, prefers not to leave a trail. He finishes the rest of his rum in a single swig and puts down the glass.

"Now, shall we indulge in a postprandial perambulation around the city of brotherly love?"

Notwithstanding Ravenscroft's assertion of being undisturbed by the presence of a possible follower, they leave the tavern by the rear entrance, past the bathrooms and through a scullery into a trash-strewn alley. From his familiarity with the exit, she thinks that this is not the first time the lawyer has left the tavern via the back door.

Ravenscroft walks quickly, as he did the night in the Inner Temple, not a man taking a leisurely stroll after a large meal but someone with a destination in mind. They cross Society Hill and head away from the historical part of the city, the surroundings progressively losing charm in proportion to age. Soon they hit an area populated with freeways and warehouses, then eventually the Delaware River, here not a bucolic stream cutting its winding way through the Appalachian wilderness but instead a broad tidal estuary, a working port of wharves and derricks, the prevailing smell an industrial mixture of fuel oil and asphalt.

They come to a chain-link fence separating them from the river, with gates and a guardhouse. Ravenscroft approaches the guardhouse and shows his credentials to the man inside; they are soon admitted. It is not until they have crossed the restricted area and rounded a large collection of rusting shipping containers that the object of their journey comes into view.

It is a ship, a large one, gleaming white superstructure above a polished dark blue hull that has been topped with a white strake running along its length, as if to emphasize her clean and purposeful lines. The ship has two funnels, squat and steeply raked, each of them sporting small wings, echoing the navigation wings protruding from the bridge.

"The SS *United States*," Ravenscroft says. "The world's fastest-ever transatlantic liner."

"Is this how you will be returning to England?"

"No, I'm afraid that her days as a liner ended long ago."

"Why is that?"

"She doesn't look it now, but she's quite old. She was laid down in 1950. The U.S. government subsidized her construction because in the recently ended Second World War the Pentagon had been impressed with the service of the two Cunard Queens, *Queen Mary* and *Queen Elizabeth*, both of which were converted to troopships for the duration. They had huge capacity and were very fast—*Queen Mary* had been a Blue Ribander—and so they were able to outpace the German U-boats. The government commissioned this ship in cooperation with United States Lines: the shipping company would operate her as a transatlantic liner during peacetime, but for war she would revert to government use. She was constructed to military specification in the naval shipyard at Newport News: thick hull, watertight compartments, no flammable materials: even the piano in the First-Class lounge was a specially-built Steinway, made with a rare species of fire-resistant mahogany. And above all she was to be fast: she was fitted with high-pressure boilers feeding steam turbines that delivered a quarter-million shaft horsepower: the same machinery arrangement that was to power the new *Forrestal*-class of superlarge aircraft carriers. The *United States* was faster than anything else afloat. In 1952, when she returned to New York after having completed her maiden crossing, the *United States* flew from her masthead a forty-foot blue pennant, twice the normal length, because she had won the Blue Ribband in both directions, eastbound and westbound, on her very first voyage. A tremendous feat of engineering at the time. Even today, for that matter. Yet, less than a decade later, she was doomed."

"By what?"

"The Boeing 707. Pan Am introduced it into their service in 1958. The jet age had arrived, and the great transatlantic liners suddenly became dinosaurs."

"Surely not all, if you've never crossed by airplane before?"

"True. Cunard persisted, for which I am profoundly grateful—I don't know what I would have done without the *QE2* and *QM2*—but gone forever were the days when one could wander down Liner Row on the west side of Manhattan and see tied up there one of the *Queen*s, and beside her the *Normandie* or the *Île de France*, and then the *Aquitania* or the *Carinthia*, the *Bremen* or the *Deutschland*. The *United States* ceased transatlantic service in 1969: she was no longer profitable."

"What became of her then?"

"A varied but undistinguished career, like an aging screen actress who had once been billed in boldface, now condemned to cameo roles as someone else's mother. She did some Caribbean cruising, and was at one stage slated to become a floating casino in Atlantic City. A Turkish shipping line took ownership for a time in the 'Nineties, and she spent a year in a Sevastopol shipyard. But most of the time she was laid up and, despite the efforts of preservationists, seemed destined for the breaker's yard."

"She looks in pretty good shape for all that."

"Indeed, she does. Let us take a walk along the wharf, shall we, and admire her from stem to stern." He continues talking as they stroll. "She's just returned from nine months in a naval graving dock at Newport News, Virginia. In fact, it was the very same dock where she was built: she was returned to her place of birth to be reborn, one might say."

He pauses, apparently expecting a reaction.

"Very appropriate," Sabrina remarks, but her response does not satisfy him. He stops walking and faces her directly.

"No, it is more than just appropriate. Entirely necessary, I would say, entirely necessary. In order to start again, one must by definition go back to the beginning. It is essential: one must have a fundamental foundation if one is to truly begin again. Think of the Renaissance—the ultimate rebirth, the very name means rebirth—how did that begin? It began by rediscovering the texts of the Ancients—that is, by going back to the beginning of civilization. You must remember that during the Dark Ages the Greek and Roman texts had largely been lost in the West, and it was often through Arabic translations—some of them acquired by Crusaders like William the Marshal—that we regained our knowledge of Thucydides and Tacitus, Epicurus and Lucretius. These were enough to kick off a recivilization of the West, at least in the crusading nations, but the whole enterprise was supercharged in 1453 with the fall of Constantinople. Suddenly, there was a massive influx of Greek scholars fleeing the Saracens, and they brought the old texts with them. We went back to the beginning, and the Renaissance was the result. It is one of history's great ironies that the rebirth of Western civilization should have been so encouraged, however unintentionally, by Islam."

It is the most emphatic she has seen the lawyer. "Are we still talking about the ship?"

"The ship, and much else. I hope that you will think about what I have said." She agrees to do so and Ravenscroft, now pleased with her response, resumes walking along the wharf, gesturing loosely toward the great ship beside them.

"In the graving dock she was completely stripped down, everything removed, the entire structure scraped back to bare metal. Her hull was found to be fully seaworthy, notwithstanding years of neglect, a testament to her sound design, and the skilled work of the great-grandfathers of those who were refurbishing her. Although the hull is steel the superstructure is aluminium—this is one of the things that made her so fast: the *United States* displaced only fifty-thousand tons compared to the *Queen Mary*'s eighty-thousand, although they were physically the same size. But aluminium next to steel induces a Galvanic reaction, a sort of corrosion, which required painstaking repair. The engineering spaces underwent extensive overhaul. At one time, steam was the standard propulsion for ships, firstly coal-fired, then oil-fired. But steam power at sea went the way of steam power on rail: today, almost all sea-going vessels, like almost all locomotives, are powered by diesel engines. The exception is the navy, which generally uses gas turbines—that is, marine versions of jet engines: more expensive but more powerful."

"Is that what the *United States* will use, gas turbines?"

"No, she will remain steam-powered, but no longer will her boilers be oil-fired. Instead, her steam will be produced by an atomic reactor."

This time it is Sabrina who stops walking. She stares up at the ship.

"You mean that she's nuclear-powered?"

"Not yet, but she will be. Firstly, she will complete fitting out: that is, the installation and testing of the various systems needed for a ship to function: lighting, air-conditioning, ventilation, freshwater supply, sewerage and fire main, communications, and many others—the complexity of it all quite amazes me. The power will come from shore for now; it is not until the fitting out is complete that she will again be towed down to Newport News, and the reactors will be lowered into her bowels. When she leaves there for her sea trials, she will be under her own power for the first time in twenty years."

"Nuclear power."

"Indeed." They resume walking. "An expensive choice, but it will allow this ship to sail the world's seas for decades without ever needing to refuel."

They continue walking in silence to the end of the ship, where they come to a halt. Sabrina gazes up at the elegantly rounded stern bearing the name *United States* in big white letters, and below that what is presumably her port of registration: *New York*. They are nearer the river now, and the bulk of the vessel no longer provides a windbreak. This is a good day to see the ship, she thinks, with the blustery breeze bringing the bright briny smell of the sea, the pale blue sky and wind-whipped clouds forming a dramatic backdrop, the sort of day that might make an adventurous person yearn for the limitless freedom of a life plying the world's oceans.

"The shafts were intact, but she needed new propellers: four magnesium-bronze monstrosities that are quite beautiful, like fabulous pieces of sculpture, the blades machined to a most pleasing surface finish that makes them seem to shimmer—I wish you could have seen them." He pauses before continuing. "However, I understand there is a fifth propeller that she will carry as a spare on her foredeck, and no doubt you will have ample opportunity to admire that one for yourself."

Sabrina's gaze goes from the ship to her companion.

"Ample opportunity? How would that be?"

"Let me respond to your question with one of my own. Miss Lancaster, now that you have completed your studies, what are you going to do next? Will you go into practice?"

"No, I never even took the bar exam."

"Then… ?"

"Scholarship; most likely academia, or maybe a position at an independent research institution. I've already applied for several assistant professorships, and also for a role at a D.C. think tank."

"Ah," is his immediate response, apparently one of satisfaction. His gaze goes from her back to the ship. "You haven't asked me what the *United States* will do when she finishes her sea trials."

"Won't she be going back into transatlantic service?"

"No, not at all. She is to become a floating university." It begins to dawn on her why he is showing her this ship. "She will retain her name—that is, the STEAM SHIP *United States*—and the new institution will be known plainly as the University of the SS *United States*. Much of the faculty have already been recruited."

"Are you suggesting that I should apply?"

"No, what I'm doing is offering you a position. An associate professorship, right from the start." He holds up a halting hand. "I ask you, madam, to make no comment right now. Please allow me to first make the case for what must appear to you to be a very strange proposition, and one so generous as to invite suspicion. You may of course ask questions, but I would request that you express no view on the matter, neither approval nor disapproval, so that, as you consider this offer in the days to come, no prior declarations prejudice your outlook. Can we agree on this?"

It seems a reasonable enough request, and Sabrina consents.

"Very well. Now, let us retrace our steps as I give you the lay of the land—a very inappropriate metaphor, under the circumstances." They begin walking back down the wharf. "Firstly, the nature of the institution. The university will not be accredited, at least not in the usual way. Accreditation requires conformation to a set of rules and procedures, the same rules and procedures that today produce graduates who are barely literate and completely innumerate. Worse, they are ignorant of anything outside their immediate fields: our universities are producing incomplete people. However learned they might be in their disciplines they are, as human beings, dull creatures—cogs, with no sense of the greater mechanism in which they play a part. Nor have they achieved the fundamental core attribute that should be the ultimate goal of any sound education: the ability to think clearly. It doesn't matter what whetstone one uses—be it particle physics or the plays of Shakespeare—the result should be the same: a sharpened mind ready to rationally and critically address whatever comes before it. This is the thinking behind the university: an institution whose supreme aim is to produce a full human being, fit for life.

"Secondly, it will have what no other university has: the ability to shift the campus from place to place at will. The ship will travel the world continuously during the academic year, and so students will encounter in the flesh what usually can only be studied in books. Plus, they will be exposed in their formative years to lands and cultures in more depth and in greater variety than most people achieve in a lifetime: a clever way to help produce a well-rounded person. And so, who will these people be?

"The admission process is more rigorous than for any other university in the world. Grades must be exceptional, of course, but grades alone will not gain admission. In considering applicants' qualifications beyond their grades, the admissions process at most tertiary institutions will look to references, often accompanied by a resume of suitably agreeable extra-curricular activities, not to mention those tediously dutiful admission essays: a series of hoops that any well-prepared applicant will easily jump through. This university will do none of that; instead, a formal board has been traveling the world for the last six months and will continue to do so. Every applicant will have been interviewed in person, usually in great depth, and the review board will see for themselves what sort of person they are. The academic standards are at the highest level, but so too are the personal standards."

"I assume that the tuition fees will also be high."

"All tuition will be free, as well as accommodation and meals. Services, too, from medical and dental through to laundry and cleaning. There is even a small allowance. This applies to all students, whether rich or poor. There is no such thing as a rich student, of course, just students with rich parents, but it was the aim of the founder that the well-rounded individuals who graduate from this institution should be truly individual—which is to say, free of any obligation or encumbrance, either financially or to their families.

"Who is the founder?"

"Technically, a foundation, but as I am sure you have guessed by now, the person behind it is my client."

"For what purpose?"

"Is simple philanthropy insufficient motive? My client is a very wealthy individual, Miss Lancaster: I can assure you that he will not be clipping coupons because of the cost of this university. He bought the *United States* two years ago from the group struggling to preserve her and has been engaged in getting the enterprise underway ever since. As you can see by the state of this gleaming ship beside us, it has been proceeding quite satisfactorily."

"No doubt with your help."

"It is true that I have played my part. But I would not want to give the impression that I have been central to the project: it is my client's achievement, and he is a very hands-on and capable manager." They have returned to the vessel's bow, and Ravenscroft again comes to a stop. "Which reminds me, I have not yet told you of what to my mind is his most singular achievement in the entire enterprise."

"Which is what?"

"I said that the university is unaccredited, which is true as far as it goes. However, it will have an affiliation. Can you guess what it is?"

"Should I be able to?"

"I've given you a clue."

She spends a moment in thought but can see no clue in anything he has told her and shakes her head in the negative.

"The clue is the coin," he announces. "The University of the SS *United States* will be an affiliate of the University of Oxford." He smiles at her look of surprise. "My dear *alma mater*, and also that of Mr. Bronaryre, as it happens. The ship will be a floating extension of his own college, Caiaphas. It will be a requirement that the students spend at least one academic year in residence at Caiaphas itself, and of course they will have to pass the very rigorous examinations at Oxford as well as those of the *United States*, which I imagine will be equally or even more rigorous. The degrees will be awarded jointly. One can see how appealing this arrangement is for Oxford, once academic rigor and oversight are assured: first of all, it costs them nothing—this marvelous floating extension comes for free; further, since there will be no fees, it allows the university to more readily assert that it is no longer an elitist institution; plus, as part of the agreement, the Bodleian and individual college libraries are to be fully digitized, so as to be available on board: digitizing their holdings was something they naturally wanted to do, and my client's offer to fund it as part of the proposal must have been very welcome."

"The benefits flow both ways, I think: I can see why there would be no need for formal accreditation."

"Quite so, but I think that perhaps you have failed to appreciate a significant corollary of this arrangement."

"What's that?"

"If the students are to be members of Oxford University, then it follows that so too must be the academic staff. In other words, what I am offering you, Miss Lancaster, is a fellowship at Caiaphas College. That is to say, should you accept, you will become an Oxford don."

He has no need to hold up a halting hand this time: she is rendered speechless.

Ravenscroft takes out his wallet and removes from it a calling card, which he offers to Sabrina. "I'm staying at the Explorers Club in New York. I'm hosting a small reception there on Tuesday before I head back across the Atlantic; perhaps you will join us, and we can talk more then."

She inspects the card. On top is printed *The Explorers Club*, without an apostrophe, as if the members were too busy probing the world to bother with punctuation. In smaller print on the bottom is the address, in the East 70s.

Between the club's name and the address is a stylized compass rose, with an *E* on the left and a *C* on the right. All three are printed in bright vermillion, and it does not escape Sabrina that, although neither Rosicrucian nor floral, what she is holding in her hand is another red rose.

# IX

SABRINA LOCATES the address, an ornate neo-Jacobean townhouse on East 70th Street, between Madison and Park. The front door is a Gothic arch with an iron grill set between two elaborately carved stone eminences, suggesting a fairy-tale castle. A modest plaque outside proclaims it as the Explorers Club. Inside, after having gained entrance by ringing the bell and being admitted by a doorman, she finds a less modest plaque, announcing a series of firsts: first to the North Pole, first to the South Pole, first to the summit of Everest, first to the deepest point in the ocean, first even to the Moon.

A porter takes Sabrina's coat and leads her past an enormous globe—where, he claims, Thor Heyerdahl first proposed the Kon-Tiki expedition—into a paneled salon. There is a large fireplace in the far wall, alight on a spring evening like this, still with a chill in the air. Two enormous tusks stand on either side of it—there is obviously no *ex post facto* revisionist delicacy about such matters at the Explorers Club. The room is comfortably furnished with an old-fashioned sofa and chairs, and is decorated with what are presumably artifacts of members' expeditions: crossed icepicks mounted on one wall; the head of some unlucky ungulate on another; an Emperor penguin standing in the corner, looking deeply discomfited. By the room's entrance, where in a real castle a suit of armor might be displayed, is instead something not dissimilar: a deep-sea diving outfit, including heavy lead boots and a big brass helmet with little screw-down windows.

The porter announces Sabrina and retires.

There are five people in the room. Two are standing, one by the fire and the other in contemplation of the penguin; the remaining three were sitting, but now stand and turn toward the new arrival. None of them is Aneurin Bronaryre, but Ravenscroft is among those who had been seated, and he bounces forward with a smiling face and an arm extended in welcome.

"Delighted you could join us, Miss Lancaster, delighted." He shakes her hand vigorously. "Come, let me introduce you."

The person standing by the fire is a taut figure with close-cropped ginger hair, introduced as Captain Glamis. At first, Sabrina assumes that he must be the captain of the *United States*, a role for which he would appear too young to be sufficiently experienced. He senses her surprise.

"The *captain* is because that's the rank I held in the army," he explains in a Scottish brogue. "Nothing like the naval rank of the same name. In the army, a captain is a very lowly creature. I am to be the director of security in our little enterprise: my job is to make sure that everyone comes back from their wee adventures safe and sound. Please just call me 'Glam'; that's what everyone calls me."

"Were you in the Black Watch by any chance?"

"Now how could you have known that?"

"A guess, based on the accent."

"Aye, of course." He turns toward an older man, no taller than Sabrina but so barrel-chested as to give an impression of great bulk. "Now here is a real captain."

"John Dunning," the older man says, shaking her hand with his huge paw. "And it is true that I am to have the honor of commanding the *United States* in her new life, but you mustn't put too much into it: I'm just a glorified bus driver."

"I've seen the ship," Sabrina says. "I know nothing of the sea, but I know that to take charge of such a complex immensity is a very long way from driving a bus."

She is introduced to the third person who had been seated, Judith Pearson, a slender woman of a certain age who inspects Sabrina with a long look of cool appraisal as they shake hands.

"Professor Pearson is the Vice-Chancellor of the university as a distinct institution," Ravenscroft explains, "and is also the Head of College in our Oxford role, so in the Oxonian tradition we address her as *Master*."

Sabrina understands the reason for the woman's evident reserve: she is not pleased to have had a position under her offered to someone whom she has never met.

"I thought you showed great restraint in not uttering the usual rejoinders when introduced to Glamis," she says.

"You mean something along the lines of *but Cawdor thou shalt be*? No, I assumed that he would be bored with hearing such things every time he meets someone."

"*Brava*," Glamis says quietly, and Sabrina has the sense of having just passed a small but important test.

Meeting the last person comes as a relief after the Master. She is a young woman dressed with a flamboyance that only a certain type of female can bring off: drop-waisted dress, high heels, and abundant costume jewelry, all coming together in a careless jumble—someone who has dressed to please herself alone. She is a student, the only person in the room younger than Sabrina, full of open good humor and brimming with energy, obviously delighted that another woman near her own age has joined the company.

"My name's Penelope de Vere," she says, her words tripping over each other in their rush to come out. "Of the St. John's Wood de Veres, which is to say we're terribly bourgeois and no relation whatsoever to Edward de Vere, no matter what Papa pretends, and whom you've probably never heard of anyway—he was Lord Chamberlain to Elizabeth—so what? I say: does that mean he made her bed?—but of course Caiaphas was founded by Elizabeth and he was Earl of Oxford and so it all ties in we've got a portrait of her in the Great Hall—at Caiaphas I mean, not St. John's Wood, goodness, we don't even have a great hall—Papa's just a GP and Mummy bakes—she has the most magnificent dress—Elizabeth, not Mummy—brocaded silk and one of those astonishing starched collars that looks like the thing veterinarians put on dogs to stop them biting their sutures I say, you won't call me Penny, will you?—I do so dislike it; sounds like a Sainsbury's checkout chick—but Penelope I'm quite fond of I hope someone will rush home over the sea for me one day."

The flood of unpunctuated stream-of-consciousness has come to a sudden halt, and everyone in the room seems momentarily stunned that the storm should have so abruptly abated. Sabrina is the first to recover.

"Penelope's a lovely name, and no one would leave you for ten years. I hope you'll call me Sabrina."

Through it all, Penelope of the St. John's Wood de Veres has not let go of Sabrina's hand, and now she grips it with her other as well. "I'm sure that we'll be friends. I can't wait until we're on the ship togeth—" The deluge that had seemed poised to resume stops mid-sentence, and Penelope releases Sabrina to bring a hand to her mouth: it is apparent that she has been told Sabrina has not yet agreed to join the enterprise and was instructed to keep her enthusiasm in check.

"I'm certain we'll be friends," Sabrina assures her.

"Penelope has been placed in charge of the research for the first leg of our maiden voyage," Professor Pearson interjects, perhaps wishing to ensure that the floodgates do not reopen. "It's a major undertaking: multidiscipline, logistically challenging, something that will require much planning and then responding to circumstances as they change—one of the things that will distinguish USSUS from other institutions will be the requirement that our students manage large real-world projects: that is, to successfully direct people and material to a single purpose." She pronounces the acronym as YOU-siss—apparently, this is the accepted way of avoiding the mouthful that is 'the University of the Steam Ship *United States*.'

"Where is the first voyage to go?" Sabrina directs the question to the Master, but it is the ship's captain who responds.

"The South Seas," Dunning says. "I was just voicing some concerns about it when you arrived."

"Please don't let me interrupt."

"Why don't we resume our seats?" Ravenscroft suggests. "Miss Lancaster, can I fetch you a drink?—anything you like as long as it's gin. Martini? Gibson? Gin and tonic? We're all drinking Gimlets—the scurvy-preventing citrus seemed fitting for discussing sea-faring."

"Yes, a Gimlet, please."

He goes to the adjoining bar to mix the cocktail. Glamis remains standing by the fire, leaning lightly on the mantle. Captain Dunning and Professor Pearson retreat to their spots on the sofa, revealing what had been concealed behind them: a low table, situated between the sofa and the fireplace, bearing a scale model of the SS *United States*. It is large, mounted on two stumpy columns above a broad wooden base, and extremely detailed: as she inspects it Sabrina can see millimeter-sized shutters on the bridge wing signaling lanterns, and tiny paper flags in what must be her pennant locker. On the floor next to the table is a large wood-framed glass box, evidently the top of the case in which the model is usually displayed, but now removed to allow closer examination. Much of the remainder of the table—whose top, Dunning tells her, is a hatch cover from the Coast Guard cutter *Explorer*, an unlikely survivor of Pearl Harbor—is occupied by serving plates stacked with finger sandwiches. This is evidently a working cocktail party, with easy-to-consume food placed close at hand to avoid unnecessarily interrupting proceedings.

Dunning moves along the sofa, offering room for her to sit with a good view of the ship. "Shall I give you the tour?"

"Yes, please do."

She takes the seat next to him. Penelope de Vere sits on the arm of the sofa, apparently wanting to join the tour. Ravenscroft returns from the bar with the Gimlet, placing the cocktail on a little paper napkin bearing the club's logo.

"Help yourself to the sandwiches," he says. "The Explorers Club usually serves exotic dishes, but there's no alligator tail or yak tongue tonight: we have simple ham, cucumber, and devilled egg salad," he says, pointing to each salver in turn.

Sabrina tries the Gimlet, which she professes to be extraordinarily good. Ravenscroft explains that instead of using lime cordial he makes them with pamplemousse syrup and a touch of finely ground white pepper. "I picked up the recipe from the Savoy," he says. "They do them that way at the Beaufort Bar."

Sabrina helps herself to a deviled egg sandwich. Dunning takes out a pen, which he uses as a pointer.

"This is a one-to-two-hundred-and-fifty scale model," he says, "which means that the near one-thousand-foot length of the ship is here represented as four feet. Fifty-three thousand tons gross registered tonnage. She was built to accommodate about two thousand passengers and one thousand crew, but in the refit was considerably reconfigured. The university will have five hundred students, living here in what used to be 'cabin' class, which is what they called second class." He indicates the rear of the vessel. "Ahead of that on the higher decks within the hull will be classrooms and lecture theaters and laboratories, with machinery spaces below. Midships, where there is the least motion, is the main dining room. Right forward in the hull will be crew quarters. Just one hundred twenty crew in total: modern systems require much less manpower. The superstructure will have accommodation for academic staff, which including support staff will be three hundred, I understand." Pearson nods in agreement. "My officers' cabins are below the bridge—two dozen in total—plus their wardroom. So, all up, about a third of the number she was designed to carry: we will have a rare luxury at sea, that of space.

"Her beam is one hundred and one feet, six inches. The width of the Panama Canal is one hundred and ten feet, so that means we can make it through with just enough room for the fenders on either side. She is a PANAMAX: that is, built as big as possible while still being able to transit the canal." Dunning's patter is firm but not emphatic, clear but not didactic, delivered with the calm authority of someone who is an expert on his subject—the same tone of presentation that Sabrina had tried to project at her oral defense. "She draws thirty-four feet, which is quite deep, so we'll be keeping well clear of any shallows. Propulsion is steam, four turbines and four shafts." He points to the underside of the model as he speaks, where the shafts emerge from the hull, and Sabrina notices that the model's propellers have been rendered in what might have been the same magnesium-bronze as the full-scale versions, right down to the shimmering surface finish Ravenscroft had mentioned.

"All four are independent, so there is excellent maneuverability, as well as redundancy. A quarter-million shaft horsepower in total, enough to drive the ship at thirty-five knots if required; most seagoing vessels can only make half that. There are diesel generators for electricity when the ship is not under main power, plus she has been fitted with two retractable and rotatable thruster pods, one in the bow and the other aft between the shafts. These are intended for coming alongside, allowing docking and undocking without need of tugs, but in an emergency they could also be used for propulsion."

"Where is the nuclear reactor?"

"There will be four of them, down here, in the old boiler spaces. The reactors themselves are quite heavy, and the lead shielding is heavy too, so we made sure to fit them down as low as possible in the hull, to maintain a good righting moment." He answers her puzzled expression at this last term. "It's what keeps a ship from capsizing. All ships have a center of gravity, which is pushing down, and a center of buoyancy, which is pushing up." He holds up his hands, one above the other, illustrating the action. "The center of buoyancy is above the center of gravity so when a ship rolls these two forces, moving out of their vertical alignment, will act together to try to twist it back upright. The further apart they are, the greater the force, and therefore the more stable the ship. The *United States* was already very stable, given her lightweight aluminum superstructure, and putting the reactors down as low as possible makes her even more so—which is just as well, given what they're proposing to do with her." His eyes move to Penelope de Vere as he makes this last remark, and Sabrina's gaze follows his.

"We're going into a hurricane," she says, a prospect that might worry Captain Dunning but delights Penelope de Vere.

Professor Pearson explains. "The dynamics of tropical cyclones over the ocean are poorly understood: any ship unfortunate enough to be caught in one is too busy surviving to be undertaking scientific study. But the *United States* is bigger than ordinary vessels, and we are proposing to purposely sail into a hurricane, fully instrumented. It's the feasibility of this project that we've been discussing tonight." From the look on Dunning's face, Sabrina sees that *feasibility* is here a euphemism for persuading the captain to deliberately take his ship into danger. He answers her questioning look regarding his opinion on the matter.

"Size is important, but what counts in a storm is the ship's power. As long as it can remain pointed into the sea, most any ship can ride out a storm." He turns his attention back to the model, pointing to the bows. "The waves come from ahead, you see, and so she can simply ride up and over them, plunging down the other side, what we call pitching. That might swamp some vessels as the bows dig into the following wave, but the *United States* was built for North Atlantic duty and that, coupled with her watertight compartments, will allow her to slough off the wave and keep her safe. The danger is if the sea comes from the side, a beam sea." He gestures from the side of the model now, mimicking waves hitting the ship at ninety degrees. "That changes the forces from longitudinal to lateral, inducing a rolling motion which is much harder to counteract than a pitching motion, and with the result that if the next wave hits before she has recovered from the last one she may be swamped. Even when pointing into the sea, vessels without the power to fight through might lose steerageway—that is, the ability to maintain a heading—and so inadvertently end up beam-on, particularly when sliding down the face of a wave after having topped it out—this is what seafarers refer to as broaching, and it is about the worst thing that can happen in a storm. No amount of size will help you then."

The party is silent a moment, all eyes on the model, each of them imaging such a fate.

"Given plenty of sea room, and as long as I have power plus those four shafts to help steer her, the *United States* will survive any storm, including a tropical cyclone. The real danger, as I've been explaining, is if something goes wrong. Anything that results in loss of power, or fouling of the screws or rudders, would be catastrophic. Redundancy is the key here: the ability to lose a system but still have control: that's why she has multiple shafts and multiple rudders and multiple reactors."

"So you're not opposed to the idea?"

"I'm not in favor of it; no captain of any ship could be expected to. But I don't rule it out, given certain conditions. The ship must be completely serviceable, with no systems down for maintenance or repair. The crew must be fully worked up: most of them I've recruited myself and they're good seamen, but they will need to have learned their new ship and gotten comfortable with her. No lee shores, nor shoals, nor atolls—I would only be willing to undertake it with an abundance of sea room. And then there is the storm itself: not all cyclones are the same, indeed not all quadrants of any single cyclone are the same. And, lastly, there must be time to properly prepare. These boats, for example," he says, sweeping the pointer past the row of lifeboats running along the ship's side. "We'll need to secure them with extra strops, which our sailmakers will probably have to fabricate themselves. The aircraft, too." He points to a helicopter deck down aft.

"This was not part of the ship's original design; it was added in the refit. We'll carry two aircraft: a helicopter, which can land directly on board, and a seaplane, which can land alongside and be recovered by derrick. Both of them will have to be folded and stowed in their hangers, and I'll want to double the tie-downs on them as a precaution. And then there are a thousand other items, both on the upper decks and down below, that will need to be fully secured before we venture into any typhoon." He sits back with a sigh, as if already feeling the weight of responsibility. "I will not hazard over a thousand souls unless I am sure of things."

"Over a thousand? I counted around nine hundred and fifty."

"I left out two groups of supernumeraries. The first is what the university calls 'porters and scouts.'"

Professor Pearson takes up the explanation. "We have them at Caiaphas; every college does. Porters are the general administrators of the college: they look after the non-academic aspects of running it. Scouts are essentially janitorial staff, but in Oxonian tradition they are held in higher regard than that term usually connotes—they are well-respected members of the college: porters and scouts are akin to the staff of a great house or country estate, part of its collective identity."

Sabrina turns back to Dunning. “You said there were two groups of supernumeraries?”

“Yes, and before explaining the presence of the second I should tell you that civilian use of nuclear reactors at sea is quite rare—there are some nuclear-powered icebreakers and such—but since the *Savannah,* nuclear power has not been much used in the merchant marine. You can’t just go and buy a reactor, the way you can a marine diesel: you have to undergo certification. There are two parts to this: firstly, design and installation must pass a host of regulatory hurdles. That was relatively straightforward in our case: we are using an old naval design that has been well tested over many decades of use, and it will be installed at the Newport News shipyard, which does the same work for the navy. But the second part is being able to operate it competently: the reactors are complex, and you have to be able to take care of them. There are many requirements for this, and most of the engineering team are ex-navy, recruited because of their nuclear experience. But you must be able to physically protect them, too, and so we will embark a security team whose primary function is to guard the fissile material against misappropriation. All ex-military: mostly special forces trained, ex-army or ex-marine—both U.S. Marines and Royal Marines—about thirty of them. Well trained, no-nonsense people, all in the capable hands of Captain Glamis here, who will be commanding them.”

All eyes go to Glamis, who nods and raises his glass in salute.

“Glam mentioned that he was in the Black Watch,” Dunning continues. “He did not mention that he was recruited from there into the SAS—the Brit equivalent of our special forces—and I have to say that I have nothing but pity for any Somali pirate who attempts to board the SS *United States*.” Looking again at Glamis, ever alert but with little to say, Sabrina is inclined to agree.

The tour has concluded, and the gathering moves smoothly along loosely connected threads of conversation, the way a good cocktail party does. More Gimlets are mixed and the sandwiches are consumed. At one point the conversation moves to the Explorers Club itself.

“I see from the plaque at the entrance that they are claiming first to the moon,” Sabrina says. “I thought it was NASA.”

"Actually, it was both," Ravenscroft says. "The way the club operates is by flag expeditions. Shall I show you?" He stands and leads her out into the lobby, accompanied by Penelope de Vere, who has evidently attached herself to Sabrina. Ravenscroft takes them past the globe and pauses to admire the ceiling.

"These wooden beams are from HMS *Daedalus*, a 19-gun frigate laid down in 1826."

"An appropriate name for a ship whose timbers ended up in the Explorers Club."

"In 1848, the captain and crew reported sighting a sixty-foot sea serpent off the Cape of Good Hope," he says. "The creature circled the ship for fifteen minutes before disappearing, apparently curious. It was nothing like a whale, an animal familiar to seafarers. They can't all have been making it up, but no satisfactory explanation has ever been offered."

He leads them up a staircase guarded by a polar bear—donated to the club by the actor Rudolph Valentino, who shot it, according to Ravenscroft, while on an expedition in the Chukchi Sea—and into a room on the second floor, bigger than the one downstairs, barrel-vaulted, and fitted with an even grander fireplace. On the wall are mounted a series of flags, all similarly designed as a diagonal triptych, the lower left red, the upper right blue, and with a white diagonal between them bearing the club's red compass rose in the center, with the *E* above and to the left, and the *C* below and to the right.

Ravenscroft resumes the explanation. "When an expedition is planned, the leaders will apply for a flag from the club which, if awarded, they will take with them on the journey and bring back to the club on their return. The cost is the requirement to write up a scientific account of the expedition, a 'Flag Report.' Roy Chapman Andrews—the inspiration for the fictional Indiana Jones—took this one with him on his historic trip across the Gobi Desert in 1923, returning with the first known fossilized dinosaur eggs. Thor Heyerdahl took that one on the Kon-Tiki expedition in 1947, proving by practical demonstration that Polynesians could have sailed from the Americas across a thousand miles of open ocean with no technology beyond balsa wood and bamboo." He points to the two flags in succession, and Sabrina stares at them in fascination, wondering at the heroic hardships they must have been witness to. Ravenscroft moves to a third flag. "This one was with Edmund Hillary when he climbed Everest, and also with Jacques Piccard when he descended into the Challenger Deep, and so it has been to both the highest and lowest points on the surface of the earth. And note that the *E* for *Explorers* could also stand for *Everest*, and it is located in the *upper* part, high up. The *C* stands for *Club*, but could also stand for *Challenger*, and it is in the *lower* part, deep down. A coincidence, is it not, to have captured so much meaning with such elegant simplicity?"

"Where's the one from the moon?"

"The Apollo Eleven one is in a display case in the lobby—I'll show you when we go back down. This one is from Apollo Thirteen, which of course never made it to the moon, but miraculously returned to Earth, a feat of rare skill and courage."

All three stare at it for a moment in silence.

"Perhaps one day our own will be displayed somewhere inside the club," Ravenscroft says.

"Our own?"

"Certainly. The *United States* has been granted an Explorers Club flag for her maiden global circumnavigation, given that we'll be undertaking scientific studies like the tropical cyclone research. That's why we're having the gathering here, at the club: today, we received our flag. Would you like to see it?"

Penelope speaks up before Sabrina can respond. "Oh yes, may we, please?"

Ravenscroft takes them next door into the library, a beautiful room of dark wood and soft light. "This ceiling comes from a Fifteenth-Century Italian monastery," he says, "and the stained-glass windows are quite a delight. But now I recall that I took the flag upstairs, in case a member wanted to use this room." He leads them further up, taking a staircase lined with black-and-white photographs of past members, and into an attic trophy gallery packed with display cases and artifacts. "A yeti scalp," Ravenscroft explains, pointing to a rather grisly object in a nearby vitrine, "and these are prayer wheels from Tibet." He takes them on a circumnavigation of the room. "This book is a first edition of Napoleon's *Description of Egypt*; here is a mammoth tusk that was unearthed in Alaska; these native totems were sent back from New Guinea by Michael Rockefeller—he himself never returned, apparently having been eaten by cannibals; and these peculiar items are from a four-tusked elephant encountered on an expedition to the Congo."

Ravenscroft leads them from the trophy gallery into another room, the boardroom. "This board table was given to the club by Theodore Roosevelt," Ravenscroft says, indicating the broad polished piece of furniture in the center of the room. But it is not the table that commands the women's attention, it is the object lying conspicuously on top of it: a soft parcel, bound in brown paper and string—curiously old-fashioned in an age in which everything is shipped in cardboard boxes plastered with logos and secured with tape. The parcel has already been undone, but the paper refolded, concealing the contents. Ravenscroft pulls aside the wrapping, revealing the flag: the same simple design in coarse cloth with which they are by now familiar: red and blue triangles at the corners, and in the white space between them the compass-rose-and-club-initials insignia.

"Usually the flags are reused, as the Everest flag was reused for the Challenger Deep mission. They are only retired, if ever, after having represented some particularly significant expeditions, like the ones we saw. But ours will be flying from the yardarm day and night for a year, including—if all goes as planned—through a tropical cyclone, and so the Explorers Club commissioned a new one for us, number two hundred and nine: that is, the two-hundred-and-ninth flag in the club's one-hundred-and-twenty-year history." Ravenscroft unfolds the flag on the table. "It was made by a local seamstress, and then sent up to a sailmaker in Newport to fit the ropework and shackles that will allow it to be hoisted on the halyards, plus they added a leather sleeve at the leading edge and some extra reinforcing on the seams so that the wind won't tear it apart."

Sabrina stares at the flag. It is new but rough-made—the Explorers Club is not the sort of place that would order flags from a factory in China. The number 209 has been written in black marker on the leather sleeve. She runs her hand over the fabric. She likes that it is coarse, and that it is the work of a local seamstress and Newport sailmakers.

Ravenscroft catches her eye and smiles, and she realizes that he understands what she herself had not yet perceived: that she has decided to accept the offer. Penelope de Vere grips Sabrina's arm in two hands and hugs: apparently she has sensed it, too. It seems that between her arrival at the Explorers Club and the inspection of this flag, she has made up her mind without being consciously aware of having done so.

# X

SABRINA AND RAVENSCROFT are left alone in the members' lounge, sitting together on the sofa, facing the ship model and the dying embers of the tusk-flanked fireplace behind it. The others have gone to dinner; perhaps the exit had been planned to give them privacy to discuss arrangements.

Ravenscroft has come prepared with a briefcase brimming with documents which he takes out and places on the table. Most of them are from the University of Oxford, some are British government forms, several are from Caiaphas College.

Sabrina holds one of these last in her hand, staring at the letterhead. "How did a college come to be called Caiaphas?" she asks. "Wasn't he a Biblical bad guy?"

"Indeed: he was the high priest who presided over the Sanhedrin—the trial—that condemned Jesus. When the college was founded in the Sixteenth Century there was a bit of Biblical revisionism about his role. Caiaphas's reasoning was that the Jews should not challenge Roman political power—that is, that religious authorities must subordinate themselves to the state: a very appealing doctrine to Elizabeth, a Protestant monarch who had just taken over from her Catholic half-sister and needed every support in enforcing the Act of Supremacy, which established her as the head of the English church, something bitterly opposed by Rome and the entire Catholic world, who insisted that only the Pope could occupy that role. And besides, it was argued, had not Caiaphas been an instrument in bringing Jesus to his ultimate destiny, the salvation of mankind—should he not be lauded rather than villainized. Strange to say, this view is not without precedent: to this day Pontius Pilate is venerated as a saint in some Christian churches, including that of the Copts. The chief proponent of this Caiaphine revisionist theory was the theological scholar Hugh Rhys-Evans. It was he who convinced Elizabeth to found the college, and he became its first dean. St. Giles College had been established under Bloody Mary not long before, specifically to train priests in aid of the Marian Counter-Reformation, and despite the change to Protestantism it remained a conservative Catholic-minded force in Oxford for many years, well into the Twentieth Century. One of the motivations for Elizabeth's establishment of Caiaphas was to offset that conservative influence, and the two colleges entered into a fierce rivalry, often resulting in street brawls. These days, the violence is usually confined to the playing fields."

Only one document is from the University of the SS *United States*, but it is the primary one: her contract of employment. It is many pages thick.

"I'll need time to review this," she warns.

"Of course. I expect that you'll find it is all in order, but I must tell you, Miss Lancaster, that there exists an additional role, should you choose to accept it, that is not mentioned in that contract, or anywhere else."

"What role?"

"That of amanuensis."

"To whom?"

"My client."

"Bronaryre? Why would he need someone to take dictation?"

"Rather more than take dictation, I think. He will tell you his story, and you—should you so choose—will write the book. What you write and how you write it will be entirely up to you. I have been instructed to make this condition very explicit: my client will not have any editorial input whatsoever; indeed, he will not even read it. You are to have complete license to write what and how you will."

"But why? And why me?"

"To ensure independence. And you, because you are trained in the precise and objective use of language. It is your area of expertise, is it not?—you are about to become an Oxford don whose field of study this is. Your academic discipline is the forensic exactitude of expression, the use of precise and subtle composition, the articulation of the issues at hand with clear-eyed and sober impartiality. These are the very qualities that my client is looking for."

"Why would Bronaryre need all that?"

"Because it is to be an apologia."

"An apologia for what?"

"For himself."

"Why would he need to defend himself in print? Or at all, for that matter?"

"For a very simple reason. You see, Miss Lancaster, my client is the Devil."

A long interval of silence follows this declaration, during which Sabrina searches Ravenscroft's face for a sign of humor or irony, but his expression remains impassive—once again she realizes what a very good lawyer he must be, to utter such an absurdity without any apparent self-consciousness.

"You mean that he is a devil to deal with?" she asks. "Someone who is difficult? Moody and ill-tempered, maybe?"

"I mean no such thing. My client is the Devil, madam, with a capital *D*."

"Are you saying that he genuinely believes himself to be the Devil?"

"Of course."

"*The* Devil?"

"Is there more than one?"

"Rather less, I would think." Sabrina takes a sip of her cocktail, giving Ravenscroft, who up until the last minute has seemed a perfectly rational man, the chance to admit that this is some sort of joke. But he remains silent, his expression blank, revealing nothing.

She recalls Bronaryre's observation that his lawyer was sporting with him. "This is the thing that you didn't tell me in London, isn't it?"

"On the contrary, as I've already explained to Mr. Bronaryre—who, I'll admit, was somewhat displeased with me—I faithfully executed his instructions, as my profession obliges me to do. You forget that at the point when I questioned your business in enquiring into my client, I explained that I was the Devil's advocate."

Sabrina recalls it. "But that's just a turn of phrase: playing the Devil's advocate doesn't mean that your client is literally the Devil."

"Quite so, but that was not the expression I used. I did not say that I was *playing* the Devil's advocate. The specific phrase I used was 'I am speaking *as* the Devil's advocate.' The difference in meaning is clear, and I cannot be held accountable if you—an expert in the precise use of language, after all—failed to register the distinction."

Sabrina begins to understand now: as counsel, he was required to carry out his client's instructions, but he engineered the revelation to pass unnoticed under a cloak of common idiom.

"And what did your client say when you explained this subtle difference?"

"He said that, according to Dante, counselors of fraud occupy the eighth circle of Hell, and therefore he and I would very soon be close neighbors."

Despite the absurdity of it all Sabrina cannot help laughing out loud, and even Ravenscroft allows himself a smile.

"My thinking is that you thought the chances of recruiting me would be improved by leaving the revelation that your client believes himself to be the Devil to as late as possible."

"Others might say so. I couldn't possibly comment myself." Sabrina understands this to be the English for *Yes, of course: I didn't want to scare you off by revealing that my client is a nut case*.

"So this whole thing is just a setup. You needed someone to participate in your client's fantasy, and the ship and Oxford was the price."

"My dear Miss Lancaster, I certainly hope that you don't believe any of what you just said." He stands and walks to the bar. "It is perfectly true that when you first came to my attention, it occurred to me that you might be a person suited to what would be a very unique undertaking."

"There is no such thing as *very unique*," Sabrina interjects automatically. "Either something is unique or it is not."

"There you go: evidence of your acuity with language, the very reason that I first thought you might be suitable. But then it became clear that your academic work was of the highest standard, and that you did not intend to go into practice but instead remain in academia—in short, it was obvious that you would be a real find for USSUS. I've already told you that I have read your dissertation. More importantly, so has Professor Pearson, who was deeply impressed—in fact, she hopes that you might turn it into a book. NYU is one of the world's top law schools, and has been so for a long time: it does not award a J.S.D. to anybody who doesn't deserve one. I should also tell you that we have obtained your academic records: Pearson says that your undergraduate results would have earned you a First at Oxford. You mustn't think that she is displeased to have had you thrust upon her, so to speak—quite the reverse, she is delighted to have been able to acquire such talent."

"Does she know that the person who is bankrolling the enterprise believes himself to be the Devil?"

"No, of course not. That knowledge is restricted to just us, and I do hope that we can keep it that way."

Ravenscroft returns from the bar with two small glasses filled with a clear reddish-brown liquid. "Madeira," he says. "I sometimes prefer it to port, which can be a little heavy."

He sits and they sip their Madeira for a while in thoughtful silence.

"There's no link between the two," Ravenscroft says. "The academic post is yours, whatever you decide on the other thing."

"No, I'll do it," she says quietly.

He leaves a pause before responding, perhaps giving her time to change her mind.

"You'll do it?"

"Yes. You sound shocked."

"I am a little."

"How can that be? You asked me to do it, and I have agreed to do so."

"But I haven't yet explained the terms."

"What terms?"

"Miss Lancaster, as I said, this is all quite separate from your academic role. No one is expecting you to undertake this task unrecompensed. There will be the matter of royalties."

"Royalties? Mr. Ravenscroft, I hope that your client is not under the illusion that anyone is actually going to buy his book."

"On the contrary, the Devil giving an account of himself is likely to be a global bestseller. You will receive industry-standard royalties for co-authors who are not themselves the principal."

"Fine. I won't plan my retirement around it."

Ravenscroft ignores her dismissive tone. "And naturally you will also receive an advance on those royalties." He reaches into his briefcase and withdraws a leather writing portfolio, which he opens on the table. On one side are pockets with envelopes and cards, the other is occupied by not a writing pad but a checkbook, larger than usual. He takes a pen from his coat pocket, laboriously writes out the check, tears it from the stub, and hands it to Sabrina.

The check is elaborately engraved, like an old stock certificate. The central field bears the image of a beast of benign disposition carrying a banner bearing a St. George's cross, and the remainder is surrounded by an elaborately articulated ivy border studded with variously patterned heraldic shields. It is drawn on the Banque Savoie-Didier—*maison fondée* 1321—with an address on the rue de la Corratorie in Geneva. Check is spelled *chèque* and is denominated in Swiss francs. Ravenscroft's scribble is no more legible than the last time she encountered it, but the numbers are clear enough. Whether francs or dollars, Sabrina has never seen a check with so many zeroes before.

"This is absurd," she states, holding out the check for him to take back, but he declines to do so.

"No, it is a transaction freely entered into. I can assure you that advances are entirely the norm in the publishing industry, and while it is true that no royalties are paid until the advance is earned out the inverse is not the case: advances are never returned if the subsequent royalties fall short—in other words, the money is yours, no matter what."

"This is not an advance. This is a bribe to humor a man suffering from a delusion."

"Is it?"

"You're surely not suggesting otherwise?"

"I'm suggesting that, unless things have been demonstrated to be patently false, one should accept them at their face value."

"That's the old religious catch twenty-two: you cannot understand without faith, but faith is acceptance without understanding."

This observation just makes Ravenscroft smile. "Miss Lancaster, I do think that you and my client are going to engage in some lively discussions. Meanwhile, accept the advance for now. If after six months you are still of the same opinion, then I undertake to agree to whatever lesser sum you might deem appropriate. But for now, I think we should move onto the subject of logistical arrangements. I'm hoping that you have not yet made plans for the summer."

"I have not."

"Very good. If convenient, I propose that you come up to Oxford at the end of Trinity Term, which is to say mid-June, although I must warn you that summer in England can be very much like a particularly damp April anywhere else: don't neglect to pack your woolies. There will be a program at Caiaphas to prepare the core of students and staff for the inaugural academic year aboard the *United States*. Since it is out of term, the college will have ample accommodation available."

"When does the academic year begin?"

"Early September—the USSUS academic year will be identical to that of Oxford, so instead of the two semesters that you are used to there will instead be three terms: Michaelmas, Hilary, and Trinity—what for some absurd reason the other place calls Michaelmas, Lent, and Easter."

"The other place?"

"Cambridge," he whispers disapprovingly.

Accomplished barrister he may be, but Sabrina thinks that at heart Ravenscroft is not far removed from the student who had once scaled

Magdalen Tower while exceedingly tight. He continues quickly, as if to move the conversation on from a slightly distasteful topic.

"The undergraduate degree course will be more familiar to you: it will be an American-style four-year program, rather than the U.K.'s usual three, since students will have to meet the demands of two institutions."

"Will the demands be so different?"

"I rather think so. I liken it to a military or naval academy, where in order to graduate the candidate must not only meet the highest academic requirements—the Oxford emphasis, in this case—but also the somewhat more difficult-to-define fitness-for-service requirements—that will be the *United States*' emphasis, but of course it will not be military service that they must demonstrate fitness for."

"Fitness for what, then?"

Ravenscroft does not immediately answer, instead choosing to sit back on the sofa and finish the remainder of his Madeira before responding. "The answer to that question, Miss Lancaster, I believe you will discover in Oxford."

# XI

SABRINA STANDS on the terrace, looking out over the scene before her. The flags of Somerset House fly nearby, whipped by the breeze blowing up from the Thames, close enough for their flapping to be audible. Waterloo Bridge spans the river to her right, beyond it Blackfriars, and then eventually Tower Bridge, wonderfully ornate. Watercraft come and go upon the ever-busy river. Past Somerset House and the Temple is arrayed the City of London, a curious mixture of old and new, stretching down to the East Docklands.

She goes back inside and reads again the strange welcome note that, along with an ice-bucket holding a bottle of champagne, had been waiting in the suite.

> *I often take this room when in town: it is not the Savoy's most magnificent—by their standards it is quite modest—but it is the only one with a balcony, and the view is instructive, is it not? What an unattractive hodgepodge of oddly-shaped modern buildings it is that now mars the horizon downriver, as if each new edifice had tried to outdo the hideousness of its neighbor. But nothing can detract from the jewel at the center of this view: St. Paul's, with Wren's glorious dome rising like a beacon of enlightenment amid the ugliness surrounding it.*
>
> *K. Clark thought it the most beautiful building ever.*

*A car will come for you on Friday at 11:00 A.M. to take you up to Oxford.*

*Bronaryre*

The handwriting is a flowing copperplate in black ink: anachronistic but not flowery; a clean cursive script intended not to be admired but understood—this last a contrast to Ravenscroft's illegible scribble. The envelope is ecru colored, stiff and thick, and the interior is lined not with foil but marbling, in this instance a luminous abstract in gray-greens and soft blues, corresponding to the colors of the river and sky in the view outside. The ink is curiously glossy, glistening as if still wet. The notepaper matches the envelope, and now when studying the letter Sabrina sees what she had missed earlier: a watermark. She holds the letter up against the light from outside and finds that she recognizes the design, last seen etched onto Bronaryre's cuff links.

It is interesting that *neighbor* should have been spelled without the English addition of a *u*—she wonders if this indicates an American upbringing, or whether in a form of epistolary good manners the Devil spells in the style of his intended recipient. *K. Clark* she has already looked up: Kenneth Clark—'Lord Clark' after having been made a peer—a famed Twentieth-Century art historian who at the tender age of twenty-eight had been appointed director of the Ashmolean Museum, that same institution whose stolen property is currently sitting in her pocket.

She refills her champagne glass and goes back out onto the deck.

Her eyes move again to St. Paul's, the natural focus of the view from the balcony, and a joyful one. In the pure English sunlight the pale stone of the cathedral seems almost to glow—the beacon analogy was apt. The air is so clear that she can read the time on the south tower's clock face, although it is at least a mile downriver: that fresh breeze seems to have cleansed all impurities from the air, bringing with it a faint smell of the distant sea. But then her gaze moves across the river. There, on the opposite bank of the Thames, and at the opposite end of architectural function, lie the smokeless chimneys and grime-darkened walls of what had once been a huge powerplant, and whose hulking brick mass now houses the Tate Modern. Architectural *chiaroscuro*, she thinks of them: the light-filled cathedral on the one hand contrasting with the old powerplant on the other, dark and brutal and forbidding.

She is destined to visit the latter, for folded inside the envelope with Bronaryre's note was a brochure: a gallery map from the Tate Modern, with an addition by hand: gallery number 10 on level two has been circled—not in pen or pencil but something thicker, what appears to be dark maroon paint, applied impasto, perhaps extruded straight from the tube, mimicking the texture of the Pollock she had seen in Bronaryre's *pied-à-terre*. She is apparently meant to go to the gallery, and wonders what is in there to have warranted this wordless invitation.

Sabrina is roused from her reverie by the snap of one of Somerset House's flags. The one further from her is the familiar national flag of the United Kingdom, a Union Jack, but the nearer one—an elaborate design rendered in a blaze of red and gold—she had needed to look up, and found described in heraldic terms: *gules, three leopards passant guardant in pale or and langued azure*. This had required further research to decipher. *Gules*, she discovered, is the armorial term for red; *leopard* means not just leopard but also lion, as in this flag; *passant guardant* means depicted from the side, walking with the far foreclaw raised; *in pale* means arranged vertically; *or* in heraldry is not a conjunction but represents the word's French meaning: gold; and *langued azure* means with a blue tongue.

That is indeed the flag that now flaps before her—three fanciful golden lions on a red background, although she cannot be sure of the blue tongues. It is the royal blazon of the House of Plantagenet, she has learned—that same line of English kings two of whom William the Marshal had unseated, one figuratively and the other literally, some eight hundred years previously, and whose last monarch was the malevolent hunchback Richard III, from the same House of York that had long warred with the House of Lancaster, itself a Plantagenet branch. It would be her family flag if she had a family: she wonders if she is being mocked, to have the thing practically flying in her face. Or maybe the

Fates have arranged for it to be hoisted here as an obscure vexillological omen, soaring in the sky before her, as if the warning were heaven-sent. Sabrina goes back inside and makes an entry in her journal.

*London. Bronaryre is right about the buildings: the result of a striving to break with the past, I expect, but history is heavy here, and they just look ridiculous.*

*I'm trying to break with the past, too, I suppose—new country, new university, soon to sea in a new life—but it has left me likewise ridiculous: what compelled me to agree to Ravenscroft's ludicrous proposal? Perhaps it was the very absurdity of it: I can tolerate almost anything except dullness, and whatever else Bronaryre might turn out to be—pseudo-scholar-adventurer? self-indulgent misanthrope? dangerously deranged lunatic?—I do not believe that he will prove dull. There is the challenge, too—it will be something of a game, I expect: who will be the first one no longer able to keep a straight face?*

*Besides, Ravenscroft's many-zeroed check remains uncashed: if the business becomes intolerable I can always just return it and quit.*

*That check is not the only monetary instrument in my possession whose ultimate disposition remains undetermined. The Oxford Crown is now back in its country of origin; come the weekend, it will be back in its city of origin. What then?—I will have run out of excuses.*

SABRINA DINES that night with Thomas Ravenscroft at Simpson's-in-the-Strand, a location chosen by him because of its proximity to the Savoy. Joining them is a third person, a small serious woman in her fifties who introduces herself as Dorothy Aran.

"Dr. Aran is a medical doctor," Ravenscroft explains. "She will be the ship's surgeon aboard the *United States*."

"One of them," Aran corrects. "George Carruthers is the other one, and he's a genuine surgeon—that is, a member of the Royal College of Surgeons. There are bound to be some broken bones on our adventures, and I expect him to do the setting—not my thing."

"What's your specialization?"

"Ob/gyn. I'll be looking after the girls."

"Who'll be looking after the boys?"

This innocuous question leaves them both momentarily dumbstruck. Ravenscroft, who had been tasting and approving the Châteauneuf-du-Pape, is the first to recover.

"I just now realize that I have not told you—how clumsy-minded of me. All of the students will be women. I can't believe that I never thought to mention it."

"Only women? Why is that?"

"It was originally intended to be coeducational, same as Caiaphas itself. But the advisory board convinced everyone that cramming five hundred young men and women together aboard a ship at sea for a year was probably not the best idea for a new and somewhat experimental academic undertaking. Plus, it makes the accommodation arrangements so much simpler. Thus it was decided that, at least for now, the student body will be restricted to women alone."

"Does that apply to the academic staff, too?"

"No, they will be mixed, but there has been active recruitment of women for teaching roles, and they will be in the majority. But that was not the driving factor in their selection; excellence was the driving factor."

"Does it bother you that all of the students are female?" Dr. Aran asks.

"No, not at all. If they're like the one I met—a girl called Penelope de Vere—then I doubt their sex matters much: they're destined to do well in life, whether male or female."

"My thoughts exactly. I've had many of them come through my office already, and I have to say that on the whole they're an impressive bunch: vigorous and intelligent—and as healthy as horses, too: I shall be quite bored. Which reminds me, I have you down for an appointment at noon on Tuesday."

"Me?"

"I took the liberty of arranging it," Ravenscroft says. "On Thursday, you are scheduled to have an interview at the Home Office in Whitehall for the granting of your residency status—you're required to jump through this bureaucratic hoop, I regret to say, despite spending the first nine months at sea. They'll expect you to bring a document declaring that you are not infected with the bubonic plague."

"Medical certification," Aran clarifies. "It's basically intended to protect the NHS from taking on responsibility for non-citizens with pre-existing conditions. The examination is quite routine and will only take ten minutes. But there's a second thing we'll also need to take care of, something far more important: immunizations."

"Against what?"

"Cholera, typhus, typhoid fever, diphtheria, tetanus," she says, counting them off on the fingers of a hand. "Plus onboard the ship you'll have to take a daily malarial prophylaxis whenever we're sailing near infected areas. Don't worry: the immunizations are combined into just two shots, and they're quite painless. Many of the places in the world where we'll be going are far off the beaten track, and in the close confines of a ship at sea disease can travel quickly—much better to be safe than sorry." She takes a card from her purse and passes it to Sabrina. The address is on Harley Street.

The discussion is interrupted by the arrival of the trolleys, surrounding the table like a wagon train under attack from Apaches. Each bears a large serving platter that, when the silver-domed cover is rolled back, reveals a roast from which an apron-draped waiter begins to ceremoniously carve: beef and Yorkshire pudding for Ravenscroft and Sabrina, lamb with mint sauce for the doctor. At the conclusion of the performance, Ravenscroft pulls from his pocket a fistful of coins from which he selects three heavy gold-and-silver examples: £2-pound coins. The first two of these he gives to the ladies.

"At Simpson's," he explains, "it is customary to tip one's carver at table, an acknowledgment of the accomplishment in preserving a rare skill." And so saying he leads by example and hands the coin to his carver, who accepts it with the evident pleasure of a man less interested in the pecuniary value than in having the proprieties correctly observed. Sabrina and Dr. Aran follow suit.

By the time dinner is over the jet lag is starting to catch up with Sabrina, and the conversation is primarily between the other two. She excuses herself before coffee, allowing them to discuss mutual friends and enemies at their leisure. But when Sabrina returns to her room and goes out onto the balcony she suddenly feels revived. The city is a carpet of light; below her, a jubilant throng streams across Waterloo Bridge—playgoers returning from the National Theatre, and whatever they just saw must have amused them—and in the distance a floodlit St. Paul's invites contemplation.

The remainder of the champagne is still in the ice bucket; still bubbly—she pours a glass and takes a seat outside to gaze over the view. It feels dreamlike perched up here above the city, she thinks: not a midsummer's night dream but a summer's-eve night dream: tomorrow is June 21.

Sabrina is too far removed from religious sensibilities to 'count her blessings,' but she can take stock. At the beginning of the season whose last day it is today, she could not have imagined being where she is now. She has landed an associate professorship at one of the world's premier universities. For the first time in her life she is not poor: her salary began with the signing of the contract; not a huge amount but certainly more than she is used to and—given that everything from her airfare to this hotel room is paid for—more than enough to cover her needs. And as for the room: the suite may not be the Savoy's finest, but it is certainly the finest that she has ever stayed in. So far the people she is to work with have been interesting and even engaging—Sabrina is not an introspective woman, but she knows herself well enough to be aware of how rarely she finds anyone genuinely engaging.

All in all, a happy situation—if only her benefactor did not believe himself to be the Devil.

SABRINA LAYS OUT upon the table the many books that she has pulled from the shelves, twelve volumes in total—one for each side of the dodecagonal reading room in which she now sits. High above her rises a splendid glass dome, fifty feet in diameter, and below it is a series of narrow railed mezzanines ringing the circumference, allowing precarious access to the books that are shelved there.

She has only one day to herself in London—a day without official or medical appointments—and she wants to use it wisely. It had been a toss-up between the British Museum and the Maughan Library; in the end, she opted for the Maughan. One consideration was crowds: the BM is open to the public and would likely be packed at the beginning of summer, but the Maughan is the main library of King's College London, and only admits staff and students affiliated with KCL, or outside researchers if they present valid academic credentials. Sabrina's NYU postgraduate identification card satisfied the second requirement and so now, at this early hour and with the academic year concluded, she has the reading room to herself.

The room itself had been another factor in her choice. The Maughan's is one of the world's great reading rooms: intricate but practical—as in Bronaryre's apartment, the mezzanines are not merely decorative additions but also a logical solution for storage, ornate yet rational; and although the glass dome is an object of beauty its purpose is entirely pragmatic: to allow natural light to flood in, an important consideration for a reading room built in the days before electricity and still performing its purpose admirably, for the place is brilliantly illuminated, with no need of artificial lighting; but it was the library's collection that had primarily persuaded her to the Maughan, holdings dating from the time when the Weston Chapel had housed the office of Master of the Rolls under that same Henry III in whose name William the Marshal had once ruled England, growing steadily through the centuries, and then hugely augmented in 1998 by having had turned over to it, along with the glorious neo-Gothic building which it now occupies, the entire archive of the office of public records, colloquially referred to as 'the strong-box of the British Empire,' a trove so vast as to have not yet been completely cataloged. Amid this immensity of documents, she hopes there must be answers to at least some of her questions.

Sabrina places by her books the items that she came here to investigate: the seal from the letter Ravenscroft first sent her, carefully glued back together after she had returned to New York and currently secured with a cotton ball in a small round tin that had originally contained lip balm; a Bank of England £50-note; two slips of Savoy notepaper on which, with a pencil also supplied by the hotel, she made rubbings of the Oxford Crown, obverse and reverse; a printout of the Securities and Exchange Commission Form 13-F for Pendle Hill Investments; and lastly a color photocopy of the Savoie-Didier check whose original now resides in her room safe.

Beside them she lays out her tools: a *cahier*, one of the plain brown cardboard-covered notebooks of the type she habitually uses; the same pencil with which she had made the rubbing—the Maughan's Foyle Archive, the location of especially rare works, does not permit pens—a magnifying glass bought from a Bond Street stationer; and lastly a bookmark, also from her hotel room, not strictly necessary to her work but whose guilloche pattern—vaguely recalling Bronaryre's Breguet, but here vibrantly emerald green—she finds uncommonly pleasing.

Sabrina begins with a notaphilic monograph on British bank bills, but it turns out to be a dead end: the current £50-pound note was introduced only in 2011, with the purpose of adding security features to combat counterfeiting rather than facilitate the transmission of obscure warnings to the Established Church. It is to be replaced by a new note, she learns, this one made of polymer instead of paper, and on which Watt and Boulton are to be exchanged for Adam Turing—a Cambridge man, she recalls from the movie biography: Ravenscroft will be displeased.

There are no attributions for either the selection of motifs or the execution of design: apparently, the decisions on such things are taken by bureaucrats inside the Bank of England, probably a committee, and are not subject to public scrutiny.

The banknote had been a long shot, and so she is not especially disappointed.

A directory of Swiss financial institutions reveals that the Banque Savoie-Didier is a small but well-regarded institution, established in the Fourteenth Century and privately held ever since, headquartered in Geneva, and whose primary business is 'wealth'—a banking euphemism meaning an institution that caters only to the rich. A footnote beneath the contact details warns that Savoie-Didier receives new clients strictly by referral alone.

Not entirely a surprise that Satan should have highly confidential Swiss bankers, Sabrina supposes—another dead end.

Next, maintaining the theme of money, Sabrina turns to a century-old numismatic paper, mouthfillingly titled *The Gold Coins Issued at the Mint at Oxford, 1642-46, in the Reign of Charles I.* It gives a detailed account of the Oxford mint, including a section on the Oxford Crown, complete with photographs, even though the coin is made of silver rather than gold. The author is a Philip Nelson, M.D., F.S.A—F.S.A., she discovers, stands for Fellow of the Society of Antiquaries, a learned association headquartered at Burlington House in Piccadilly. Nelson begins his paper by setting the background, and the doctor is a skilled author—Sabrina soon finds herself enthralled with the adventure of the English Civil War, or at least the Oxford part of it.

In 1642 King Charles I—who had been intending to lay siege to London—was checked at Edgehill, one of the earliest of his many humiliations, although this one not at the hands of Oliver Cromwell, who arrived too late to take part. Charles withdrew to Oxford with his battered army and two sons—themselves destined, after many hardships, to become kings of England.

The city possessed two things that Charles desperately needed: a loyal garrison and a full treasury—*plenteously endowed with cash and rich stores of plate*, as Dr. Nelson put it. From that time until its surrender in 1646, Oxford became the capital of royalist England.

Sabrina is familiar with some of the Civil War arrangements in the city from the *Telegraph* article that reported the Oxford Crown's theft—Christ Church was converted into the king's palace; Merton College became that of the queen; Magdalen College hosted an artillery battery; New College was used as an arms magazine; the royalist parliament sat in the Bodleian Library's Convocation House. The townsfolk were conscripted to build fortifications; undergraduates were pressed into military service.

In the end, the choice of Oxford was to be Charles's undoing: it lies far from the sea, which rendered resupply from his European supporters difficult. Bristol was the only convenient port available for this purpose, and when it fell so too did the king. He had failed in that most fundamental tenet of war: keeping the lines of supply open—Napoleon's disastrous retreat from Moscow had precisely the same cause. Charles fled Oxford in late 1646 and gave himself up to the Scots. They in turn gave him up to parliament, and when parliament dallied in dealing with him, Cromwell simply came and took Charles from them by force.

The New Model Army now possessed the king, and Cromwell possessed the New Model Army: from that moment the fates of England in general, and Charles in particular, were sealed.

Precious-metal plate was an important method of storing wealth at the time: it was portable and could be conveniently melted down and used as needed. Dr. Nelson's paper details the plate contributed by the various colleges, listed by weight and broken out into 'white' or 'gilt,' meaning silver or gold. Ravenscroft's college, here spelled *Magdalene*, was the most generous, at nearly 300-pounds' weight of plate. Balliol was last, at just over 40. Caiaphas ranked seventh out of the twelve colleges listed, at 86 pounds. A thirteenth, Exeter, apparently delayed complying due to 'conscientious scruples' but these were eventually overcome, as guns tend to do with scruples.

Charles established the new mint shortly after retreating to Oxford. Thomas Rawlins had been apprenticed at the Tower Mint but fled London for Oxford where he first engraved dies for medals awarded to

Cavaliers. He began engraving coins in 1644 *in which year was struck that celebrated coin "The Oxford Crown," upon the obverse of which appears, beneath the horse, a view of the city of Oxford.*

Sabrina made the rubbings to precisely record the abbreviated Latin of Rawlins's coin, intending to make an exact translation, but she finds in a coin catalog that the translation has already been done for her. She begins with the obverse:

> CAROLUS♦D♦G♦MAG♦BRIT♦FANC♦ET♦HIBER♦REX
>
> *Charles by the Grace of God King of Great Britain, France, and Ireland.*

The reverse is wordier, with the center of the coin declaring his war aims:

> RELIG♦PROT♦LEG♦ANG♦LIBER♦PAR
>
> *The religion of the Protestants, the laws of England, the liberty of Parliament*

The circumference is pithier, revealing his desires regarding Cromwell and the Roundheads:

> EXURGAT♦DEUS♦DISSIPENTUR♦INIMICI
>
> *Let God arise, let his enemies be scattered.*

Sabrina wonders if this last is something that the Devil, or someone who believes himself to be the Devil, would take personally.

She puts aside the coin rubbings and moves on to the Form 13-F.

When Sabrina entered *Pendle Hill* into the catalog's search function, it had been with no greater expectation than to learn something about the place after which Bronaryre's investment fund is named—if such a place exists, then presumably there would be a connection: an area he once enjoyed visiting; or the location of the fund's offices; perhaps he was born there. But from the returns in the catalog she had quickly realized that Pendle Hill was more than just a place: it was an event, a name given to a series of Seventeenth-Century trials for witchcraft.

She retrieved two books on the subject: one a general history of persecution for witchcraft in Britain; the other a first-hand account of the Pendle Hill trials.

Sabrina begins with the general history. There is a chapter devoted to Pendle Hill, apparently the most infamous of the English witch trials, the British equivalent of Salem. The trials took place in 1612. Similar to Salem, much of the testimony against the accused was given by a young girl. Twelve people were accused; ten were found guilty and hanged; an eleventh died while awaiting trial. Four of the victims were from a single family, convicted on the testimony of a fifth member of that family, Jennet Devize, who was just nine years old at the time.

The strife began when an itinerant peddler from Halifax, John Law, encountered Jennet's elder sister, Alizon, while crossing a field near Colne. She beseeched Law to sell her some pins—an item used in magic ceremonies but which were in those days handmade and therefore expensive. He refused, either suspecting her of being a witch or believing her too poor to pay. Soon after he was struck down with what modern analysis of the symptoms would consider a stroke, but Law accused her of having bewitched him, and she was arraigned on a charge of *maleficium*—causing injury by witchcraft. Alizon complicated the matter by admitting to having done so.

Such trials seem appalling now, the author states, but this was an age when the reality of witchcraft was taken for granted, not just among the unlearned common folk but also by the leading lights of the age: as worldly and well-traveled a man as Raleigh believed in witches; in the second chapter of the *Leviathan* the rationalist philosopher Thomas Hobbes recommends that they be vigorously prosecuted; and the founder of modern chemistry, Robert Boyle, arranged for a translation of François Perreaud's *Démonologie, ou traitté des démons et sorciers*, for which he wrote a preface proclaiming that Perreaud had *overcome...all my settled indisposedness to believe strange things*—the author of *The Sceptical Chymist* was not so skeptical after all. Even that great prophet of reason, Francis Bacon, had found time between tracts calling men to science to list the ingredients of witches' ointment: henbane, hemlock, mandrake, moonshade, tobacco, opium, saffron, and poplar leaves. Topping it off was the monarch himself, James I, who wrote a book on the subject, *Daemonologie*. The persecution was especially bad in the north. Before becoming king of England, James I was James VI of Scotland, a land where, between the years 1560 and 1600, eight thousand women were burned as witches—this in a population of barely a million. Witches were an integral part of the culture; *Macbeth* opens with three of them. It is only by appreciating the depth of this belief that it can be understood how, with no compulsion of torture, half of the defendants at Pendle Hill professed themselves to be witches.

The other book is an eyewitness account of the Pendle Hill trials written by the court clerk, Thomas Potts, titled *The Wonderfull Discoverie of Witches in the Countie of Lancaster*—the second time in a week, Sabrina notes, that she has coincidentally encountered her own surname.

She finds in the book an account of the testimony of the nine-year-old Jennet Devize that had condemned her mother to hang:

> *Iennet Deuice, Daughter of Elizabeth Deuice, late wife of John Deuice, of the Forrest of Pendle aforesaid Widdow, confesseth and saith, that her said Mother is a Witch, and that this she knoweth to be true; for, that shee had seene her Spirit sundrie times come vnto her said Mother in her owne house, called Malking-Tower, in the likenesse of a browne Dogge, which shee called Ball; and at one time amongst others, the said Ball did aske this Examinates Mother what she would haue him doe: and this Examinates Mother answered, that she would have the said Ball to helpe her kill Iohn Robinson of Barley, alias Swyer: by helpe of which said Ball, the said Swyer was killed by witch-craft accordingly.*

Potts authored the work in 1613, shortly after completion of the trials, but Sabrina's edition is from 1845, commissioned by the Chetham Society—an association specializing in Lancastrian history—and contains a long introduction by the editor, James Crossley. Crossley makes his conclusions regarding Jennet Devize abundantly clear:

> *A more dangerous tool in the hands of an unscrupulous evidence-compeller, being at once intelligent, cunning and pliant, than the child proved herself, it would not have been easy to have discovered.*

He notes that in 1633, as if some retributive punishment awaited her, Jennet Devize was herself condemned to death for witchcraft, although there is no record of the sentence ever being carried out.

A strange business to have named an investment fund after, Sabrina thinks—perhaps the two are unrelated, and there is another Pendle Hill somewhere.

The next book is a compendium of London's medieval churches that survived the Great Fire. Temple Church is as Ravenscroft described it, built as the headquarters of the Knights Templar, but the site already had a long association with military might cloaked in religious creed: it was the location of the Roman temple in Londinium, and so was the center of imperial power in England a thousand years before the Crusades. Even today it retains an independence: the Temple Church is characterized as a 'Royal Peculiar,' which in the Anglican lexicon means that it is outside any episcopal or archiepiscopal jurisdiction: the head of the church—whose formal title is the 'Reverend and Valiant Master of the Temple'—answers only to the Crown.

Sabrina wonders whether a church without ecclesiastical oversight might be useful to the Devil and his agents.

She moves on to the Rosicrucian angle, beginning with a general overview. The movement arose to public prominence with a series of publications in the early Seventeenth Century—contemporaneous with the Pendle Hill witch trials, she notes—but it certainly existed earlier, as exemplified by an engraving of the hermeticist and astrologer Paracelsus in the *Philosophiae Magnae Paracelsi* of 1567, known as the 'Rosicrucian portrait' for its many Rosicrucian symbols, including eight 'crosses patty'—a term Sabrina learns is etymologically an anglicization of the French *croix pattée*, meaning a cross with splayed feet, and signifying a Greek cross whose arms widen as they move outward from the center, either in straight lines or more usually curves, as in the broad red cross that the Templar Knights wore on their surcoats as a symbol of their martyrdom.

It is also the type of cross featured on her seal.

The sect's origins were evidently much older. The putative founder of Rosicrucianism was a perhaps apocryphal German, pseudonymously Christian Rosenkreutz, who traveled to the Middle East in search of esoteric knowledge—presumably with the Crusades—and on his return to Europe founded the Fraternity of the Rosy Cross. But the symbol of the rosy cross long predates even this, to at least as far back as the Louvre's 'Harbaville Triptych,' a Byzantine ivory dating from around the year 1068, in whose central panel the rosy cross features prominently. There is a Templar connection: following their suppression, many Templar knights are supposed to have joined this new and secret order. Rosicrucianism died out with the Enlightenment, but much of it survives in modern Freemasonry.

She moves on to her last item: the seal that Ravenscroft identified as Rosicrucian. After searching the catalog on the term *Rosicrucian seals*, she selected the two volumes that from their entries appeared most heavily illustrated, and therefore most likely to allow her to identify the precise source. Both volumes are indeed heavily illustrated, but after an hour spent searching through them she finds nothing to match the seal—her last item, the one she thought most likely to succeed, has met with disappointment.

Sabrina sits back, considering this failure.

The Freemasonry reference had rung a bell, and after a while she recalls the source: it was her map. She pulls it out and soon locates the 'Freemason's Library,' an item she saw earlier when figuring out how to find the Maughan, and noted for its strangeness. The library is situated in Covent Garden, just a five-minute walk away.

# XII

SABRINA ROUNDS DRURY LANE into Great Queen Street, suddenly coming face-to-face with the Freemasons' Headquarters. She had expected a modest establishment, something befitting the secretive nature of the order, but the building is the opposite of modest: it is a large limestone edifice occupying a triangular corner location, dwarfing its neighbors, jutting forward proudly like the prow of a great ship, and topped by a tower as if to proclaim its presence for all to see. She crosses the street and enters through a mighty bronze door.

The library, she learns from the receptionist, is located on the first floor, which in England means the second floor. Sabrina reaches it via a broad staircase and a series of corridors, empty but for her.

It is a library in the traditional style: a long straight room, high-ceiling to accommodate tall windows, and with bookshelves arranged at right angles on either side, forming little alcoves in which one may sit at a table and study undisturbed.

To the left is the librarian's desk, and behind it is the librarian: an elderly gentleman in a buttoned cardigan who greets Sabrina with an inquiring smile. She explains the purpose of her visit, and in return is handed a sheet of paper and a ballpoint pen, which he refers to as a *biro*. No electronic registration here: the Freemasons do things the old-fashioned way.

After she completes the form the librarian disappears for five minutes. When he returns it is with her new library card: a piece of paper on which her name and address have been typed by a machine that is dropping the C-key, and which was subsequently laminated in clear plastic and then cut to size by an unsteady hand. He presents it to her proudly.

No barcode, no magnetic strip, not even an ID number—Sabrina resists an urge to hug the librarian. Instead, she takes from her bag the little lip balm tin, removes the lid, and offers the reconstructed seal lying in its cotton-ball bed for the gentleman to inspect. He leans forward, just inches above the seal, and pushes his spectacles to the end of his nose. He shows no particular reaction, as if being asked to identify obscure seals were an everyday occurrence for a Masonic librarian, as indeed it might be.

"Ah, yes," he says, after a minute's minute inspection. "*Agnus Dei.*"

"*Agnus Dei*?"

"The Lamb of God."

Soon Sabrina is ensconced in an alcove, so sunny that the dust particles are visible, going through the books that the librarian retrieved for her. The first is a catalog of Templar symbology. She discovers that the Agnus Dei was a theme commonly adopted on English *Templi Sigilla*—Templar Seals—as opposed to those of the French Grand Masters, who favored the more common representation of two knights mounted on a single horse, emphasizing the order's vow of poverty. She finds three close matches: the seal of Robert of Sandford (original in the British Library); William de la More (original in Durham Cathedral); and Richard of Hastings (unattributed). But it takes her another hour before she finds Ravenscroft's seal. It is in a volume titled *Cartulary of the Monastery of St. Æthylwine at Easton Grey*. A cartulary, she learns, is a copy of the original charter of an ecclesiastical establishment, a document detailing their rights, duties, privileges, and so on. The Monastery of St. Æthylwine had been established in the year 875, when Alfred the Great ruled Wessex and half of England was still under Danelaw. It was shut down in 1538 as part of Henry VIII's dissolution of the monasteries.

The book's frontispiece is illustrated with an engraving of the abbot's seal at the time of the monastery's closure, approximating the one in Sabrina's tin. But the author contends that this seal was a copy of a previous design, and he included a lithograph depicting the earlier example to demonstrate his point. It matches Ravenscroft's exactly.

It is the seal of Aymeric de St. Maur, the Master of the Knights Templar in England from 1200 to 1219. The creature seems more a goat than a lamb, slender and without wool, shown in profile, moving left to right. What she had taken for horns is actually a halo—wholly opposite in symbolic meaning—although the animal's countenance retains a knowing superciliousness more in keeping with her original impression. Above it rises a staff bearing a diamond-graved banner and topped by a cross, a so-called cross patty. There is no mistaking it: the peculiar horn-like bend in the halo; the banner's second-from-bottom streamer flowing upward while all the others go down; the odd offset of the Greek cross in the inscription above the Latin cross of the staff.

Now she knows why she had found no trace of it earlier: the seal is not Rosicrucian, as Ravenscroft claimed; it is Templar.

She looks up Aymeric de St. Maur. He was Master of the order in England during that period when King John gave control of his treasury to the Templars. He was also an executor of John's will when the king died in 1216, and was no doubt well acquainted with William the Marshal—in fact, together they had achieved supreme power: St. Maur had the treasury; William had the regency. Along with the signing of the Magna Carta in the previous year, it seemed that by 1216 the pair had brought off a successful coup d'état—the most successful coup of all: when the people do not even realize that a coup has taken place.

Sabrina returns the books and thanks the librarian for his help. She is about to leave when he clears his throat meaningfully.

"I wonder if you might like to see the museum?"

"There's a museum?"

"Oh, indeed. It would be a shame to have come to the library but missed the museum."

He has been too helpful for her to refuse, so she follows his directions down to the other end of the library, where an adjoining room does duty as the Freemasons' museum.

As with the library, she is the only visitor.

She wanders from display case to display case, dutifully inspecting the Masonic artifacts which, while usually decorative and sometimes artful, are of no particular interest to her. Mostly they are ceremonial items: clothing; trophies; drinking cups; silver trays.

One case catches her eye: it contains an exhibit of what are termed 'tracing boards'—plaques the size of her notebook depicting surrealistic scenes: pillars on a checkerboard floor with a ladder leading up into nothingness; an interior of a fantasy palace in which the passages do not quite connect; a coffin with a skull and crossbones, bearing a strange scroll. But most items are medallions and similar trinkets, referred to by the exhibit labels as 'jewels.' It is while glancing through a case of these last, wondering how long good manners requires her to spend in the museum before she can decently leave, that she comes to a sudden halt.

She recognizes the design on one of the jewels: it is the same motif that she had first seen etched into Bronaryre's cuff links, and then again as a watermark on his writing paper.

At the time she had supposed that the pattern was a pair of triangles, but the explanatory card beside the jewel identifies it as a 'unicursal hexagram,' a supposedly cosmic symbol. The five-leaved flower-like object at the center is a 'pentacle,' an earth symbol.

Sabrina looks up *unicursal hexagram*. The *unicursal* part means that it can be drawn as a single line, that is, without lifting pen from paper. In 1639, the French philosopher Blaise Pascal wrote a treatise on the pattern, *Hexagrammum Mysticum Theorem*, expounding the mathematical properties of the unicursal hexagram, including the fact that if the six points lie on a conic section, then the points at which any set of three opposing sides meet will always form a straight line—more astonishing that someone should discover this than the discovery itself, Sabrina thinks. Still, it was enough for the unicursal hexagram to be regarded as mysterious, as Pascal's title suggested, even occult.

There is no attribution or provenance, just a note that the object had been discovered by a farmer in a field in Gloucestershire in 1953, and then subsequently purchased by the local Masonic Lodge and donated to the museum.

Sabrina wonders how the unicursal hexagram would have come to adorn Bronaryre's cuff links.

# XIII

## A Mystery

GALLERY NUMBER TEN on the Tate Modern's second level is a big room containing just nine paintings, all by the same artist, all monumental, all identical in subject matter, and all of them equally baffling.

The artist is Mark Rothko, an American Abstract Expressionist whose working life spanned the middle of the last century, and about whom Sabrina knows nothing beyond a hazy recollection that he favored rectilinear color fields.

That is what she sees before her now as she stands in the middle of the gallery, going from painting to painting: brutalized rectangles. Stranger than this apparent need to endlessly repeat abused quadrilaterals is the color choice: just two: black but not quite, a black unsure that it is not really gray; and red, varying from subdued amaranth to a dark, saturated maroon, rust-hued, a color that looks like it is aging on the canvas in front of her; a color that if a smell would be musty and vaguely repellent.

It is the same color that had ringed the gallery on the brochure. Someone wittier might instead of circling the gallery have used a rectangle when highlighting it on the brochure, but maybe the Devil is disinclined to irony.

She retraces her steps to the room's entrance and reads there the Tate's introduction to the gallery. As their similarity suggests, the paintings are a set, the result of a commission from the Seagram company in 1958. Seagram had just completed their new headquarters in New York—a handsome, bronze-clad building on Park Avenue designed by the master modernist Mies van der Rohe and his young acolyte, Philip Johnson, a landmark in the Internationalist school of architecture. The paintings were intended for the Seagram's crown jewel, the Four Seasons, destined to become the most celebrated restaurant in New York. It was a highly prestigious commission, and well paid, too.

Yet with all the hard work done and on the verge of delivering the commission, Rothko had suddenly balked. He refused to hand over the paintings—instead, he returned Seagram's money and put the paintings into storage until, many years later, donating them to the Tate.

As a gesture it was recklessly dramatic: Rothko was throwing away reputation and wealth, something it is hard to imagine a struggling artist doing. But why?

Sabrina returns to the paintings for a clue. The rectangles are not punctiliously rectilinear, the edges never quite straight and somewhat fuzzy, not clearly defined. And their interiors are variable in tone and texture: one color palette, but not quite coherent. There is a sense of movement—notwithstanding that they are simple color fields—a sense of evolution on the canvas, particularly with the red. Energy, she supposes, but it is cheerless energy, a brooding presence beneath the surface, obfuscated and perhaps destructive, something best not revealed to plain view.

Somewhere there is a key to understanding these, Sabrina thinks, but she does not know what it is: for her, the paintings remain opaque and incomprehensible—a sullen, vaguely disquieting cipher.

What is it that Bronaryre wanted her to see in this room, she wonders. What is it that she missed?

## An Epiphany

THE ROTHKOS ARE still on Sabrina's mind that evening at St. Paul's. She has come to the cathedral not as a sightseer, nor less a supplicant, but as an auditor: from time to time St. Paul's hosts musical performances—usually but not necessarily of sacred music. This is not uncommon in Anglican establishments, Sabrina has learned, the prime example being the church of St. Martin-in-the-Fields in Trafalgar Square, a major musical institution in England, and one that in no way limits itself by shunning the profane.

Tonight's program is just a single work, that same oratorio whose title she first came across during her oral defense when a stranger in the audience had claimed to be from 'Sancta Civitas'—a stranger who asked about the Doctrine of Necessity, a question that helped propel the series of unlikely events leading her to a new life.

The oratorio is being performed on the 100th anniversary of its premiere, and when Sabrina saw it advertised in the morning paper she had called right away to get a ticket, believing that such coincidences should be at least acknowledged, if not humored. Given that the title means *Holy City* and that the libretto is taken entirely from the Bible, the work was obviously deemed suitable for a performance in the old cathedral, notwithstanding the awkward fact that, according to the program notes, Ralph Vaughn Williams professed himself to be 'a cheerful agnostic,' and when they were up at Cambridge together Bertrand Russell referred to Vaughn Williams as 'the most frightful atheist.'

Sabrina puts aside the program and surveys the interior of St. Paul's. It is hard to see how 'Sancta Civitas' could be performed anywhere other than inside a cathedral, she thinks: nowhere else would have enough room. There is a full orchestra in front, surrounded by tiers of choristers, completely occupying the apse's American chapel and the two side chapels flanking it, more than could be accommodated on the stage of a normal venue. There is a boy's chorus occupying the actual choir, and then a second semi-chorus—the 'distant' chorus—in the transepts. Add to that the cathedral's organ, whose great gilded pipes rise just before the choir, plus the two soloists—all of this for not much more than thirty minutes of music.

But what music! From the hushed opening notes—somber but wondering, willing to find resolution—Sabrina realizes that this is to be a work the likes of which she has never heard before. The choruses weave and murmur for a while, hinting at what is to come, swelling inevitably into vast waves of sound, lush and glorious, almost overwhelming even St. Paul's. Striving, endlessly striving, seeking reconciliation—but the plaintive English horn at the end of the *Allegro moderato* suggests the hopelessness of this task. And finally, after much searching, the solemn and sorrowing close, lamenting what has been lost and what will be lost to come, but accepting, too: understanding that loss is the undying accompaniment to ever-dying life, and finally the choruses' last echoes slowly fade away into nothingness, as one day so shall we.

She is transported: it is a supreme work of profound contemplation, full of melancholy beauty, music performing its highest purpose: expressing that which is beyond language to express. She has never been so moved, by music or anything else.

It occurs to her that the calm acquiescence of the 'Sancta Civitas' is the very opposite of this afternoon's Rothkos, which had been all deep, sullen, unreconciled rage.

Sabrina's eyes are streaming as the lights come back up, too soon, far too soon; but at least she is not alone: there are handkerchiefs and tissues everywhere.

As she walks back through the empty streets of the City toward her hotel—no possibility of the tube after that music, no possibility of other people at all—she weeps still and is grateful for the darkness, for she is becoming self-indulgent. She is not normally given to such displays, and chides herself for it now. But if tears then let them be like these, she thinks; she is not at all despondent; to the contrary, she feels strengthened. And if one is destined to deal with the Devil, she thinks, then there could surely be no better fortification for it than the music that she has just listened to.

# XIV

## And I Saw an Angel Standing in the Sun

SABRINA EMERGES FROM the Savoy's lobby, marble-paved and wood-paneled, into sunshine and warmth—two properties that have eluded her so far in England, the last week having been all gray skies and, at the Whitehall office where she was granted residential status, similarly gray officials. The entrance to the hotel is located at the end of a short lane running off the Strand, terminating in a circular drive at the center of which is a fountain, burbling away.

The front desk had called up to let her know that her car had arrived, but downstairs there is no sign of either it or her driver, just a scattering of parked vehicles and, stopped right in front of the portico, a bright red sports car.

This last appears to have come to a halt involuntarily, for the hood is up, and the car is surrounded by a small cluster of spectators watching someone working on the engine. The spectators include the doorman.

Sabrina walks over, and the doorman tips his top hat in greeting.

"They told me my car was here."

"And so it is, Miss Lancaster." He smiles broadly and gestures toward the stranded sports car.

"This?"

"Beautiful day for a jolly in a roadster, ma'am."

*Roadster* she assumes must mean *convertible*. The hood, which in this vehicle comprises the entire body in front of the windshield and tilts forward instead of opening in the usual way, has so far concealed the identity of the driver/mechanic bent beneath it, but now he stands to look at the new arrival. It is Aneurin Bronaryre.

"Lancaster," he says in greeting. "Did you bring a scarf?"

"No."

"There might be one in the glove compartment."

"What is this?"

"An E-Type."

"What's wrong with it?"

"Nothing."

"Then what are you doing?"

"Watering it." He holds up a bottle, which from the label she recognizes as the hotel's brand of bottled mineral water. "E-Types have spent twenty-four hours racing at Le Mans without overheating, but that's with plenty of air flowing through the cooling system. They don't like being stationary, and so before negotiating London traffic it's best to top up."

"With mineral water?"

It is the doorman who replies. "Nothing but the best for a fifty-year-old Jaguar." He pronounces the vehicle's marque with three syllables instead of two: JAG-YOU-ARE. "Shall I get your luggage, ma'am?"

All eyes turn to her bag—recently purchased for the trip and large enough to accommodate the clothing required for an extended period abroad—and then toward the Jaguar's tiny trunk. It is clear that the latter cannot possibly accommodate the former. Bronaryre is the first to break the ensuing silence, addressing the doorman.

"Have it sent up to Caiaphas, will you, Johnson?"

"I'll get someone to run it up now, sir." He gestures to a porter, who quickly takes her bag and disappears. Johnson the doorman gives

Sabrina a reassuring look. "Don't you worry, ma'am, we'll have your baggage there before you arrive." If they will need to make stops to water the car, she does not doubt it.

"Come and I'll show you the engine," Bronaryre says, "then you can help close her up."

Sabrina walks around the raised hood and joins him. Guests coming and going from the hotel have paused to admire the car, swelling the crowd, and the score of people now surrounding it close in, realizing that this will be the last chance to see what lies beneath the hood.

Bronaryre gives Sabrina a brief tour of the engine.

"Four-point-two-liter straight-six," he says. "That's a considerable displacement for a six-cylinder. It's a continuation of the engine that powered the D-Types to outright victory at Le Mans three years in a row—William Lyons wanted to retain the same configuration, but the engineers had to increase bore to keep up with the ever-more-powerful Ferrari GTOs that Enzo was building. Double overhead camshafts," he says, pointing to two polished aluminum covers running longitudinally along either side of the engine. "And these are the carburetors, triple SUs." To Sabrina, they look like a row of shiny little tea kettles. "Let's button her down."

Closing the hood is a two-person operation: Sabrina's role is to remain outside and apply pressure to the rear corner, forcing it down against the rubber weather strip, while inside the cockpit Bronaryre manipulates a chrome-handled rod running through the front firewall to latch it down tight. They circle the car and repeat the operation on the driver's side. She wonders what someone driving alone would do; probably they would never open the hood, knowing that they could not close it again, and supposes that the mechanism must have been designed with racing in mind, in which there is always a pit crew on hand to accomplish the task.

Bronaryre stands back and, with a glance toward the now buttoned-down vehicle, silently invites Sabrina to contemplate her ride.

The Jaguar is long and slender and tautly drawn, like the animal after which it is named. It is very low. The hood has a central bulge, required to accommodate the large engine that she has just seen lying beneath, and a series of louvers are cut in on either side, no doubt needed on a car prone to overheating. Chrome wire wheels with white-wall tires. The windshield is so low that three stubby wipers are required for coverage. There are none of the wings or air scoops or exaggerated body shapes that one might see on a modern car, added to advertise sporting pretensions, but instead just a cool simplicity of purpose expressed in elegant, flowing lines.

"It's beautiful," she says.

"The man who designed the body, Malcolm Sayer, was not an automobile stylist but an aircraft engineer, hence the aerodynamic shape. Enzo called it the most beautiful car ever made, and he wasn't one to give easy compliments to competitors."

"A sculpture, really."

"Indeed; the Museum of Modern Art in New York has one just like this, except theirs is navy blue."

"I suppose yours has to be red." It is the first time that she has referred to his delusion, however obliquely, but he makes no comment in response.

The porter who took her luggage returns. He carries a small paper bag from which he extracts two bottles of mineral water. "For the journey," he says, but whether they are intended for consumption by the passengers or the car is not clear. He places them in the center console and then withdraws a third item, which he offers to Sabrina. "Compliments of the Savoy, ma'am."

It is a scarf, still in its packaging. She thanks him and unwraps it. The scarf is pure silk and bears a pattern that on closer inspection is revealed to be a stylized rendering of the hotel's logo.

"How very kind of you." Sabrina puts it on Audrey Hepburn-style, tied beneath her chin, and then adds a pair of sunglasses to complete the look.

The doorman opens the passenger side and she takes her seat, a foot lower than in a normal car, and requiring a semi-gymnastic performance to curl her long legs into the E-Type's narrow footwell. Bronaryre avoids this awkward operation by the simple expedient of stepping over the door and directly into the cockpit. He slides in under the steering wheel, a stylish wood-rimmed artifact from the days before airbags, and when the only button on a steering wheel was for the horn.

The dashboard is as purposeful as the rest of the car: a simple black metal backing studded with a broad array of dials and buttons and switches, more like an airplane cockpit than an automobile interior. Between the seats is a floor-mounted stick shift and a chrome brake handle. The whole thing feels highly complex and slightly industrial, something that would require more than just a driver's license to operate competently.

"Ready?"

"Ready."

Bronaryre pulls down a lever to the left of the steering column, as if selecting flap for take-off, and then engages the starter. The engine cranks huffily for a turn or two and then bursts into vibrant mechanical life. With the top down there is nothing to suppress the snarl from the exhaust, loud enough to sound as if purposely designed to annoy the neighbors, but it draws smiles of delight from the gathered crowd; one small boy bursts into cheers.

Bronaryre engages gear, releases the brake, and away they go. The booming exhaust echoes off the buildings on either side.

They come to the red light at the end of the lane, where it meets the Strand.

"You're on the wrong side," Sabrina shouts, the only way in which conversation is possible. "They drive on the left here."

"Not in the Savoy Court: this is the one street in England on which—by an act of parliament—you must drive on the right." He jerks a thumb over his shoulder, back toward the hotel. "It's because ladies traditionally sit right behind the chauffeur, and driving on the right allows them to get out directly under the hotel's portico, and thus never be rained upon."

She looks back and sees how it would work. "How very considerate of parliament."

The light turns green and they shoot out into the Strand. Since normal conversation is impossible, Sabrina sits back in her sun-drenched seat and enjoys the passing scene. Bronaryre seems to sense her pleasure in this and so, after entering the traffic circle at Trafalgar Square, keeps going around for three complete circumnavigations: once to view Nelson's Column; a second to take in the National Gallery; a third to admire the church of Saint Martin-in-the-Fields. At last, they leave Trafalgar Square and head into Saint James's. The traffic is not particularly heavy—a result, no doubt, of London's congestion pricing scheme—although an occasional double-decker bus, bright red like the car, comes threateningly alongside as they drive down Piccadilly, towering above the Jaguar and blotting out the view.

In Knightsbridge, Bronaryre suddenly turns off the main road and down a narrow dead end.

"Where are we going?" Sabrina asks, but before he can respond she has seen the answer for herself: at the end of the street is valet parking for Harrods.

"I assumed that you would be tired of restaurants and room service," he says, "so this evening I thought we might picnic in the Dean's Garden."

Inside Harrods, the food hall is a crowded, bustling market.

"You select some cheeses; I'll fetch the wine." Bronaryre disappears into the crowd, leaving her alone in the cheese department, a place in which she could have happily spent an hour looking through their inventory. By the time Bronaryre returns she has chosen three cheeses: a seasonal Oxfordshire Rollright; a Stilton from the Nottinghamshire village of Colston Bassett; and finally a territorial, Red Leicester, selected because of its extraordinary color and cut fresh from a mighty round. Meanwhile, Bronaryre has fetched more than just wine, and they leave Harrods with a crusty-looking country bread, pâté, oil, black olives, prosciutto, a sausage labeled Devon that looks like mortadella, a jar of something called 'gherkins,' artichoke hearts, asparagus spears, and fairy cakes for dessert. The Devil dines well, she thinks.

The E-Type is soon retrieved and after an extended discussion about it with the parking lot attendants and admiring passers-by—an inconvenience that Sabrina is beginning to realize is unavoidable with such a car—they are once again underway.

The route west begins as Brompton Road, but undergoes several name changes as they head through Chiswick and Richmond, eventually metamorphosing into the M4 motorway. As they pass beyond Heathrow the traffic lightens, and Bronaryre increases speed accordingly. Soon the car is traveling at over 100 MPH and the wind, which until now had been a gentle breeze, has become a buffeting and shrieking force. The windshield deflects most of it, but Sabrina is grateful for the scarf. Oxford is only sixty miles from London, and before long there are signs for the exit.

# XV

SABRINA'S FIRST IMPRESSION of Oxford is that the traffic is worse than London's, but that soon changes as they cross Magdalen Bridge into the center of the city. Suddenly, it is all medieval ramparts and meandering paths and those many marvelous spires. High Street is closed to cars—except Bronaryre's, it seems—but eventually he turns off into a cobbled lane, rutted by centuries of use, and which must be negotiated at a fraction of the speed on the motorway, so slowly that even a bicyclist manages to overtake them. He names the high-walled colleges they pass by while bouncing along the cobblestones: Merton, Oriel, Corpus Christi. Two turns later they come to an archway, just wide enough to accommodate the E-Type, and giving onto a small courtyard where amid several parked cars there is a single unoccupied space, conspicuously signed as private.

Bronaryre parks. Sabrina unfolds herself from the car and stretches gratefully. While he puts the top up, she looks about at the city that is to be her new home. There is a square tower behind them—Merton Chapel, she will discover—and ahead a prominent spire rising above one of the colleges. Despite the warmth of the day the air feels cool here, still and shadowed, ensconced within the many stone walls of the ancient city. Cool or not, there is a small stream of water trickling out from under the E-Type: Sabrina had noticed the temperature gauge creeping higher while they were buried in traffic, and she had sensed that the car was coming to the end of its tether.

Bronaryre leads the way through a narrow passage back to High Street. That first spire turns out not to be a college: it belongs to Saint Mary's—the official church of the university, Bronaryre tells her, despite the fact of Christ Church cathedral—and is a feature that Sabrina realizes she should have identified from its depiction on the Oxford Crown. Next to it is a distinctive domed building, the Radcliff Camera, and then the Bodleian Library and Sheldonian Theatre. Any of them, plus neighboring All Souls College, could be hit by a pebble tossed from the same spot—she had not realized that everything would be so close together.

They take the lane bordering Brasenose and, after turning into Turl Street, find Caiaphas College now suddenly right in front of them. Sabrina takes an instant liking to the place, even before having entered it: a small, walled haven tucked away deep in the heart of Oxford, without the magnificent portals and mighty bell towers of the grander colleges, a place whose entrance is just a simple Gothic archway protected by two big green-painted main doors pierced by a smaller person-sized door—a convenience that she will learn is called a *wicket gate*.

No sign: either you knew this was Caiaphas or you did not.

They enter the college. The first stop is the porters' lodge, where Sabrina is introduced to a Mr. Collins, the head porter, fully fitted out in livery, including an elegantly embroidered waistcoat, but whose manner is the opposite of what his clothing might have suggested: welcoming without being gushing, deferential without being obsequious, practical and to the point—he tells her right away that her baggage has arrived and already been taken up to her room, relieving her of the lingering anxiety of what to do if it did not show up—as with the college, she takes an instant liking to its head porter. After introductions are complete, Collins turns to Bronaryre.

"Did she behave herself on the way up, sir?" he asks.

It takes Sabrina a moment to realize that he is referring to the car, not herself.

"Overheated on the way in."

"Just as well it wasn't tomorrow: they're forecasting record temperatures."

"Perhaps you can ask the garage people to flush the cooling system and replace the radiator belt?" The porter agrees to do so and Bronaryre hands across the car keys before turning to Sabrina. "I'll leave you in Collins's capable hands. If you would care to join me in the Dean's Garden at six, we'll set about consuming all of this." He indicates the bulging Harrods shopping bags.

Collins gives Sabrina three sets of keys: one is a key to the main gate, including an electronic fob for opening the door leading from the porters' lodge into the first quadrangle. The second is to the Dean's Garden, the only access to which, apart from the Dean's Residence, is via an external gate located around the corner on Ship Street, thus allowing the dean the singular privilege of entering and exiting the college without having to do so under the watchful gaze of the porters. The third key is for her rooms, located on Staircase VIII in the second quad. Collins briefs her on mealtimes and explains the operation of the Great Hall. She is given a sheaf of documents, including various registration forms that he invites her to fill out at leisure and return to the porters' lodge later. Lastly, Collins gives her a map of the college and marks the location of her room with a red *X*, but he does not offer to accompany her, perhaps sensing that she would prefer her first exploration of the college to be conducted alone, or maybe he is simply too busy to leave the porters' lodge.

Sabrina thanks him and, using her new fob, passes into the college grounds.

The quadrangles, like Caiaphas itself, are more modest than those of the larger colleges like Christ Church or Magdalen: each of them is about a hundred feet square, the first crossed diagonally by paths but in the second, hers, the central lawn is left undivided, allowing half a dozen students to enjoy a lively game of croquet in the afternoon sunshine. On all four sides the honey-colored walls rise high, the differing parts—Dean's Residence, Chapel, Great Hall, Senior Common Room, Junior Common Room, Library—all melding together seamlessly with the students' and fellows' accommodations, as if it had been the work of a single unified conception rather than the accumulation of centuries that it actually was.

Sabrina locates Staircase VIII and begins the long climb to the top floor, thinking that at least she will keep fit while in residence at Caiaphas. On one of the landings a small wooden sign is fitted above a door, noting that those rooms had once been the student quarters of a well-known English Prime Minister.

Her room turns out to be two rooms, a bedroom and a sitting room, and has something that she did not expect in a five-centuries-old college: her own bathroom. The windows are small but there are sets front and back, allowing in abundant light and air. She goes to the windows facing the quad and gazes out over her new academic world, about as far removed from the busyness and bustle of NYU as could be imagined.

She should unpack, but instead she leaves her rooms and goes exploring.

# XVI

SABRINA IS SURPRISED to find on the quadrangle wall at the base of the stairwell a graffito, but it is a graffito of a benign type, rendered in chalk rather than paint, depicting a red dragon and, below it, a large Roman numeral with a series of colored pennants and college names. One of the croquet players, sensing her puzzlement, comes over to explain.

"Rowing," he says. "These are the results from Eights Week, and you can see that our team did rather well: they won their 'blades,' which is to say they bumped another boat on each of the four days of the regatta, hence these four blades with the colors of the colleges they bumped." Sabrina sees that what she had taken to be flags or pennants are in fact the stylized blades of boat oars.

"What's the dragon mean?"

"It's the symbol of our college, on our coat of arms." His companions call him over for his shot, so Sabrina thanks him and continues her circumnavigation of the central lawn.

The two quads are separated by the Great Hall, empty in the late afternoon with lunch finished and preparations for dinner yet to commence, and she has the place to herself. It is a large, long room with a magnificent roof high overhead, coffered and barrel-vaulted. The windows are fit for a cathedral: triple-tiered with the top of each arch fancifully carved in a triplex pattern, echoing the three-level arrangement of the panes or, in those religious times, perhaps intended to invoke the triune nature of the Christian deity.

Tables and benches are arranged longitudinally for the students, and at the end of the hall there is a raised dais with a real dining table and chairs, the High Table that Collins had explained is where fellows of the college, like her, dine. The paneling is dotted with portraits, and pride of place above the High Table is occupied by a full-length rendering of Elizabeth I in all her finery, looking very worldly with sparkling jewels and luxurious raiment, casting her cool gaze upon the viewer, tolerant enough but brooking no nonsense, every inch a queen.

Sabrina is circling the first quad when she hears music. It is coming from the direction of the Chapel. She supposes that a service must be underway and enters cautiously so as not to disturb the congregants, but once inside she finds the Chapel empty. Not entirely empty, for directly above her is a gallery, evidently reached by the small wooden staircase rising from the vestibule, and someone is up there now, invisible from below, apparently practicing on the organ—probably rehearsing the Sunday program. Other than the unseen player, she has the place to herself. She takes a seat on a nearby pew and sits back to enjoy the impromptu concert while admiring the Chapel's interior.

The instrument is a powerful one: the low notes make the pew tremble beneath her.

The Chapel, like the rest of Caiaphas College, is Gothic: that curious combination of the richly ornate redeemed from excess by resting on a background of cool, dignified stone. The pulpit is lavishly carved, the floor a wonderfully intricate mosaic, and even the misericordiae of the choir are works of art. The walls that rise to support the soaring vaults are pierced by tall, slender, light-flooding windows, topped by the pointed arches—sometimes ogee, sometimes ogive—that give the style its characteristic theme.

The organist comes to a stop. The sudden silence is jarring. Sabrina looks up to see if her presence has been perceived, half expecting a look of stern disapproval at her unwelcome intrusion, but no face appears. In the echoing chamber of the chapel the only sound is her own breathing, punctuated after a long pause by a page of sheet music being turned over in the gallery high above her.

The music resumes. It is a heavier piece this time, clashing counterpoint on a brooding theme that rattles the furnishings, threatening to shake the whole place down. The deluge continues apace, aiming for but never achieving resolution, always falling back into a dark foreboding dread. Whatever it is, Sabrina thinks, it is not a church hymn.

The voluminous music fills the Chapel, seems to flood it, as if not just moving the air but actually displacing it. It flows forward, relentless and unstoppable, a crushing physical presence, entirely irresistible. The hurtling repetitions become hypnotic, mesmerizing, contrapuntal variations on a single trance-inducing theme. Sabrina realizes that she is taking short sharp breaths, and for a moment, just as the piece reaches a crescendo, she has the sudden sensation of drowning.

The piece ends, and after a moment a head pops out, a man. He does not seem to be annoyed at the intrusion; he is smiling. He says something, but Sabrina's ears are still ringing, and she cannot understand him. He repeats himself, louder this time.

"Welcome to Caiaphas College," he says. "I hope I wasn't playing too loudly."

"No, I enjoyed it, the second piece especially."

"Strange to say, they were the same piece. The first time I played it in the style of Albert Schweitzer, the great humanist who was also a concert-level organist. The second time was in the style of Richard Wagner, who wasn't much of a humanist at all—nor an organist, for that matter—but he certainly knew his *Sturm und Drang*."

"What was the piece?"

"Bach. The 'Fantasia and Fugue in G minor.'" The organist leans his arms on the railing. The light is pouring in through the window behind him, and so she cannot see him clearly, but she can tell that he is inviting the conversation to continue.

"I'm amazed that the same piece of music could sound so different, just from the style of playing."

"That's because it's Bach—he's like Shakespeare, endlessly interpretable, hiding a hundred possibilities in a single line. Think of the

Goldberg Variations, which for two centuries after Bach's death was mostly dismissed as an obscure keyboard exercise, with little utility beyond musical training, until Glenn Gould astonished the world by revealing the piece in its full glory in 1955. Or Casals a generation earlier, happening upon the cello suites in a dusty Barcelona book store while still just a youth, and realizing that he had discovered an overlooked treasure—an event that was to ensure his fame, and the music's, too."

"I've been in Oxford less than a day, and already I've learned a dozen impossible things before dinner."

Her interlocuter claps his hands. "Very good, Doctor Lancaster. You will do well here, I perceive."

She can sense rather than see his smile, and feels a pang of pleasure in having successfully pulled off her first literary allusion in Oxford, even if only to a children's story.

"Do you know, that is the first time anyone has addressed me as *Doctor*. What's your name?"

"Wilkins, Roger Wilkins."

"Are you a college fellow?"

"Yes, but not at Caiaphas; I'm at Campion Hall. However, Caiaphas needed an organist, and I needed an instrument on which to practice, and so here I am. Tell me, what's an impossible thing that you learned today?"

"I learned that the word *blades* has a very unusual but highly specific meaning in Oxford: it means having achieved a deliberate collision in a rowboat on four consecutive days."

This time Wilkins laughs out loud. "Well, that's what it means alright, but you must refer to them as *racing eights*—a *rowboat* is something to take Aunt Harriet and the children for a jaunt—and an outright *collision* is to be avoided: they merely *bump*."

"I'm also learning that language is very particular here."

"Everything has hidden meanings in Oxford. It is not only the city of dreaming spires, it is also a city of narrow lanes and short sightlines, where everything is shadowed or occluded. One must navigate with care.

Oxford is the city of subtle deceptions, and nowhere more so than with language."

"The city of subtle deceptions?"

"Certainly. Take, for example, those racing eights. The river on which they race is the Isis. For the rest of that river's course it is known to the world as the Thames; only in Oxford is it called the Isis. The other river that runs through Oxford, the one on which one usually punts, is spelled CHER-well but pronounced CHAR-well. The main street is called High Street, but is only ever referred to in conversation as *the High*. Or consider the curious case of Saint Mary Magdalen. There are five places in Oxford that are named for the saint: a church, a street, a road, a bridge, and a college. Firstly, the thoroughfares: the *street* is pronounced in the normal way—MAG-dah-len—but not the *road*: that's pronounced MAUD-lin. Same juxtaposition for the buildings: the *church* is MAG-dah-len, but the *college* is MAUD-lin. And the bridge is MAUD-lin, too."

"It seems to be designed to baffle the unwary tourist."

"Or perhaps, as a system of nomenclature, its real function is to distinguish the *us* from the *them*, by which I mean the initiated from the uninitiated, the Oxbridge from the Redbrick. There are a thousand misuses or mispronunciations, any one of which will serve to quietly reveal education or class or status or background, without requiring the bad manners of overt questioning. Who would guess that Pembroke rhymes with *cook*, or Balliol with *granule*? Christ Church is technically not a college because it is the cathedral seat, and so anyone using the term *Christ Church College* is immediately identifiable as an outsider—most Oxonians simply refer to it, quite deceptively, as *the House*. One doesn't even *go* to Oxford, you *go up*, and when joining you do not merely *enroll*, you *matriculate*. Nor do you leave Oxford, instead you *come down*, unless of course you are expelled, in which case you are *sent down*. You do not *major* in a field of study, you *read* it. At the end of your doctoral studies elsewhere, you are awarded a PhD., but not at Oxford: here it is a DPhil. In the rest of the world, a *scout* is a boy in a funny uniform; in Oxford, it is likely an elderly man who 'does for you,' which is to say he cleans your rooms. College dues are *battels*. Reunion dinners are *gaudies*. In Oxford, even the term names are designed to confuse. For the two terms following Michaelmas, Cambridge uses the perfectly logical *Lent* and *Easter*, but in Oxford these are obscurely referred to as *Hilary* and *Trinity*. And there are nominally eight weeks in each of those terms, but at Oxford the counting begins not at one but at zero—Naughth Week—so in fact there are nine. Time itself is obfuscated in Oxford: if you go to the cathedral for six P.M. Evensong, you will find that you have arrived early: Christ Church maintains a separate time zone—the old Oxford Time—which is five minutes later than standard British time. And take *subfusc*. The word *subfusc* means dusky and dull-colored, like the old tweeds one might don for a walk in the countryside. In Oxford it means the opposite: a formal black-and-white outfit, and which always includes cap and gown. Sometimes a carnation must be worn, and the color of the carnation must be correct: depending on the occasion, white or pink or red. It seems designed to confuse and embarrass: one can imagine someone uninitiated turning up for an event in his country duds, and finding everyone else in formal wear. Even everyday errands are different here: Oxford is surely the only place on earth where one could profess an intention to 'go to the plodge and check the pidge on the way to the Bod' and be perfectly well understood."

Sabrina laughs, wondering what pidges and plodges are, although she can guess that 'the Bod' means the Bodleian Library.

"Thanks for the briefing. Are you going to come down from there?"

"I'm not sure I should risk it."

"What's the risk?"

"To my soul."

"Huh?"

"You admired the second rendering of the Bach. To be frank, it made me slightly queasy to play it that way: all darkness and dread and despair—I just did it as an exercise, and then only because I thought I was alone; I would never play that way in public."

"So I've caught you out?"

"So you have. I suppose I have no choice but to come and face you now."

His silhouette disappears, and there is only light. Sabrina hears the sheet music being packed away, followed by the sound of his footsteps leaving the gallery. She returns to the vestibule to meet him at the bottom of the stairs.

Roger Wilkins is tall, having to duck as he comes down the little staircase, and still retains something of the gangliness of youth. Early thirties, she would guess, that age when a man has reached the full confidence of adulthood, but not yet acquired the cynicism of long maturity—the ideal age for the male, she thinks, the period when he will be at his productive best. Head of thick, unruly hair above what seems an open, honest face.

He comes to the bottom of the staircase, and as he stands fully upright Sabrina receives a surprise: he is wearing a clerical collar. The concern for his soul is suddenly explained.

"I didn't realize that you were a priest," she says. "I'm not even sure if that's the correct term in the Church of England—should I say 'minister' instead?"

"No, not at all: Anglicans do use the word 'priest.'" Wilkins's mood seems unimpacted by her evident shock—Sabrina supposes that he must be used to it—and he continues good-humoredly. "However, I must tell you that I am neither Anglican nor a priest. It's another of those Oxonianisms, I'm afraid—I assumed that as soon as I said where I was from you would understand."

"Do you mean Campion Hall?"

"Yes. You see, *hall* is one of those words with a special meaning in Oxford. There are forty-five constituent colleges and permanent private halls that make up the university. Colleges and halls are essentially the same thing—that is, they are both residences and places of instruction—except that permanent private halls are also religious establishments: So, for example, Wycliff Hall is Anglican. Regent's Park is Baptist. Saint Benet's and Blackfriars are both Roman Catholic, the former run by the Benedictines, the latter by the Dominicans."

"What's Campion Hall's affiliation?"

"Campion Hall is also Roman Catholic, but it is Jesuit."

"You said that you're not a priest, but you wear a clerical collar?"

If he is put out by her to-the-point American directness, he is too well mannered to show it. "I am what they call a Jesuit Brother: that is, I am a member of the order, but unordained. I normally wear regular clothing, but for church or chapel I think it proper to wear clerical attire, even if the service is Anglican rather than Catholic—to tell the truth, there's not that much difference between them, especially High Anglican, which is what they practice here. Unordained brothers are common in our order, especially for those members who are destined for a career in scholarship rather than ministry—I'm very happy to deliver an academic paper, but quite frankly I couldn't manage a sermon if I tried."

"Is music your field of study?"

"Oh, no—the organ playing is just for pleasure. My academic field is genetic anthropology."

She considers this for a moment. "Isn't genetic anthropology a little hazardous for those of your persuasion—I mean, likely to lead to doctrinal contradictions?"

He laughs out loud again. "Well, we reach conclusions where the science leads us. It might not suit a Benedictine, who would simply deny the conclusion, or those wretched Dominicans, who would happily burn you at the stake for having reached it, but we Jesuits are much looser with these things. We don't fuss about what doesn't matter. Consider the case of Edmund Campion, for whom Campion Hall is named. He was an English Jesuit who, at Tyburn, was hanged, drawn, and quartered under the reign of *this* college's founder, for the crime of having questioned her legitimacy. Yet here I am, a member of the same order happily participating in services in this bastion of High Church Anglicanism."

Sabrina's initial guardedness on discovering his vocation begins to fade—whatever his beliefs, he is uninterested in pressing them upon other people. At last she is able to disregard the immediate fact of the collar and pay more attention to his face, and in doing so receives a second shock in as many minutes.

"I recognize you," she says.

"I was wondering if you would."

"You were at the oral defense of my dissertation. You asked the question about the Doctrine of Necessity."

"Indeed, I did."

"How come?"

"I was already in New York: I was completing a sabbatical at Rockefeller University."

"You said you were from *Sancta Civitas*—I looked it up; there's no such institution."

"In fact there is: *Sancta dei Civitas* is another name for the Catholic church. Pope Leo XIII—who was instrumental in shepherding the church into the modern world—applied the term in his encyclical of the same name, and ever since modernists such as myself tend to use it."

"But why would you show up at my oral defense at all? How did you know that it would take place? How would you even know that I existed?"

"I was told of you."

"By whom?"

"Justice Scaglietti."

"Scaglietti?" Her voice registers astonishment, but even as she says it she is already beginning to see the logic: the Jesuits were obviously courting the Justice—successfully, as his sister had made clear—but it seems they were wise enough to have realized that Scaglietti would make short work of anyone not up to the Justice's level of academic rigor, and so had pulled one of their sharpest knives from the drawer: an Oxford-trained scientist, someone who could intellectually go toe-to-toe with Scaglietti.

"How did you know the Justice?"

"We met at a dinner hosted by the general of our order in New York. It turned out that the Justice and I shared an interest in music. He invited me to come up to his estate, Netherly, where he was hosting a recital. I accepted and arrived at his house at the appointed time. Immediately after the recital ended he briefly pulled me aside from the other guests. What he told me was very alarming: he said that he expected to die, quite soon and quite suddenly. I feared that I was going to be called upon to give spiritual guidance, which as I've mentioned I'm perfectly hopeless at, but it soon became clear that what he wanted was something else entirely. He took one of his cards from the desk and wrote your name on the back, explaining who you were and that he was the subject of your dissertation. He asked that, were he suddenly to die, that I attend your oral defense and, during questions, ask about the role in his opinions of the Doctrine of Necessity. He requested that I make no further contact, and that the question appear to be entirely natural and unplanned. He said that you would understand."

"Understand what?"

"I have no idea."

"Didn't this seem strange to you?"

"A little, of course. But not so much. I supposed that he simply wished to give you an easy question during what was no doubt to be the most important academic day of your life. He had obviously taken an attachment to you."

"An attachment?"

"He told me about the codicil."

"What codicil?"

This time it is Wilkins who is surprised. "Apparently there was a codicil to his will, one that he drafted himself earlier that evening—I suppose if anyone was in a position to competently append a codicil to their own will it would be a Supreme Court Justice. He told me that it stipulated that in the event of his death the cataloging of his papers was to be offered to you on a first refusal basis, and it specified the sum that was to be paid by the estate, which I gather would be generous. You didn't know?"

"I did catalog his papers, and I was well paid. I just didn't know that it had been in the will." His sister had deliberately concealed that part, Sabrina realizes, probably to maintain the authority of employer over her, and therefore someone with the final say in the disposition of her brother's papers. A petty deception, she thinks, but the weightier matter right now is the fact that Scaglietti had apparently wanted to ensure that, in the event of his sudden death, she had access to his papers. It must have been because he wanted her to find that letter, hidden in the section of Blackstone's *Commentaries* dealing with the Doctrine of Necessity, and whose location he arranged to have hinted to her at her oral defense. But why go to all the trouble; why not just tell her outright?

"Do you recall the date you went to Netherly?"

"Vividly," Wilkins answers. "Justice Scaglietti was found dead the very next morning. I was shocked: he had appeared to be in robust good health that evening although, considering the conversation, presumably sensing death at hand."

Sabrina returns to her pew and sits down. Wilkins joins her but has the good sense to remain silent as she considers these strange new revelations.

Scaglietti had not spoken to her directly because he never saw her again. Perhaps he had been intending to call her the next morning, or maybe he just did not feel safe sharing confidences over a telephone at all. He could have written her a letter; for all she knows he did, but it was never mailed. In any case, it had obviously been a last-minute decision, executed in urgency, a hasty arrangement designed, if all else failed, to allow her to find the hidden letter in a manner that would arouse no undue suspicion—she was an obvious choice for the cataloging—and the Justice must have counted on the fact that she was writing a dissertation on his opinions as being sufficient motivation for her to pursue the matter, as indeed it had been.

She wonders if there had been something else in the library, something she missed, something that would have explained what was going on. If there was, that opportunity is gone forever now: if she is to discover what the business was with Bronaryre, she will have to get it from him directly.

# XVII

THE ENTRY GATE leading from Ship Street into the Dean's Garden, half obscured by the overhanging branch of a large beech tree growing on the other side, is a sturdy sheet-metal-clad structure completely filling the portal, presumably to ensure privacy and obviously rarely used: the old lock into which Sabrina inserts the key is flecked with rust, and the peeling green paint was probably last applied in the Edwardian era. The hinges squeal loudly as she pushes it open.

The sun will not set for another three hours, but much of the garden is already in shadow, and when Sabrina closes the gate behind her she has the sense of having entered another world. The tall stone walls suppress all sound from the city outside, and also limit the external view: there is the tip of Exeter's spire visible across Turl Street, and Lincoln's much more ornate one a little further away, but mostly it is just sky, silken and cloudless and blue.

The garden is not much smaller than a quad, but here instead of plain lawn and stone paths there is a riot of plant life that has the effect of compressing the space, turning it into an intimate hideaway in the heart of the city. The trees here are not the spare London planes favored for lining Oxford's sidewalks, but instead big country trees on the brink of full summer foliage: an oak in the far corner, towering over the chapel, a pair of stately horse chestnuts at the other end, and beside her the mighty beech with which she is already acquainted, branching beyond the wall and threatening to block Ship Street. Between the trees are bushes and flower beds and a little rose bower, with the climbing varieties clinging to an arched trellis of the type people like to get married beneath, and the freestanding rose bushes planted in surrounding beds.

Two men are by the roses, standing back to her and apparently engaged in discussion when she arrived, but now having turned at the sound of the gate. One of them is Bronaryre. He has exchanged the khaki chinos and white button-down shirt of this morning's drive for navy chinos and a blue button-down shirt this evening, and her first thought is to hope that her clothing—a plain but well-cut Ralph Lauren outfit resulting from her recent first foray into the boutiques of Madison Avenue—is not too dressed up.

If the man standing beside him will be joining them for dinner then she has certainly overdone it. He wears a waxed cotton vest over a rough flannel shirt, buttoned at the sleeves despite the warmth of the day, and corduroy trousers tucked into big rubber boots of the type the British refer to as 'Wellies.' As if that was insufficient to keep him warm, he also wears one of the flat woolen caps favored by the English. He is quite short and looks very old.

She walks over to join them.

"Lancaster, let me introduce Old Tom."

Old Tom touches his cap in greeting. His hand is as gnarly as the beech tree, the knuckles enormous and probably arthritic.

"Please call me Sabrina," she says, and removes her shoes so as to get lower down.

This gesture amuses Old Tom and he smiles, revealing a ruin of English dentistry. He smells a little, not sharply malodorous but earthy, like the smell of a barn or a stable. His face is covered in gray stubble made all the more prominent by the deep color of his skin, so darkly brown as to be almost mahogany, and she wonders how he could get that color in the English climate.

"It is to Old Tom that we owe this luxuriant oasis," Bronaryre explains. "He is the head gardener."

"I was taken aback by how beautiful it is as soon as I opened the gate," she says. "It's like a little hidden dell, an amazing thing to find in the middle of a city."

"Aye, that it is—all that's missing are the faeries and sprites."

"I hope that I didn't interrupt you. Were you discussing the roses?"

The old man nods and turns his attention to the trellis. "I was just telling Mr. Bronaryre here what needs to be done. Not much at all really—they'll mostly take care of themselves—but we've got a hot spell coming and so I wanted to make sure they'll get their water like they'll need."

"I could smell them as soon as I came in, all the way from the other side of the garden."

"This is their time, late June, these ramblers particularly."

"Is that what the climbing roses are called?"

"Aye. Technically your climbing rose blooms multiple times a year, but the flowers are not as spectacular nor the perfume as strong. 'Ramblers' are climbers that bloom just once, but when they do it's worth the wait: deep color, like these Goldfinches here." He points to a group of brazen-petalled blossoms, so metallic in appearance as to give the impression of having been cast rather than cultivated. "Or these Veilchenblau, or these Phyllis Bides." The Veilchenblaus are more purple than blue, the Phyllis Bides apricot, both of them neon-like in the profound vibrancy of their coloration. Old Tom nods toward the freestanding flowers. "For the shrub roses I only plant Old English Garden Roses, which is to say varieties that pre-date 1867."

"What happened in 1867?"

"The first hybrid was successfully cultivated. *La France*, it was called." In Oxford, Sabrina thinks, even the gardeners are erudite. "What people think of today as roses are really hybrids: they look pretty enough, but they've got no bottom."

"No bottom?"

"Not hardy. And no smell. Not like these. Take this Maiden's Blush: no hybrid will ever give off a fragrance like she does."

Sabrina steps over to the nearby bloom, easily identifiable from its name by the coloration: pale pink in the center fading to cream at the tips, and inhales deeply. The smell is heady, rich, and opulent.

"What an amazing scent," she says. "What are the other shrub roses?"

"That's Old John," he says, pointing to a bright orange flower. "He's 'Old,' like me."

"You're not so old."

"Ah, I've always been 'Old,' even when I was a young'un: name's Bell, you see."

Sabrina plainly does not see, and so Bronaryre speaks up.

"There's a famous bell above the entrance to Christ Church, formally cast as Great Thomas but sometimes referred to as Old Tom, as in the Morris dance reel 'Old Tom of Oxford' and indeed also in the name of a pub across the street from the bell, The Old Tom. So, anyone in Oxford whose surname happens to be Bell is liable to be nicknamed Old Tom, no matter their age."

Sabrina nods in understanding, and Old Tom resumes his survey of the shrub roses.

"The fair ones nearest us are Duchess of Sutherlands, and those to the right are Parson's Pink Chinas. The yellows are Harrisons, and that purple rose is called The Bishop. The ones at either end are Yorks and Lancasters. Got to keep them well separated, of course—but you'd already know that." He chuckles handsomely, not above laughing at his own quip.

Sabrina thanks him for showing her the roses and Old Tom, after a few last instructions to Bronaryre, takes his leave. The gate closes behind him, leaving Sabrina and Bronaryre alone.

"Shall we dine?"

There is a wrought-iron table and chairs by the northeastern corner, the spot that would receive the most sunlight, and though now in shadow the metal retains some warmth. The food is still in the Harrods shopping bags, but Bronaryre has brought out proper plates and silverware. He sets about opening the wine while Sabrina lays out the food.

They eat mostly in companionable silence—in Sabrina's case she is too hungry to talk, having had nothing since the previous evening—with just an occasional comment or question passing between them: "Be sure to try the Rollright: it's only made in the spring and is at its peak now"; "Are these gherkins the same as cornichons?" (they are, but he has to correct her pronunciation—she had them as JER-kins, which he explains is the name for the type of vest that Old Tom had been wearing); and, when Sabrina is trying unsuccessfully to retrieve the last of the olives from the bottom of the jar, "I suppose I should have brought a long spoon," a remark that draws a smile of appreciation from Bronaryre, sufficient to acknowledge the *double entendre*, but he makes no comment.

They finally sit back, sated. The light is softer now. The birds are active, not the pigeons that dominate Oxford's public areas but plump little perky-tailed wrens, very communicative, and robins smaller than their American cousins, comically red-bibbed rather than truly red-breasted.

Bronaryre tops up the wine glasses. Sabrina delves into her bag and pulls from it the booklet that he gave her in New York, the copy of *The Numismatic Chronicle and Journal of the Numismatic Society*. She lays it on the table.

"According to this, the provenance of the Ashmolean's Oxford Crown is well documented: it was, at the time the paper was published in 1855, in the possession of the Bodleian Library, having been acquired by the Bodleian as a bequest from a coin collector, a Mr. Browne Willis. I looked him up: Willis was, in addition to being a Member of Parliament for Buckingham, a well-known numismatist. He died in 1760. The Bodleian subsequently transferred the coin to the Ashmolean, from which apparently you or your lawyer arranged to have it stolen."

"Not stolen. Recovered."

"But the provenance is very clear."

"And incomplete. How did this Browne Willis come into possession of the coin to begin with?"

"Since he died in 1760, surely that doesn't matter."

"It matters a great deal. Do you have the coin?"

"I do."

"May I see it?"

Sabrina hesitates, but only for a moment: she is probably so much an accessory after the fact by now that were he not to give the coin back it would make no difference. She takes from her pocket a little felt sleeve, intended for the safe storage of earrings but now containing the Oxford Crown, and hands it over, hoping that he will take as much care with the coin as she has done.

He removes it from the sleeve and stares at the thing for a long time in silence. Sabrina wonders if he is examining it for some type of telltale mark or imperfection—perhaps an artifact of the uneven manual minting used when the coin was struck in 1644—that would identify it uniquely.

"Is it yours?"

"Oh, yes, certainly."

"How could that be, given that its provenance has been established for over two hundred and fifty years?"

"Because it was given to me earlier, before this Browne Willis ever acquired it."

"Earlier?"

"I came into possession of this coin on the afternoon of Tuesday, January 30, 1649, a few minutes after the hour of two o'clock."

Sabrina is about to raise the obvious objection when she suddenly understands: the story, and her role as amanuensis to an illusory Satan, has begun. Perhaps Bronaryre is exploring some new experimental technique for writing prose fiction: to fully immerse oneself into the character—the writer's equivalent of the actor's Stanislavski method—in order to tell the story. She wishes she had brought a notebook.

Another long silence ensues. Bronaryre continues to stare at the coin. A good amanuensis should prompt, she supposes.

"You remember the date very clearly."

"It's Old Style, of course—Julian. England, ever suspicious of the papacy, didn't move to the Gregorian calendar until 1752."

"What made the date stick in your mind?"

"It was the day that King Charles I was beheaded. I was a very young boy at the time, and it is my earliest distinct memory—no doubt a result of the gruesome circumstances. I was taken to Whitehall that morning by William Hendrick, a Colonel in the New Model Army and whose ward I then was. I remember that his wife objected strongly, but he insisted. I don't know whether she was worried for me because of the beheading or because of the weather: it was a fearsomely cold day, as if the heavens were rendering their opinion on the execution of a lawful monarch. The Thames was completely frozen, and we walked along it from Holborn to Whitehall. It was just as well, because the streets were packed, everyone feverish with the import of what was to come, and eager to see it for themselves. The mood was against the execution, and the threat of riot was in the air."

He takes a sip of wine and glances at her briefly, but without real interest: she can tell that he is fully back in time, even if only imagined time, on the day they killed a king. His attention returns to the coin in his hand, and he continues the story.

"We made our way through the palace to the Banqueting Hall, Inigo Jones's architectural masterpiece. I had never been in such a magnificent building, had not even known that such buildings were possible, and it impressed me deeply. It's the only part of Whitehall Palace still standing, do you know it?" She does, having visited the place after being interviewed for her residency, but he does not wait for a reply before continuing. "It was packed with Puritans that day, never a lively bunch but especially solemn now. Determined, too: they were hard men, and if there were any second thoughts or notions of a last-minute reprieve I saw no evidence of them in that hall.

"The scaffold had been set up outside, ringed by soldiers to separate it from the immense crowd. Hendrick was an important commander and so we were at a window with a prime view. A little before two P.M. Charles was escorted to the scaffold.

"The crowd fell silent. My first reaction was surprise at his very long hair; having been in the company of Roundheads this struck me as highly unusual, although it was the fashion of the day among the aristocracy. He was very impressive: dressed in a shirt with a blue sash but not shivering, despite the extreme cold—I later learned that he had worn two shirts that day, so as not to give any impression of trembling with fear.

He gave a short speech but there were so many soldiers surrounding the scaffold that I doubt many in the crowd could hear.

"He put on a nightcap, and that action chilled me: I realized that it was to give the axman a clear shot at his neck. Until then it had all seemed a little unreal to me, but that gesture with the hair brought home the hard truth: that a man was about to have his head violently cleaved from his body. The king spoke quietly to his executioner for a few moments—their heads bent close together, strangely intimate, as if two old friends in amiable discussion—and then he lay down upon the block. He gave a signal—even now he was still a king, it seemed, with the execution unable to proceed until he had given the royal assent. The executioner lifted the ax and brought it down, a single swift blow.

"As the echo of that blade burying into the wood died away, the immediate effect was silence, as if no one could quite believe what had just happened. But then an enormous moan arose from the crowd, all together, as if they had rehearsed it to get the timing right. I looked up at Hendrick: he was speechless, horrified, his face streaked with tears—I had never before seen a man so undone.

"Curious as to whether this was a common reaction, I looked around. I was stunned by what I saw: these men who moments ago had appeared to me so grimly adamantine were now as visibly appalled as Hendrick. One of them was retching in the corner. But then I looked at the man standing next to me, on the other side from my guardian. He was dressed like all the others—white shirt, black coat and black trousers stuffed into black boots, broad-brimmed Puritan hat—but he showed no reaction whatsoever, neither revulsion nor satisfaction. In his own way he seemed as stoic as the king had been, self-contained and impervious to the world, except that there was none of the air of the martyr about him—he gave the impression of being a practical man of the world, fully capable of taking care of whatever might come his way, and with little need of, or tolerance for, demonstration.

"He must have sensed me staring at him. He looked down, apparently noticing my presence for the first time. He regarded me for a moment with mild curiosity, then asked what it was that I had just witnessed. I answered that I had just witnessed, Sir, the killing of the king. He shook his head. 'Nay, boy, that was but the surface. What you saw today was the fate of those who would place themselves above God and their fellow man.' He fished a coin from his pocket—this coin—and gave it to me. 'Keep it as a reminder of this day, boy. Once this coin was very valuable, worth a whole crown. Now it is worth nothing, and the head of he who issued it will never again a crown wear.' He looked outside, where on the scaffold the executioner was holding up the king's severed head to the crowd. I was very pleased with the coin, although there was one thing still troubling me. 'But who will rule us now?' The stranger smiled, and silently mouthed a single word: *me*. Then he winked. Someone called to him, and he left. I'm sure that by now you've guessed the identity of the man who gave me this coin. That was the first time I had ever laid eyes on Oliver Cromwell."

THERE IS A LONG SILENCE after the story is finished. Sabrina has a hundred questions, but it was a tale well told and she does not want to spoil the conclusion by quizzing its logic. The long dusk of the high northern latitudes has fallen, and the previously blue sky has taken on a luminous pink wash, turning it into a pale violet. The birds are quiet now, and the air has become still, as if settling for the night. Sabrina finishes her wine; Bronaryre continues to stare at the coin. She supposes that—to his mind at least—it is his property after all.

"It's your Rosebud."

Bronaryre is stirred from his reverie. "Rosebud?"

"*Citizen Kane*. Rosebud was Kane's last dying word; it turned out to have been the brand name of his sled when he was a little boy, the sled that was left behind when he was taken away."

The observation seems to animate Bronaryre.

"Strange that you should mention it: I knew Orson Welles at the time he was making that film, although I can't say that I had any creative input into it—as opposed to the infamous *War of the Worlds* broadcast, which he made at my suggestion."

"You suggested it?"

"The world seemed destined for another war at the time, although it had barely gotten over the first one, and I hoped that the broadcast might spur some perspective: show how stupid it is to endlessly fuss over petty political disputes when there was so much happening on a grander scale—the theory of relativity was still quite recent, as was quantum mechanics: the door to a new and unexplored universe of knowledge lay open before us—indeed right then in a Berlin lab the atom was being split for the very first time—yet all people could talk of was Munich and the Sudetenland. It felt to me like the Greek city-states indulging in their endless squabbles while beyond the Bosphorus Persia loomed. But as to the Rosebud reference, then yes, I suppose you're right: for me, this Oxford Crown is something of a Rosebud."

And so saying, he hands back the coin. It is warm from his touch, almost hot, as if the Devil ran at a higher temperature than the 98.6 degrees of normal human beings.

"How did you lose it?"

"It was taken from me when I was imprisoned in the Tower, and not returned when I was released. Some fat Beefeater kept it, I suppose, and eventually the crown found its way into the hands of Mr. Browne Willis, by which time it was worth much more than its face value. I wonder what Cromwell would have made of that—coin and king both restored—although he was long dead by then."

"You were imprisoned in the Tower of London?"

"Yes."

"Wasn't the Tower for political prisoners?"

"Indeed it was, but let us leave that for another time."

He takes the wine bottle in hand and briefly inspects the label, perhaps, like Sabrina, having enjoyed the contents and wanting to commit the producer's name to memory. He pours out the remainder into their glasses. Sabrina sits back and puts her feet up on the chair opposite, still bare since she removed her heels when talking to Old Tom. She feels comfortable in this hidden garden, the evening pleasantly warm, the taste of the wine on her lips, the friendly heft of the coin in her hand. It is darker now and a little breeze has arisen, unfelt by them in the lee of the garden wall, but enough to gently rustle the foliage of the treetops high above, almost lulling her to sleep.

"Does the dean always vacate his quarters for you when you're in Oxford?"

"Not at all: I'm not staying here, just borrowing his garden for the evening, and then only because he's not in residence. I have a place not far away, in Gloucestershire."

"If I was the dean then I would never leave the college. I would live in this garden. It feels like Old Tom said: the only thing missing are the faeries and sprites, and I wouldn't be surprised if they showed up, too."

"Oxford is certainly the right place for them: something about the air here seems to give rise to the fantastic. J.R.R. Tolkien lived his whole adult life at Oxford: he was across the street at Exeter when he came up, and then went on to become a fellow at Pembroke and later Merton. Same for C.S. Lewis: he was at University College, and then afterward was a fellow at Magdalen. The author of the wonderful *Wind in the Willows*, Kenneth Grahame, went to St. Edward's School—I wonder if Ratty and Mole and the outrageous Mr. Toad could have been conceived without that Oxford exposure. And, of course, there was Lewis Carroll."

"How interesting that you should bring him up: I was just thinking about *Alice in Wonderland* earlier today."

"There you go: just a day in town, and already you're infected with the fantastic, too. Are you familiar with the story of how *Alice* came to be written?"

"No, please tell me."

"It involves a Dean's Garden, very much like this one—the Dean's Garden at Christ Church. Carroll was a fellow there, a mathematician. There is a school of literary criticism contending that *Alice in Wonderland* is a mathematical allegory: her many size changes being analogous to the concept of the limit of a series; the Cheshire Cat's persisting grin an example of algebraic abstraction; Alice herself, while swimming in the sea of her own gigantic tears, performs multiplication computations that apparently don't make sense—*four times five is twelve, and four times six is thirteen, and four times seven is—oh dear! I shall never get to twenty at that rate!*—but in fact, in a modular series increasing by three at each step, the calculations are all correct: four times five is twelve in base eighteen arithmetic; four times six is thirteen in base twenty-one; four times seven is fourteen in base twenty-four; and so on—and it really is true that no matter how high you go, you will never get to twenty, a curious phenomenon. Only in Oxford would someone write a children's story that delves into the mysteries of advanced number theory.

"But as to the Dean's Garden: the dean of Christ Church at the time—the 1860's—was Henry Liddell. He had three daughters: Lorina, Alice, and Edith: the Prima, Secunda, and Tertia of *Alice in Wonderland*'s prefacing poem. Carroll's rooms overlooked the Dean's Garden, and he would have seen the girls playing there. He became a family friend of the Liddells. One summer's day, in 1862, he and the Reverend Duckworth (Ducky in the poem), took the girls for a picnic, rowing five miles up the Isis from Folly Bridge. To pass the time Carroll made up a story, in the way that travelers have done since Chaucer and Boccaccio. It so delighted the middle daughter, Alice, that she asked Carroll to write it up for her. He did so and presented it to her as a Christmas present in 1863. And that is how *Alice in Wonderland* came to be."

"That's a lovely story. It sounds so idyllic—something that couldn't happen anymore. The world is no longer innocent enough to enjoy gentle arithmetical absurdities, or to entrust one's daughters to two grown men, especially if one of them is wearing a clerical collar."

"People no longer communicate as they did then—there were only two ways to communicate in those days, in conversation or by letter, both of which are now lost arts, as dead as Sanskrit. There's a scene in *Alice*, early on, where she looks through a door and sees beyond it a hidden garden, which she wishes to enter and explore but cannot—she is too big to fit. At Christ Church, beyond the Dean's Garden, there is a second walled garden, the Cathedral Garden. It was off-limits to the rest of the college, including the dean's daughters, but not to the dean himself. It was also the shortest route from the Dean's Residence to the Cathedral, and so every Sunday Alice saw her father open that door, and would have briefly glimpsed the forbidden garden that lay beyond before he shut it behind him, and she longed to explore it for herself. Alice, although just ten years old at the time, had been able to communicate that longing to Carroll sufficiently for him to have alluded to it in the story. I can't imagine that happening with the average ten-year-old today."

"What became of her?"

"Alice Liddell? She went on to lead what would have been considered the proper life for a Victorian woman of genteel upbringing: the grand tour, followed by marriage and children, society dinners and charities."

"I wonder if she ever got to see what was beyond the garden door."

"Literally?—probably. Metaphorically?—I doubt it: she would have been too bound by the strictures of her class and time."

"Then I feel sorry for her."

"Perhaps she would have been unhappy had she done otherwise."

"Maybe, but what value is a riskless life?"

"Did you go to the gallery at the Tate?"

"Yes."

"Did you enjoy the paintings?"

"No."

"Good: only a fool would *enjoy* them: their purpose is to disturb. Do you know, the same morning that they arrived at the Tate their creator was found dead in his studio, lying in a broad pool of his own blood, having slit both wrists not crosswise but right along the forearm—there was to be no chance of a last-minute rescue. He left no note because there was no need for one: those paintings were the note. Mark Rothko had gone through the door, and look what happened to him. He committed what he saw to canvas, and then he killed himself."

Sabrina suddenly understands what that dark, rust-hued, many-toned red must represent: Rothko had been painting what was to be the color of his own drying blood. The revelation astonishes her. She marvels at the nerve of it, the grim commitment, the uncompromising audacity.

"Do you think," she asks, "that if he were to be miraculously resurrected he would take up a career in accountancy instead?"

"He might consider it."

"I know nothing of him, but I somehow doubt it. Taking risk means that you sometimes lose, perhaps even terminally, but life without risk is not living, it is merely existing."

"So you would go through the door?"

"Yes."

"Well, there it is." Bronaryre nods toward the far end of the garden, where there is a little green-painted wooden door that Sabrina had noticed earlier, almost hidden by the two horse chestnuts flanking it.

"But this is Caiaphas, not Christ Church."

"That door is not Alice's door. It is *your* door."

"Mine?"

"Yes."

"Where does it lead?"

"To risk. To hazard. Perhaps to Hell, given that it is I who is offering it to you. It's always possible that you will end up in a Wonderland of your own, but don't forget Rothko's color field of his own blood."

"It leads to nothing," she says. "It leads to Old Tom's gardening tools, or the utility meters, or a fuse box."

"Perhaps it normally does, but not right now—tonight, it has been transformed into a portal that opens into another world."

Sabrina takes her feet from the chair and stands. "I think you're spreading a little midsummer's eve pixie dust, but I'll give it a try." She begins walking toward the door. "Need a garden tool while I'm down there?"

"Given Rothko's fate, I would avoid anything sharp."

Sabrina continues through the garden. It is almost dark but the moon has risen, near full, providing enough illumination not to trip. The garden is less fragrant now and she wonders if, in their own way, plants go to sleep, too. She approaches the door. There is less lawn under the chestnuts and she slows, still barefoot, walking on gravelly dirt now.

The door is painted the same green as the big iron gate she came through earlier, but this one is much smaller, made of wood, and has no lock nor even a normal door handle, just a simple latch—it is only a garden shed after all.

She glances back before opening it. Bronaryre is looking not at her but up at the moon, as if in contemplation, maybe already wondering how the 'Devil' is going to explain having had his bluff so easily called.

Sabrina lifts the latch, opens the door, and steps forw—

# First Circle

Thalia

## A Water Sprite

SABRINA AWAKENS IN A FIELD.

The sun is rising in a sweep of blue sky, and it is already warm, the prelude to what will be a hot summer's day. She is on the edge of a meadow, lying supine in soft grass. By her are trees, ashes and sycamores, soaring a hundred feet high. Their foliage quivers in the breeze, spilling dappled light down upon her: probably it was that light, flickering bright and then shadowed on her eyelids, that awakened her.

She sits up and wonders how she came to be here.

Her last memory is of opening the green door in the Dean's Garden. She assumed that it would be a door to storage space for Old Tom's gardening equipment, and had been on the verge of stepping through into the darkness on the other side, but she can recall nothing more.

Sabrina examines her surroundings: gently rolling countryside with grassy expanses of meadow separated by groves of trees, what the English call *downs*. But then she realizes that it cannot be quite true: unlike those cultivated rural landscapes, here there are no roads or paths, no poles or fences. It seems that she is alone in nature—a very mild and complaisant nature. Notwithstanding her stranded state, she feels a surge of joyful exhilaration.

Sabrina stands and performs a self-inspection. She is unharmed, although a little gritty: it has not rained here for a while, she guesses, and the breeze has kicked up the dust. She is barefoot. Her only clothing is a cotton garment, white, more a nightgown than a dress, and she briefly wonders whether she has experienced an extreme case of somnambulance, but then quickly dismisses the idea: no one would sleepwalk all the way out of Oxford, and in any case the clothing is not hers.

She removes it to read the label: Braithwaite & Slether, York, and beneath the maker's name is a coat of arms with the words *Suppliers of Girls' Pinafores to H.M. Queen Victoria.* All at once she remembers the conversation from last night, and the circumstances she finds herself in become, if not entirely clear, somewhat less obscure: she has been invited to play Alice, or some facsimile of Alice, in her very own adventure. She has even been dressed in period costume.

Perhaps it is a form of college hazing ritual: extreme orienteering with a historical Oxford theme, and so she has been deposited in the middle of nowhere, stripped to ensure that she has no resources such as cash or a cellphone or even identification (it better have been the girls at the college who performed that particular operation, Sabrina vows, or the Devil really will get his comeuppance.) The task now before her is to make her way back to Caiaphas.

She looks again at the label, which makes her laugh out loud—prim Victoria wearing a girl's pinafore!—and she realizes that she is in surprisingly good spirits for someone who has apparently been rendered unconscious and ended up, lost and barely clad, in the middle of the countryside.

However, Sabrina has always wanted to wear a pinafore. She puts it back on.

She is also exceedingly thirsty. Whoever had the good sense to place her in the shade had not thought to leave water as well.

She sets out across the meadow, heading for the crest of a nearby ridge, likely the place from which she will gain the broadest view, and therefore the best chance of locating a town or village. No livestock graze upon the slope—something for which she is thankful, given that she is barefoot—and the high grass is dotted with wildflowers.

Sabrina begins picking a posy as she proceeds: there are anemones by her; and beyond them daisies, not much different; but then she finds some wildflowers to add color: bluebells more powder-blue than the deep hue of the American version; a cornflower-like plant that she mistakes for a columbine (it is chicory, she will learn later when looking it up); and lastly a reddish flower from whose single distinctive tongue-like petal—so different from the others and thrust forth as if to blow a rude floral raspberry—must be one of the countless species of orchid.

She comes to the top of the rise and gazes over the countryside: on one side the terrain dips before continuing further upward, with trees lower down but a bare bluff at the top, a better viewing spot than her current one. On the other side the ground slopes gently away, ending in another line of trees at the bottom. She sees meadows and fields, and in the far distance an ancient drystone fence, partly collapsed, but no sign of current habitation. To see further she will need to climb more, but among the trees down below there is a willow, and willows mean water.

Sabrina sits on the grass and fashions a garland from her nosegay while considering the next move. The daisies have good strong stalks, easy to thread through without tearing, and when the ring is complete she weaves in the others, making a fragrant little floral wreath. Meanwhile, thirst has won out over immediacy: she stands, solemnly crowns herself Queen of May, although it is late June, and then makes her way downslope.

The willow has not deceived her: there is a stream, swift-flowing, with water so crystalline that she can clearly see the shallow bottom—pebbles, scoured by the force of the flow. But how to drink from it: the bed is clean, but the banks are muddy.

Sabrina contemplates the breadth of bank from grass to stream, and decides that a broad step from one directly into the other is achievable. She hitches up her pinafore in preparation, but when making the attempt stumbles, ending up on her knees. The lower halves of both her and the pinafore are now streaked with mud, but Sabrina finds herself laughing:

had she not slipped she would not have thought of bathing, but now a necessity has been made of virtue.

She looks around to confirm that she is alone and then takes off the pinafore. Since half of it already requires drying she decides to remove the grit from the entire thing and submerges the garment in the stream. She briefly leaves the brook to lay it on the grass to dry, and then returns to the water.

The stream is not very deep, two feet at most, and so she kneels to bathe, splashing away for a little while and then remaining perfectly still to observe the occasional fish swim by, surprisingly large for such a shallow waterway, and sometimes inquisitive, coming right up to her with mouths opening and closing as if in noiseless greeting. The water feels cool and refreshing, more slippery than tap water, like liquid mercury.

She lies down, floating, head upstream so as not to lose the garland, hands on the pebbles of the bed beneath to help anchor her, the flow of water on her scalp almost a massage, tendrils of hair streaming out either side, the willow branches waving overhead, pattering light, and above them the limitless ultramarine canopy of sky.

Sabrina closes her eyes. The cooling stream flows by and she drifts into a floating dreamscape of caressing water and billowing light. She is weightless, suspended. Soundless, like space, the only sound that of deep space, deep echoing space, space echoing in the void. She is outside of herself here in this stream, released from the corporeal world, a spirit-being, a water-sprite.

There is a sudden flash of lightning.

Sabrina immediately opens her eyes, mindful of the old adage never to swim during a thunderstorm, but she finds that no clouds have gathered above her. She sits up and turns to the bank. There she sees five legs, all coming together at a polished wooden box. Three of the legs are also wooden, evidently a tripod. The other two are encased in trousers, long and skinny, not much thicker than the first three. The box has a glass lens at the front, and behind it a curtain of black material from which emerges a single crooked arm whose hand holds a flash pan, still smoking, evidently the source of the lightning. Sabrina is looking at some sort of old-fashioned camera, she realizes, and the camera is pointed at her.

Her pinafore is no longer on the grass. It has been hung from a tree branch, perhaps the better to dry, but the photographer is between her and it.

The remainder of the figure comes out from beneath the black curtain, slowly unfolding himself like an ungainly stick insect emerging from a cocoon. He is exceedingly tall but sports a tattered top hat, as if to be taller still. He wears a disreputable black suit whose cut is many decades out of date, a white shirt with a black tie in the form of a large loose bow, and black leather shoes whose long-pointed toes have begun to curl skyward. An emaciated and somewhat clownish Abe Lincoln, Sabrina thinks of him.

He doffs the top hat and attempts an awkward bow in greeting.

"Mortimer Pence," he announces. "*Daguerriste de la nature*."

"More than just nature, I think." Sabrina has arranged herself as modestly as possible in the circumstances, with crossed arms for coverage above while relying on the stream for coverage below.

"Ah, but what could be more natural than you as you are now? Eve before the Fall, one might say, although personally I am reminded more of that remarkable painting recently put on display at the National Gallery, John Everett Millais's *Ophelia*. Perhaps you are familiar with it?"

"No. Please bring me my pinafore."

"I see no pinafore."

"There."

"Hanging from the branch?"

"Yes."

"I believe that garment is a nightgown, madam—something of the type one imagines Macbeth's sleepless wife wearing while slinking hand-wringingly through the midnight halls of Castle Cawdor, slowly turning insane."

"Fine, then please bring me my nightgown."

"If you wish, but I must tell you that it is still damp, which is why I hung it up in the tree so that the breeze might more readily dry it. And you yourself are of course wet. To put on clothes that are still damp while one is already wet is to invite calamity in England, even on a day such as today. May I suggest that both you and the nightgown should be allowed time to dry, an interval during which we may profitably employ my apparatus, *n'est-ce pas*?"

"Where am I?"

"Immersed in the River Windrush, upstream of Bourton-on-the-Water."

*Windrush*—what a beautiful name, Sabrina thinks, although the *river* part seems a little grand for so modest a stream.

"Is it far to Oxford?"

"Oxford? Oh, yes, ten leagues at least, a full day's ride. I can take you into Bourton in my little pony trap after we're done, should you wish, or better yet drop you at the big manor house, which is closer still. Now, I wonder if you might arrange your right arm like so?" He raises his right arm above his head, in a gesture that might precede a swoon.

Sabrina supposes that this must be a continuation of the theatrics that began with the door in the Dean's Garden, and in any case the prospect of a pony trap is certainly to be favored over the alternative of wandering around barefoot in search of civilization. She assumes the posture of a swoon.

"And arrange the other arm like so."

She arranges her other arm like so.

"Now hold that pose."

Sabrina is forced to hold it a long time as there is much adjustment to the apparatus, and the flash pan needs to be refilled with powder, but eventually the photograph—presumably a daguerreotype—is taken.

"What do you do with your shots?" Sabrina asks.

"With what?"

"Your daguerreotypes."

"I have a small business in photogravure."

Sabrina assumes that this is meant to suggest that he is some sort of itinerant Victorian-era pornographer, creating a certain style of postcard once sold surreptitiously from bookstalls along the banks of the Seine. She wonders where they found this creature—too old to be a student;

presumably an actor, although his extraordinary height and extreme slenderness would severely limit his roles, which is probably why he accepted this one.

A dozen watery daguerreotypes follow, each one taking several minutes to set up and accomplish, and punctuated by much discussion about his devotion to this amazing visual medium, assertions as to its artistic merit, and encouragement to 'inhabit the spirit of the heathen Naiad, unacquainted with either modesty or embarrassment.'

At length, Mortimer Pence exhausts his supply of silver plates, and the photography is complete. For all but the first few daguerreotypes Sabrina has stood, and so she is now dry from the knees up. Pence fetches her nightgown from the tree and extends a long thin arm to help her up the bank.

He packs his photographic apparatus into a leather suitcase, and places the boxes of flash powder—with the alarming brand name BlitzLichtPulver—into a separate tin container, chatting all the while, comparing his daguerreotypes to "that wonderful new painting, Waterhouse's *Hylas and the Nymphs*—oh, you're unfamiliar with it? You really must see it, although I have no doubt that our own fine work done just now will soon surpass it in illustrious fame."

The *daguerriste* takes the suitcase and tin in hand while Sabrina picks up the now folded tripod, and they begin walking back along the bank, upstream, Pence prattling cheerfully all the way, until after several hundred yards coming upon a clearing on the other side of the trees. There a horse, still harnessed to a light two-wheeled carriage, looks up at their approach. It is a fine-looking animal but its expression is somewhat desultory, as if it would just as soon have been left alone to contemplate whatever it is that horses contemplate.

"Horace," Pence says, noticing her looking at the horse. "Fine bay coat, don't you think, and never fractious: he's a gelding." The horse does indeed have a fine coat—a deep shining chestnut color, darkening to black at the extremities—and the gelding part probably accounts for the aimless expression.

Mortimer Pence packs his equipment into a trunk attached to the rear, and then politely hands Sabrina up into the carriage. It is lightly sprung and bows as she puts her weight on the step. Pence is soon seated beside her, and they get underway. He asks if she is staying at the manor, his first expression of any curiosity about her other than as a photographic model—an omission that reveals him as part of a charade, she realizes, for surely anyone coming across a naked woman in the middle of nowhere would have been more inquisitive, diligent pornographer or not.

She replies that she is not staying at the manor, but expresses a hope that the people there might assist her in returning to Oxford.

"I know nothing of them," Pence admits. "No one is ever quite sure what the Devil's going on at Temple Slaughter Preceptory."

"Temple Slaughter Preceptory?"

"Rather a mouthful, isn't it? There's no genuine preceptory anymore, just the manor house these days. Quite a pile, or so I'm told—can't say that I've ever seen it for myself."

"Who owns it?"

"A Mr. Sacheverell Edgewater. Not your traditional country squire; spends most of his time in London, or even *abroad*." Pence's expression puckers at this last word, as if repeatedly venturing overseas was something that no prudent Englishman would do. "He only occupies the house in the summer. The money's a bit of a mystery; something in the colonies, I'm led to understand."

They have been going steadily uphill as he talks, taking a narrow track through wooded country rising from the river, but now Pence comes to a stop. There is a pair of squared stone posts on the right, rising to the height of a man, and with an iron gate between them. A set of steps on the other side leads further upward and disappears into the forest, but they are moss-covered and obviously rarely used. That and the gate's isolation here in the woods suggests a purpose more as a boundary marker than a true entrance to the estate, perhaps something intended to serve as a warning to poachers.

"This is as far as I can take you, I regret to say, but if you go through the gate and continue up the hill you will no doubt come to the preceptory."

Sabrina feels like complimenting him on a fine performance but supposes that it would be bad form to demonstrate disbelief, however obliquely, and so she simply thanks him for the ride and dismounts from the carriage. Pence salutes in farewell, urges the unmanned Horace onward, and soon disappears from view.

Sabrina approaches the gate. There are words carved into the stone posts, darkened with age and difficult to read without tracing the letters with a finger. The one on the left turns out to be the estate's name, the spelling of the middle word of which—*S-L-O-U-G-H*—seems a long way from Mortimer Pence's *Slaughter*: perhaps it is one of those strange English place names that seems over the centuries to have veered wildly from the original. She does not need to trace the inscription on the right: it is a single word, *private*, and whose point is emphasized by the gate being locked. This is more a gesture than a hindrance—Sabrina simply walks around the gateposts—but as she climbs the steps she wonders how welcoming the reception above will be.

Fifty yards from the gate Sabrina comes to a sudden halt. She is abreast a large stone sculpture, fifteen feet tall and depicting a dragon, but placed well off the path and in the shadow of the trees, the reason she almost missed it. The beast is depicted poised on its haunches, mouth open and wings starting to unfold, as if about to pounce upon or perhaps roast a victim. She steps off the path to inspect it more closely. The stone was originally brown but has darkened with age, now almost black in parts, and is pitted by the weathering of what must have been many seasons of exposure, perhaps centuries. There is no explanatory title or attribution carved into the stone base, but given the creature's posture there can be no doubt as to the intended purpose: it is a warning to turn back.

Sabrina continues onward. The steps twist and turn but always lead further up through the forest. She spots deer, but even her barefoot and moss-softened tread is audible to them in the reigning silence of the trees, and they quickly scatter at her approach. It is dark and a little eerie—walking alone and ill-clad through such a place, she can now understand how tales of witches and trolls seem always to be set in forests: even on as bright a day as this one, these woods feel slightly enchanted, as if an elf might suddenly pop out and poke a pointy tongue at her.

Sabrina emerges at last from the forest, and the steps fade into lawn sloping yet higher. She mounts this last rise, and suddenly Temple Slaughter Preceptory is laid out before her.

SABRINA IS STANDING on the grass verge of a long, graveled drive, broad enough to warrant the term *parade*. To her left, marking the beginning of the drive, is a large fountain featuring a sculpted Neptune and attendant Nereids, arising bare-breasted from the spume—something that Mortimer Pence would have appreciated. Beyond it is a neat little red-brick building, evidently a gatekeeper's lodge and no doubt the primary entrance to the estate. London planes line the parade. The house is a quarter of a mile distant at the other end: a grand Palladian manor built of honey-colored stone, a three-story box with a pillared portico, and flanked by two lower wings reaching out from either side and then squaring off, forming a three-sided forecourt.

Pence would have found at the fountain more than just the Nereids to appreciate. By it is a girl in shorts and a T-shirt, crouching, with a camera to her eye. She is photographing a second figure perched on the fountain among the nymphs, another girl, slender and dark and completely naked.

Sabrina thinks that at least now she need not feel self-conscious about being dressed in only a nightgown.

The photographer finishes the shot. She notices Sabrina and smiles broadly. Sabrina realizes that it is a smile of recognition: the girl was one of the croquet players from the second quad yesterday. She comes forward.

"Hello, Dr. Lancaster. I saw you arriving at Caiaphas yesterday."

"Sabrina, please."

"I'm Katy Telford, and that's Sesuna." They shake hands, and the sylph-like Sesuna waves in greeting from her precarious perch on the fountain. "Sesuna doesn't have a proper surname—she's Ethiopian."

"Eritrean," Sesuna corrects.

“I mean Eritrean. I’m photographing her.”

“So I see.”

“Luckily, we’ve got sunshine today: I wanted to capture the gloss of her skin against the white marble of the sculpture, and if it had been overcast we might have had to wait all week for another opportunity.”

“Why’s that?”

“No grounds staff on the weekend.”

“Ah, I see.”

“I’m glad you’ve joined us; Mr. Bronaryre said you might come.”

“Bronaryre is here, too?”

“Yes, he usually summers here, apparently, although if I owned it I don’t think I’d ever leave.”

“He owns this place?”

“He does, and he’s letting us use it. Can you imagine a more wonderful place to spend the summer?”

“You’re staying here all summer?”

“A lot of us USSUS girls will be spending at least part of the summer here; Sesuna and I all of it. We have academic assignments but the workload is much less than during term—quite leisurely, really. Are you coming to the play tomorrow night?”

“I didn’t know there was one. Are you and Sesuna going?”

“Oh, we’re in it. Sesuna is the *star*, and one of my photographs will be in the playbill, I hope.”

“Then I shall certainly attend. Now, don’t let me interrupt you any longer while the light is still good.”

She leaves them to continue their photoshoot and heads toward the house, keeping to the grass to avoid walking barefoot on gravel. On the way she passes a third girl, sunbathing prone on a towel but too engaged in the book she is reading to be aware of Sabrina’s passage, and then further on in a small clearing two more girls practicing what appears to be kick-boxing.

She approaches the house. There are several cars parked in front, one of which she recognizes: Bronaryre’s E-Type Jaguar, radiantly red as if freshly waxed, and parked in the prime spot: right beside the portico and shaded by it.

A man emerges through the front door, late fifties or early sixties, wearing a business suit rather than livery or formal clothing, but from whose bearing and demeanor she takes to be the butler.

"Dr. Lancaster, allow me to welcome you to the preceptory. My name is Ronson. May I show you to your room?"

If Ronson is surprised by Sabrina's appearance he does not show it. He leads her through the hall, oak-paneled and haphazardly decorated with marble busts and monumental oil paintings and a Persian rug or two, but which is nevertheless slightly shabby—the hall of a country house that is actually lived in, accumulating its character over many years, not the pristine everything-in-place perfection of an arriviste's trophy mansion.

They mount the stairs—more paneling and paintings—to the second floor. The butler leads her to a room at the end of the hallway, accessed through a set of double doors.

"The blue room," Ronson announces.

Sabrina stands still a moment, taking it all in.

It is a corner room, the two interior walls of which are paneled in white-painted wood for the first eight feet of their height, thence in a pale-blue wallpaper for a similar distance to the ceiling high above—evidently the source of the room's name. But it is the other two walls that immediately attract her attention, both pierced by many large windows allowing light to flood into the room. The long wall faces the south side of the house—the opposite direction from which she approached—onto an area which has been formally landscaped in the French or Italian fashion: an orderly arrangement of shrubbery carefully trimmed into strict geometrical obedience—topiary, she supposes—and all laid out on a lawn so immaculate that a golfer might practice putting upon it.

"The parterre," Ronson says, answering her unasked question, "said to be one of the finest in England, and certainly the pride of our grounds staff."

The far wall has French windows that open onto a broad private terrace. Given the situation and size, it must be the best bedroom in the house.

"I hope that I haven't caused Mr. Bronaryre to vacate his quarters," she says.

"Not at all, ma'am. He occupies apartments at the other end of the hall."

No, this room would not be Bronaryre's, she thinks: it is too light-filled for that dark brooding presence, too feminine. This is a woman's room, and she wonders who might have occupied it in the past.

"The fireplace is Jacobean, quite a special example."

Sabrina steps over to inspect it. The fireplace is immense, six feet tall, and carved in high relief with a complex riot of grotesquely imaginative creatures roaming among dense foliage, a gathering of ghouls and gremlins in the undergrowth. A fascinating and somewhat ghastly thing, strangely out of place in this light-filled woman's boudoir.

"Must be the Devil to keep dusted," she comments.

She is alert for any reaction to the word *Devil*, but Ronson merely smiles, appreciating the implied compliment to the household staff. "The maids use makeup brushes, I'm led to believe."

There is a knock at the door and a girl enters, about the same age as the Caiaphas students, but even before she shyly bobs in greeting Sabrina can tell that this is not a college girl but a sturdy country lass.

"Allow me to present Polly, who will be at your service while you're in residence," Ronson says. "I should note that Polly will only be available during daylight hours, as she is required to assist her family with the evening milking." Polly's open countenance briefly clouds at this last part: she does not like being identified as a dairymaid rather than a lady's maid.

Sabrina is tempted to say that she does not need a maid, but clearly Polly is looking forward to the prospect, so instead she steps forward with her arm outstretched.

"Please call me Sabrina."

Polly shyly shakes hands. "Yes, ma'am." It is apparent that she has not the slightest intention of addressing her as Sabrina.

"Dinner will be at eight o'clock," Ronson says. "Mr. Bronaryre sends his compliments and wonders if you might care for cocktails at seven, and if so whether it would be convenient for him to join you on your terrace at that time."

Sabrina agrees to this proposal and Ronson withdraws, leaving her alone with Polly.

"Do you know what the dress code is for dinner?"

"I was told 'black tie,' which doesn't make much sense: what woman wears a tie?"

"It means formal, which of course I don't have—do you know if my things were brought over from Oxford?"

"No, nothing came from Oxford, Miss."

"So I'll be dining barefoot in a pinafore then."

"Ooh, but you haven't seen what came from *London*. I put it all in there."

*There* turns out to be a two-chambered space leading off the main room, with the bathroom to the left and a dressing room to the right. The latter is littered with shopping bags and boxes bearing the names of the boutiques from which they must have come, plus a bevy of garment bags crowded into the closet.

"I'm sorry I haven't had a chance to unpack yet: they just arrived this morning."

"Let's do it together then."

This delights Polly, who has obviously been looking forward to discovering what is inside these many colorful packages. They start with a group of bags whose distinctive green-and-gold coloring Sabrina recognizes: they are from Harrods. They contain makeup and toiletries, as if whoever made the purchases had wandered from counter to counter in that vast cosmetics space beside the food hall, bags open, inviting the saleswomen to thrown in whatever they thought might be useful.

Next come the boxes: gloves and belts from a well-known leather goods supplier; a dozen small, prettily wrapped packages, all of which contain jewelry; Scottish woolens; a waxed outdoor coat—an item that Polly assures her is necessary for the English countryside, even in summer; several scarves; a belted raincoat; an evening purse and a handbag; a score of boxes containing footwear, everything from ballet slippers to sturdy brogues; and lastly, lingerie in a broad variety of styles but a narrow range geographically: all of the undergarments are Italian.

While they open boxes Sabrina invites Polly to tell her about herself. Polly's last name is Mumford, and her family are tenant farmers. She is just sixteen, but Sabrina senses that the hardships of rural life have already made her a little less carefree than typical in girls of her age. She has been to London precisely once: a school outing when she was twelve. She has never before been in the grounds of Temple Slaughter Preceptory, let alone inside the main house, and for Polly a summer job working here is something of a treat, and left unsaid is that the extra income, however modest, would be welcome. Sabrina is thankful she did not tell Ronson that she had no need of a maid.

After all the boxes have been opened, they begin an exploration of the garment bags. There is a selection of summery print dresses from Liberty; several stylish suits, some with pants and others with skirts, all beautifully cut; a lady's shooting outfit in fine tweed, and bearing a famous gunsmith's brand; a cocktail dress of the sort that one would not wear while taking tea with the queen; and a dozen or so other dresses in various styles, all *haute couture*, things that Sabrina would never have bought for herself.

The last item is a large box on the shelf above the hangers which turns out to contain a broad-brimmed, beribboned hat—an item that sends Polly into peals of laughter—but Sabrina imagines it is the sort of thing that might go with one of the Liberty prints, if playing croquet of a Sunday afternoon.

Polly sits back, dazed by the explosion of clothing, boxes, ribbons, and tissue paper surrounding them, and emits a single extended syllable of exuberant astonishment, "Corrrhhhh."

Sabrina casts a cooler eye over it all. She is being led into temptation, she realizes—this bewildering assortment is just Bronaryre playing the part of his imagined alter ego.

"When you leave, you can take all the Asprey boxes with you and give them to Ronson, with my thanks, but I'll have no need of jewelry. Meanwhile, we must select a dress for tonight. What about the Chanel?"

"You said it was formal."

"The Chanel is mid-calf, that's good enough."

"It's a Saturday night."

Polly Mumford, Sabrina realizes, tends to become peevish and nasal when not getting her way.

"All right, what do you think I should wear?"

In response, Polly goes to the closet and pulls from it the item that Sabrina suspected she had in mind, a spectacular Art Deco-inspired dress of silver-accented layered chiffon, not quite opaque and exceedingly *décolleté*.

"The Temperley gown," Sabrina says. "It's a little..." She allows a vague hand gesture below her throat to complete the sentence.

"You'd knock the boys for a sixer, I reckon."

"I couldn't lean forward to eat—I'd starve."

"This weather won't last, miss: tonight might be the only chance you'll ever get to wear it."

True enough, Sabrina thinks: considering the lack of coverage, it is a dress that could only be worn on the warmest of evenings—and a Temperley gown at Temple Slaughter Preceptory does have a certain ring to it.

"Very well," she says, "the Temperley it is."

AFTER POLLY LEAVES for home to help with the milking, Sabrina sits at the big desk. She does not have her journal, still back at Caiaphas, but there is a blank Moleskine notebook on the desk, presumably intended for her use, plus a nibbed pen and a bottle of ink labeled Diabolo Menthe, which turns out to be green. Given the turn of events, a fresh notebook for this new phase seems appropriate.

*What was rigged behind the Alice door? An aerosol of some kind, or maybe just a vial of knock-out powder placed above the lintel, and set to tip when it was opened? Or perhaps there was a substance on the door latch, something I had to touch.*

*How did Bronaryre steer the conversation to* Alice in Wonderland *in the first place?—it was I who initiated the topic of fantasy, with talk of faeries and sprites. Perhaps that was just convenient, and if I hadn't brought it up he would have found some other way to engineer my going through that door.*

*Old Tom must have been an actor, too, like Mortimer Pence—if he really was the head gardener then it would mean that he was a collaborator in the abduction, since the Alice door had to have led to the place where he normally keeps his tools. I saw nothing of him around the rest of the college; Bronaryre could have admitted him through the Ship Street gate, avoiding the porters. And why would the head gardener be working on a Friday evening?*

*He knew those roses well enough, though; perhaps Bronaryre briefed him. I will ask Collins about it when I get back.*

*Was all the play-acting meant to persuade me that Bronaryre is the Devil? That feels like too facile an explanation; whatever else he may be, Bronaryre is not trite: he would not seriously expect me to base belief on a little piece of theater, however well performed. There is something more to it, I'm sure, part of a larger scheme whose purpose is not clear, nor yet meant to be clear. As a gesture it was certainly extravagant: the actors, the props, a script flexible enough to adjust to the unpredictable behavior of a principal character who is unaware that she is in a play—it was an accomplished piece of improv.*

*The photography must have been planned all along, given the fact of the daguerreotype equipment on hand, and the Mortimer Pence actor must have been delighted when I went bathing, an excellent chance to work in some extemporaneous ribaldry. But after the initial surprise at discovering his presence, I soon realized that I was being practiced upon, as the English say, and took quiet pleasure in being such an easily persuaded model—now it was me doing the improv. It took Mortimer Pence aback, I saw, both the character and the actor, but hadn't he suspected that I would realize daguerreotype plates could not have been produced these last hundred years, and so there was no possibility of the thing being real.*

*The extravagance seems less surprising now that I have seen Temple Slaughter Preceptory: anyone who owns a place like this can afford to indulge his whims, however excessive.*

*The clothes and the maid are an extension of this, I suppose—partly the showman making a grand introduction to his estate, partly an attempted bribe to good behavior with the book, partly a game of dress-up, with me as the doll.*

*No matter; I am content to play the game for now.*

By the time she completes her entry it is too late in the day to explore the grounds, but there is enough time to explore the house. Sabrina dresses in riding breeches and a cotton shirt and then makes her way downstairs. Beyond the hall is a pair of salons, the first furnished in big comfortable chairs and sofas suitable for sitting back and reading, the second with a grand piano in the corner, evidently a music room. The dining room is not much smaller than the Great Hall at Caiaphas, and beyond it is a billiards room smelling faintly of cigars. Next to it is the library, giving onto the main terrace and the parterre beyond, and at the far end a light-filled conservatory.

There is a map of the estate mounted in the hall, and Sabrina pauses to study it. There are many features to explore later: a 'Water Garden'; beyond that a hedge maze—no doubt a complex one, as it occupies several acres; a circular Roman temple, apparently imitating that of the Vestal Virgins in the Forum; and an amphitheater, presumably the venue for the upcoming play.

The estate's properties are far larger than she had supposed, extending well beyond the bounds of the manor itself, where Mortimer Pence had dropped her off, and all the way down to the banks of the Windrush, including the area where she had encountered the photographer. Likely the land was once farmed by tenants—hence the remnants of that drystone fence—but is now abandoned, and thus a convenient stretch of unoccupied country in which to stage impromptu theater.

Sabrina steps out onto the main terrace. It is twenty feet wide and a hundred feet long, flanking the entire southern side of the house and separating it from the great sweep of the parterre, sunk fifteen feet below the level where she now stands, and reaching southward in a smooth expanse for a hundred yards or more.

She walks the length of the terrace to its eastern end and takes a set of steps down to the parterre.

The base of the terrace, now looming above her, is walled with brick, artfully laid to suggest a series of arches, although not disguising its fundamental architectural role as a buttress. But crossing back to the other side, Sabrina comes upon a feature sunk into the center of the wall that is not utilitarian: a magnificent iron grill, fifteen feet wide and equally as high, stretching right up to the level of the main terrace. It is a fabulously sumptuous piece, ornate crests intermingled with delicate leaves, embellished with elaborate finials and sculpted roundels and extravagant baroque curlicues that, given its size, must have required a considerable foundry to fabricate. The ironwork is finished in black and gilt, with the gilt dominant, and in the late-afternoon light it glows golden, gloriously radiant, as if it were the very entrance to Heaven, notwithstanding the earthen situation leading off the parterre and into the base of the house, suggesting another destination.

Sabrina approaches to see what lies on the other side. It is too dark beyond the grill to discern much detail: she has the impression of a considerable space scooped out from the earth, vaulted but undecorated, like a small chapel but without sacerdotal appurtenances—curiously plain, considering the magnificence of the grill. Part of the ironwork is hinged, forming a small gate facilitating passage without requiring the entire thing to be opened, like the wicket gate accessing the porters' lodge at Caiaphas, but she finds that it is locked. It is only then, while inspecting the ironwork more closely to see if there might be another such entrance, that she realizes the gilt is not gilt-colored paint but true gilt—this is, gold leaf—which, given the extent of the coverage, must have cost a fortune.

Sabrina finds it strange that such grandiose ornamentation should have been endowed on the entrance to what is apparently just empty space.

She continues across to the steps on the western side and takes them back up to the main terrace. She lingers there for a while before going inside, looking out across the parterre and the forest beyond, stretching all the way down to the river, a mile or more away. A big estate for such a small, densely populated country, she thinks, particularly one that had more-or-less taxed the great land-owning families into extinction—she knew that most such places were now in the hands of the National Trust. It would have taken great wealth to have maintained Temple Slaughter Preceptory in private ownership—that, or particularly useful connections.

On the way back to her room Sabrina makes a stop in the library, intending to choose a book to read before bed. She surveys the collection.

One wall is given entirely to reference works: dozens of atlases—political, historical, geological, oceanographic, even architectural; a pharmacology index; Strunk and White; philatelic and numismatic catalogs; a Debrett's; several sets of encyclopedias, from Diderot's original *Encyclopédie,* dating from the mid-1700s, up to the fifteenth and final printed edition of *Britannica*; and dozens of dictionaries, many of them specialist or foreign-language, plus two full sets of the Oxford English Dictionary: all twelve volumes of the first edition and twenty of the second. Most of the books look well worn, even those more recently published—some have been perused, examined, and consulted to near destruction, the way a good reference work should be—but which seems an anachronism in the electronic era.

Below the shelves is a series of broad flat drawers containing hundreds of maps, naval charts, and ordnance surveys.

Sabrina moves to the other shelves. There are many volumes of architecture—she is beginning to suspect that architecture is to Bronaryre what the thermometer is to a physician: a way of quickly assessing state of health, in this case of the body politic.

There are numerous histories and memoirs, plenty of poetry but a paucity of fiction (Sabrina had hoped for an Agatha Christie, preferably set in a country manor), a good collection of classics, a surprisingly large number of books on the sciences—especially pure and applied mathematics: both Fourier and Laplace in the original French; Leibniz and Flamsteed in Latin; a book by that same Nobel-laureated Heisenberg who was to lead and perhaps sabotage the Nazi atomic program, in English, summarizing his lectures delivered at the University of Chicago in 1929, and laboriously titled *The Physical Principles of the Quantum Theory*—it is a thin little volume, visible proof that, when it comes to the profundity of ideas, size does not matter.

She finds both *Principia Mathematica*s located next to each other: Newton's original *Philosophiae Naturalis Principia Mathematica*, and then, in three separate volumes, Whitehead and Russell's similarly and rather self-consciously titled work of more than two centuries later.

Most of the books are old, but those on mathematics look especially well worn. Sabrina inspects a few to see when they were published, and what she finds astonishes her: they are almost all first editions, even the Newton.

It is irresponsible that these are not under lock-and-key, she thinks, and unforgivably reckless that they are not stored in a fireproof vault. Sabrina sits and considers this discovery, staring at the front cover of the *Principia* in her lap (and surprised to find there the diarist Samuel Pepys's name below that of Isaac Newton—the book was published under the auspices of the Royal Society, whose president Pepys was at the time, and apparently it had required the old lecher's imprimatur to be legally published—something that strikes her as being superbly ludicrous).

These math books would likely be worth more than all the gilt on those gates below, Sabrina thinks, probably more than if the gates were made of solid gold. She replaces the *Principia*, finding herself irrationally annoyed that it is not better cared for, and surveys the remainder of the collection.

There are no travel books, no cookbooks, nor anything that might conceivably be shelved in the 'lifestyle' section of a typical bookstore;

nor are there, despite a large selection of art books, any volumes of photography, something that seems odd, given the encounter that had been engineered with the *daguerriste de la nature*.

This apparent anomaly gives Sabrina an idea.

While photographing her, the Dickensianly named Mortimer Pence had specified two paintings. In a volume devoted to the Pre-Raphaelites, she locates a plate depicting the first of these: John Everett Millais's *Ophelia*. According to the introduction, the Pre-Raphaelites were a group—'brotherhood,' they termed themselves—of mostly English mid-Nineteenth-Century artists who wished to do away with the mannerist conventions that in their view had hobbled art since Raphael and Michelangelo. In Millais's painting, Ophelia lies floating in a stream not unlike the Windrush, having found peace at last, beautifully garbed in an elaborate dress whose lustrous fabric reminds her of the Temperley. According to the notes, *Ophelia* was completed in 1852 and exhibited at the Royal Academy, where it was hailed by Ruskin, although not universally acclaimed.

In a second book, Sabrina finds the other painting—John William Waterhouse's *Hylas and the Nymphs*. There is no elaborate clothing here: the nymphs, all seven of them, are as naked as she had been in the stream this morning, and Hylas seems not very alarmed.

The painting was completed in 1896, and so Sabrina has found what she was hoping for: a factual inconsistency, in this case, an anachronism: how could Mortimer Pence have just seen the 'recently put on display' *Ophelia*—which would presumably have been around 1852—and yet be aware of a picture painted half a century later?

She returns to the Pre-Raphaelite book to confirm her facts. *Ophelia* is at the Tate Britain, which occupies the museum's original building on the Embankment, known simply as the Tate before the collection was split with the establishment of the Tate Modern across the river. She checks the provenance, and receives a disappointment: although it was painted in 1852, *Ophelia* only came into the Tate's possession in 1894—as part of Henry Tate's original gift to the nation—and therefore it is not an anachronism after all: the fictional Mortimer Pence could have legitimately come across it as recently put on display after *Hylas and the*

*Nymphs* was completed. But then she realizes that there is a second inconsistency: Pence claimed to have seen it at the National Gallery, but clearly it is at the Tate: two separate institutions, one on Trafalgar Square, the other down by Vauxhall Bridge. It is a small slip, but sufficient to dispute any assertion by Bronaryre that what she experienced today was something other than play-acting.

She sits back, pleased with having this little fact at her disposal, ready to deploy, like a prosecutor who knows that he has in his possession the means to undercut the defense attorney's primary witness. But as Sabrina continues to read she receives a second disappointment: at the time of the Tate gift, the museum to which Henry Tate gave it was known as the *National Gallery* of British Art—it was not until 1932 that the name was changed to the Tate.

So Mortimer Pence had identified the institution correctly; in fact, he had named it in a way that few contemporary people would have known to do.

Sabrina puts aside the book and thinks on this for a long time, wondering what the odds are of an unknown actor in a minor role putting in the time to research British art history to the extent of getting such an obscure detail correct.

# Second Circle

Melpomene

♄

THERE IS A SECOND ENTRANCE to Sabrina's terrace, an external staircase coming up from the back with a little gate at the top, allowing access for staff without the need to go through Sabrina's room. At precisely seven o'clock Bronaryre arrives on the terrace via these stairs, shortly after the maid who laid the table for cocktails had completed her task and left. He is wearing a dinner suit, well cut and sharply pressed, with brightly polished shoes. There is no hint of country casual, and Sabrina is suddenly grateful that Polly had badgered her into the Temperley, however revealing.

"Mr. Sacheverell Edgewater, I presume."

"As once I was, but that was long ago."

"I take it that you have found a new valet."

"Indeed, I have—a Filipino gentleman who for some reason has chosen to forego that Pacific paradise for the cold mists of Albion."

"Another fallen angel, perhaps?"

"Then he and I shall get along famously. Now, a dry Martini?"

Besides the shaker and ice, the maid brought up only a single bottle of gin and a little tray of cocktail olives, so Sabrina assumes that the question is rhetorical. Given the absence of vermouth, the *dry* is a given.

Bronaryre begins mixing the drinks.

"Here, smell this." He offers her the uncorked gin bottle.

She leans forward—but not too much: the Temperley is not a dress in which one may safely lean very far forward—and inhales. The smell is gin-like but more so, as if it had been distilled again and again, concentrating it into a liquor that is deep, rich, and herbal. She can feel it faintly burn the back of her nasal passages.

"Remarkable. What is it?"

"Physic Gin. It's made and bottled entirely in Oxford, and the botanicals are derived from those planted in that city in 1648 by Jacob Bobart the Elder in what was then called the Physicke Garden—so named as it was intended to cultivate plants for their medicinal qualities—and which today is the Oxford Botanic Garden. It's located on Rose Lane, on the other side of the High from Magdalen. I knew Bobart when I was up, and since tonight I propose to tell you something of my time in Oxford I thought it would be an appropriate cocktail."

He finishes mixing and hands her a glass.

"Will this knock me out like the wine did last night?"

"The wine didn't knock you out; as far as I know, nothing did."

"Then what happened?"

"Surely only you can answer that?"

"It was like *Alice in Wonderland* on acid."

"Your adventure was a result of your own mind. I suppose that *Alice in Wonderland* must have been in your thoughts." Sabrina recalls the literary allusion that she had been so proud of delivering earlier that day. "Are you given to trances?" Bronaryre asks.

"Trances?"

"A predisposition for entering transcendental states. Some people are, you know, but no matter."

He raises his glass and drinks; she is reminded that he is not a man for extraneous civilities, like offering cheers before drinking or explaining his abductions.

"*Ignoratio elenchi*."

"What refutation do you accuse me of ignoring?"

Sabrina is impressed: anyone else confronted with an obscure Latin phrase would probably have asked for it to be repeated, and even if familiar with the language would have at least hesitated, but Bronaryre responded with the comprehension of a Cicero. "Your Latin is very fluent."

"It was required when I was up at Oxford. Latin was the language of instruction in those days, and usually of authorship, too—it was what allowed scholarship to be international, the way English does today."

"In this case, your Latin is literally too correct. In jurisprudence we use the term *ignoratio elenchi* in a more general sense, to mean arguing a point which may or may not be true, but which does not bear upon the question at hand."

"You mean a red herring?"

"Yes."

"Then perhaps you misunderstood the question at hand."

Sabrina assumes that this tangential obscurantism is his way of telling her that she can expect no explanations. But she does not care: on the whole she enjoyed the day, a day unlike any other that she has experienced: waking in a wildflower-strewn meadow and bathing in a clear country stream—the sort of day one could not arrange for oneself: the very act of arranging would undo it, removing all the surprise and wonderment—analogous to the observation of a quantum particle, where the act of observation destroys the properties being observed. It was a form of performance art, she supposes, but it brings to her mind a more archaic term, *masque*, alluding as that word does to a sense of the Ancients and their secret Mysteries—Eleusinian and Dionysian—carefully guarded and enigmatic; although perhaps *mummery* is a better term: there was certainly much in Mortimer Pence that was ridiculous. In any case, if Bronaryre chooses to illustrate his fictions with further masques and mummery, then Sabrina is resolved that from now on she will not object, but simply be entertained.

"Well, I enjoyed the day, trance or otherwise."

They move to the corner of the terrace, where light from the lowering sun still skims in from above the treetops. Sabrina sits on the broad stone balustrade, Bronaryre remains standing but leans back upon it.

"What's that?"

She is looking at a bird, the size of a large chicken but much more colorful, having emerged from the grasses at the edge of the weald and now pecking away on the parterre.

"A pheasant," Bronaryre says. "A cock, of course, the hens are quite plain—the opposite of humans, where it is the female that is given to extravagant display." She wonders if this is an oblique comment on the Temperley. "We have a lot of them on the estate, and tonight we will be dining on some of his relatives."

"Poor fellow," Sabrina says. "He's all alone."

"The cocks always are."

"I suppose that must be your natural state. Do you feel an affinity for him?"

"Other than a desire to consume his brethren, no."

She takes her first mouthful of the Martini. The gin seers her throat and she can feel it enter into her nervous system, sparking through her synapses like a tiny lightning bolt. She looks at her glass in amazement.

"I've never tasted anything like it."

"Jacob Bobart would be very pleased to hear you say so—he took great care in the cultivation of his Physicke Garden, and the botanicals in this gin were foraged from it."

"Do you know what they are?"

"Some of them: there is wormwood, which as you may know is the primary ingredient in absinthe, sweet woodruff, calamus root, oil from the seed of the opium poppy—"

"There's opium?"

"A trace, no doubt, but not enough to be pharmaceutically effective."

"What else?"

"Gentian root. Rue."

"Rue? I've never heard of it."

"It's also called herb-of-grace. Little known today, but once common enough to have been mentioned in four of Shakespeare's plays. In Hamlet, it is referred to under both names in the scene where Ophelia, mad with grief, distributes flowers among the courtiers:

*There's fennel for you, and columbines:*
*There's rue for you; and here's some for me:*
*We may call it herb-grace o' Sundays:*
*O you must wear your rue with a difference"*

The Ophelia reference echoes Mortimer Pence's mention of the painting of the same name, and Sabrina suspects that Bronaryre has led the conversation to that character on purpose—but then she realizes that it was she who asked him to name the botanicals in the first place. She briefly wonders if she was somehow subtly hypnotized in the garden last night, and her question had been the result of a post-hypnotic suggestion.

"What was the medicinal quality attributed to rue?"

"It was used to treat impaired vision—appropriate, since my hope is that by telling you my story you will come to see things more clearly. Milton uses rue in this sense in 'Paradise Lost,' when the Archangel Michael employs it to help Adam:

*Then purg'd with euphrasy and rue*
*The visual nerve, for he had much to see*

You too, Lancaster, have much to see. But first I must explain how it is that *I* came to see, by which I mean to see myself for what I am. Are you familiar with Hegel?"

"Hegel?"

"Georg Wilhelm Friedrich Hegel—the German philosopher."

"No. Did you study under him?"

"He was born a century after I was sent down."

She recalls that the expression *sent down* was among the Oxonian subtleties the Jesuit organist had explained: Bronaryre was expelled from the university.

"I'm afraid that I know little of philosophy, and nothing of Hegel."

"His idea was that all human progress, whether in thought or deed, is the result of a conflict between opposing forces, a dialectic. Fichte, a fellow German Idealist, termed these opposing forces *thesis* and *antithesis*, and the resulting outcome of their conflict as *synthesis*. This is a useful idea for framing many things: as various as, say, modern constitutional democracies arising as a result of the resolution of the conflict between the highest ideals of freedom, as in the storming of the Bastille, and the negation of those ideals, like the Reign of Terror; or, to pick something wildly different, the peculiar power in the paintings of Rembrandt as being the result of the clash between light and shade. Marx and Engels famously married the idea with materialism, and out popped the Communist Manifesto. In my case, my understanding arose through such a conflict of two sides. The first of these, the one that I will characterize as *light*, was Oxford."

Sabrina sees a bird of prey soaring gracefully above the parterre, primaries extended like the fingers of a hand, circling watchfully: a beautiful creature—vigilant, totemic, vespertine.

The strutting pheasant cock has quietly disappeared.

The bird suddenly dives, swooping down low and close, skimming past the balustrade, as if to inspect this woman with her impertinent gaze.

"What is he?"

"A harrier. And this particular one is a she."

"How can you tell?"

"*Circus cyaneus*—the hen harrier. It's a species that displays a high degree of sexual dimorphism. The males are much smaller, with dull gray plumage above and white below. The females weigh half as much again as the males, and have brown plumage, darker above, tawny and distinctively streaked below, as if to emphasize their speed. And the tail coverts are white, which makes them appear ring-tailed like this one—watch."

The harrier dives for another identification run, and this time she swoops by so close that her flight is audible, with a rush of air felt by them on the terrace as she flashes by—a windrush, Sabrina thinks. Once past and clear the bird banks steeply away and glides gracefully skyward, tail feathers extended, its white ring plain to see. Sabrina watches her for a while, effortlessly aerobatic, but dusk is upon them and she turns from the bird to Bronaryre. "Tell me about your light, while we still have some with us."

He takes a large mouthful of the cocktail before continuing, as if recalling his Oxford days had given him taste afresh for those botanicals from long ago.

"I went up in 1660. I was at Caiaphas, of course. I have already told you that I knew Jacob Bobart the Elder. I was better acquainted with his son, Jacob Bobart the Younger, who was near my age. He was a fellow student, but in addition to his studies he spent much of his time assisting the elder Bobart in the cultivation of the Physicke Garden, which is how I became acquainted with it. He also helped his father compose the catalog that lists, among others, the botanicals that you are now consuming: the *Catalogus plantarum horti medici Oxoniensis*. The son went on to become a professor of botany at the university, as well as to run the garden that his father had established.

"Courses of study were not as formalized as they are now. There were four general fields: theology, law, medicine, and philosophy. The first three were for the professions, none of which, given my close association with a regicide, were open to me in those revengeful Restoration years, and so I read philosophy by default. However, the term *philosophy* had in those days a much broader meaning, encompassing what today are termed the STEM studies: science, technology, engineering, and mathematics. The last of these, mathematics, came to me with special ease, and I concentrated my studies there."

Sabrina almost smiles: of course that cold and abstract field would have been a natural for the Devil. Then she does smile: she has started mistaking fiction for fact.

"However, I sampled broadly from the fecund grove that is the University of Oxford, including botany. Botany was not then a science of ordering and nomenclature but of experiment and investigation. As the name Physicke Garden suggests, plants were studied not so much for what they were as for what they could do, particularly when ingested. This was a major field of investigation, so much so that the university's garden was not the only *horti medici* in town. There was another physic garden, a private one behind Crosse Hall, that belonged to a wealthy apothecary. At that time many new plants were arriving from the Americas, some examples of which had ended up in that second garden, and one of which—a plant that was purported to impart great vigor simply by chewing on the leaf—Jacob Bobart Junior and I longed to study.

"Crosse Hall no longer exists—the site is now occupied by the Shelley Memorial, University College's specious attempt to bathe themselves in the reflected glory of a student they had in fact expelled for atheism—but in those days the apothecary occupied the ground floor and rented out the rooms above. This gentleman did not become wealthy by mistake: our pleadings with him to allow us to study this plant were denied, unless we were to pay handsomely for the privilege: five guineas, a sum far beyond our means—I was quite poor, and Bobart's father had to sell fruit from the Physicke Garden to pad out his meager income. Neither of us had ever even laid eyes on one of these marvelous new guinea coins, machine struck, it was said, from a quarter ounce of pure gold.

"While we were haranguing, and being harangued by, this niggling money-grubber, a figure came down the stairs. He was a man in his prime in every sense: mid-thirties, dressed soberly but expensively, wearing polished boots that unlike our own were not in need of a cobbler's attention, and wearing both a genial smile and a resplendent wig, one which was unlikely to be colonized with nits.

"Evidently this was the apothecary's lodger, and he had been listening to the argument, perhaps disturbed by it while in his rooms. At the bottom of the stairs, he wordlessly reached into his purse and withdrew five guineas. The apothecary was astonished but not so astonished that he was unable to hold out his hand. The coins gleamed brilliantly and made a fine deep clunk as they were dropped into his open palm. The lodger then turned to us and said, 'I, too, have felt a desire to study this interesting new antipodean specimen. Gentleman, shall we do so together?' And so we proceeded directly into the garden, right then and there.

"The apothecary's lodger—our benefactor—turned out to be Robert Boyle. The five guineas meant little to him: the father of modern chemistry was a very wealthy man—his people were Anglo-Irish plantation owners; his father was the Earl of Cork—but nevertheless he chose to rent meager rooms and live a life of scholarship in Oxford when he could instead have bought a Chelsea mansion and lived a life of leisure in London. By that stage, he and Hooke had already developed their famous pneumatic pump, and he had published *The Sceptical Chymist*; soon he was to formulate the scientific law that still bears his name. But he was more than just a chemist. For a start, he was an alchemist: he never ceased in the belief that it would be possible to transmute one element into another—how pleased he would have been with the particle accelerators of today, where such things are routine. But all knowledge was of interest to him: he yearned to know everything.

"The group that gathered around Boyle was referred to as the 'Invisible College'; Bobart junior and I became minor satellites in their orbit. This 'Invisible College' was at that time in the process of becoming the Royal Society, of which Boyle was to be a founding member. In their repository today one can still see a document in his hand, unheaded but commonly referred to as 'Boyle's Wish List,' which enumerates twenty-four things that he hoped might one day be made possible through science. The first of these was *The Prolongation of Life*."

"Then he might find you of even more interest than a particle accelerator."

"Indeed he would—but the prolongation of life is at the top of all people's wish lists, is it not? Let's sample some of the others." Bronaryre adopts a thoughtful pose, head slightly cocked, which gives Sabrina the impression that he is pulling to mind the original document as if he had a photographic memory—something aided by what follows, for he articulates each of Boyle's items with the precision of a person reading out loud.

"*The Art of Flying*," he says. "A dream at least as old as the legend of Icarus; *The Transmutation of Metalls*: predictable, given his alchemical activities. *Potent Druggs to alter or Exalt Imagination, Waking, Memory, and other functions, and to appease pain, procure innocent sleep, harmless dreams, etc.*: a clue as to why he might have chosen quarters by a physic garden; *Freedom from Necessity of much Sleeping exemplify'd by the operations of Tea and what happens in Mad-Men*: you see now that the five guineas to access this wondrous new Coca plant was not entirely free of self-interest; there are many others: *The Art of Continuing long under water, and exercising functions freely there*; *A Ship to saile in All Winds*; *A perpetuall Light*; *The practicable and certain way of finding longitudes*; *the making of Armor light and extremely hard*; *The Acceleration of the Production of things out of Seed*—now, varied as they are, what do all these have in common?"

"Besides being on Boyle's Wish List?"

"Yes."

"I don't know."

"They've all been done. Achievements that would have seemed miraculous to Boyle are so commonplace today that we do not even think about them. Imagine if he were suddenly to appear in the modern world. What would he make of GPS, of Kevlar, of airliners, of the light bulb, of genetic modification, of a nuclear submarine? I assume that even modern dentistry would seem amazing to him."

"As for many an Englishman, both ancient and modern."

"The point is: civilization has achieved many things that are truly remarkable, not to be dismissed lightly. We sometimes forget to appreciate these, and must remind ourselves of them when assessing humankind."

"Is that what we're doing, assessing humankind?"

"For me, it is an occupational hazard."

Sabrina finishes her Martini. The olive remains stuck in the base of the glass, and she is contemplating how best to coax it out when a knife suddenly appears in Bronaryre's hand, an ebony-handled weapon whose slender blade he opens with a single sharp snap of the wrist.

"Allow me."

He uses the tip of the knife to impale the olive in her glass, and then holds the blade up, inviting her to pluck the fruit from it.

Bronaryre expects her to use her fingers—the blade is held at the convenient height to do so—but instead Sabrina leans forward, using a hand to hold back her hair while ignoring the feel of the Temperley falling away, and lightly plucks the olive from the tip of the blade with her teeth.

The blade has been forged with a pattern of banded swirls, and Sabrina thinks of Ravenscroft's shimmering magnesium-bronze propellers.

She stands back up straight and regards her tormenter in silence, slowly chewing. He holds her extended gaze, matching her silence and with no particular expression, but Sabrina senses that for once she has gotten the better of him.

He refolds the knife with the same single-handed efficiency, returns it to an interior pocket where a less well-equipped man might keep reading glasses, and finishes his Martini. He holds out a hand, inviting her to give him the empty glass.

"So Oxford was half of the story, the side of light," Sabrina says. "What was the dark?"

"Let's leave that for another day. We're dining formally tonight, and it would be ill-mannered to be late."

SABRINA AND BRONARYRE join the rest of the party in the salons below. Bronaryre introduces Sabrina to an unusually tall oriental woman and then leaves her. The woman's name is Malavalaya, although whether this is a first or last name is unclear, and describes herself as Bronaryre's executive assistant. She is evidently playing the role of hostess for the evening, but from her dress—a tight sheer gown, vaguely fetishistic, and whose leather bustier top is so stiffly stayed that every breath is a startling sight: her chest pressed firm against the fabric on inhale, but then withdrawing on exhale, revealing when standing next to her a series of coffee-colored curves and two nipples, very dark and prominently erect—Sabrina wonders if in this case executive assistant is not a euphemism for mistress.

It is a large party: at least a dozen Caiaphas students, including not just Katy Telford and the unsurnamed Sesuna of the afternoon, but also the Penelope (not 'Penny') de Vere Sabrina had first met at the Explorers Club, and many other guests.

Dinner is announced with a gong, and the guests drift into the dining room. It has been arranged as a single long table, flowers and candlesticks down the spine, and on either side an array of glittering silverware and sparkling crystal, crisp linens and gleaming porcelain.

Bronaryre takes the host's position at the head of the table. Sabrina's seat, designated by a little handwritten card bearing her name and whose cardholder is a miniature silver replica of the Neptune fountain, is two-thirds down the table. While the guests settle themselves Sabrina counts the items in her place setting: a broad white porcelain plate rimmed in a complex pattern of red and black forms the focus, and is surrounded by five knives, five forks, three spoons, an implement resembling pliers, four glasses variously sized, a side-plate patterned similarly to the first, a napkin in an engraved silver ring—along with the place card and holder, twenty-four pieces in total; she has never sat at such a magnificent table setting.

The man to her left—a Col. Swinton, according to his card—is a round, ruddy-faced gentleman whose army days are evidently behind him. While the first course is served the colonel introduces himself with a marked northern accent, explaining that he is a native Northumbrian who, having no fond memory of his childhood climate, retired to this corner of Gloucestershire, only to find the weather no better.

"Bourton-on-the-Water should be called Bourton-*under*-Water," he asserts. "Still, can't complain about it today—feels like it's going to be a real Battle-of-Britain summer this year."

"A Battle-of-Britain summer?"

"The summer of 1940, when Hitler was trying to bomb Britain into submission during the Second World War, was an unusually fine one. In overcast weather the German bombers could hide in the clouds, you see, safe from our fighters, but in that uncharacteristic summer of cloudless blues skies day after day they had no cover, and so the Hurricanes and Spitfires were able to pick them off. If it hadn't been for the peculiar weather the whole thing might have turned out very differently, and we'd be eating an appetizer of pickled herring instead of these rather excellent potted prawns."

Sabrina agrees that the potted prawns are very good, and asks the colonel if he has taken up military history in his retirement.

"History, yes; military, no. I'm something of a local historian now; authored an article or two. That's why I'm here, in fact. I wrote to Mr. Bronaryre recently to ask if he might allow me to inspect some of the old stones from the preceptory—the manor was built over its ruins, you see, and supposedly in the basement there are still some parts of the original walls. I didn't have much expectation that he would agree—didn't even expect a reply, given that he has such a reputation as a recluse—but he agreed to give me access and invited me to dinner to boot: terribly kind of him."

"Did you see the old stones?"

"Aye, and much else." Swinton is interrupted by the pouring of a new wine, more deeply straw-colored than the crisp Chablis that had accompanied the prawns.

"Ah, hock," he says after tasting it, and then noticing her look of unfamiliarity, "*Hock* is the English name for Riesling, of which I must say this is a fine example—from the Mosel, I imagine."

Sabrina follows his example and tastes the Riesling: deeper and sweeter than the wine that had preceded it. Swinton continues his story.

"It turns out that there is much more than just a few old stones: it seems the manor was built not so much on top of the preceptory's ruins as it incorporated those ruins into the design, so that the old preceptory formed a sort of preconstructed basement. The cellar is very impressive: the entrance is situated below the terrace, on the same level as the parterre. It is built in the form of a large niche, and going through the gate one has the sense of entering a portal into a secret underground world. Inside, Bronaryre was kind enough to show me several rooms in which the walls are partly or even completely original to the preceptory. The floors, too: flagstones upon which crusaders once stood."

The soup course arrives, a seafood bisque whose transport from bowl to mouth is something of a challenge to Sabrina, sitting rigidly straight-backed. The colonel pauses to consume a spoonful or two before resuming his account of the cellar.

"One wall still has iron hooks embedded into it that may have originally been used to hang their broadswords. I was surprised at how much has been preserved. There were more rooms, leading even deeper, but Bronaryre said that they had been closed due to safety concerns—apparently there has been some subsidence. Perhaps even more surprising was the stone itself. Cotswold stone is highly characteristic: it is a pre-Cambrian sandstone, famed for its golden color, and is what gives the villages around here their vibrant butter-tinted hue. But the preceptory walls are built of ironstone, which is very different to our local Cotswold stone: dark gray when freshly cleaved, but after becoming weathered it often turns into a deep red due to the oxidation of the ferrous content for which it is named—in short, it rusts."

The Colonel pauses as the soup bowls are removed and the larger of the wine glasses, empty until now, are filled. "Claret," Swinton remarks approvingly, "that will go admirably with the game."

Since the wine has been decanted and is thus anonymous, Sabrina wonders what it was that allowed the colonel to identify it—perhaps the shape of the glass is specific to Bordeaux—but he soon provides an explanation.

"I should say that the cellar is a cellar in both senses of the word, for that is where Bronaryre stores his wine, including this wonderful 'Fifty-nine Haut-Brion that the staff were taking upstairs while I was down there."

They pause to taste it, amazingly flavorful for a wine two-thirds of a century old, before the colonel continues his account.

"Ironstone is very hard and so was a suitable building material in dangerous times, but the nearest quarry is in Hook Norton, twenty miles away. Twenty miles doesn't sound much to us, but there is no navigable water route, and so those blocks would have had to be transported overland by ox cart—a considerable undertaking in the Twelfth Century, when there were no roads and much of the countryside was still forest."

"Perhaps they liked the color?"

"Or the pattern: most of the stone in the cellar is a particular type of ironstone called tiger stone, which has alternating bands of dark gray and deep red—striped, like a tiger—and I could see that there had been an effort to match the pattern between blocks. Or maybe there was another reason: ironstone has ferromagnetic properties—the lodestone of a primitive compass was made of ironstone—and so maybe they perceived magnetism as a mystical quality that they wanted to incorporate into the building of their preceptory."

The pheasant is served, roasted to a deep golden brown, followed by salvers of vegetables making the rounds, and then finally silver sauce boats brimming with dark gravy.

Sabrina's first mouthful is a revelation: she had expected it to be somewhat bland, like chicken, but the pheasant has a very different taste: pungent and gamey, seemingly unrelated to that of its domesticated cousins.

"What a remarkable flavor," she says. "I've never tasted anything like it."

"Neither have most people," the colonel says, "including those who eat pheasant."

"What do you mean?"

"I mean that wine wasn't the only thing that I found aging in the cellar." He leans closer and taps the side of his nose with a forefinger, apparently an English gesture indicating that a secret is about to be imparted. "These birds were down there, too," he says, *sotto voce*. "They had been hung, using those very same hooks that I was describing just now. About three days, I would guess."

"Is that a long time?"

"Most pheasant aren't hung at all, and those that are only for a day, or two at most. But there's more: I checked the spurs. The cocks have spurs, you see, and their length is a simple and reliable indicator of the age of a bird. I can assure you that these birds were quite young, which is to be expected if shooting in late June."

"Is that unusual?"

"It's more than unusual, it is illegal. Pheasant can only be shot from autumn through mid-winter; to take them at the beginning of summer is a serious offense in England, where we understand the need to preserve our fowl in a land with ever-dwindling habitats in which they may thrive. The only pheasant one can legally eat now has been frozen. I mentioned to Bronaryre that he would have trouble with the authorities if they caught him, even though he was shooting on his own estate."

"What did he say?"

"He said the Bible teaches us that the meek shall inherit the earth, and he assured me that his pheasant were indeed poised to do so—I wasn't sure what to make of that, and as his guest I naturally let the matter drop. I have to say though, however criminal its history, I'm certainly enjoying this fine bird." And so saying he resumes the meal with relish.

Sabrina resumes hers, too, thinking that the Devil really can cite Scripture for his purpose.

The dessert is called 'trifle,' but the item that occupies Sabrina's bowl is anything but trifling: it is a mighty concatenation of strawberries, custard, fruit jelly, whipped cream, and sponge cake so heavily doused with sherry as to make her eyes water when eating it, and she needs the Sauternes that has been served as the dessert wine to help wash it down.

"I've been wondering what a preceptory is—I assume a religious establishment, like an abbey or a friary."

"It's the equivalent of an abbey or friary, but run by one of the military orders. *Preceptor* means teacher or instructor, and so in this case *preceptory* meant a military academy, a place where the knights lived and were trained in the martial arts." Now Sabrina understands his crusader comment from earlier. "The preceptor was the commandant, and preceptories were sometimes known as commanderies. Up where I'm from we still have the ruins of one, Chibburn Preceptory, that was run by the Hospitallers, and there is a Bodmiscombe Preceptory down in Devon that was run by the Hospitallers, too—that is, the Knights of the Hospital of Saint John, as they were originally dubbed, later known as the Knights of Malta, after the retreat from Jerusalem. Temple Slaughter belonged to a different order: the *Temple* part comes from their name: they were the Knights Templar."

The Knights Templar keep coming up, Sabrina thinks, as in one of those cheap conspiracy novels.

"And *Slaughter*?"

"Nothing to do with the modern meaning of the term, despite the presence of those bellicose knights. It's derived from an Anglo-Saxon word, meaning a wet place."

"Slough?"

"Yes," he says, beaming with surprise. "We normally pronounce it to rhyme with plow, but the truth is that no one knows how those ancient

Britons of Wessex would have said it. Presumably, the name is a reference to the River Windrush. A pretty stream: it's worth taking a stroll along it if you get the chance."

Sabrina decides against explaining that she is already well acquainted with the Windrush. She had hoped that the meal was over, but triangles of cheese-on-toast are served.

"Welsh rarebit," the colonel explains. "In England, we often finish the meal with a savory, which must seem strange to an American, but I suppose that given our host's background it was inevitable."

"What's his background?"

"I confess I don't really know—the truth is that his background is something of a mystery around here. I meant only that since Bronaryre's name is obviously Welsh, then the Welsh rarebit makes sense."

Dried fruits and nuts are served after the savory, and Sabrina thinks that the meal will never end, although at least she discovers what the pliers-like instrument is for when the colonel uses it to open an almond: it is a nutcracker.

At last, the feast is complete, and the party retires to the salons for coffee and liqueurs. Bronaryre invites several of the men to join him for billiards, including Swinton. Most of the girls head for the music room, and the others drift variously into the drawing-room, or the library, or the terrace outside where Malavalaya and a handful of guests have formed a chatty group by the balustrade, drinking brandy and smoking cigars. The other three are men and much younger than the colonel: they are the most eligible-appearing of the male dinner guests, and no doubt were drawn to the terrace more by Malavalaya's laughing presence than the need for tobacco.

Sabrina climbs the stairs back up to her room—it has been a long and extraordinary day, and she has been stuffed like a Gascon goose: she is exhausted.

## The Blood Sacrament

A FIRE HAS BEEN set, despite the fine weather, and now dancing flames illuminate the deeply sculpted forest of demons, making carved stone come to life. She watches it for a little while, thinking that the man who fabricated this fireplace four hundred years ago must have hoped for this effect: his vision of Hell, no doubt.

Jacobean, Ronson said: that same James who had ruled England at the time of the Pendle Hill trials and authored a book called *Daemonologie*.

Sabrina decides to read by the fire before retiring, and turns to the bedside table to retrieve the book she chose from the library that afternoon—*Alice in Wonderland*, not read since childhood but due for a review now, given her recent adventures.

She discovers that a small silver tray has been left on the table beside her book. The tray bears three items, each sitting on its own little linen napkin. The first is a bottle of mineral water; the second is a cut-crystal glass into which to pour the first. But it is the third item that catches her attention: an apothecary's bottle, just three inches high, and sealed shut with a tiny cork. Sabrina picks it up, surprisingly hefty, obviously made with thick glass.

There are two labels. The first of these is affixed to the face of the bottle in the normal manner, but the small print is faded with age, and in the low light Sabrina cannot read it. There is no such problem with the second label, a stiff brown strip of cardboard longer than the bottle is tall, and attached to its neck with a piece of rough twine, the way in which a corpse in a morgue might once have been labeled, around a big toe. It bears just two words in large emphatic hand-drawn capitals: *DRINK ME!*

Someone has been reading her *Alice*, she thinks. She uncorks the bottle and sniffs the contents: dark and herbaceous, like an Italian *amaro*, and she supposes that it must be some sort of elixir intended to help settle the stomach after a large and illegal meal.

Sabrina drinks the contents in a single swift gulp. The fluid is bitter-tasting and highly alcoholic.

She neither shrinks nor grows.

Sabrina returns to her place before the fire and resumes reading, getting as far as the hookah-smoking caterpillar before her eyes will stay open no longer. She undresses, laying the Temperley carefully over a chair for Polly to deal with in the morning, and gets into bed, but after a long period of tossing and turning discovers that sleep does not come: whatever benefits the *digestif* might have had for her stomach, a side effect is wakefulness, despite fatigue.

Eventually, Sabrina gets out of bed and redresses. There is a flashlight in the bedside table drawer—Temple Slaughter Preceptory suffers the occasional blackout, Ronson explained, something to be expected in an isolated country house whose wiring is a century old. She takes the flashlight in hand and heads back downstairs.

The main hall is deserted, but inside the salons the evening is still in full swing. In the music room someone is playing a rousing rendition of 'Bohemian Rhapsody' on the piano, and the girls are singing along enthusiastically. Sabrina enters the empty dining room and takes the French doors out onto the terrace, now unoccupied.

The house is floodlit, although the moon, on the verge of full, would have provided sufficient illumination. She goes to the end of the terrace and takes the steps down to the parterre.

It is much darker below, beneath the floodlights and in the shadows of the buttress.

Sabrina goes to the large gilded grill she had admired that afternoon, the entrance to what Swinton described as the cellar. She uses her flashlight to inspect the space on the other side, an arched recess sunk into the earth behind the terrace's buttressing wall. It is too large to be called a niche; perhaps *alcove* is the correct term.

This time when Sabrina checks the wicket gate embedded into the grill she finds it unlocked, no doubt deliberately left that way during a large dinner party in which staff would need access to the cellar.

She enters the alcove and closes the gate behind her. The air is colder in here, smelling of bare stone. The floor is laid with broad tiles. The space feels vaguely religious, the walls carved and molded with complicated care, like a side-chapel in a cathedral, but there is no cross, nor ornamentation of any kind beyond the baroque design of the interior itself.

There are no doors or portals, but part of the wall to her left is ajar, an opening whose existence would not be apparent to a casual observer when closed.

Sabrina approaches and slowly pulls it open.

On the other side is a passageway, three feet wide, stucco lined and barrel-vaulted. The passageway is unlit, but she will not need to rely on the flashlight's narrow beam: a kerosene lantern sits on a ledge immediately inside, already alight, and whose soft glow bathes the whitewashed walls in a warm golden light. The tunnel runs west, disappearing into shadow beyond the loom of the lantern. Sabrina tries the flashlight, but it penetrates no further: she cannot tell what lies beyond. A faint waft of air comes from the other end, smelling of dank earth.

She takes the lantern in hand and proceeds cautiously along the passageway. At the end it turns right, leading deeper beneath the house before eventually widening into a small room whose walls, stucco to begin with but soon transitioning to stone, apparently mark the beginning of the preceptory's ruins.

She holds up the lamp to closely inspect a block of stone. It is roughly hewn and coarse to the touch, broadly but unevenly banded in horizontal layers of rusty maroon and graphite gray.

An archway at the far end leads into a second, much larger space. No stucco or cement here, just ironstone: it is a room unchanged for a thousand years. A refectory table stands in the middle, much used but currently bare, and wooden crates are stacked by the walls, with various estate names branded into their end timbers: Château Vaudieu, Bartolo Mascarello, Lynch-Bages—evidently this room is now used as the wine cellar.

The next room, although empty, was obviously where the fowl were recently hung: there are rusting iron hooks embedded into the walls, and on the flagstones below is a large, slowly congealing pool of blood. The sight of it jogs Sabrina's memory, and she suddenly makes a connection: the colors of the walls and the colors of the Tate's Rothkos are identical shade palettes: almost-black grays and drying-blood reds.

Embedded into the far wall is a small iron door. On it is a bright yellow sign with large black lettering: *Warning: Subsidence! Unsafe! Do Not Enter!*

Sabrina crosses the room and opens the door.

On the other side is another passageway, narrower and lower than before, so constricted that two people would have difficulty passing each other, and disappearing beyond the lamplight into blackness. It is not an inviting view, and the warning sign is unambiguous, but having come this far Sabrina wants to find out what lies at the end.

She steps through the doorway.

The tunnel is low enough that Sabrina, already tall and wearing high heels, needs to duck. The air cools as she proceeds down the passageway, and her flesh puckers. In the lamplight she sees her breath misting, visible evidence of how much colder it has become.

She is soon shivering. The claustrophobia she has felt at the back of her mind since entering the labyrinth now becomes all-embracing, almost a physical force, and she fights to contain it, counting her steps as a way of distracting her mind.

At step thirty-four she hears the echoing sound of the iron door slamming shut far behind her, and wonders how it could have done so in this breezeless air.

Sabrina decides that if the door has been locked she will discover it soon enough, and so there is no point in retracing her steps now. She presses onward, trying to keep thoughts of entombment at bay, and finds that ahead of her there has indeed been subsidence: one wall has partially collapsed, revealing bare earth oozing behind. The stones have tumbled across the floor, barring passage, and if she is to continue then she will need to climb over them.

Climbing is not something achievable in the Temperley. She takes it off, blows the dust from one of the blocks, and carefully lays it on top.

Sabrina clambers over the obstruction, now bare-breasted but still wearing high heels to protect her feet.

The passage on the other side is as narrow as before, but it begins to slope subtly downward, and twists and turns in serpentine fashion, destroying whatever sense of orientation she had retained. The lantern is dimmer here, as if there was less oxygen. The slope steepens sharply, and now the twists become full circles: she is spiraling downward, plunging deeper into what feels to her to be the entrails of the earth.

The path straightens and flattens. It is warmer now, the result of being nearer molten magma, Sabrina imagines. Soon the passageway broadens, and she is at last able to stand without hitting her head. The walls here are no longer simple rough-hewn unfinished stone but instead smooth surfaced, and some are carved in low relief with symbols. She pauses to inspect them: a few are vaguely celestial—one appears to be a star, another with a tail could conceivably be a comet—but the others are completely unfamiliar to her, indecipherable.

She continues down the passage and comes to a door, thick timber bound with iron. She lifts the latch and pushes it open.

The room on the other side is not large, perhaps twenty feet square. It is lit with flaming torches mounted in wall sconces; she has no further need of the lantern, and places it on the floor—here not the paving stone of the tunnel, but instead a mosaic of some kind, Byzantine-like. The room is bare of furnishing. The air until now has been dry, but in this room a faint mist hangs, dulling the edges of vision, but not so much that she cannot see the startling sight in the center of the room.

Sabrina sees herself. Her eyes are closed, and her skin is tinged blue. She is naked, lying supine as if upon a table, but she floats unsupported, and tendrils of her hair gently waft, like marine creatures slowly undulating on a coral reef.

Sabrina remains standing in place and surveys the room for the source of what she assumes must be some sort of projection or hologram but, finding nothing, returns her gaze to the thing in the middle of the room.

She approaches and reaches out a hand. Her floating self is solid—no hologram—but cold; dead.

Sabrina stares for a long time. She decides that she will inspect this creature, her own corpse, to discover how she died, or perhaps how she herself will die. She begins at the feet and works slowly upward, her head low over the body so as to miss nothing. She finds no sign of wounds or puncture marks, indeed no blemishes at all—not even the now barely visible scar on her left knee, the result of a bottle tossed carelessly into long grass, and upon whose broken remnants she had received the cut as a small girl when running in pursuit of a ball; nor at the crook of her left elbow the more recent bruise from when she had her blood taken at Dr. Aran's office—this is herself in some sort of abstracted form, freed from the frailties of the flesh. She comes to the face.

Is this really me, she wonders, and recognition seems to momentarily retreat: the features are the same, indeed identical, but this creature is somehow unfamiliar to her, newly foreign, like reacquaintance with an old friend not seen for many years, only to discover that one no longer knows this person, nor particularly cares for their company.

She leans down very close, her nose brushing the creature's lips, and inhales deeply: if there is no visible wound then death might have been by poison, and perhaps she will smell it.

There *is* an odor, and she recognizes it: that same exotic smell she had first detected in the back of the Bentley, and then again on the Black Watch raincoat. She stands up straight and looks down upon her dead self. You did not die of poison, she thinks, you died of Bronaryre.

I am dying of Bronaryre. I will die of Bronaryre. I died of Bronaryre. *Ego morior, morieris, mortuus Bronaryrius.*

The creature's lips suddenly part and the tip of a tongue emerges to gently lick them. Then the eyes open.

Sabrina steps back. They stare at each other for a long moment in silence.

"I art thou, thou art I," the creature says, not as a pronouncement but merely an observation.

"Who are you?"

"I am the keeper of truths."

"How did you come to be here?"

"I am here because it is my destiny to be here. Why are you here?"

"I don't know."

The creature sits up, although sitting upon nothing, and then stands, facing Sabrina.

"You are here to be sanctified. You are being sanctified now. You will continue to be sanctified and when you have completed your consecration you will bring forth that which must be. This is your destiny; it is why you are here, and it is also why you are."

A pool of blood appears on the floor, fresher than that of the fowl earlier, rapidly growing, and soon it is inches deep, splashing in from some unseen source. The creature cups her hands to form a bowl, then bends her head and vomits blood into them. It overflows, joining that on the floor. She holds out her hands in a gesture of offering.

Sabrina leans forward and drinks from the cupped hands.

The creature reaches out and prints a single bloody palm print upon each breast.

A demon appears, large and fierce, red-scaled and rampant. He descends upon Sabrina, wrapping one clawed limb around her waist and the other her neck, taking her weight. Sabrina reaches out her right leg and plants her shoe firmly on the wall, burying her heel into a crack between blocks for purchase.

Her dead self watches her, without expression.

Sabrina bends backward. The blood rushes from her head, and then all becomes blackness.

# Third Circle

# Terpsichore

SABRINA WAKES UP WITH the sun streaming through the south-facing windows, illuminating the white marble horrors of the fireplace at the far end of her room so that it seems almost to glow—she forgot to close the curtains last night, but daylight has obviously not disturbed her sleep since, despite going to bed early the previous evening, she can tell from the slant of the sunlight that it must already be late morning.

She checks the time on the bedside clock and sees there the bottle on her nightstand, empty. She picks it up and, now that there is an abundance of light with which to read the faded print, studies the old label with the careless leisure of someone ensconced in a feather bed and feeling no particular need to get out of it. *Doctor Thoroughgood's Laudanum Admixture for the Inducement of Dormitive Restoration!* it gleefully announces, *Three Grains of the Extract of the Opium Poppy in Every Tablespoonful!*—it seems that Doctor Thoroughgood was the effervescent and emphatic French Connection of his day.

The empty bottle accounts for the good night's sleep, she thinks, and also the vivid dream during it—a result, no doubt, of a four-way combination of hallucinogenic opiates; dinner conversation descriptive of a mysterious Templar cellar; the presence when going to sleep of a fire-lit, demoniacally-inspired Jacobean fireplace; and an extended celibacy born of Sabrina's single-minded determination to earn her doctorate, one that had brooked no distraction.

She now understands why laudanum was so popular in the Nineteenth Century: such dreams must have come as a welcome respite to those repressed women in straitlaced Victorian England.

Sabrina reluctantly gets out of bed. The Temperley lies carelessly discarded on the bathroom floor: she was evidently too tired last night to bother hanging it. She goes out onto the terrace, enjoying morning sun on naked flesh, and hopes that the staff do not choose this moment to come and clean her room. She leans on the balustrade and gazes out over the parterre. It is empty: today is a Sunday, and so there will be no grounds staff.

It suddenly occurs to Sabrina that there might be an observation area on the roof, like a widow's walk, and she looks back up above her, hoping not to find that it is she who is now being observed. There is no widow's walk, but she discovers that embedded into the entablature crowning the house, directly below the cornice, is a frieze. It is not carved in relief but instead inscribed, apparently in Latin. Sabrina goes inside and returns with her new notebook. She transcribes the inscription:

QVOD SI MEA NVMINA NON SVNT

She supposes that the *V*s are really *U*s, which would make the meaning something along the lines of *when my something is not*, but she has no idea what that something—*numina*—might be. She puts aside the notebook and returns her gaze to the parterre. It is no longer totally unoccupied: strutting about in his usual spot by the corner nearest her room is the pheasant, highly colorful but peering about somewhat quizzically, as if wondering where all his friends got to.

Thinking of their fate reminds her that she is hungry; in fact, she is famished. She quickly dresses and heads downstairs before breakfast is finished.

THE DINING ROOM is unoccupied but the sideboard is still laid for breakfast. Judging from the emptiness of the chaffing dishes she is the last to rise this morning. There are no eggs or bacon or sausages left, but she finds that baked beans with mushrooms and grilled tomatoes make for a satisfying meal, especially with grainy toast slathered in plenty of butter and marmalade.

Ronson the butler enters.

"Good morning, Doctor. I trust that your room has proven satisfactory?"

"Very satisfactory, especially the bed—I hope that I haven't caused you to extend breakfast when you need to prepare for lunch."

"Not at all. I should explain that we don't usually serve lunch here at Temple Slaughter, at least not in the traditional sense. Mr. Bronaryre considers it an interruption, an unwelcome intrusion into the activities of the day. When there are guests at the estate we normally lay out sandwiches and so forth for those who do not share Mr. Bronaryre's beliefs or metabolism, a sort of early take on afternoon tea, but today not even that."

"What's happening today?"

"There is to be a play at the amphitheater this evening, ma'am, should the fine weather hold, and for which we will supply picnic hampers. That's why the house is empty: all the young ladies are up there now, preparing for the performance. In the meantime, is there anything that I can do for you?"

"Are there any newspapers?"

He shakes his head. "Another peculiarity of the preceptory: Mr. Bronaryre does not take in the newspapers. Nor are there any televisions or radios on the estate."

"Surely a redundancy in these days of wireless communication?"

"Ah, but you see we don't even have that: coverage is spotty enough out here in the countryside, but in an estate as large as this one, where the master rebuffs all approaches from the telecommunications companies wishing to install their devices, there is no coverage at all. The one thing we have is an old-fashioned landline telephone in the main hall, which anyone is welcome to use. I'm afraid that when it comes to communication with the outside world, Temple Slaughter Preceptory is still in the Edwardian era, but Mr. Bronaryre likes it that way."

The abundance of reference works in the library is now explained: there is no other way to look things up.

Malavalaya enters the room; Sabrina is not the last to rise after all. She is the definition of disheveled, eyes barely open, hair all astray, and wearing a fabulously embroidered but loosely tied Oriental robe, obviously thrown on in a hurry so as not to miss breakfast. She goes to the sideboard, quickly stacks a plate, then comes and sits opposite Sabrina.

"Paya, paya, what a night," she says, tucking into the toast with gusto.

"The party carried on late?"

"I was up till dawn," she says, in her curiously accented English. "We ended up going over to the Roman temple so as not to disturb anyone, and played what you might call a form of pin the tail on the donkey, but I was outnumbered three-to-one."

"I'll bet none of them were demons," Sabrina says to herself, realizing how absurd the boast is.

"What about you?"

"A quiet night," Sabrina lies. "I went to bed early," she adds, cleaving closer to the truth now.

Malavalaya emits an enormous yawn, stretching her arms up and her head back, a gesture which causes the robe to open sufficiently to reveal a single brown nipple that, with her body stretched taught, briefly appears to be yawning itself.

"What a lovely robe," Sabrina says.

"It's from Macau, as am I. My father was a Macanese witch doctor; my mother was a sorceress from Borneo—a natural pairing."

"Is Macau where you met Bronaryre?"

"Yes, he won us in a card game there."

"Won us?"

"Hippolyte and me: we came as a pair, and were valued at twenty-thousand patacas. This was back when it was still Portuguese; the Chinese authorities frown upon such things now."

Sabrina locates the telephone after leaving the dining room. It is in a booth set into the paneling at the far end of the main hall, accessed via a varnished wooden door embedded with small glass panels. The apparatus itself is a big black affair with a rotary dial, like a wall-mounted version of the one in Ravenscroft's office, and Sabrina wishes that she had someone to call, just for the pleasure of using it.

She steps outside. The E-Type is missing from its place by the portico: perhaps Bronaryre has gone to church to keep tabs on the other side. Sabrina can tell by the oil-stained gravel that it is the Jaguar's regular spot, or that of some other old car. A big black Bentley is parked beside it, looking identical to the one in New York, and then another Bentley, this one smaller, a two-tone coupe in silver and gray with a sweeping fastback tail: she wonders if the Devil got a bulk buyer's discount.

There is a scattering of half a dozen other vehicles, several of them sports cars but also a Range Rover and a big squared-off Land Rover with a heavily lugged spare tire attached to the hood and a large winch mounted on the front bumper, a vehicle that looks capable of crossing the Kalahari if required.

Sabrina walks out across the gravel to the middle of the forecourt, a position that will give her a pleasant perspective to look back upon the house. She comes to a halt and lifts her sunglasses.

It is very quiet. There is birdsong, and the occasional faint sound of people somewhere in the distance by the woods at the northern end of the estate, evidently the location of the amphitheater. She turns around to inspect the house. The inscription on the frieze continues on this side, as she had guessed it might, and she opens her notebook to write it down:

MAGNA SATIS DVBITEM HAVD EQVIDEM

Evidently, it is a fragment: the line must continue around the corner. To her right is the west wing, forming a long *L* leading off from the main house, and ending in a tower with an ornate gilded clock face at the top, something that makes an architectural virtue of utilitarian necessity (it is actually a water tower, Ronson told her, built high to ensure adequate pressure in the plumbing). To her left is the east wing, much shorter, so she heads in that direction, circling the house. Sabrina comes to the main terrace running along the south side, with the parterre spread out below. Above her on the top of the southeastern corner is her room.

The pheasant has disappeared—perhaps he has chosen to be less conspicuous following last night's feast, or maybe the harrier has returned. Sabrina transcribes the southern side of the inscription:

FLECTERE SI NEQVEO SVPEROS ACHERONTA MOVEBO

She walks the length of the terrace until coming to a point at the southwestern corner from which she will be able to see the fourth and final side, and looks up. The corner rooms here are Bronaryre's, if Ronson's description of his quarters as being at the other end of the hall is accurate—perhaps he prefers evening light over morning light, which seems a reasonable choice if you are the Prince of Darkness.

She transcribes the remainder of the inscription. Assuming that the east, being the direction of beginnings, would be the first line, it reads:

*quod si mea numina non sunt*
*magna satis dubitem haud equidem*
*implorare quod usquam est*
*flectere si nequeo superos acheronta movebo*

Sabrina knows or can guess at much of it, but her recollection of Latin conjugations and declensions is rusty, plus some words escape her entirely, and so the overall sense eludes her. If there was a wireless connection she would soon have the thing translated, but Sabrina supposes that she will have to work through it the old-fashioned way. She returns to the house and in the library locates a well-worn Latin-English dictionary.

The translation exercise turns out to be less successful than she had imagined. Some words, like *magna*, she does not need to look up, and others have a reasonably straightforward meaning, like *numina*, which turns out to be the accusative plural declension of *divine will*. But too often there are multiple meanings, so that s*atis*, for example, can be a conjugation of *serere*, to sow or plant, but it can also simply mean *enough*. The word *acheronta* does not appear in the dictionary at all. In the end, she finds that she has made little advance on unraveling the inscription.

Sabrina returns the dictionary to the shelves and decides that she will join the girls at the amphitheater to see if they need any help setting up.

She goes back up to her room to return the notebook and finds Polly tidying up.

"I thought you had the day off."

"It was this or church."

"Don't let the vicar hear you say that."

She is fetching her sunglasses when Polly cries out from the dressing room.

"My goodness, how did you get the dress so dirty?"

Sabrina freezes for a moment, but then forces herself to join the maid. Inside the dressing room, Polly is holding up the Temperley. The hem is ringed with what looks like dried blood.

DOWNSTAIRS IN THE main hall, Sabrina presses the butler call and Ronson soon appears.

"I'd like to go out," she says. "I wonder if I can have a car."

"Certainly, Doctor. I can have one of the lads take you in the Bentley, or if you'd prefer to drive yourself you can pick one of the others."

"I'll drive myself."

"Would you like the TVR so that you can take the top down?"

"Is the Range Rover available?"

"The Range Rover it is." He leaves her momentarily, soon returning with a set of keys and a map. "The petrol tank was topped up Friday. There's satellite navigation, of course, but here's a map just in case. Do you need any directions?"

"I'm going to Oxford."

"Then turn left out of the gate and just follow the signs—thirty-five miles; shouldn't take long. Registration and insurance papers are in the glove compartment. Remember to drive on the wrong side of the road."

WHEN SABRINA successfully turns left onto the road after leaving the estate, she has answered the first question whose purpose the journey was intended to establish: no one tried to stop her, and so she is not a prisoner at Temple Slaughter Preceptory.

The Oxford traffic is less bad than when she first arrived in the city, a passenger in Bronaryre's E-Type, just two days and what feels like a lifetime ago. How turned upside down her world has become in those intervening forty-eight hours, she thinks—whatever else one might say of the Devil, he cannot be accused of not living each moment to the full.

Sabrina comes in over Magdalen Bridge and slips down Merton Street and Magpie Lane into the little court behind the High. She half-expected to find the E-Type sitting there, as if Bronaryre had read her mind and was already ahead of her, but the reserved spot is empty and so she parks the Range Rover in it.

Mr. Collins is not on duty today, but the porter manning the lodge recognizes Sabrina and doffs his bowler in welcome as she passes through the main gate at Caiaphas. She rounds the northern side of the first quad and enters the chapel.

Sunday service is underway. With Trinity Term completed, Sabrina would have expected a mostly empty chapel, but the place is full and so as a latecomer she takes a little seat in the vestibule rather than force a space in the pews.

The service plods along. A hymn begins—Psalm 68, according to the hymn board—and Sabrina finds that she is familiar with the first line: *Let God arise, let his enemies be scattered.* It seems that, when inscribing the Oxford Crown, Charles I had borrowed from the Bible to express his sentiments concerning Cromwell. She is alarmed to find that the psalm is unaccompanied. However, following the closing benediction, the mighty organ above her begins to sound, as if from the heights of heaven itself. A few parishioners file out of the chapel, but most of the congregants remain seated to enjoy the post-service organ recital.

Sabrina recognizes the music, that same 'Fantasia and Fugue in G minor' that Wilkins had been practicing on Friday—played in the style of Schweitzer, naturally. The Bach proceeds for ten minutes and then, after a short pause, is followed by a second piece, more ominous than the first, and Sabrina briefly wonders if Wilkins has not decided to chance a repeat in the Wagnerian style after all. But she soon realizes that this is a different work, formal and orderly in its construction, yet the tone is brazen and relentless as if the composer were suffering an urgent but unredeemed sense of menace—suitable music, she realizes, for the conversation to come.

The piece ends and the congregation politely applauds, as if they had been attending a concert rather than a religious service—apparently they came not so much for spiritual comfort as for the free music, and Sabrina understands how a Jesuit interloper has come to be welcomed into this venerable bastion of High Anglicism: he fills the pews, even out of term.

Soon after the chapel empties Roger Wilkins comes down the stairs from the gallery, a sheaf of sheet music under an arm. Today, in addition to the clerical collar, he is wearing both a cassock and an academic gown, a sartorial representation of his twin—and surely often conflicting—allegiances. He spots Sabrina right away and comes over, smiling with pleasure.

"What did you think of that last piece?"

"Shades of Wagner."

"Indeed, although in fact it is more Bach: the Toccata and Fugue in D minor—most often heard today, I'm sorry to say, in the soundtracks of horror movies, right about when Dracula makes his first dramatic appearance. I was considering what you said the other day, and decided that perhaps these voluntaries could use a little more variety."

"Fitting music for the reason I'm here then."

"Which is?"

"I have two questions for you."

"Shoot."

"How would you identify the Devil?"

Wilkins laughs, until realizing that she is not sharing it. "You're not serious, are you?"

"Perfectly. Say you met someone who claimed to be the Devil, or whom you suspected of being the Devil, how would you know? Is there a secret question that he must always answer in a particular way, say, or—speaking of Dracula—something like no reflection in a mirror; or perhaps a telltale mark—isn't there a six-six-six thing?"

Wilkins studies Sabrina in perplexed silence for a long moment before responding.

"Sabrina, there's no such thing as the Devil."

"What?"

"There's no such thing. It's a myth."

"But how can you say that—surely *you* would be required to believe in the Devil?"

"I believe in *evil*, certainly—there is abundant evidence of it every day. But a leering fellow with a pitchfork and tail: no, of course not."

Sabrina steps back and crosses her arms in annoyance. "Well, that's just wonderful—of all the Jesuits in the world, I get the one who doesn't believe in the Devil. What are the odds?" The chapel is not quite empty—an usher, who has been collecting hymnals from the pews, stops and looks up at them. Sabrina steps closer and lowers her voice. "Don't they kick you off the team if you don't believe in this stuff?"

"I'm afraid it's not really a Christian doctrine: the general conclusion of comparative religious scholarship is that the concept crept in through Zoroastrianism. The Bible doesn't have much to say on the subject, you know; there's nothing in the Old Testament."

"How can that be? What about the Garden of Eden?"

"Technically a *serpent*—whether or not the serpent represents the Devil is a matter of interpretation."

"Okay, the Apocalypse, then?"

"A dragon or serpent—again, interpretation."

"But isn't the Devil an angel who rebelled, and was expelled from Heaven?"

"Yes, there's Lucifer. But nowhere in the Bible is it explicitly stated that Lucifer and the Devil are one and the same—he's a fallen angel, certainly, but the identification of Lucifer with the Devil is... extracanonical."

"Wasn't Christ supposed to have been tempted by the Devil?"

Wilkins nods. "Yes, I suppose everyone agrees on that part, but it is generally understood to be a parable or allegory, not to be taken literally."

"I can't believe that I'm standing here trying to convince someone wearing a clerical collar to believe in something that I don't even believe in myself."

"Sorry to disappoint you."

Sabrina sits, considering this response. Wilkins remains standing and eventually breaks the silence.

"There are always teeth, I suppose."

"Teeth?"

"Like a horse."

"I'm not following you."

"It's the way people estimate the age of a horse, by checking its teeth. The older the horse, the more ground down and discolored they will be—it's the origin of the expression, 'Don't look a gift horse in the mouth.'"

"And so?"

"And so, the Devil is presumably very old, right? You were asking for a way to check. That's a way: look at the teeth. If they're not worn with age, then no Devil, wouldn't you say?"

Sabrina leaves a long pause before responding. "I was hoping for something more theologically rigorous."

"As I said before, that side is not my strength."

Sabrina resumes her thoughtful silence, and eventually Wilkins prompts her. "You said that you had two questions?"

"Yes, I do. On the night Justice Scaglietti died, the night of the recital, who else was there?"

She can tell that the abrupt change of subject has surprised Wilkins, but he answers levelly enough.

"Between thirty and forty people, I would say. There was the soloist, a young woman with a Greek surname but who I think was English—I never spoke to her, but she introduced each of the *lieder*, and she had an English accent. The songs themselves were all in German: Schönberg, mostly. The pianist who accompanied her was an Oriental gentleman, Chinese, I would guess, and an excellent keyboardist, but I never spoke to him either. The arrangement for the evening was the recital to begin with and then the reception afterward—I suppose there were too many people to consider a full dinner party. Scaglietti pulled me aside for the private interview soon after the recital ended, and by the time we rejoined the others the reception was well underway. I spoke to an orthodontist and his wife—I can't remember their names, but he and Scaglietti had been at school together. There was a contingent from the Kennedy clan, and they passed by me briefly, in the way that political types do—careful to meet everyone, but engaging with no one. I left rather early, to catch the train back into town."

"Do you remember what any of the other people there looked like?"

"Not specifically. I had the overall impression of a well-heeled and worldly crowd, the sort you might encounter in a typical Upper East Side social gathering. And there was catering staff, of course. But the truth is that I didn't pay anyone much attention that night: during the recital my focus was on the performers, and afterward I was too disturbed by what the Justice had just told me to concentrate on other people."

Sabrina says nothing for a while, wondering if there are further questions she should ask but, unable to come up with anything, she stands to leave.

"I suppose there is one other person I recall," Wilkins says.

"Who?"

"When I went outside and began walking down to the front gate, there were the guests' cars parked on either side, and at one of them the driver was polishing the vehicle."

"What did he look like?"

"Well, that's what makes me remember: the driver wasn't a man, it was a woman. I was thinking what an unusual occupation that is for a woman, but she was definitely the driver because she was dressed in traditional chauffeur's livery: peaked cap and gray uniform, knee-high brown boots."

"Do you remember what sort of car it was?"

"Actually, she told me. I made a comment in passing—'You've got the shiniest car on the block' or something of the sort. I expected an equally innocuous reply, but instead she stopped polishing and stood up straight, as if my comment required careful consideration. She turned to me, serious-faced, and said, 'It is a Bentley.' She was quite striking but there was something slightly off-kilter about her; I wondered if she might not be simple. I said that it was a very impressive vehicle, and she said, 'My name is Hippolyte, which means unleasher of horses, and so you see it is quite appropriate that I should be the driver.' Odd response, don't you think?"

BACK IN THE parking lot and sitting in the Range Rover, thinking of what else she should do before returning to Temple Slaughter, Sabrina takes advantage of the available wireless signal to look up the inscription on the preceptory's frieze. The search engine quickly identifies it as a quote from the *Aeneid*, Book VII, whose Virgilian dactylic hexameters John Dryden had rendered into English heroic couplets of rhyming iambic pentameter:

*If native pow'r prevail not, shall I doubt*
*To seek for needful succor from without?*
*If Jove and Heaven my just desires deny*
*Hell shall the pow'r of Heav'n and Jove supply*

According to a footnote, that last line— *flectere si nequeo superos acheronta movebo*—whose sense might be better translated as *If Heaven will not answer, then to Hell I will apply*, had been used by Freud as the epigraph to his *Interpretation of Dreams*, something that feels vaguely coincidental to Sabrina, given the nature of her potent and vivid nightmare of the previous evening—one that might have been of interest to the author—but Freud's choice would have long post-dated the construction of Temple Slaughter Preceptory.

The E-Type is back in its usual parking spot when Sabrina returns to the preceptory. Upstairs in her room, she finds three objects waiting for her on the desk.

The first item is a flat wallet made of thick saddle leather, just three inches square, and secured with a strap. Inside it she finds the Oxford Crown—the Devil showing that he can be trusted, she thinks, even to returning objects he clearly covets. The second item is a printout of a long newspaper article whose subject is the Tate Rothkos. The third is an envelope. Inside it is a note, the strong cursive script as familiar to her now as the marbleized lining of the envelope.

*I had my bootmaker stitch up this pouch to protect my property while it unreasonably remains in your possession. As a lawyer, you will be fully aware that there is no legitimate ownership of a stolen object, regardless if received in good faith—a clear case of* caveat emptor. *Since my claim prioritizes that of the Ashmolean, I expect the coin to be returned to me when you have overcome your stubbornness on this subject—unwillingness to face facts squarely is the curse of humankind, and I hope for better from my Boswell.*

*To assist you in this latter duty I have provided you with an essay I came across some years ago—I have never met the author but I don't need to: he and I understand each other perfectly.*

*We are to enjoy a play tonight, prefaced with a short lecture. I propose that we meet beforehand in the Long Garden to finish that bottle of Physic Gin.*

*Bronaryre*

She takes the article and sits back on the sofa to read it. It is an extract from the *Guardian*. The author is Jonathon Jones, the newspaper's art critic, and begins by painting the scene on that morning in the winter of 1970 when Rothko was found dead, *the pool emanating from him on the floor of his studio measured 8ft x 6ft. That is, it was on the scale of his paintings. It was, to borrow the art critical language of the time, a colour field.*

Sabrina is soon immersed in the essay, a lively combination of story-telling and art criticism. But then she slowly comes to a stop.

According to Jones, Rothko had sailed to Italy after being given the Four Seasons commission, and in Florence he visited, and was deeply influenced by, Michelangelo's vestibule to the Laurentian Library. Rothko admitted as much: *He* [Michelangelo] *achieved just the kind of feeling I'm after—he makes the viewers feel that they are trapped in a room where all the doors and windows are bricked up, so that all they can do is butt their heads forever against the wall.*

Sabrina has seen that same room. At her school—'convent boarding school for foster girls,' they called it, but 'orphanage' was the unvarnished reality—the nuns had taken them to Italy when she was twelve, the purpose no doubt to inculcate the true faith in impressionable minds with a visit to holy headquarters.

In Florence they had dutifully done the sights, including the Basilica of San Lorenzo, curiously unadorned on the outside—just bare brick in seeming disrepair—but inside a Baroque gallery of monumental works, fitting for the favored church of the Medicis. She remembers the vestibule to Michelangelo's library clearly and, like Rothko, had found its narrow immensity overwhelming and claustrophobic.

It was the same feeling she had last night while wandering through the hidden Templar labyrinth in her dream, if it was a dream.

She goes downstairs to the library and locates a volume on Michelangelo. The photographs do not do the vestibule justice: there is no place to stand and properly capture that crushing weight: it is not photographable, she thinks: one has to stand in it and feel the place first hand. But there is no mistaking the colors: the somber grays of the steps and columns and pilasters, and beneath them the dark red porphyry of the floor, the shade of slowly congealing blood.

So that was where Rothko found his color palette, Sabrina realizes—both for the Four Seasons commission, and his own suicide.

She flips the page.

The Basilica of San Lorenzo holds a second set of Michelangelo masterpieces, located in the New Sacristy, which contains the tombs of the Medici, and the page she has turned to has photographs of a pair of sculptures from this room, figures carved atop a tomb, both naked, one male and the other female. Nominally they are *Dusk* and *Dawn*, but both lie back in what appears to be post-coital exhaustion, something that had shocked the twelve-year-old Sabrina, although the nuns seemed to like it.

The female figure, Dawn, is at once noble and earthy, a goddess having temporarily come down from Olympus to slum it among mortals. But it is the male figure that transfixes her, overmuscled and unrefined, a massive figure with huge hands, gazing without sympathy or humor, a contemplative but ultimately unforgiving creature.

His face is exactly that of the demon from her dream last night. Michelangelo has even carved his hair so that there are two bulges at the fore, budding horns reminiscent of his Moses, that correspond to the more developed pair adorning the head of the figure in her vision. Same physique as well, beneath the scales and claws: a brute too large to be human, all thick knotted muscle mass, and with hands capable of crushing bone.

Bronaryre—Devil or not—could have no way of knowing how deeply this sculpture had affected her as an impressionable girl, which means that last night was only an opium-induced nightmare after all: just an echo of a childhood experience, released from memory by the Rothkos, and forcefully returning in a drug-soaked dream.

The stain on the Temperley could be anything: the hem had been trailing on the ground all evening. And in any case in her dream she had not been wearing it at the time of her encounter in the labyrinth, so even if blood then not from that strange blood-soaked chamber in which she had encountered her own dead self.

Sabrina returns to her room and finishes the *Guardian* article while taking a leisurely bath. In the end, she agrees with Jonathan Jones's assessment of the Tate Rothkos:

*But this mystical Rothko is unapproachable. He is pompous, grandiloquent, asking to be cut down to size. For many visitors to Tate Modern—you can see them walking quickly past the best art in the place—Rothko is a closed case.*

So it had been for her: just colored rectangles, without genuine meaning. Now she sees the Rothkos for what they really are: an anguished and profoundly vivid vision of Hell.

THE LONG GARDEN AT Temple Slaughter Preceptory is walled—a common feature of English gardens, Sabrina is starting to realize, perhaps a reflection of the national character: that unwillingness to come out into the open, and manifested by a habit of language in which true meaning is implied rather than explicitly expressed.

She enters through a gated arch and sees at once that this is where the grounds staff indulge themselves. There are the marble statues and topiarized shrubs of a formal garden, but here the main show is the flowers: large beds of them on either side of the long central alley, hosting a dozen varieties, and now in early summer they are in glorious bloom, the evening air rife with their perfume. Most of the flower beds have little verdigris signs identifying the varieties, and Sabrina reads them as she strolls along—golden calendula, larkspur, St. John's wort, marigolds, amaryllis, an odd-looking flower called Jack-in-the-pulpit whose name makes sense when observed with a sufficiently willing imagination, bright red poppies, yellow-white asphodel, blue pearl hyacinths, and a strange flower called sea kale, with bunches of white blossoms perched atop tall reed-like stalks.

Sabrina thinks that the Long Garden must be bee heaven.

Bronaryre is sitting at a round table at the far end of the garden. He is wearing khakis and a white cotton shirt open at the collar; Sabrina is relieved that she selected a simple Liberty-print wrap dress, and opted for sandals and bare legs.

"Did last night's laudanum originate with those poppies?" she asks as she approaches.

Bronaryre looks up from the document he has been reading, extraordinarily fine-printed on long foolscap paper, and Sabrina thinks that he has very good eyesight for a four-hundred-year-old.

"No. I fund a small pharmaceutical research lab."

"Surely they're not permitted to provide you with a controlled substance?"

"I imagine not." He looks down at the paper in his hand. "Forgive me for a moment, but I must sign these. Perhaps you might entertain yourself for a few minutes in the garden."

Sabrina strolls back to the lone bed that did not have a sign identifying the varietal. The flowers here are red-petalled, vermillion at the base and gradually deepening into a deep maroon at the tip, so dark as to be almost black. They look something like a long-fingered hand reaching up, vaguely tulip-like but more elongated, and the stem is not tubular but gnarly and thorned, like a rose. She leans forward to smell one: it is highly perfumed, but not at all sweet, nor even particularly floral—something deeper and more earthy.

Sabrina would have looked them up if there was wireless service, but now while on the estate she no longer bothers carrying a phone.

These flowers would go well with her dress, she decides. She plucks one, and then a second—let that be a lesson to Bronaryre, sending her off to *entertain herself*—and removes the thorns to fashion them into impromptu boutonnières, opening the top two buttons of her dress to provide holes.

Meanwhile, Bronaryre now has a pen in hand—an elegant old-fashioned instrument, a fountain pen; perhaps the same one he used to write the note to her earlier today—and is signing the document. Bronaryre is a man for mechanical things: the pen, the Breguet, the E-Type Jaguar. Each in its way is a pinnacle of the past era, she supposes: the Industrial Age; the period immediately predating the current Electronic Age. They are all beautiful objects, aesthetically pleasing, and she decides that her initial instinct when first meeting him was correct: the Devil chooses to be surrounded by things satisfying to the eye and touch. She strolls back toward the table.

"What are these flowers called?"

"*Fleurs du mal*."

"Flowers of evil?"

"I was reading Baudelaire at the time."

"You mean *you* named them?"

"I created them. They are the result of an experiment."

"A hybrid?"

"Something like that. Genetic manipulation, certainly." He does not expand on this answer.

"You're not a fan of the internet, I gather."

"I'm not a fan of being under electronic surveillance. Which, among other things, is why my lawyer deals in physical documents, like this." He blows on the paper to dry the ink and then puts it into a box secured with a bright scarlet ribbon, a type she recognizes from Ravenscroft's office. "Opium I can get away with," he says, "but unfortunately there is no way to park a transatlantic ocean liner without marine insurance."

Sabrina sits in the chair across the table.

"Are we going to sail on schedule?"

"Yes. Tomorrow, I go to London to negotiate arrangements for the docking. A ship the size of the *United States* would normally dock in Southampton, but I want to begin from Greenwich—longitude zero degrees, and the home of Wren's great observatory: a suitable place from which to commence a marine odyssey. The ship's agents would normally see to such matters, but it's an unusual request and it is important to me that we begin properly, so tomorrow I will accompany them. What about you?"

"I have a meeting with Professor Pearson to review what it is that I'm going to teach."

"Then our leisure is at an end. I hope that you had an interesting day exploring the estate?"

"I discovered that you have an advertising slogan circumscribing your home."

"I do?"

"Four lines of Virgil."

"Ah, four lines of Dryden, but as it happens less than three of the original Virgil: from the masculine caesura in line 310 to the end of line

312, although I—which is to say Jameison à Bocages, the name that I was going under at the time—considered ending it at the last hephthemimeral caesura, so as to exclude the overt reference to the underworld."

"And what made you-as-Jameison-à-Bocages not do so?"

"I guessed that most people wouldn't realize that *Acheronta* is a Latinization of the river Acheron, thus signifying Hell, and those who figured it out wouldn't care. It turns out that I was right: in the more than two centuries since I rebuilt the house, no one has ever questioned the purpose of the inscription—once one avers that it is from the *Aeneid* all inquiry ends, as if the legitimacy of any Virgil quotation was beyond question. A common shortcoming: to mistake shibboleths for explanations."

"As is failing to squarely face facts, I'm led to believe."

"You're on a journey. Understanding will come to you."

"Not before a drink, I hope."

So chastened, Bronaryre stands and begins mixing.

"Gin and tonics this evening—suitable for a picnic."

"We're having a picnic before the play?"

"No, we're having a picnic *during* the play—one of the benefits of having one's own theater is that one can use it however one chooses, including having a picnic while the performance takes place."

"What play are we to see?"

"Something the girls wrote themselves. More a ballet than a play, I'm led to understand—an excuse for them to dress up and dance about. I hope you don't mind."

"Not at all. I used to do ballet at school." She can tell from Bronaryre's expression that this is something that has genuinely surprised him: Ravenscroft's research into his client's amanuensis was not so complete after all. "The nuns made me do it," she explains. "I was considered willful, and they thought that I needed physical activity to correct it. I had no aptitude for sports, but I was tall and skinny, so dance it was."

"Why were you considered willful?"

"There were several attempts at foster parent placement, all of them unsuccessful. On each occasion I found myself in the midst of people marveling at their self-sacrifice in tolerating my presence, along with the implicit demand that I was to demonstrate an appropriate level of gratitude. I would not have been able to articulate it at the time, but I sensed it well enough: my purpose was to polish their self-esteem. How I despised their pious conceit. Needless to say, the expected demonstrations of gratitude were not forthcoming. These occasions never lasted long—none more than three months—and I was soon sent back to the convent school."

"Was that any better?"

"Immeasurably so. A convent school for foster girls sounds Oliver Twistish, but in fact it was very different: I was happy there. How much easier it is to do what one is asked when the demand is merely institutional, not personal. It was highly regimented: we wore uniforms whose hems were required to touch the knee; you stood when the teacher entered the room and did not sit again until given permission to do so; there was no tolerance of inattention or talking in class—but after that they left you alone: there was no requirement, for example, to attend a neighbor's birthday party and pretend not to be bored. The discipline was strict: they still used corporal punishment, and I was on the receiving end of it a couple of times. The level of academic instruction was first-rate; my few brief acquaintances with public schools left me unimpressed, but the nuns took their avocation seriously. Sister Aloysius, who taught us Latin, could have given Cicero lessons—not that I've retained much of it: I couldn't translate your Virgil without looking it up. I was lucky to be at the convent school: it was their education that allowed me to earn the scholarships without which I would have gotten nowhere. And the nuns did not expect overt demonstrations of gratitude; they looked elsewhere for their reward."

"What was the form of corporal punishment?"

"Caning, bent over a desk, dress up, pants down."

"Discipline, or sexual fantasy?"

"If the latter then I must have been an unsatisfying subject: I made it a point of honor to never cry out, and bore my punishment in stoic silence."

"Do you still practice dance?"

"Not since I was sixteen."

"Perhaps you will take it back up."

"I think that unlikely."

Bronaryre completes the cocktails by adding a slice of lemon, cut with that same ebony-handled folding knife with which he had spiked her olive twenty-four hours ago. He hands her a glass, resumes his seat, and they drink without ceremony.

"I have a question," Sabrina says. "How can you have been a boy at the execution of Charles I? Doesn't the Devil always exist?"

"No, at least not in the sense you mean—a single manifestation—although I must admit that the question troubled me for a time, too, until I discovered the truth. But we are getting ahead of ourselves. I told you that understanding came to me in Hegelian fashion, that is, as the result of a conflict between thesis and antithesis, and last night I recounted the first part, the thesis, which I characterized as *light*. That took place in Oxford. Now I shall tell you about the other side, the antithesis, the *dark*."

"Where did that take place?"

"London."

Bronaryre pauses to take a long swallow before putting the glass on the table.

"Perhaps I should explain what happened to me after that world-shaking execution in 1649. That winter was especially severe, as I've mentioned, and one of its victims was my guardian, Colonel Hendrick. The widow was barely able to support her own brood, she certainly could not support me. It was arranged that I would be raised by the family of someone abler to bear the expense, someone whose fortunes had taken a sudden and dramatic turn for the better.

"Despite his silent and surreptitious assertion to me that day, Cromwell was not yet dictator—he did not become Lord Protector until 1653—and executive power was assigned to a Council of State, of which he was the president and dominant member. The first order of business was to prevent external war: the Continental powers—being mostly monarchies—were naturally horrified by the beheading of a king. There were many calls for invasion, not least by Charles's son, the future Charles II, now holding court in exile in France.

"The Council needed to present a vigorous justification for the regicide to help subvert this threat. That required a good Latinist, Latin being the language of diplomacy in those days, and if the Latinist was also fluent in French and Italian, then so much the better. And lastly, as you would expect, he had to be unimpeachably a supporter of the cause. There was one such man, a poet, who had suffered for his stubbornly oft-expressed views under the Royalists but always held firm, and he was appointed secretary to the Council. He was, of course, John Milton. Milton put aside his poetry—he was famously to take it up again after the restoration of the monarchy, when he was old and poor and blind but still as fierce as ever, and penned the greatest of English poems, 'Paradise Lost.' But in 1649, he instead took on the cause of defending the new republic. His official title was Secretary of Foreign Tongues."

"Did you become a republican, too—small-*r* republican, I mean? Are you as opposed to kings as your lawyer?"

"I certainly see few principles as self-evidently absurd as that of position by birth, and I suppose that I must have absorbed some of it in that house in Charing Cross, a pebble's toss from the present Trafalgar Square that we thrice circumnavigated the other day. However, despite the patriarchal Puritanism of the head of the household, it was a *ménage* dominated by women: Milton's wife, Mary, was very young—seventeen years his junior, and to me more of an elder sister than mother. The daughter Anne was a little younger than me, and there was a second daughter, another Mary, still just a baby. Add to them servants and wet nurses, and I had the impression that Milton was glad to be on his way to work each morning, no matter the weather. But in any case my tenure there was not long. Being a male, I had to be educated: as soon as I was old enough I was packed off to a boarding school, and returned only to the Milton household during holidays, experiencing each time a snapshot of what had become of them, rather than sharing in the contemporaneous reality of their disturbed lives."

"Which school?"

"Winchester: I am an Old Wykehamist—no doubt the oldest. By the end of 1649, the household had moved into apartments in Scotland Yard, and Milton had begun a long battle of vituperation with the leading Continental scholar of the time, the great humanist, Salmasius. Milton more than held his own in this contest, although he had already lost sight in his left eye; by the Easter of 1652, he was completely blind. His daughters and nephews, and occasionally me, became his amanuenses. A third daughter was born in that year, but the mother, Mary, did not survive the childbirth. Meanwhile, the commonwealth was coming undone: in 1653 Cromwell took full power, and England became a protectorate. Milton married again in 1656, but in 1658 she also died. So, too, in that same year did Cromwell, and thereafter the republic was doomed. It was then, as if to rage against fate, both personal and political, that Milton began 'Paradise Lost.'

"By the summer of 1659, it was clear that the monarchy would be restored, and parliament, now thoroughly royalist, was in the mood for revenge. That June, Milton's works were publicly burned by the London hangman. Milton went into hiding, but in October he was found and arrested. I was in my last year of school and planning to go up to Oxford. As an Old Wykehamist I should have gone to New College, but I was tainted by my association with the Roundheads, and only Caiaphas would accept me—it was a poor college in those days, mostly Welsh. Now, thanks to a settlement made as part of the agreement establishing the University of the SS *United States*, it is by far the most well-endowed college in Oxford."

"So you paid them back for what they did all those centuries ago," Sabrina says, *and which explains how you get access to the Dean's Garden*, she silently adds.

"It was an easy generosity: money doesn't mean much to me anymore, but again I'm jumping ahead. At the end of what was my last term at Winchester I returned to London as usual, except now I had no household to temporarily rejoin. The city had changed with the

Restoration—the taverns were full and the theaters had reopened following the republican interregnum: I suppose I must have retained from my early years a sense of Puritan reserve, and all around me it seemed that there was a flood of newly released wantonness—in any case, it was not the London of my childhood, and it seemed to me an unreal city.

"I found lodging in the Liberty of Savoy, which theoretically protected me from arrest by the Crown, but I was arrested anyway: as a young man associated with the great defender of the revolt, I was an obvious target. Strange to say, my imprisonment was not an unpleasant experience: indeed, my accommodations in the Tower were more comfortable than those in the Liberty; I had ample time to pursue my studies while sitting in the sunshine atop the parapets, and for assisting the Ravenmaster with his duties I was permitted to share his table—I can assure you that Beefeaters really do eat beef, and plenty of it.

"In the May of 1660, Charles II crossed the channel and resumed the throne: the Restoration was complete, to the general approval of everyone except John Milton. At the end of August, Charles issued a wholesale amnesty. The only exceptions were the documented regicides: those who had signed his father's death warrant. I was released. The timing was fortunate: I was able to go up to Oxford before Michaelmas term began, and so there was no delay in taking up my studies. Milton had already been released, and was now living in much reduced circumstances on Jewin Street, in St. Giles-without-Cripplegate.

"I spent that Christmas with him. Cromwell had paid Milton handsomely when he was alive, and the Whitehall apartments in which Milton spent most of the republican years were provided at the commonwealth's expense—he had even decorated them, before his total blindness, with paintings from the decapitated king's collection. All that was gone now, and Milton was poor. The decline of the commonwealth and the many deaths in the family were beyond his powers to have altered, but his own certainties did him no favors either: he refused to bend to the new reality, like the fallen angel of his poem: *All is not lost; the unconquerable Will*, as he put it, *And courage never to submit or yield*. He was not just the author of *Eikonoklastes*, he was himself an innate iconoclast: who but a natural contrarian would have used blank verse for the greatest epic in the English language? Shakespeare and Marlowe and others had mastered the form for drama, but no one used it for poetry, casting aside in a single gesture rhyme and feet and meter—even Shakespeare had rhymed his sonnets. Milton was a man who never crossed a bridge that he didn't wish to burn behind him, but his repeated misfortunes, deserved or otherwise, never deterred him; indeed, they only hardened him, made him all the more uncompromising, determined to seek retribution in the only way now available to him, via his pen: thus, 'Paradise Lost.'"

"I suppose that his stern religion would have made him a very difficult man to live with."

"I think that he had no genuine religion, at least not in the traditional sense. He professed a harsh, predestinarian Puritanism, to be sure, but I never once knew him to attend any church or chapel, or listen to any sermon. Nor did he practice any of those quasi-religious ceremonies in the household, as so many of them did: there were no family prayers or anything of that kind, and if he himself privately prayed he never gave any hint of it to me. His real religion was the sanctity not of gods but of the human mind. He admits as much in the first canto of 'Paradise Lost':

*A mind not to be chang'd by Place or Time.*
*The mind is its own place, and in it self*
*Can make a Heav'n of Hell, a Hell of Heav'n.*

"Those lines describe Satan. The theme is, of course, the loss of Paradise, but not just for Adam and Eve. Satan himself lost Paradise when he was cast from Heaven, and in the poem Satan feels not just the sting of that loss, but its unfairness, too. Why should knowledge be forbidden? Why should one not be permitted to question? There is a passage in Book VIII, in the Garden of Eden, where Satan invites Eve to consider the divine ban upon knowledge:

*Why then was this forbid? Why but to awe*
*Why but to keep ye low and ignorant,*
*His worshippers; he knows that in the day*
*Ye Eate thereof, your Eyes that seem so cleere,*
*Yet are but dim, shall perfectly be then*
*Op'nd and cleerd, and ye shall be as Gods*"

And now another Satan has just said it, Sabrina realizes, in another garden, and to another Eve, surely one as fascinated and confused with her surroundings—one whose eyes *yet are but dim*—as had been the mythical original. She wonders if Bronaryre is aware of the parallel.

"It certainly supports your assertion that he had no real religion: he seems to be making the case for the other side."

"Quite so. One of the criticisms of 'Paradise Lost,' right from when it was first published, is that Satan is represented not as the villain, but as the hero."

"You mean… you?"

"Yes. He knew who I was well enough: he told me plainly that Christmas of 1660, and he said that he had known it for years. I think that his disability did more than the unusual sharpening of the other senses that blindness is often reported to result in. It also sharpened what one might term the subliminal intellect, that ability to subconsciously process very small variations in sensory perception, and draw valid conclusions—a subtle art that I doubt would have come to him, a man of such certainties, unless he had been blind."

"Did this startle you, to be told that you were the Devil?"

"No, not at all."

"Not at all?"

"No—by then I had already figured it out for myself."

Bronaryre empties his glass before continuing the story.

"On that Christmas in 1660, Milton was up to Book IV. After a fine dinner of roast goose and a good Hermitage, both of which I had obtained and both of which we knew could not have been obtained legally, I took his dictation, as I had as a child. He looked at me and smiled—I should mention that although he was blind there was no visible evidence of it; he looked perfectly normal. But it was the smile that caught me short—such a rare thing to adorn that obdurate man's face—and I had the impression that he was actually seeing me, as if his sight had suddenly returned. That was when he told me that he knew who I was. Neither of us pretended that we didn't know exactly what he was talking about. Then he began his dictation. It was a declaration from Satan:

> *Knowledge forbidd'n?*
> *Suspicious, reasonless. Why should thir Lord*
> *Envie them that? can it be sin to know,*
> *Can it be death? and do they onely stand*
> *By Ignorance, is that thir happie state,*
> *The proof of thir obedience and thir faith?*

And then that crystal-clear statement of intent:

> *I will excite thir minds*
> *With more desire to know*

From that moment on, I knew my purpose: to excite men's minds with more desire to know."

Bronaryre continues to recite the poem, and Sabrina wonders if he has memorized all ten thousand lines. He has a voice suited to recitation, firm but not harsh, expressive but not histrionic, and she can feel the rhythms of the verse as he speaks, despite the lack of rhyme or meter and the endless enjambments as Satan, fallen but still loquacious, makes his case. Sabrina sits back and puts her feet up on a second chair, eyes closed, glass held two-handed in her lap. The dress falls away from her legs, and she realizes that undoing the buttons for the boutonnières has left more of her on display than she may have wished: she feels a little Eve-like herself. It becomes mesmerizing, a semi-dreamscape of seeming to float on the verse among the perfumed flowers in this Garden of Eden, listening to Satan reciting his splendid self-defense in firm empirical verse, noble and epic.

A distant bell rings, and Bronaryre comes to a halt. Sabrina opens her eyes.

"Is that for us?"

"*Send not to know for whom the bell tolls,*" Bronaryre says, switching poets.

"*It tolls for thee,*" she responds, completing the verse, and Bronaryre smiles, as rare an expression on his face as on that of his long-ago poet-guardian.

THE AMPHITHEATER AT Temple Slaughter Preceptory is cut into the side of a defile leading down toward the River Windrush. Stone steps and benches curve in an arc around and above the proscenium, but unlike a traditional amphitheater there is grass-covered ground between the stone seats, little half-hillocks connecting each level with the row above, and forming a natural bolster on which viewers may lie back while watching the show. It is small, just a dozen or so tiers, and is surrounded by forest. It feels curiously isolated, as if set apart from the rest of the world—an intimate little arena suitable, Sabrina thinks, as a setting for art that invites imagination to run wild.

The bell is a big one, two feet in diameter, and housed in a campanile off to the side of the stage. A stagehand continues to pull on the bell rope, calling attendance in rhythmic somber tones.

There are thirty or forty people in the audience: those students who are not participating in the performance; Malavalaya and her band of admirers; several others that Sabrina recognizes from the dinner last night; plus a pair of curious squirrels, quietly chewing nuts while looking on from the far side at the edge of the wood. At the top of the theater, laid out on trestle tables, are picnic hampers, rugs, cushions, tea candles in sand-blasted glass bowls, and a big galvanized tin tub filled with ice and bottles of champagne. Bronaryre grabs a hamper and champagne; Sabrina gathers the cushions, candle, and rug. They settle themselves a third of the way down.

The bell stops tolling as the sun dips below the treetops, leaving the sky still a clear pale blue, but the amphitheater is now in shadow. The bell-ringer disappears behind the stage, and the silence is ripe with anticipation.

Bronaryre pours champagne. Sabrina lies back and eats a sandwich—grainy country bread filled with cheese, chutney, and smoked ham carved straight from the bone.

Two girls emerge from backstage carrying a large blackboard mounted on a frame and deposit it stage-left. They disappear for a moment before returning with a second blackboard, similar to the first but this one is covered with a cloth. They place it stage-right, and then fetch a third blackboard, also covered, this time placed center-stage.

A spotlight comes on, illuminating the first blackboard, which is blank.

A man appears and mounts the stage from the steps at the side. Sabrina was briefly introduced to him last night; she cannot recall his name but remembers that he is a fellow at Christ Church. He wears an old-fashioned suit, and his hair is cut in a curious bob: he gives the impression of being a somewhat effete dandy, an effect that is not helped when he begins to speak, for he has a prominent stutter.

"G-g-good evening. My name is D-D-Dodgson, Charles Dodgson, and I would like to talk to you tonight about the number n-n-nine."

He writes the number *9* on the blackboard in white chalk.

"I wonder if anyone can v-v-volunteer a common use of this splendid number?" He gazes out at the audience with expectation. A short silence is eventually broken by one of the shyer girls, offering an answer in the form of a question.

"Nine lives of a cat?"

"Yes, indeed—very good. Now, any others?

"'Revolution 9,'" offers another girl, "from the White Album," she adds. This does nothing to resolve Dodgson's obvious puzzlement, and he moves on without comment.

"Surely we have one or two Greats scholars with us tonight?"

"I think you must mean the Muses," someone responds.

"Indeed, I do. There are, of course, n-n-nine Muses, and is it not curious that, when seeking to explain the very wellspring of human creativity, the Ancients conceived of it as being ninefold. Now, what about in cosmology?"

"Nine planets!"

"Exactly: there are nine planets: Mercury, Venus, Earth, Moon, Mars, Jupiter, Saturn, Uranus, and Neptune." The inclusion of the moon draws a few chuckles. "And is it not remarkable that the Ancients, who knew nothing of Uranus and Neptune, nevertheless still conceived of the cosmos nonologically: they imagined that the earth was at the center of a series of transparent spheres in which were embedded the planets then known to them, plus one for the sun and another for the stars: nine layers in all. The *composition* has changed, but the *number* has remained the same."

And perhaps equally curious, Sabrina thinks, is that when Pluto was capriciously demoted by some self-styled astronomical arbiters, a replacement 'Planet IX' was soon discovered, even if only by inference from its gravitational effect.

"Now," Dodgson continues, "what other examples can we come up with?

Bronaryre leans over and says, "You've got one, haven't you?" Sabrina does, and so prompted she puts aside her sandwich and speaks up.

"The nine Justices of the U.S. Supreme Court."

"Is that so? Thank you, Dr. Lancaster."

She turns back to her champagne and catches Bronaryre's expression, as superficially neutral as always, but something about it—perhaps the cast of an eye or the turn of his mouth—makes Sabrina think that her answer was not the one he was expecting. She tries to think of what else it could have been but can come up with no candidates.

On stage, Dodgson continues. "I believe that there is at least one other significant use of the number nine that we have not yet identified. Are there any medievalists in the audience?" and then, adding as a hint when no response is forthcoming, "Proto-Renaissance Italians of the T-T-Tuscan persuasion…"

"The nine circles of Hell," someone says.

"Why, yes indeed, sir, precisely so. In his *Divine Comedy,* the great Dante Alighieri conceived of the Inferno as a series of circles, *nine* in number. And so now we see how basic the number nine has been in the Western canon: whether in imagining the Heavens, or Hell, or the fountainhead of human creativity, when describing the fundamentals of existence Man has consistently reverted to the number nine. Why should this be?

"Well, to begin with, the number nine has an integer square root, and not just any old integer square root, but the number three, surely a blessed number given it is that of the Trinity, which should impress everyone, except of course those at B-B-Balliol." Dodgson smiles broadly, delighted by his *double entendre*—Balliol and Trinity have famously feuded for centuries—and there is appreciative laughter from the audience.

"But here is a curious feature: let us add nine and nine, and we get eighteen. Now, sum the digits—the one and the eight—and what do we get? Nine again, back to where we started. Very well, let us try with three nines instead. That's twenty-seven. Now we add the two and the seven and… Oops: here we are back at nine again. Is there no escape? Let's see, four nines equals thirty-six. Three and six, oh dear: back at nine. Five nines: forty-five, no: that's no good. Six nines: fifty-four—no, still at nine. Seven nines, sixty-three—oh, blast!"

The audience is laughing with him now, enjoying his inability to escape the accursed nine.

"Enough of this hesitant pussy-footing about, I say! Let us do three thousand, two hundred and fifty-six nines." He writes it on the blackboard.

*3,256 x 9*

"Now, let's see." He scratches his chin comically, as if doing the calculation mentally, which earns a few titters, and then starts counting on his fingers, which gets a full laugh. "Why, that's twenty-nine thousand, three hundred and four." He begins writing it on the blackboard, but then pauses and looks over his shoulder at the audience. "But you'd already figured that out, hadn't you?" He finishes writing the product.

*29,304*

"Let's sum the digits. Two plus nine, that's eleven. Add the three: fourteen. Then four: that's eighteen."

*18*

"Now all we need do is add that one and eight and... Oh, goodness gracious, here we are again!" He throws down the chalk in mock frustration, and Sabrina thinks that this Christ Church don could have had a stage career as a comic actor, in the mold of a Stan Laurel.

"As it turns out, there is no escape: no matter how many nines we do, the sum of the digits will always regress to nine. No other n-n-number exhibits this curious attribute, and I would hazard a guess that Dante decided on *nine* circles because of its distinctive qualities, like this one, as well as its being a perfect square of the Trinity. But I will go further.

"Dante completed the *Divine Comedy* in the year 1320. A century earlier, Leonardo Fibonacci of Pisa—a fellow Tuscan, and someone with whose work Dante would have been well acquainted—had discovered another curious facet of number theory. Let us begin at the two most fundamental of concepts: those of nothingness and unity." He writes the numbers zero and one on the board.

*0 1*

"Now add the two numbers together, and we get one. Then again add the last two numbers, and we get two."

*0 1 1 2*

"Keep adding the last two numbers, and we form a sequence, like this."

| | | | | | | | | | | |
|---|---|---|---|---|---|---|---|---|---|---|
| *0* | *1* | *1* | *2* | *3* | *5* | *8* | *13* | *21* | *34* | *55* |

"Now take the ratios of each pair."

| | | | | | | | | | | |
|---|---|---|---|---|---|---|---|---|---|---|
| *0* | *1* | *1* | *2* | *3* | *5* | *8* | *13* | *21* | *34* | *55* |
| *0* | *1/0* | *1/1* | *2/1* | *3/2* | *5/3* | *8/5* | *13/8* | *21/13* | *34/21* | *55/34* |

"And convert them into decimal notation." Dodgson walks across the stage to the far blackboard and, with a theatrical flourish, whips away the sheet to reveal the resulting computations already completed beneath.

| | | | | | | | | | | |
|---|---|---|---|---|---|---|---|---|---|---|
| *0* | *1* | *1* | *2* | *3* | *5* | *8* | *13* | *21* | *34* | *55* |
| *0* | *1/0* | *1/1* | *2/1* | *3/2* | *5/3* | *8/5* | *13/8* | *21/13* | *34/21* | *55/34* |
| *0* | $\infty$ | *1* | *2* | *1.5* | *1.6667* | *1.6000* | *1.6250* | *1.6154* | *1.6190* | *1.6176* |

"Is this not a beautiful series?" he asks. "Look at it: all the universe encompassed by the first few items: nothingness, infinity, singularity, duality, division. But then look at what happens as the series continues. The variation mysteriously reduces: it starts narrowing down. Now let's see how that continues as we extend the series."

Sabrina thinks that Dodgson must have very full classes, since he obviously has a flair for lecturing, and now that he is enthusiastically into his subject the stammer has disappeared.

With a single dramatic thrust, Dodgson rotates the blackboard, which is hinged about the horizontal axis, revealing on the other side the same Fibonacci series, but with two additional rows.

| | | | | | | | | | | |
|---|---|---|---|---|---|---|---|---|---|---|
| *0* | *1* | *1* | *2* | *3* | *5* | *8* | *13* | *21* | *34* | *55* |
| *0* | *1/0* | *1/1* | *2/1* | *3/2* | *5/3* | *8/5* | *13/8* | *21/13* | *34/21* | *55/34* |
| *0* | ∞ | *1* | *2* | *1.5* | *1.6667* | *1.6000* | *1.6250* | *1.6154* | *1.6190* | *1.6176* |

| | | | | | |
|---|---|---|---|---|---|
| *89* | *144* | *233* | *377* | *610* | *987* |
| *89/55* | *144/89* | *233/144* | *377/233* | *610/377* | *987/610* |
| *1.618182* | *1.617978* | *1.618056* | *1.618026* | *1.618037* | *1.618033* |

| | | | | | |
|---|---|---|---|---|---|
| *1,597* | *2,584* | *4,181* | *6,765* | *10,946* | *17,711* |
| *1,597/987* | *2,584/1,597* | *4,181/2,584* | *6,765/4,181* | *10,964/6,765* | *17,711/10,964* |
| *1.618034* | *1.618034* | *1.618034* | *1.618034* | *1.618034* | *1.618034* |

"We see that the series soon converges to a single number which, when rounded to six decimal places, is 1.618034. Is this not strange: why would a series, which had begun by spanning the vast breadth from nothingness to infinity, happen to converge at all, and, if so, why to this particular number? The series fascinated Fibonacci when he came upon it, and he published the results in 1202, in the *Liber Abaci*—literally, the book of calculations—a work which not only described the sequence that now bears his name, but also introduced into Europe the Arabic numbers that we use today. Until the *Liber Abaci*, Western Europe was constrained by clumsy Roman numerals.

"And what about this number that is approximately 1.618034? What makes it so special? The Ancients had a vague awareness of it: to them, it was the mysterious 'Golden Ratio,' a number representing perfect symmetry, and all the more baffling because it could not be clearly grasped, for they had no concept of irrational numbers. That did not stop them from using it: Euclid in geometry; Vitruvius in architecture; but it wasn't until Fibonacci that the thing could be precisely pinned down. Three centuries after Fibonacci, another Leonardo, Leonardo da Vinci—also hailing from that same region of the Arno valley so fertile in soil and mind—illustrated a book dedicated to this number: Luca Pacioli's *Divina Proportione*: literally 'divine proportion.' It was not until Johannes Kepler that the link between the Fibonacci sequence and the Golden Ratio was clearly defined. However, until tonight, I don't believe that any connection with Dante's *Inferno* has ever been identified.

"Now, as I hope to demonstrate, Dante did more than just conceive of Hell as nine circles. Some of the circles were themselves subdivided, one into rings, another into rounds, a third into *bolge*—that is, into ditches—the last of which was further subdivided into three categories. And here is what it looks like."

Dodgson goes to the central blackboard and, like a magician completing a particularly clever trick, removes the covering sheet, revealing Dante's Inferno.

# **Dante's Inferno**

| | | | | | | |
|---|---|---|---|---|---|---|
| Circles: | 1 | Upper Hell | Incontinence | First (Limbo) *(after crossing Acheron)* | | |
| | 2 | Upper Hell | Incontinence | Second (Lust) | | |
| | 3 | Upper Hell | Incontinence | Third (Gluttony) | | |
| | 4 | Upper Hell | Incontinence | Fourth (Greed) | | |
| | 5 | Upper Hell | Violence & Bestiality | Fifth (Wrath) *(in the River Styx)* | | |
| *(Dis)* | 6 | Lower Hell | Violence & Bestiality | Sixth (Heresy) | | |
| | 7 | Lower Hell | Violence & Bestiality | Seventh (Violence) | Ring 1 | Against Neighbors |
| | | | | | Ring 2 | Against Self |
| | | | | | Ring 3 | Against God, Art & Nature |
| | 8 | Lower Hell | Fraud & Malice | Eighth (Fraud) | Bolgia 1 | Panderers & Seducers |
| | | | | | Bolgia 2 | Flatterers |
| | | | | | Bolgia 3 | Simoniacs |
| | | | | | Bolgia 4 | Sorcerers |
| | | | | | Bolgia 5 | Barrators |
| | | | | | Bolgia 6 | Hypocrites |
| | | | | | Bolgia 7 | Thieves |
| | | | | | Bolgia 8 | Counselors of Fraud |
| | | | | | Bolgia 9 | Sowers of Discord |
| | | | | | Bolgia 10 | Falsifiers: |
| | | | | | | Category 1: Falsifiers of things (alchemists) |
| | | | | | | Category 2: Falsifiers of persons (imposters) |
| | | | | | | Category 3: Falsifiers of money (counterfeiters) |
| | | | | | | Category 4: Falsifiers of words (perjurers) |
| | 9 | Lower Hell | Fraud & Malice | Ninth (Treachery) | Round 1 | Traitors to their kindred |
| | | | | | Round 2 | Traitors to their country |
| | | | | | Round 3 | Traitors to their guests |
| | | | | | Round 4 | Traitors to their lords |
| | | | | | Round 5 | Traitors to God |

"Now, firstly you will observe that Dante divides Hell into two parts, Upper Hell and Lower Hell. For the section of the Inferno that lies beyond the *Fifth* Circle, Lower Hell, Dante has a special name, 'Dis.' You also see on the second blackboard that in the Fibonacci sequence, it is at the number *five* where the ratio no longer derives a basic concept—nothingness, infinity and so on—but instead begins moving toward the Golden Ratio. This is Dante's first hint that he has Fibonacci in mind. Dante further distinguishes Dis by separating it from Upper Hell by the River Styx, a signal that we are now entering new and uncharted territory. You will also note that it is in Lower Hell—this 'Dis'—that all the strange subdivisions occur.

"Now, let us examine the first circle in Dis. It is the Sixth Circle, reserved for *heretics*. Dante is warning us here that we are crossing from the trivial, the minor sins of Upper Hell, into more serious ground, and that a very great *heresy* lies ahead.

"We progress to the Seventh Circle, and the subdivisions begin. This Circle is divided into three Rings: Ring One to begin with—transgression against neighbors—so the number *1*." He writes it on the blackboard.

*1*

"Plus a second Ring—transgression against self—so another *1*, and which brings the total transgressions to *2*."

*1  1  2*

"Plus a third Ring, so *3*, but this Ring itself has three transgressions—against God, art, and nature—and so the total number of transgressions is now *5*."

*1  1  2  3  5*

"And so the sum of divisions—that is, transgressions plus Rings—is now equal to *8*. Thus we have arrived at the first numbers of the Fibonacci sequence."

*1 1 2 3 5 8*

"We move on to the Eighth Circle. In the Eighth Circle there are nine undivided *Bolge* plus the four Categories of the tenth *Bolgia*, for a total of thirteen items."

*1 1 2 3 5 8 13*

"And then, in the Ninth and final Circle, we simply sum all the divisions of Dis: three Rings in the Seventh Circle; nine undivided Bolge plus four Categories in the Eighth; and finally the five Rounds of the Ninth Circle, for a total of twenty-one."

*1 1 2 3 5 8 13 21*

"And so there we have it: the Fibonacci sequence, revealed in all its naked splendor, and suddenly Dante's many awkward and rather artificial divisions and subdivisions make sense. We have arrived at the great heresy that he hid inside the *Divine Comedy:* the heresy that Perfection—represented by Divine Proportion, and described by the Fibonacci sequence—is embedded in the ultimate Corruption, which of course is Hell itself. Now, to understand the weight of this heresy we must recall that in the medieval world of Dante's time, men believed that all that was human was corrupt, tainted by original sin, and that the purpose of life was to reach redemption through faith. Faith was the only path to Heaven, which is to say, to Perfection. This is the secret proposition of the *Divine Comedy*: we do not need to entrust our destiny to faith, we can use our minds instead. Divine Proportion does not require divine revelation: it can instead be attained by mathematics, a product of the ingenuity of supposedly tainted Man. Or, to put it in more modern terms, do not look to the heavens for the way forward, humankind, find it in yourself instead.

"So, ladies and gentlemen, in as much as a humble mathematics don may presume to the role of literary critic, I will assert that Dante Alighieri constructed his Hell based not just on the number nine, but also on the Fibonacci sequence, and he did so as a clarion call to his fellow man. Yes, it was all carefully wrapped up in a coating of protective orthodoxy—Dante did not wish to burn for his beliefs—but it was there, available to those whose intellects were equipped to see. We do not need faith, he is saying, we can find perfection in ourselves: just look at these numbers, defining perfection, derived not from the heavens but from the mind of my Pisan cousin, Leonardo Fibonacci. And, when you consider it, we can surely guess at Dante's reservations regarding the church by those with whom he populated his *Inferno*, including a friar, an archbishop, and no less than three popes. But perhaps the time has come to see this Inferno for ourselves." He opens his arms in a gesture of introduction.

"Ladies and gentlemen, welcome to Hell."

Dodgson leaves the stage to the appreciative applause of an audience surprised that they should have found a mathematics lecture entertaining, although no one would have wished it any longer. Beside her, Bronaryre picks a bright green Granny Smith from the picnic hamper, polishes it briefly on his khakis, and then loudly bites into it, tearing away a third of the apple's crisp flesh with a single mouthful: there is nothing wrong with those four-hundred-year-old teeth.

Dusk has gradually faded while Dodgson delivered his lecture, and now at its conclusion night has fallen, the only illumination coming from the candles and theater lights. The latter go dim, leaving the stage in darkness.

Music begins, not from directly in front but off to the side, and Sabrina sees that in the shadows to the right of the stage a string quartet has gathered. All four musicians are young women—students—but however young they may be it quickly becomes apparent that their standard of play is concert-level. The music begins with the viola, emphatically stating the theme in a minor key, and then the others join in, but the viola remains dominant, weaving in and out of the other three in tense, unresolved agitation: suitable music, Sabrina thinks, to accompany a descent into the underworld.

A spotlight hits the stage, illuminating a single figure. She is clad in toga-like classical attire, her hair up and secured with a golden fillet, and shod in what appear to be golden sandals but which Sabrina can see are actually ballet slippers secured at the ankles with gold satin ribbon. It takes a moment for Sabrina to realize that beneath all the theatrical make-up she recognizes the performer: it is Penelope de Vere, but a different Penelope now, confident and striking, a world removed from the brash eager girl at the Explorers Club. This effect is aided by the thin material of the toga, not quite opaque under the harsh glare of the spotlight.

She remains perfectly still, staring out above the audience.

A second girl emerges. She wears a white collared shirt with a bow tie, the sleeves rolled to the elbows and further secured by elasticized metal bands, old-fashioned men's trousers cut high at the waist and secured with suspenders, plus a thin, Clark Gable-like mustache. A microphone drops from the darkness above, which she grabs and uses to announce proceedings.

"Ladies and gentlemen, tonight, in nine rounds, for the heavyweight championship of the eternal soul, in the corner of Blessed Light, Beatrice!" She pronounces the name in the Italian manner—bee-ah-TREE-chay—apparently in this interpretation of the *Divine Comedy*, the lifelong object of Dante's devotion will be substituted for the poet himself.

The audience cheers and whistles. De Vere briefly clenches both hands above her head and bounces on her toes, the way a boxer might, before resuming her stationary pose.

"And, in the corner of Sinister Darkness, that famed agent of damnation, The Unspeakable One!"

A second spotlight comes on, illuminating Sesuna. She wears a man's dinner suit, complete with tails, top hat, and walking stick, and leans upon this last in a casual, self-confident pose while smoking a cigarette in a long thin ebony holder.

The crowd, prompted by the other girls hiding behind the stage, boo loudly. Someone hisses, but all the fuss only serves to amuse The Unspeakable One.

A fourth figure comes on stage, dressed in a sequined bodysuit with tights and high heels. She struts across the stage while holding above her head a sign bearing a large number *1*, announcing the round number in the manner of a prize bout.

A bell is rung, the supernumeraries leave the stage, and the quartet resumes playing.

The show gets underway with a *pas de deux* in which Penelope performs traditional ballet moves while Sesuna, sassy and taunting, dances free form around her. Sesuna is as handy as Astaire with the stick, using it successively as a prop, baton, and finally cane, employing it in this last mode to deliver, with exquisite timing, an audible smack to the Blessed One's behind as Penelope passes her *en air* while performing a *grand jeté*. At the conclusion a video begins, projected onto the background, showing the two of them in a punt in precisely the same pose as they ended the dance, probably filmed on the Cherwell but no doubt meant to represent crossing the Acheron. Charon is played by a Japanese girl in a sailor's suit, and who while the film runs comes on stage live to perform a series of cartwheels from one side to the other.

The performance proceeds: part ballet, part pantomime, part *Commedia dell'arte*, part gymnastic demonstration, part Radio City Rockettes, part psychedelic circus, part haute-couture fashion event, part Bedlamesque vaudeville, part Grand Guignol horror show. There is a progression of scenes, with background video filling out the sparse stage scenery, loosely depicting the various sins of each circle of the Inferno: a strip club for the Second Circle, Lust; an obscene version of the mass for the Sixth, Heresy; a lush Victorian house of ill repute, all satin and lace, for the Eighth, Fraud, the first *bolgia* of which features panderers and seducers. The Seventh Circle, Violence, features the two girls Sabrina had seen on the lawn when first arriving at the manor, practicing what she had thought at the time was kick-boxing. Virgil never appears as cicerone; instead Sesuna as The Unspeakable One acts as Beatrice's guide/tormentor in the Netherworld. Each round/circle is announced by the ringmaster, but otherwise there is no spoken word: just posturing and mime, music and costume, gymnastics and dance.

In the strip club scene of the Second Circle there had already been two girls bare-chested but for pasties, the tassels of which they had set twirling with the careful coordination of synchronized swimmers, but by the Eighth Circle any notion that this play would be condoned by the university authorities has been dispensed with: most of the courtesans wear tight corsets with breasts exposed, two perform for a 'customer' wearing nothing but pearls.

At the conclusion of the Eighth Circle scene the stage is left in momentary darkness. When illumination resumes it is not from stage lights but lanterns, lining the front of the stage with their reflectors facing rearward, bathing the final scene in dancing golden light. The music resumes, that same grave but forceful *agitato* that had introduced the play. On the backdrop a series of sparklers begin to light up and, when they are all aflame, spell out Dante's famous exhortation at the gates of Hell: *Abandon all hope, ye who enter here.*

Beatrice comes on stage. Penelope has discarded the toga and now, besides ballet slippers, wears nothing but a single gold-colored body-hugging leotard—or perhaps not even that, just body paint: it is hard to tell in the low lamplight. Either way, the result is to cover her head-to-toe in a glittering gilt sheath that reminds Sabrina of the cellar grill.

The Unspeakable One comes in from the other side. Sesuna is now covered in a coating of shining black latex, turning her svelte body into something as smooth as a river rock, like an unusually slender Henry Moore, almost asexual in its lack of definition or detail, despite the nakedness.

The switch to lamplight is explained: harsh theater spots might have revealed imperfections, but in the soft glow of the lamps it is possible to imagine them as abstractions, as unblemished ideals—personifications of Dante's hidden heresy: perfect forms arising from a corrupt Hell.

The two dance, and Sabrina sees that both of them have held back until now, saving their best for last: Sesuna displaying her athleticism to the full; Penelope, sustained technical excellence—she must have trained for years. It ends with them both spinning side-by-side *en pointe*, faster and faster, matching the ever-increasing tempo of the music until they seem almost to blur.

Then suddenly all the lights extinguish, and the music devolves into discord. Behind the stage drums and cymbals sound irregularly, and an overamplified electric guitar is brought close to a speaker, causing a screeching feedback squeal. There are indistinct crashing sounds, and Sabrina wonders if they are prerecorded, or if the girls had prepared actual stacks of plates and china and glassware backstage.

In any case, the meaning is clear: in the end, Chaos reigns.

The last of the noise echoes away. A gong sounds in resolution, and Sabrina wonders if they are quoting from the 'Bohemian Rhapsody' that they had been singing and dancing to the previous evening.

The lights come back on and the players mount the stage. Penelope and Sesuna are now robed. The audience is not large but the loud cheers and whistles and applause make it clear that they enjoyed the show.

The quartet is illuminated and the players stand to make their bows. Sabrina turns to Bronaryre.

"That was something well beyond the usual undergraduate romp, don't you think? At least off-Broadway level."

"Fit for the Acropolis itself, although I would have wished they had expanded the catastasis."

"Catastasis?"

"The ending: the third part of a classical tragedy. It begins with *prostasis*—an introduction, usually a speech in ancient Greece but in our case the Fibonacci lecture; then *epistasis*—the main action, which was the tour of the underworld; and finally *catastasis*: the climax. There wasn't much in the way of catastasis, but this is a common problem, and since the word has the same root as *catastrophe* you can see how things are usually resolved: from Sophocles through Shakespeare, pretty much the entire cast ends up slaughtered. Here, they relied mostly on the music for resolution."

"What was that piece they played at the start, and then again at the end?"

"Vaughn Williams," he replies, and Sabrina had somehow sensed that Vaughn Williams was going to be the answer. "The 'String Quartet No. 2 in A minor,' which has an unusual subtitle: 'For Jean on her birthday.'"

"Who's Jean?"

"Jean Stewart, who was the viola in the Menges Quartet, the musicians who premiered the work."

"A little macabre for a birthday gift."

"It was the technical challenge of playing it that was the gift. As for the content: it was premiered in October 1944. The D-day landings had been successful, and at last the end of the great struggle was in sight. It was a time for review, for summing up. The work was premiered in London, at the National Gallery, which K. Clark was then running. Like St. Paul's, the National Gallery had miraculously survived the Blitz, but much of London lay in ruins. The paintings had all been packed off to the countryside for safekeeping, and so K. held concerts there to help keep spirits up."

"You knew Kenneth Clark?"

"Yes."

"Vaughn Williams, too?"

"Yes, Ralph, as well." He pronounces the composer's first name as Rafe, rhyming with *safe*. "And I knew Jean Stewart, too, for that matter. But all of that is a story for another time."

Sabrina realizes that this acquaintanceship might explain how the agnostic Vaughn Williams—Bertrand Russell's 'frightful atheist' of his Cambridge days—had come to compose an oratorio whose libretto was Biblical: he had known Bronaryre. No wonder it had been entirely from the Book of Revelation.

More food is brought and more champagne is opened. Soon music is playing and dancing has begun: there is to be an after-show party, it seems. Sabrina joins in for long enough to congratulate the various players on their performances, but then quietly leaves—the day has exhausted her.

Sabrina returns to the house, silent and still. She is slowly mounting the stairs while ruminating on the evening when an idea occurs to her. She turns around and goes back down to the library.

Most of the art books are oversized, too tall for the regular shelves, and so occupying their own bookcase built to accommodate them. She goes along the rows, reading the spines, but comes to one volume too narrow to bear a title, and which she must have missed before. She pulls it out. Although narrow it is broad, double-folio, like the Gutenberg Bible. This book is not quite as ancient, but is old: the dark blue cloth binding of the cover is fading unevenly, and the black-bordered title label attached to the middle, no doubt once white, has aged to a soft mold-stippled cream.

A popular book: the corners of the cover are worn with use, and the top of the spine is bent back where countless fingers have pulled it from the shelf over the years.

The title is *The Wonders of the Windrush.*

Sabrina settles herself into the sofa with it, intending to spend a few minutes leafing through this book that has obviously been enjoyed by many people before her, but after opening it to the first plate she comes to an abrupt halt.

It turns out that the 'Wonders of the Windrush' are her.

Each right-hand page—recto—contains a large black-and-white photograph of herself, naked but for the floral garland, disposed in or about the stream: Mortimer Pence's work. She flips back to the title page and finds him credited as the *daguerriste*. The author is listed as Mr. Sacheverell Edgewater, esquire. No publisher; the volume was privately printed in the year 1898—probably the only way something of this nature could be published in prudish Victorian England.

But then Sabrina checks herself: of course it could not have been published then; it was printed in the last two days, and aged to play the part.

She returns to the photographs. There are just a dozen, hence the slenderness of the volume, each accompanied by text on the verso. There is a hint of sepia, no doubt induced as part of the counterfeit. The Daguerre technique is sympathetic to naked flesh, she decides: it imparts a clean sheer metallic luster, as if some quality of the silver on the photographic plate was somehow imparted to the subject. If truly Victorian she would have expected in the text much nonsense about ivory breasts and heaving bosoms, but instead it is, if not exactly anachronistic, then at least incongruent, more *tanka*-like than purple prose.

*Along the Windrush*
*Water washes away words*
*And with them all care;*
*Indulge in the precious now*
*And lament not for beyond*

In the accompanying photograph she stands in the stream, side-on and seemingly unposed, straight of posture, staring back at the photographer with a blank knowingness—there is something childlike in the penetration of that gaze, and indeed she appears childlike herself: slender, as if still a teenager; a face not just unlined but unadult in its lack of guile; the face of someone impervious to the deviousness of men, an effect added to by the garland, as if to signify allegiance to simpler things. It is a look that might quietly unnerve a thoughtful viewer.

Sabrina wonders if she is seeing herself objectively in this photograph, in a way that she never would before a mirror; seeing herself as others must see her. If so, she thinks, what a strange creature I am: detached and distant, not quite human.

She returns to the bookshelves, putting aside self-reflection and the *Wonders of the Windrush.*

After further searching she finally locates the volume that she came here to find, one that she was aware existed from her first survey of the library: a catalog of the permanent collection at the Tate Modern. It takes only a moment to find the photographs of the gallery in question, and Sabrina counts the paintings with care, to be certain of the result.

It is as she had guessed: there are *nine* Rothkos in the Tate Modern. And she knows instinctively, without exactly understanding why, that when Dodgson was asking for examples this is the one Bronaryre had expected her to give.

## The Sacrifice of the Moon Wraith

SABRINA AWAKENS WITH A START.

It is two A.M. She has again failed to close the curtains, and the light of the moon—fully risen—must have woken her: the room is bathed in bright silver luminescence.

The fire is extinguished despite the extra fuel, in the form of *The Wonders of the Windrush*, that Sabrina had added to it after returning to her room last night.

She feels agitated, perhaps disturbed by the play, or with lingering annoyance at finding that volume in the library. In any case, the laudanum—the bottle had been refilled in her absence, again with an emphatic *DRINK ME!* label tied around its neck, an instruction she had once again obeyed—is not working tonight.

A moonbeam falls upon the fireplace, illuminating its Jacobean horrors in a gloomy ethereal glow: she can almost see the grotesque creatures in it slinking slowly through the foliage, nocturnal ghouls stalking the unguarded, ready to snatch from them their souls while they sleep unaware.

She gets out of bed and goes to the terrace. Here, unobstructed by casement and glass, the lunar light falls unimpeded upon her naked flesh. I am a phantom, she thinks, and she performs an impromptu spectral ballet for her personal pleasure, her body remembering a flow of movement last practiced a decade ago—*jetés* and *pirouettes* if not quite *en pointe* then at least *en* sole—passages remembered by her body even if they have long since slipped from her conscious mind.

Sabrina completes the exercise, breathing hard now. She goes to the balustrade and lies supine upon it while regaining her breath. The moon is right above her, so bright that she must close her eyes against it.

She is moonbathing, she realizes, and wonders if it will turn her mad.

There is a song somewhere on the breeze, plaintive like Vaughn Williams's 'distant' chorus, so faint as to be barely audible. Ghostly, like her. It is not the music of a party.

Her flesh bristles, and she imagines that her skin must now be as puckered as a freshly plucked pheasant.

She goes back inside and locates the Liberty print, carelessly removed and discarded over a chair last night. She puts the dress back on, hastily securing it with a couple of buttons at the waist. No shoes; if she is to go sneaking out of the house late at night, it would best be done with bare feet.

Sabrina leaves her room and goes downstairs. The main hall is always lit but it is deserted now, and the lights have been turned low. She goes outside and quickly crosses the gravel onto the grass verge: quieter, and gentler on bare feet, too.

She follows the main parade all the way down to the Neptune fountain, its burbling amplified by the stillness of night into something resembling a thunderous waterfall. The gate to the Long Garden is still unlocked, and Sabrina makes her way down the shadowed central alley, the many statues now barely perceived shapes looming eerily, until finally emerging onto the broad lawn at the far end.

The song is a little louder now, sufficient to confirm that it is a chorus, but not loud enough to distinguish the lyrics. It is coming from the direction of the amphitheater.

Sabrina heads downhill, descending into the deep ravine that leads down toward the river, until coming to the great scoop of the theater. The arc of seats is shadowed by the trees behind, and in the cool of the night a little mist has been precipitated by cold stone and moist earth, but the stage is bathed in an unearthly pale radiance by the moon, perfectly full, as if having engorged itself in order to illuminate the events to come.

There is an altar upon the stage: stone, ancient, primeval, Druidical. There had been no such prop in the play.

The music is present but still distant; it has no source, she realizes—it will always be distant, no matter how close she approaches.

Sabrina takes the center steps slowly down, descending from the lip of the theater into the pit. At the bottom she looks back up and sees that the theater is crowded now, the seats filled with faceless wisps here to witness whatever is to follow.

A sacrifice, of course—what else could it be?

She turns and mounts the stage. This will be the missing catastasis, she thinks: a ritual, something archaic, primordial, antediluvian. She lies supine upon the altar, as she had earlier on the balustrade, but the stone is much colder against her back here, even though she is now wearing a dress.

There are two of them this time, soon emerging from the woods as if they had been lurking there all along, waiting for her to arrive, fast-moving and heavy-horned. They are green, not forest green, as might be expected of demons emerging from the trees, but the color of verdigris, like a pair of ancient copper gargoyles suddenly come to life. They begin leaping and bounding down the face of the amphitheater like cloven-hooved goats negotiating an alpine chasm—they are not demons, Sabrina realizes; they are satyrs.

Her hand moves to undo her dress but the first to fall upon her simply tears the two sides apart, buttons flying off, a wild beast ripping away hide to feast on flesh. She can feel the metallic cold of their copper skin as they assail her. She tries to keep silent but cannot, emitting inarticulate yelps and cries that echo in the amphitheater, so loud that she fears they must be heard from the house.

She has the sense of being gorged upon, of being consumed by these creatures—*flesh unto my flesh*, she hears, or thinks she hears, but who could have said it?

Sabrina feels herself drowning, breathless, of being engulfed in a sea of sensation. But then the impression gradually subsides, and her sense of asphyxiation slowly dissipates. She is no longer sinking. She is instead suspended, floating beneath the surface of the sea, and looking up through gently rippling water at a shimmering star-cast sky, like a mermaid wondering at the strange world of light and air above.

# Fourth Circle

Calliope

# ♃

SABRINA WAKES UP IN her bed in the Blue Room with no memory of how she got back there. The first thing she does is locate and inspect the Liberty-print dress. Next, she goes to the dressing room, briefly examines herself in the mirror, and then returns to the desk and opens her journal, wanting to make a record while things remain fresh in her mind.

> *How very real last night's ravishing dream seemed, and seems to me still—it was a dream: the buttons of the dress, whose moonlit flight through the air as it was torn apart I vividly recall, are intact. Besides, I have none of the bruises or scrapes that had it been real would have resulted from all that stone. But for the hard physical evidence, I would have sworn that everything I dreamed last night actually happened, even that satyrs existed—I perceive that opium is a tempting portal, as enticing and hazardous as the Alice door.*
>
> *Malavalaya's breakfast account of her Saturday evening escapades was no doubt the inspiration. I was thinking on it much of the day: how uninhibited some people are, so extrovert, so ready to engage with others; how very opposite to my own closed disposition—I had been considering this difference, a difference in general outlook, wondering at the causes, and the relative merits of one versus the other.*

*The dancing on the terrace part is easy enough to explain: the conversation with Bronaryre in the Long Garden unearthed the memory of those long-ago ballet lessons, not thought of for many years. During the show I had been recalling the five basic positions, and trying to remember the names of the various attitudes and movements:* plié, jeté, pirouette, en pointe—*dance was on my mind.*

*The music, too: it was 'Sancta Civitas'—with the distant chorus now truly distant, calling from deep in the woods—a piece of music that has been swirling around in my head since hearing it that evening at St. Paul's. Hardly ballet music, although in my imagination I had managed a flowing adagio-tempoed moondance suitable to that plaintive chant.*

*As for those satyrs...*

*I had come across metallic flesh earlier in the evening—seemingly my own, as rendered in* The Wonders of the Windrush *daguerreotypes. (Bronaryre presumably placed the book in the library for me to find, still trying to sell the Mortimer Pence encounter as something other than an amusing piece of theater, I suppose—I'm not opposed to treasure hunts, but he will need to place his clues more discreetly if he doesn't want them incinerated.) It was not just the substance of the satyrs' flesh that was recently suggested, but the finish as well: that same verdigris as on those little copper signs embedded into the Long Garden, naming the varieties—gray-green in tone, coarse-fine in texture.*

*Perhaps I should rearrange the bed so that the last thing I see before falling asleep is something other than that fireplace, with its demons in the flames.*

*Perhaps I should give up opium.*

OXFORD COMES AS a relief. Here is normalcy, Sabrina thinks, as she walks along the narrow streets busy with activity—or at least what counts as normalcy compared to Temple Slaughter Preceptory. She is comfortably in her own clothes again, old and familiar. People come and go around her, bustling on their way, and she feels the quiet pleasure of anonymity that only a city can provide.

Even the weather has returned to normal, for England: it is raining, but a soft rain so light that it seems to hang in the air rather than fall, and Sabrina finds pleasure in walking umbrella-less and bareheaded through it: fairy-tale rain in a fairy-tale city.

The first appointment of the day is with Professor Pearson, alone to begin but as the forenoon progresses they are successively joined by two other people. The first of these is a Professor Davis, Regius Professor of Civil Law, a genial man who offers a few minor amendments to her teaching proposal, mostly bibliographical additions, but he generally approves of the structure.

"Frankly, you probably know better than me," he says diffidently. "NYU is a first-class law school and, as I expect you're already aware, here in England much of the heavy lifting in the instruction of law is handled not in the universities but at the Inns of Court, or in Chancery."

Sabrina is initially surprised by the second person to join them: Bronaryre's lawyer, Thomas Ravenscroft, but then she realizes that he is an obvious person for the Master to have invited, given that he is a practicing QC.

Ravenscroft swiftly carves away the spare fat from her proposal, and soon arrives at bone—Sabrina wishes that she could see him in action in a courtroom, for she suspects that his razor-sharp incisiveness must leave many a poorly prepared witness bleeding hopelessly on the stand. Apparently, he maintains an emeritus role with the university—Pearson's secretary refers to him as 'professor'—but the precise nature of the position is not made clear, although whatever it is qualifies him as a fellow of his alma mater, for when the morning's meetings are satisfactorily concluded Ravenscroft invites her to lunch at his old college.

They walk together to Magdalen, taking the long way despite the damp weather, strolling under Hertford Bridge and past New College into a large park, where they amble lazily by the banks of the Cherwell. Fallow deer graze nearby. A harrier circles above, this one gray with black wingtips, a male. Through the willows a racing eight is briefly visible, rowing by on the water, and Ravenscroft raises a cheer of encouragement to the crew.

"*Floreat Magdalena!*" he cries, before turning in explanation to Sabrina. "At Magdalen, it is customary to cheer for one's team in Latin."

They approach from the north—the same aspect as the view of the city rendered on the Oxford Crown—and Sabrina sees why Ravenscroft chose to come this way: the great green swathe of grass forms an elegant prolog to the college buildings, rising in stately calm in the distance. Soon they are upon them, and Sabrina has an opportunity to see what the bigger colleges are like. Magdalen is one of the grandest, and the buildings are suitably to scale, cathedral-like—even the gargoyles are gargantuan, and luridly grotesque: lurking imps and bizarre fiends, although one she is surprised to see depicts a pair of lovers, embraced. They make their way through the quads—always by the paths, even though Ravenscroft's status as a fellow would have allowed him onto the grass; presumably its avoidance is a habit born of his undergraduate years. They arrive at a central cloister.

The Hall is on the second floor of the south side. It feels like an aircraft hanger in comparison to that of Caiaphas, and here everyone gets an individual chair in contrast to the shared benches of her own college, but what the latter lacks in size it makes up for in charm, she thinks, already partisan in such matters. They are seated at the high table, which since it is out of term they have to themselves.

Sabrina discovers that lunch at Oxford is very different from lunch at NYU: they are brought a hearty stew, served by a liveried steward.

"Venison," the man announces, somewhat somberly, as he places the plates before them.

Ravenscroft looks up sadly at the steward.

"Who was it, Willoughby?"

"Professor Atkins, I regret to say, sir."

"Chuffy Atkins? By God, I had him for Mods when I was up—I had no idea the old fellow was still at it. He certainly had a good innings, Willoughby—we should hope to do as well, eh?"

"Indeed, your honor," but the glum Willoughby does not seem any cheerier as he begins uncorking the wine.

Ravenscroft turns to Sabrina and offers an explanation for this strange reaction to venison stew. "You recall that there were deer in the Grove, the park we just came through? It is a tradition at Magdalen that on the death of a fellow one of the deer is taken. The beast is slaughtered, and a feast made of it. We are no doubt lunching on the leftovers."

"Oh."

"I hope that hasn't spoiled your appetite. The idea is that we should eat heartily, celebrating the memory of our dear colleague, although my main recollection of old Chuffy Atkins is laboring through Latin declensions."

The wine is poured, a claret whose bottle is so dust-covered that the label is rendered illegible—'Eighty-nine Latour, Ravenscroft tells her, and it is clear that he is an important alumnus to have commanded such a bottle from the college cellars.

"To old Chuffy Atkins," Ravenscroft says, raising his glass.

"To Professor Atkins," Sabrina responds, copying his gesture, "to whom you no doubt owe the ability to cheer for racing eights in grammatically correct fashion."

They drink to the dead don.

"Now tell me," Ravenscroft says as they begin the meal, "how are you settling in?"

"Fine. I like Oxford. I like Caiaphas, too. Not as magnificent as your Magdalen, I now see, but that's part of its character, I think. It feels quite apart from everything: a compact little private domain set down right in the heart of the city."

"Enchanted?"

Sabrina stops eating. She suspects that the word was not chosen by accident.

"Yes—literally, as it happens."

"Oh, yes?" It is clear from his tone that he is not surprised.

"I dined with Bronaryre in the Dean's Garden. At its conclusion, he invited me to go through a door. After doing so, the next thing I remember is waking up the following morning. In a field. In Gloucestershire."

"What happened next?"

"A performance, something set in the Nineteenth Century, supremely well choreographed considering that it had to have a high degree of improvisation."

"For what purpose, do you think?"

"It could have been intended to persuade me that I had somehow been transported back in time, or more likely was just an entertaining introduction to Temple Slaughter Preceptory, although why I should be entertained I don't know. Your client is fond of performances, I think—whether presented plainly as a play upon a stage, or more surreptitiously folded into reality."

"Do you have any concerns?"

"For myself, none. And the students are obviously enjoying themselves immensely, although I doubt that the university authorities would approve of every aspect. But they seem to bloom there: Temple Slaughter Preceptory is Coleridge brought to life—*In Xanadu did Kublai Khan a stately pleasure-dome decree*—I wouldn't deny them that."

Ravenscroft takes a thoughtful sip of wine. "Anything else?"

"I am supplied with laudanum."

"Are you taking it?"

"Yes."

"And the effect?"

"Dreams, extraordinarily vivid."

"Where does he get it from?"

"He says that it's provided by a pharmaceutical research lab he funds."

Now it is Ravenscroft's turn to stop eating.

"It would be very interesting to know whether or not that is true, and if so the name and location of this laboratory."

"You mean you don't know of it?"

"I do not."

"I assumed that as his lawyer you would."

"In general, people share very little with their lawyers, and given the nature of this particular client one may safely assume that he has a good deal to hide. Which reminds me, how goes your other work?"

"You mean the 'apologia'? Well enough, I think. So far it's taken the form of story-telling, accompanied by strong cocktails. Maybe the liquor helps; certainly the tales are well told."

"Perhaps they're true."

"You're still determined not to contradict your client? Even in private, and even when your client's assertions are palpable nonsense?"

"You're assuming that they cannot be true."

"He claims to have been present at the execution of Charles I."

"Perhaps he was."

"He also says that's where he obtained the Oxford Crown, given to him by Cromwell, no less." She leans across the table and lowers her voice. "The same coin that his lawyer arranged to have stolen, by the way."

"I am merely a facilitator, Dr. Lancaster. I have acted entirely in good faith, and possess no prior knowledge of provenance."

"I'm not sure that the Benchers of the Inner Temple would see it your way."

This last makes Ravenscroft smile broadly. "I perceive that you're becoming familiar with our somewhat arcane institutions of English jurisprudence. And, yes, you are quite right: the Benchers would have little tolerance for such jejune nonsense from one who has taken silk, and I have no doubt that they would make short shrift of any appeal to reliance-based estoppel with a swift *nemo dat quod non habet*."

Sabrina finishes her venison stew with the plate left clean, something she would not have thought possible. "That was delicious," she says. "Do Oxonians always eat lunch like this?"

"I hope you left room for pudding."

*Pudding* turns out to be a dense treacle-soaked affair served with bright-yellow custard and clotted cream, generously proportioned, and which to her amazement Sabrina manages to entirely ingest. She sits back in exhaustion at the meal's conclusion, estimating that she has consumed more calories at this lunch than she normally would in three days.

But Sabrina is mistaken in thinking that the meal is over: after leaving the Hall they retire to the Senior Common Room, a sumptuously decorated inner sanctum for the fellows, rather dark, with something of what Sabrina imagines would be the atmosphere of a gentlemen's club on Pall Mall. They have the place more or less to themselves and take big wingback seats on either side of the fireplace, alight on a damp day like this, where they are served coffee.

There is a strange contraption between the two seats, an odd little copper carriage on wooden rails passing in front of the fire, vaguely steampunk. In the carriage is what appears in the low light to be a glass replica of the Eiffel Tower.

"What is it?" she asks, looking at the device.

"Do you know the Bishop of Norwich?" Ravenscroft replies.

Sabrina is momentarily nonplussed by this question. She dislikes the common habit of exclaiming 'Excuse me?' as a knee-jerk response to something that one has not understood but heard perfectly well, and so instead considers the question for a moment in thoughtful silence, trying to figure out what bearing the Bishop of Norwich might have, but any thread of relevance eludes her.

"No," she eventually admits, "never met him."

"He's a terribly good chap, but he always forgets to pass the port."

Her eyes go again to the little carriage. She reaches out to the Eiffel Tower, which when she lifts it is revealed to be the long tapering neck of a cut-crystal decanter, one whose broad bulbous base is filled with a deep-purple liquid that was not visible when inside the carriage.

"How ingenious."

"Pour some for yourself first, and then pass the thing over."

She takes a glass from the side table, fills it, and then sends the little carriage on its journey across to Ravenscroft.

"Quinta do Noval Nacional, 2000," he says, pouring himself a generous glass. "The first vintage of the new millennium, and also the greatest, at least so far. I asked Willoughby to decant a bottle for us."

The port is thick and unctuous, like liquid velvet, a contrast to the sharper Madeira Ravenscroft had urged upon her at the Explorers Club, and is so effective as a *digestif* that the lawyer is soon helping himself to a second glass.

SABRINA STRUGGLES TO stay awake for the remainder of the afternoon—mostly taken up in meetings with university administration—before returning to her rooms at Caiaphas.

At the porters' lodge—'plodge' in Oxonian parlance, she now knows—she checks her pigeon hole—'pidge'—and finds there an envelope. It is not Bronaryre's marbleized handmade stock, but instead a standard-sized envelope whose rear flap has a shield printed on it, emblazoned with a golden-winged crown placed above a black wolf's head.

She turns the envelope around. On the top left is printed *Campion Hall*. Inside is a note written on similarly printed letterhead.

*Dear Lancaster,*

*Following our conversation the other day, I got in contact with the agency that represents Johanna Missonatis, the soprano who sang that night at Justice Scaglietti's house. Since it was a private recital I asked if they had been given a guest list. I didn't expect a response, but Missonatis herself called me. To sum up what turned out to be a long conversation, she does indeed have such a list and undertook to forward it to me.*

*Missonatis told me that she had been troubled ever since that evening. She had been returning from the bathroom when she happened upon Scaglietti talking with another man. They had just emerged from the library. She overheard nothing of what they said, but from the tone of their parting she had the sense that the conversation had not been a pleasant one. The other man moved on, and the Justice returned to the room. Neither of them noticed Johanna. Needless to say, the next day after discovering that the Justice had died in the early hours of the morning she immediately thought of the incident, but given that the death was due to natural causes there was no action to take.*

*Missonatis only saw the other man briefly, and then only from behind. He was solidly built, had a big shaved head, and what she described as strangely pointed ears. She guessed that he was in his forties, but can't be sure. By the time the performance was over he had disappeared, but the accompanist had been putting names to faces during the evening, and so together they were able to identify the man by a process of elimination against the guest list. His name was Aleister Crowley.*

Aleister, *not* Alastair—*how many of those could there be?*

*I looked him up. Sure enough, there's only one Aleister Crowley. The first name is pronounced ah-LIST-er, and is an affectation he adopted while up at Cambridge. There are plenty of photographs, and indeed he is a solid man with a shaved head, and his ears do seem to be pointed on top, not rounded as usual.*

*His occupation: occultist.*

*He died in 1947.*

*What's going on, Lancaster?*

*In my order, it is customary to offer 'Yours in Christ' as the valediction, but since you are a self-declared Godless heathen I will refrain from doing so, and shall instead sign off with:*

*Hoping that You have not Gotten Yourself in Over Your Head I'm Here if You Need Me,*

*Roger Wilkins, S.J.*

THE WEEK BEGAN with relief at being away from Temple Slaughter Preceptory; by Friday, Sabrina longs to return. She wonders whether it is the otherworldliness of the place that appeals—the sense of being immersed in a strange epic beyond the everyday, something unpredictable and perhaps treacherous—or if instead it reflects a simple desire to be reunited with the laudanum bottle.

Ronson invited her to call when she wanted a vehicle sent to pick her up from Oxford, but Sabrina instead orders a car service, partly out of not wanting to inconvenience the preceptory staff, but also because it means that she will arrive unannounced.

THE E-TYPE IS IN ITS usual spot when Sabrina arrives at the manor, but when she inquires Ronson tells her that Bronaryre is out: with foul weather forecast he elected to take the Range Rover rather than the Jaguar. Most of the girls are still in Oxford, not arriving at the preceptory until later in the evening, and she has the sense of having the house to herself.

She goes into one of the salons facing onto the parterre. The wind outside is rising, rattling the French windows like an importunate traveler demanding to be let in, and sending occasional gusts all the way down the chimney. These act as a natural bellows, boosting the fire into bright and cheerful yellow flame. Sabrina settles into a sofa in front of it with two books, both of whose subject is the same: Aleister Crowley. The first is a 1951 biography; the second is a 1929 autobiography, which the author modestly titled *The Spirit of Solitude: an Autohagiography: Subsequently re-Antichristianed The Confessions of Aleister Crowley*, both volumes borrowed from the Bodleian, and the latter having required the staff to delve deeply into the stacks to retrieve, it apparently having been thought best to bury the thing.

Not being as convinced of Crowley's sainthood as he himself apparently was, Sabrina begins instead with the biography. Crowley was independently wealthy, which enabled him to indulge in a variety of pursuits, many of them disreputable. He was, in addition to being an occultist, an accomplished mountain climber; a heroin addict; a skilled chess player; a libertine and seducer; a poet and novelist; and a British spy who, after being recruited while up at Cambridge, was sent first to Saint Petersburg, and then later infiltrated an organization of German sympathizers in the U.S. during the First World War. He was labeled *the wickedest man in England* by the British popular press, a title to which he would unlikely have objected; he referred to himself as *Beast 666*.

Crowley was involved in a variety of esoteric groups and occult practices: Rosicrucianism; the Ordo Templi Orientis (a sect to which he had once hoped to recruit Adolf Hitler); various Hindu and Buddhist practices; the ancient Egyptian rituals around The Book of the Dead; Tarot; the Hermetic Order of the Golden Dawn, where he was entangled in a rivalry with W.B. Yeats; and then finally, perhaps finding these others insufficiently debauched for his tastes, he invented a new religion: Thelema. For this last, she is surprised to learn, Crowley adopted as a symbol the unicursal hexagram with a pentacle in the center.

His home on the shores of Loch Ness, Boleskine House, became a place of pilgrimage for devotees of the occult, and the house earned a reputation as being the most decadent residence in Britain.

An interesting although ultimately unattractive man, Sabrina decides, one whose shortcomings are adequately summed up in his favorite self-serving phrase: *Do what thou wilt*, which is no more than a sophomoric license to do anything at all. She returns to her room, having read enough, and takes up her pen and journal instead.

*What was Crowley's ghost doing at Scaglietti's house on the night of the Justice's death?*

*Obvious answer: killing him.*

*Presumably something pharmaceutical—it is clear that Bronaryre has abundant resources in that area. But how did he ingratiate himself sufficiently to get an invitation in the first place, and who did Scaglietti understand him to be? Could the Justice have really believed that he was a ghost, rather than an impersonator? The instinctive response is that Scaglietti was far too sharp-minded a realist to entertain such nonsense, but then how to square that with the fact of the Justice's Catholicism, much more than just nominal, as the disposition of his estate demonstrated—there was a certain credulity there, a willingness to believe.*

*What next? I have the sense of being a surfer on the face of an immense wave—something building ever higher, crushing and unstoppable—and where one slip means calamity. The only hope of emerging intact is to maintain perfect balance, and there can be no hesitation, no second-guessing. I feel the time has come to take the Devil by the horns.*

Sabrina closes the journal in a gesture of frustration. She stands, resolved that for once she will act instead of being acted upon. She grabs the flashlight from her bedside drawer and heads back downstairs.

There are no staff on hand in the hall. Sabrina goes to the little secretaire by the front door and opens the key drawer. She searches through it, not furtively but furiously, with fierce determination, until finding a key whose ring is labeled *cellar*. She takes it with her and goes out the front door, leaving the drawer open behind her.

The sky has lowered, sullen and darkly leaden. The ozone-laden air is heavy with the electric scent of an approaching storm. Sabrina circles the house to the parterre, now empty of birds; even the pheasant has retreated.

She arrives at the big gilt-and-black grill below the terrace. The key fits and she soon has it unlocked. The gate opens with a loud squeal, but Sabrina is beyond caring now; she enters the chamber. The place is cold and dark, notwithstanding daylight, or some semblance of it, on the other side of the grill. Sabrina uses the flashlight to orient herself.

The chamber is vaulted, about the size of a side chapel in a large cathedral, and perhaps it had once served a similar purpose here: many of the country gentry, notoriously conservative, had kept to the old religion through the Tudor Reformation, hoping for a reversion under their successors, the Stuarts—something that had taken a revolution to thwart—and so this chamber might once have served as a place in which to surreptitiously hold the Catholic mass, something that would explain its isolation from the rest of the house.

If so, there must be a priest hole somewhere.

She uses the flashlight to examine the walls. There are niches in the sides, which from the old wax she can tell usually accommodate candles, and a larger recess at the rear, which may have served as a location for the altar.

There are no doors, but if concealing a priest hole there would of course not be, and in any case Sabrina knows from Colonel Swinton's account that on the other side there is a cellar, built on the preceptory's ruins, that must be accessible somehow.

She soon finds it: a simple handle disguised as a tether ring which, when turned and then pulled, audibly releases a latch on the other side. But when she continues to pull, expecting the panel to now swing open, nothing happens. She tries it again and again, each time with subtle variations, unable to accept that having found something so suggestive it could turn out to be nothing after all.

"It won't work."

Sabrina turns to find Bronaryre leaning against the far wall and looking amused. She wonders how he got through that gate without the thing squeaking.

"It would have been too obvious," Bronaryre continues. "The king's men would have soon discovered it, and made short work of anyone found on the other side. That's why it's actually a double mechanism. To open it requires two people: one doing what you are doing, and the second to stand on this apparently loose flagstone over here." He stands on the corner of a tile. A door-sized panel swings open.

Sabrina shines her flashlight inside. It is a narrow passageway, very dark. Immediately inside on the right is a wooden shelf on which sits a lantern, just as there had been in her dream, although this time it is unlit.

She cannot recall if Swinton had described that detail or not. Bronaryre comes beside her.

"I take it that you would like the tour."

"Yes, I would."

Bronaryre soon has the lantern alight. He leads her through the passageway and around the corner into a broad chamber, much of it filled with crates of wine. The walls are made of the same dark red and gray ironstone that she recalls from her dream—but Swinton had described that feature carefully: it was the reason he had asked to come down here.

"Is there more?"

Bronaryre leads her to the next room. This is the one with the iron hooks in the wall—again as she remembers, but again Swinton had mentioned them when discussing his discovery of the illegally shot pheasants—Sabrina cannot distinguish between what she remembers from what was suggested to her by the Colonel's account.

At least someone has cleaned the pool of blood from the flagstones.

On the far side is a door bearing a sign in yellow with black lettering: *Warning: Subsidence! Unsafe! Do Not Enter!* That sign feels familiar, and surely is not something that Swinton would have described in detail.

"What's on the other side?" she asks.

"More of the same, but in a state of collapse. The contractors put in jacks as a temporary measure. They're working with a consulting firm to put together a plan for permanent restoration, one that will do as little damage as possible to the original stonework. We'll probably implement it next winter, during a dry spell, when the ground is hard."

Sabrina stares at the door, doubting every word. She could probably get to it and see for herself, she thinks. He might try to stop her, but she would get to it first if she was fast enough.

She walks to the door, briskly but not running. He makes no attempt to intercept her.

She swings the door open and shines the flashlight inside.

Before her is a sea of vertical poles, their metal shining in the flashlight. There are flat plates fixed to the top and bottom of each, distributing load. The poles are composed of two pipes, one threaded inside the other, and with drilled holes so that a handle can be inserted to raise or lower them: the 'jacks,' evidently—they remind Sabrina of the scaffolding put around buildings in Manhattan to protect pedestrians when maintenance is performed aloft.

This is not what she saw in her dream.

But then she looks again, a decides that maybe the scene is not so unfamiliar after all. Beyond the jacks, at the extreme range of her flashlight, she sees that some stone blocks of one wall have collapsed, tumbling down in a heap abutting the other side. It resembles the section of the tunnel that in her dream she had needed to remove the Temperley to negotiate.

Sabrina considers this in silence. The jacks look new; certainly the metal is shiny, and there is no evidence of dust—not that there would be much to stir up dust down here. Perhaps they were installed post-dream, an effective way of barring passage through to that inner chamber where she had witnessed herself floating unsupported in the air, dead at first, and then resurrected, spewing blood.

She turns to Bronaryre, standing unmoved on the other side of the room, gazing back at her with his usual focused yet disengaged intensity, the way a scientist might an interesting specimen.

"Rather foreboding," she says. "It might be the entrance to Hell."

"No, I wouldn't think so," he replies. "Hell is never closed."

BRONARYRE LEADS SABRINA back to the first ironstone room, the one that is used as a wine cellar.

"Since we're here," he says, "why don't you choose something for dinner tonight?"

Sabrina walks over to the wooden crates, briefly inspects the open ones, and selects a bottle based solely on the peculiarity of the label: a scribbled but emphatic *No Barrique No Berlusconi*.

Bronaryre smiles when she hands it to him.

"Bartolo Mascarello," he says. "He despised the use of *barrique*, those small French oak casks, usually toasted, that add so much wood to a wine, and which have become *de rigueur* for the international style. He made his Barolo the old-fashioned way, *cappello sommerso* to ensure plenty of tart tannins, and then long aging in big old *grandi botti* made of Slavonian oak, or even chestnut. He referred to Barolo that had been barreled in *barrique* as 'a clown with rouged cheeks.' You can see from this label that he had no more fondness for clowns in the political arena than in the oenological. He's gone now, but his daughter Maria Teresa continues the battle against *barrique*."

"Then your lawyer would like her," Sabrina says. "He has a great affection for those who would dislodge the Berlusconis of this world."

They emerge from the cellar back into the alcove to discover that the world outside has changed: the storm has broken while they were underground, and now torrential rain is falling. There is no possibility of regaining the house without becoming soaked.

"Let us take it as a sign from the heavens," Bronaryre says, "and drink the Mascarello now."

"The heavens? Surely not a place from which you would normally take a hint."

They set up in the space behind the gilded grill, sitting on a pair of upturned wine crates, drinking from two stemless and unmatched glasses hastily cleaned out with Bronaryre's handkerchief.

Rolling thunder sets a mordant bass line, while the wind howling over the parterre supplies the treble, and sometimes it suddenly bursts into a shrill wail, as strident as a shrew. Rain lashes across the landscape, occasionally sweeping through the grill and landing a few feet in front of them.

They drink for a while in comfortable silence, experiencing, in Sabrina's case at least, a quiet pleasure in sitting snug and dry, drinking an old-style Barolo by soft lamplight, while beyond the grill the skies rage.

"Why did you hold masses," Sabrina asks, "or were they black masses?"

"What are you talking about?"

"Didn't you hold masses here?"

"No. What makes you think such a thing?"

"It feels religious to me." She looks again at their surroundings. "Maybe *masses* is not quite right; it seems quieter, more a place for calm reflection or spiritual contemplation instead of overt religious display; an abbey rather than a church, if you know what I mean."

"That much is true: I built this space after having spent some time in France, where I became well acquainted with the monasteries—mainly their libraries—and at the time my mood was Cistercian, favoring simplicity of form, as opposed to the more elaborate Cluniac style. But that was purely an architectural sensibility; this space was not intended for any religious purpose."

"Then why the priest hole?" she asks, nodding toward the hidden entrance.

"It's not a priest hole. It is for concealment, certainly, but not the concealment of priests,"

"Then whom?"

"Those whom I wished to conceal, for one reason or another."

"Do you mean a dungeon?"

"Sometimes—you must realize that in my business the end always justifies the means."

Sabrina wonders if this is an obscure threat.

"Then what is this space for? Is it merely decorative?"

"Not at all. I built it, along with the rest of the original house, when I returned to England at the end of the Seventeenth Century. I had another name by then: Aubrey Greystoke. The first house burned down in 1743, but this part survived unscathed. It is a sounding chamber."

"What's a sounding chamber?'

"For concerts. It was my habit in those days to hold *soirées* on the parterre. The players would be located in here, where the shell-like structure acted as a natural reflector of sound, something useful in the days before electrical amplification. But it has a second purpose, too."

"What?"

"Look above you. What do you see?"

"The ceiling. Vaults."

"And those vaults, is there anything about them that strikes you as unusual?"

Sabrina studies them for a moment before responding. "They are elongated in some parts, and flattened in others."

"Precisely. The curvature in a traditional vault is an arc of a *circle*. In here, they are not circles, they are *ellipses*. Newton published the *Principia Mathematica* in 1687. At the time, it was said that there were less than a dozen people in the world who could actually understand it. If so, one of them was me. I fully realized what an epochal event it was: for the first time, mankind had attained a demonstrable understanding of the heavens, a monumental achievement. Almost as astounding was the mathematical method Newton devised to arrive at his conclusions: subtle in concept and enormously complex in operation—'fluxions' was the term he used, but today we call it calculus. Every curve in this room is an embodiment in stone of the principles of Newton. The ellipses share a common focus, which is this." He taps a tile with the sun etched upon it. "There are imaginary second foci beneath it, one for each curve. The inverse-square law determines the rest. So, your intuition was quite right: in a sense, it is a place of reflection and contemplation, although upon the nature not of gods but the cosmos."

Sabrina looks up again, scanning the ceiling before returning her gaze to Bronaryre.

"Nine vaults."

"Naturally."

They sit for a while in meditative silence, which is again broken by Sabrina.

"Why do you use Aleister Crowley's Thelema symbol on your cuff links and so on?"

"The unicursal hexagram? As with my coin, you have the provenance backward. I did not adopt it from Crowley; Crowley adopted it from me."

"From you?"

"More accurately, via my proxy, from Blaise Pascal. Pascal revealed the unique mathematical properties of the unicursal hexagram in 1639, when he was just sixteen years of age. I became familiar with his discoveries while up at Oxford: the Invisible College was in deep correspondence with Pascal, especially Wren, who proved the rectification of the cycloid at Pascal's prompting. Pascal was something of a heroic figure at that time, defying the Sun King, the Pope, and the Jesuits all at once, although he was still just in his thirties. Their combined weight crushed him: he never made it to his fortieth year."

"And so you adopted the unicursal hexagram in his honor?"

"More for its elegant though obscure mathematical precision, but certainly Blaise Pascal had my respect. The ultimate test of a man is to stand for right against power, no matter the cost. Pascal passed that test."

The Devil has no more admiration for authority than his lawyer, Sabrina perceives, although perhaps not for the same reasons.

"And the pentacle in the center?"

"An earth symbol. My purpose is to excite men's minds with more desire to know, but humankind exists only by the permission of nature, and thus it is to this nurturing planet that I owe ultimate allegiance."

"Did you ever meet Pascal?"

"He died in 1662; I didn't move to France until 1666."

"Why did you leave England? Was it because you continued to be persecuted under the Restoration?"

"No, something quite different: I discovered how I came to be."

Bronaryre stands, picks up the bottle, and refills their glasses before continuing.

"I've told you that by the time I left Oxford I already knew *who* I was, but what I didn't understand was the *how*. As far as the world was concerned, I was an orphan. In those days there were very few written records in such matters; to be an orphan effectively meant that one's background was erased. I had no history before being plucked from oblivion by Colonel Hendrick, and now he was dead.

"In 1666, I came down from Oxford and again took up residence in London, this time in a Ludgate garret by that stinking ditch known as the River Fleet.

"The 'Invisible College' had become the Royal Society in 1662, and through my association with Boyle I was permitted to attend their meetings in Gresham College, although not, of course, to speak. It was an exciting time: in the previous year alone, Cassini had determined the rotation of Jupiter, Mars, and Venus; Grimaldi had explained diffraction; Hooke had published his *Micrographia*, expounding the microscope; and then in 1666 Newton measured the moon's orbit. It seemed that the scientific problems which had challenged men for millennia were suddenly all being solved at once—I was like the young Alexander fretting at his father Philip's victories: I feared there would be nothing left for me.

"Two events happened in that year—one personal, the other not—which together caused me to leave England. The first, the personal one, was the death of Colonel Hendrick's wife. I had maintained no contact with the family since the death of her husband, seventeen years previously, but then one day one of her children, Abraham, now a young man, arrived unannounced at my lodgings. It was he who told me of the death of his mother: the plague had swept through London the previous year, and she was one of its victims. I made the expected expressions of sympathy, although in truth I could barely remember the woman. But it was not sympathy he had come for.

"He had with him a small package wrapped in waxed cloth and secured with twine, which he gave to me. It was a book, he told me, one that had belonged to his father, and then passed into the possession of his mother. After her death, he had gone through the library while sorting out the estate, and inside the front cover of the book he had found a note, written by his father. Abraham said that it was clear from the note that the book had been intended for me, which was why he was now delivering it. With his duty done he quickly took his leave: it was clear that he had been uncomfortable in my company. After he left I unwrapped the package, and discovered why.

"The book was titled *The Wonderfull Discoverie of Witches in the Countie of Lancaster*. It was written by—"

"Thomas Potts," Sabrina interjects, "the court clerk at the Pendle Hill witch trials." Bronaryre shows no visible reaction to her interruption, but she knows that she has gotten the better of him twice now. "You have a fund registered in the Cayman Islands called Pendle Hill Investments," she explains. "I searched for 'Pendle Hill' and made the link with the witch trials, which of course led to Potts' account. What was your connection?"

"Do you recall that the chief witness for the prosecution was a young girl, as were the accusers at Salem? Her name was Jennet Devize."

"I do remember, but at Salem they were mostly hysterical teenagers. Devize was something else entirely: a much younger girl, just nine years old, but cunning and manipulative beyond her years, condemning people with perfect calm."

"Indeed."

"What about her?"

"According to Colonel Hendrick's note, Jennet Devize was my mother."

Sabrina wishes that she had been less forthcoming with the *cunning and manipulative* comment, but Bronaryre continues evenly enough.

"Hendrick explained the circumstances of his becoming my guardian. Before the Civil War he served as a militiaman, and was stationed in Fleetwood. In 1633, Devize, now a young woman, was herself accused of being a witch. She was arrested and subsequently tried and sentenced to hang, but the sentence was never carried out. The king—that same Charles I at whose beheading I was a witness—intervened, and issued a pardon.

"Despite the pardon, Devize was kept imprisoned in Lancaster for the remainder of her short life, perhaps for her own safety. The general public was certain that she was a witch, royal acquittal or not, and were she to have been released they might have taken matters into their own hands. She was thus under incarceration when she fell pregnant, and this was taken to be further evidence of witchcraft: since she had no communication with the outside world, how could she have been gotten with child except through supernatural agency—a demon had impregnated her, it was believed; some said the Devil himself.

"Hendrick thought this was nonsense, and assumed that a prison guard was responsible. He and his wife were then childless—they mistakenly assumed that she was barren—and so the Hendricks undertook to take me on as their ward."

"What did you think?"

"I agreed with the mob. I already knew *who* I was, now I had the *how*—something that I have since had confirmed."

"Confirmed how?"

"By DNA analysis."

"What does that prove? That you have Devil DNA?"

"In a manner of speaking, yes. You know that there are twenty-three chromosome pairs?"

"Yes."

"One of these pairs is the sex chromosome. In a female child, you cannot determine which of the pair is from which parent, since in both cases it will be an X chromosome. But in a male child of course you can: the Y chromosome must have come from the father."

"I see."

"These days there are vast databases of sequenced DNA—in Britain, for example, there is the U.K. Biobank: half a million individuals in that one alone. In genetic research, scientists use these to look for statistical correlations between DNA sequences and identifiable characteristics—so-called 'genome-wide association studies'—this is how they learn what genes lead to particular traits. Take the iris, for example: if a study revealed a strong correlation between your quite unusual phenotype—violet eye color—and a specific mutation on the HERC2 gene—which you no doubt have—then it could reasonably be concluded that the mutation leads to the eye color. This makes working out the actual mechanism much easier: you know where to look—imagine how difficult it would be to figure it out from scratch, searching through all three billion base pairs in the human genome, one by one. But to perform a genome-wide association study you need huge databases so that the statistical correlations will be meaningful. And a side benefit of having these huge databases is that you can determine how unusual any particular DNA sequence is by seeing what degree of correlation it exhibits with all the rest."

"And you've had this done?"

"I have. The X chromosome, the one from my mother, demonstrates high correlation, well within one standard deviation of probability. Whether a witch or not, Jennet Devize was genetically uninteresting."

"And the other?"

"According to the models, it is outside six standard deviations of probability. By comparison, a so-called Black Swan event—which is to say one that is highly improbable—is outside just three. Statistically, to say that something is outside six standard deviations of probability is to label it is all but impossible. And not just the X chromosome: the same is true in the other twenty-two as well, where in each instance one of the pair—presumably that from the father—is a statistical outlier."

"Perhaps he was a foreigner, someone whose DNA is unlikely to be in the database."

"No, the difference in DNA between any two random individuals, regardless of race or region, is only about one-tenth of one percent. The degree of variation in my DNA is orders of magnitude greater than that."

Sabrina realizes that she has no way to challenge these assertions, and so decides on a change of tack instead.

"You said there were two reasons that you left England."

"Yes, and the second is very straightforward: my lodgings burned down. I should add that it was not just my lodgings; most of London burned down as well: 1666 was the year of the Great Fire. It began in Pudding Lane, well downriver from where I was, but the wind whipped it up and the fire burned unabated for five days. By the time it was extinguished, the city in which I had hoped to make my way no longer existed. London was to be rebuilt, better than before as it happened, but that would take many years, and I was impatient to get on with life, not yet understanding how much of it I was to have.

"I had no family, no real connection with England. Nor was it lost on me that as someone already marked by the government as an enemy, now lately revealed to have been the offspring of a convicted witch, and someone who had recently moved to the city only to have it engulfed in a fiery conflagration—in a year with the number 666, no less—it might be prudent for me to leave town for a while. I sold the only possessions I had of any value, my books, and made my way to Pari—"

Bronaryre's account is suddenly interrupted by a lightning strike, stunningly bright, the sheering bolt blinding in its brilliance. The clap of thunder that accompanies it, perhaps concentrated by the sounding chamber, is more than just loud: it is a physical force, and Sabrina is knocked from her upturned wine crate onto the floor. The actual event lasts just a second or two, but it is much longer before Sabrina again opens her eyes, and longer still before her hearing returns. Bronaryre appears perfectly unperturbed, despite what Sabrina assumes must have been a direct strike on the metal grill, but when she follows his gaze out onto the parterre she sees that in fact the bolt had terminated in a nearby topiary bed, destroying it utterly.

And then Sabrina smells an odor, a familiar one that she had first faintly detected in the back of Bronaryre's Bentley, and then again on his Black Watch raincoat—but this time she is able to identify it precisely: it is the pungent but not unpleasant odor of a freshly struck match, but one in which the stick is made of some particularly exotic and fragrant timber: sandalwood or oud perhaps, or one of those resinous desert shrubs from which the likes of frankincense and myrrh are extracted.

She closes her eyes, raises her nose to thc air, and inhales deeply.

"What you smell is sulfur," Bronaryre says, observing the gesture. "Lightning reacts with particulate sulfur, producing that distinctive odor, all the more so these days, given that mankind has chosen to pollute the planet with it, but even before, when the only source of airborne sulfur was volcanic activity, lightning was still known for that smell: Homer records it in the Odyssey: *Therewith Zeus thundered, and hurled his bolt upon the ship, and she quivered from stem to stern, smitten by the bolt of Zeus, and was filled with sulphurous smoke*; Pliny the Elder notes, rather more scientifically, that *Lightning and thunder are attended with a strong smell of sulphur, and the light produced by them is of a sulphurous complexion*—presumably he would be well acquainted with sulfur, given that Vesuvius killed him; and in 1749, Franklin cited *Sulphureous smell* as the last of the twelve attributes of lightning that attested to its electrical nature."

"When I first met your lawyer, he gave me a rhyme to help me remember how to correctly pronounce your name: it was *world-a-fire*, and that is how it smells now, as if the world was burning."

"Sulfur has always been associated with divine retribution, the Book of Revelation being a prime example."

"I don't recall sulfur being in the Bible."

"In the original Greek it is indeed sulfur, but translations often render it in more poetic terms."

"More poetic?"

"Not just poetic but alchemical. Usually, the King James Version is credited with having introduced this fancy, although it was already in Taverner's much earlier translation: can you guess what it is?"

"No."

"Fire and brimstone."

SABRINA RETURNS TO HER room and finds Polly waiting for her. The fire has been set. Polly has already chosen a dress for the evening—long-sleeved as a concession to the miserable weather—but Sabrina tells her that, after having just been knocked senseless by a lightning strike, a formal dinner is out of the question, and she will opt for sandwiches in her room instead.

After a long recovering bath, giving her time to reflect on the day, Sabrina makes a brief entry in her journal.

> *I looked up Taverner, with whose 1539 translation of the Bible Bronaryre is obviously familiar, and which Vaughn Williams used for his 'Sancta Civitas'—I don't think this is a coincidence. Rychard Taverner was an Oxford alumnus (Christ Church & Corpus Christi; Caiaphas did not yet exist) and also a member of that same Inner Temple that serves as a sanctum to Ravenscroft. He was encouraged to make the translation by Thomas Cromwell, chief minister to Henry VIII, and great, great grand-uncle of the Oliver Cromwell who supposedly gave Bronaryre the Oxford Crown. But serving Henry VIII was a hazardous business, and when Cromwell fell from grace Taverner was in trouble. In 1540, Henry had Cromwell beheaded, and in the following year Taverner was imprisoned in the Tower by the same monarch: he and his patron had both defied absolute power, and paid the price—just like the Satan of 'Paradise Lost'; no wonder Bronaryre favors Taverner's version.*
>
> *Fire and brimstone?—naturally. But as for the Devil claiming to have been in a 'Cistercian' mood: who is going to believe that?*

Sabrina settles in front of the fire with a volume she came across in the library while looking up Taverner: De Quincy's *Confessions of an English Opium-Eater*, part salutary admonition, part instruction manual. Sandwiches and a pot of robust Earl Grey arrive; she has taken a liking to the latter since being introduced to it by Ravenscroft, although she never had a taste for tea before, and still disdains the dull dishwater that the English typically serve up. Sabrina reads until her eyelids can stay open no longer. She ignores the laudanum bottle on the side table, and this time sleeps deeply, peacefully, dreamlessly.

THE FOLLOWING MORNING the weather has cleared into a bright clear day in which the air seems to have been washed so clean by last night's downpour that it has achieved a perfect crystalline transparency, the sort of air where it seems one could see forever, if only the earth were not a sphere, and pure sunlight streams unabated into Sabrina's room. On the terrace the scent of damp grass wafts up from the parterre, smelling refreshed and renewed.

Downstairs in the dining room she finds Penelope de Vere, Sesuna, and Katy Telford in eager discussion: they are going to Hampton Court Palace for the day, primarily to see how the famous hedge maze compares with their own—Sabrina notes the proprietorial tone: they have taken possession of the preceptory, or perhaps the preceptory has taken possession of them. Their plan is to stay overnight in a riverside pub and then return directly to Oxford on Sunday, for which they have arranged a Thames slipper launch to take them upstream through all thirty-three locks from Turk's Pier to Folly Bridge—but the question is how to get to Hampton Court Palace to begin with.

Sabrina agrees to drive them; she will continue into London and do some shopping.

THEY TAKE THE RANGE ROVER, a vehicle with which Sabrina is already familiar, and having plenty of room for the four of them. She turns on the ignition and goes to the satellite navigation screen. There is a location already in there, entered not in the usual way as an address, but instead as coordinates of latitude and longitude—about a hundred miles to the southeast, according to the system.

It had not been there when she took the vehicle out last weekend.

She stares at the screen for a long moment, considering this discovery. Ronson told her that Bronaryre had taken the Range Rover out yesterday, a wet day in which a four-wheel drive would be useful for what in Britain counts as a long journey. It might be interesting to know where Bronaryre went, she thinks, especially if it turned out to be the location of the pharmaceutical laboratory that had aroused Ravenscroft's curiosity—a facility that might be secretive enough not to have a published address, therefore requiring latitude and longitude for directions.

Sabrina takes out her notebook and records the coordinates before entering Hampton Court Palace as the destination. An hour later, after dropping the girls, she continues the journey not east into London, but south into Hampshire.

SABRINA FOLLOWS THE SATNAV'S smooth-voiced instructions until at last finding herself driving down a lonely country lane as the navigation system counts down the final yards. There are trees and fields, but no houses or other buildings, not even farms. The road is devoid of traffic, which is just as well: the narrow strip of asphalt is hemmed in on either side by hedgerows, and encountering a vehicle coming from the other direction would require a negotiated settlement.

Sabrina rolls to a halt. The satnav has led her to nothing.

Not quite nothing: she sees in the hedgerow ahead of her a narrow gap. It leads into a driveway flanked by a little low brickwork, one side of which bears a sign too small to make out.

Sabrina gets out and goes over to read it: *Private Property.*

She advances far enough down the drive to spot above the trees the roof of a distant house, invisible from the road: black-tiled; multi-gabled; many-chimneyed. It does not look like a pharmaceutical lab; it looks like someone's home.

Sabrina is acutely aware that in the confined lane where she left the Range Rover any car bigger than a Mini would have little chance of squeezing past. She returns to the vehicle, starts it up, and takes the driveway.

It terminates in a circle in front of the house. There is a woman in the garden, bent over a rose bush with a pair of secateurs in one hand and a flower-laden straw basket in the other. She stands and watches the approach of the Range Rover.

Sabrina comes to a halt and gets out.

The other woman wears a scoop-necked summer dress made of lemon-colored organza, more suitable for a tea party than gardening, but she holds herself with a graceful lack of self-awareness. A little older than Sabrina, mid-thirties. Her face betrays no annoyance at the intrusion, but instead a look of genial confusion at the arrival of an unexpected visitor.

"Hello," Sabrina says. "I'm sorry to barge into your driveway like this, but I couldn't find any place to pull over without blocking traffic."

"Oh, not at all," the other woman says, a little flustered. "Were you looking for us specifically? Or perhaps just a place to turn around?"

"Neither. I was following the vehicle's navigation system to find out where it led, and the point it took me to is just across from your driveway. I don't know whether the destination was meant to be this house, or somewhere else nearby."

"Did it have an address?"

"No, just the latitude and longitude, nothing else."

"You didn't program it yourself, I take it?"

"The location was already in the system."

"You mean like one of those car rallies, where you have to solve riddles about the waypoints and so on—I do so enjoy them myself."

"Something like that—a treasure hunt of a kind."

"How frightfully mysterious. I imagine that the house must be the intended destination: it's terribly notorious, I should say, and there's nothing else nearby."

"Notorious?"

"Oh, yes," she says, glancing over her shoulder at the building behind her, as if to look at it through a stranger's eyes. "This is Headley Grange. Have you heard of it?"

Since clearing the trees Sabrina has been aware of the building whose roof she had glimpsed earlier, a large edifice looming on her left, now fully revealed, but had paid no attention to it while explaining her intrusion.

Now she sees that it is much larger than a normal house, more of a mansion, designed in what she takes to be Victorian taste and not entirely coherently—the masonry is a strange mixture of stone and brick, the gently arched portal is incongruously topped with a steeply pitched pediment, and the glorious bay window on one side has nothing to counterbalance it on the other—as if the original owner had kept changing his mind or running short of funds while the house was being built. It has a slightly run-down air, in need of a little maintenance, with the roof tiles lichen-covered, and between the bricks moss is slowly replacing mortar. The garden is fecund to the point of returning to forest, but smells wonderfully wetly sweet, and the overall effect is not unpleasant: a rambling old house hidden away in the woods, forgotten, set apart from the world, a secret domain.

Sabrina likes it: despite the size it is not intended for vainglorious display; it is a house of lichen and soft moss—there is probably a small troll living under the front step.

"It seems a lovely place," she says, "but I'm afraid that I haven't heard of it."

"Why don't we have a cup of tea," the other woman offers, "and I'll tell you all about it?" She steps forward, arm outstretched. "My name's Imogen Hart."

"Sabrina Lancaster." They shake hands.

Imogen Hart leads Sabrina to the house—it seems there is to be a tea party after all.

THE FRONT DOOR IS made of solid wood, very thick, suitable for a castle, but immediately inside the entrance vestibule there are two smaller doors fitted with panels of ornately etched glass. These open onto the main hall, not very broad but it is a soaring space, with the staircase rising high above. Imogen leads Sabrina to the right, into a living room with windows giving onto the garden.

She disappears to fetch tea. Sabrina looks around the room: high ceiling and elegant moldings; the walls are neither papered nor paneled, but painted a soft mustard color and otherwise left unadorned; there is a piano by the wall through which she entered and at the other end a fireplace set with fresh logs. The furnishings are simple but comfortable.

Imogen returns with a tea tray, talking as she serves.

"Headley Grange was built in the late Eighteenth Century as a workhouse for the poor and insane—what we would now call an asylum. Strange to say, public feeling against the workhouse was high, notwithstanding that the inmates were locked away and caused no harm to anyone. There was a poor tax in the parish, coming on top of church tithes and all the rest—perhaps that was the cause. In any case, one day in 1830 a mob formed. They marched on Headley Grange and sacked it, ripping away the roof tiles, smashing doors and banisters, taking down ceilings, removing anything portable that might be of value, and destroying whatever was left. Much of the house was ruined."

Sabrina wonders if that mighty front door was fitted as a result.

"The house was eventually renovated and converted into a private home, but then gradually fell into disrepair. An aging widow owned it, and I imagine that in those days it must have been like Miss Havisham's place in *Great Expectations*: all overgrown garden and cobwebbed rooms, the air heavy with dust and disappointment."

"What an interesting story."

"But there's more. Have you heard of Led Zeppelin?"

"The band? Yes, of course."

"They made nine studio albums, of which the most famous is the fourth—it's the one with those Tolkienesque lyrics about Ringwraiths and so on, and includes the song 'Stairway to Heaven,' now regarded as something of an anthem of the era."

"I know 'Stairway to Heaven.'"

"That song, along with most of the album, was recorded here in Headley Grange."

"In this house?"

"In this room, actually."

"You mean that the house was converted into a sound studio?"

"No, not at all: they brought along a mobile recording van that was fitted with all the necessary technical equipment. By then the widow was gone and the house was offered for rent, but it was terribly run down at the time—damp, dilapidated, and the heating didn't work: no one wanted to live here. But it had two qualities that appealed to the band's leader, Jimmy Page: firstly, it had excellent acoustics; and secondly, it was haunted."

"Haunted?"

"Page is a frightfully keen student of the occult, you know. In any case, he rented Headley Grange specifically to record that album. The cables ran through the window behind you to the recording van, which was parked out by those hydrangeas. The piano over there is the one they used on the album. Robert Plant wrote the lyrics to 'Stairway' while sitting by this fireplace, all in a single evening. Shall I show you the inspiration?"

Imogen leads Sabrina back into the main hall.

"The stairway to heaven," she says, pointing up at the flights of steps leading to the higher floors.

Sabrina smiles, remembering the hedgerows that had hemmed in the car, and quietly sings,

*If there's a bustle in your hedgerow, don't be alarmed now*

Imogen joins her for the next line.

*It's just a spring clean for the May Queen*

and at its conclusion both women fall into laughter. They return to the living room and tea.

"Have you lived here for very long?" Sabrina asks.

"Two years, since I joined the institute."

"Institute?"

"Yes. Today, Headley Grange is a scientific research institute."

"In what area?"

"Biomedical research," Imogen says, and Sabrina realizes that she might have found the pharmaceutical lab after all. "We study the brain, not just memory and cognition, which are the most common fields in brain research, but the mind in full: in personality, in character, in the totality of the self."

"Totality of the self?"

"You might say that our focus is the soul."

Sabrina considers this last answer for a long moment before responding.

"It's not an accident that I'm here, is it?"

"No, I don't think so. I recognized your vehicle as soon as you arrived, but I wanted to get a feel for who you were before saying anything—what we do here is too important to be revealed without discrimination."

"You know Aneurin Bronaryre?"

"Yes."

"How?"

"He owns Headley Grange."

"Do you know who he is, or claims to be?"

"Yes. And I think that's why you're here."

"What do you mean?"

Imogen sits back in the seat, considering her answer. She has transformed from the diffident *Town & Country* caricature Sabrina first met, well-meaning but vague, full of frightful modifiers. Now she is articulate and intelligent, a scientist appraising her subject with an acute and impassionate gaze.

"The ancient Greeks believed that the entrance to the underworld—that is, to Hades—was in a cleft at Delphi. The underworld was thought of differently then—not as a place of punishment for non-compliance with religious dogma, but rather the opposite: as a place of thoughtful repose. And it was considered to be a source of deep truth: thus, the

Pythian Oracle, high priestess of the Temple of Apollo at Delphi, whose prophesies were considered infallible. Do you know the maxim that was famously inscribed above the entrance to the temple?"

"No."

"*Know thyself.* And that might equally well serve as the motto for what we do here: we have developed a technique for allowing one, at least briefly, to know oneself. That is, we can glimpse deep into a person's soul. And I think that is why you are here."

"You're proposing to use this technique on me?"

"Yes."

"What is it exactly?"

"I'm afraid I can't say. It's a psychological process, of course, and therefore it is important that the subject have no prior awareness: it might prejudice the responses."

"So, there are questions?"

"Yes, it is essentially a Q and A."

"How long does it take?"

"A few hours. You'll be back in Oxford before Sunday vespers."

Sabrina sighs—the satnav coordinates had been deliberately left for her to find, and this is just another of Bronaryre's masques—but having come here of her own accord she can hardly refuse to play her part in the performance.

"Very well. What comes next?"

Imogen goes to a drawer in the sideboard and takes from it a leather-bound portfolio. She returns to the sofa and lays it on the table by Sabrina. "It would require your consent," she says.

"A liability release?"

"Rather more than that. It consigns your soul to the Devil." She smiles at Sabrina's reaction. "Not forever," she clarifies. "Just for a day."

Sabrina opens the leather portfolio, revealing a document hand-printed on something too thick to be paper: parchment or vellum perhaps. She scans the text: it is as Imogen Hart described, rendered not in the tortuous legalese of a liability waiver, but in straightforward empirical language, the entire purpose summed up in the first line:

*I willingly commit my soul, for the term of this day, to be laid bare in such manner as the possessor of this document shall so choose.*

It is not a document ever intended to be presented in a court of law.

"Anything else?"

"Well, you should know that in a sense you will cease to be yourself. You'll lose any willfulness, any sense of limitation: it will be as if all the things you have ever been taught, and all the precepts with which you have ever been inculcated, have suddenly disappeared—the removal of ego, in Freudian terms; but perhaps Nietzsche put it better: you will be transported beyond good and evil."

"Leaving the soul bare?"

"Yes, exactly. You will be transposed outside of yourself, which is to say that you will have the ability to see yourself as a third person, analytically and objectively."

Sabrina does not mention that she is already familiar with this *doppelgänger* phenomenon, having recently witnessed the resurrection of her dead self.

"You will be prompted in various ways as you are being questioned. The process can be stopped at any stage: you merely have to say so. If you wish to proceed then you must remain perfectly silent, except in answering a question, of course. If at any other time you speak, the procedure will immediately terminate."

Sabrina is a little apprehensive about being *prompted in various ways*, but having come this far she is not going to back out now. "Do you have a pen?"

"Ah, yes, that's the other thing I need to explain."

Imogen goes back to the sideboard, returning this time with two items: a covered stainless steel pan the size of a laptop, and a smaller wooden box, from the patina an antique, and whose lid is inlaid with ivory in a pattern that Sabrina immediately recognizes—a unicursal hexagram with a pentacle at the center.

Imogen lays them on the table and lifts the lid on the pan. Sabrina leans forward to inspect the contents. Inside is some plastic tubing, gauze pads and tape, a brown bottle labeled *alcohol*, a small glass vial containing clear liquid, and a pair of hypodermic syringes.

"When consigning one's soul to the Devil," Imogen explains, "it is customary to sign in blood."

The blood-taking is performed on a vein in Sabrina's right arm, more efficiently than Dr. Aran's nurse had managed it on the left, still bearing the bruise. When the syringe is full she lifts the lid on the second item she fetched from the sideboard, the wooden box. Inside is a heavy glass inkwell, and a slender nibbed pen.

The syringe is emptied into the inkwell, and Imogen offers the pen to Sabrina. She accepts it, dips the nib deeply into her blood, and then consigns her soul with a flourishing signature suitably bold for such a reckless act.

The second syringe is used to inject the contents of the small glass vial. When Sabrina asks what it is Imogen's response is 'a sort of truth serum.' She removes the needle and tells Sabrina to count backward from ten.

Sabrina never reaches zero.

## A Trial by Ordeal

SABRINA AWAKENS. She is standing. Her mind might have been unconscious, but not so her body, and she wonders what state she is emerging from that would allow this—somnambulance? a trance? drug-induced psychotic delirium?

She is blindfolded and gagged. Her arms are secured over her head and bound at the wrists.

A long silence is broken by footsteps approaching from across the floor. The blindfold is removed, but by the time her eyes adjust whoever removed it has disappeared.

Sabrina finds that she is in the middle of a mirrored room, slightly sunken—away to her right, a few broad stairs lead up to a narrow gallery. There are no windows. The one door at the end of the gallery is the only visible exit.

She can see in the mirrors that her hands are bound by a pair of black leather cuffs from whose joining shackle runs a chrome-linked chain leading upward. Sabrina follows its course overhead: the chain is connected to a block-and-tackle arrangement hanging from the ceiling—she wonders if this was rigged only to ensure that she cannot fall, or is intended for some other purpose.

She studies her reflection. The gag is a strip of red silk tied behind her head. She is no longer wearing her own clothes, but instead a stiff corset, a small thong, fishnet stockings, and black patent-leather platform shoes. Someone has very carefully applied makeup, and her hair has been bundled up and secured with a clip, presumably to expose her neck, around which is a polished metal collar.

There is a trickle of blood running from the crook of her right arm where she was injected, but otherwise she appears unharmed.

She takes a few exploratory steps ahead until the chain above halts further progress, and then tries various other directions, but it is soon apparent that she is limited to a circle of about six feet in diameter, within reach of nothing, certainly not the gallery where sitting on the sideboard is a bag, her own, that contains her telephone.

She examines the room more deliberately, as a form of mental distraction. No rugs, just bare wooden floor, smoothly and evenly finished. On the side facing her is a sofa with two matching chairs on either side, low and upholstered in cream leather—fashionable modern furniture. There is a glass coffee table in front of the sofa, and on it are a pair of tablet computers, the hinges out to make them stand upright, but the screens are facing away from her. On either side of the chairs are lights, big studio lamps with silver umbrella-like reflectors, both pointed directly at her. Beside each lamp is a large professional-looking video camera mounted on a tripod—an echo of the encounter on the Windrush; she wonders if this is deliberate.

There are no other furnishings besides the sideboard along the gallery which, in addition to her bag, holds a length of folded black velvet fabric.

Despite the lack of windows she does not have the sense of being in a cellar, but instead a stylish living room that has been configured for the occasion—presumably for a video shoot, given the fact of the cameras.

The studio lamps suddenly illuminate, incredibly bright, and Sabrina shuts her eyes against the glare. She gradually reopens them, and when her eyes have sufficiently adjusted to allow her to again look in the direction of the lamps she sees that both cameras now have small red lights blinking on their faces: the video shoot has begun.

Imogen Hart enters the room. The tea-party dress is gone; she now wears a laboratory coat. *Dr. Hart* is embroidered on the pocket. She comes to a stop in front of Sabrina, and halts Sabrina's noises of protest with a finger to her lips.

"The gag will be removed now," she says, "but remember that, except to answer questions, you must not speak. If you do, the procedure will immediately terminate."

She steps over to the sofa, now plunged into deep shadow by the bright studio lamps on either side, and takes a seat on the right. Sabrina realizes that there is someone already sitting there, at the other end, the tips of his casually crossed legs just visible in the boundary of the shadow, someone who must have quietly entered immediately after those lamps were turned on. She can make out nothing of him other than he is male: the shoes are men's shoes, highly polished oxblood.

Two people, hence the two tablet computers.

The door opens and a third figure enters. He is dressed in robes and wears a full leather face mask, elaborately figured as a bull, including a pair of horns rising high above his head: it is the mask of the Minotaur. He comes to a halt in front of Sabrina and removes the gag; she feels a wave of relief in being able to breathe unhindered. He steps back and stares at her in silence for several minutes before speaking.

"What is thy nature?" he asks, in a deep commanding bass.

She does not answer. He nods, as if having expected no response, and walks over to the sideboard where, with his back to her, he carefully unfolds the black velvet cloth. When he turns around he is brandishing a length of rattan cane, six feet long, half an inch in diameter. He returns to a position in front of Sabrina.

"What is thy nature?"

She says nothing. He gently runs the tip of the cane from her left knee to hip, an insolent gesture, at once both caressing and threatening, but his eyes do not leave hers.

"What is thy nature?"

This time when she does not respond he gives a quick flick of the wrist, just an inch or two, but this is sufficient for the cane, stiff but flexible, to whip against the side of her buttock, delivering a sharp sting. Sabrina briefly flinches, an involuntary recoil, but quickly resumes an upright posture.

A long pause of expectation.

"What is thy nature?" he eventually repeats.

Sabrina remains mute.

The Minotaur steps to the side, taking a position from which a strike of the cane would come down squarely on her rear. She makes no move to twist her body away.

"What is thy nature?"

A pause, and then he brings the cane down hard across her behind. There is no hesitation, no holding back: it was delivered with full force, and she staggers under the blow.

A long silence follows, with no sound apart from Sabrina's labored breathing.

"What is thy nature?"

The second blow arrives a little lower than the first, but no less harshly—she could hear the rushing whoosh of the cane the instant before it landed—and Sabrina bites her lip in the effort to not cry out. She recovers herself and stands erect, and mute.

"What is thy nature?"

She spread her legs a little, bracing for the next blow. This time she feels the sting reverberate through her body, as if to absorb it, almost to be energized by it; something related to but not exactly pain. Nevertheless, her body reacts: her breathing becomes shallow and swift.

She repeatedly swallows. She breaks out in a sweat; feels it gather and flow down her temples and between her breasts and down her back; tastes the salty tang of it in her mouth.

"What is thy nature?"

With the fourth strike of the cane, she becomes fully bifurcated. She is two beings now: the psychological creature, absorbing the blow with a defiant satisfaction, even joy; and the physical, reeling under the assault, barely able to stand.

"What is thy nature?"

This time she would have collapsed were she not strung aloft. Tears run down her face, but she smiles, for the answer has suddenly come to her.

"What is thy nature?"

"Insatiate," she quietly croaks, "I am insatiate"—and the room goes dark.

SABRINA AWAKENS.

This time she is horizontal, lying supine. She runs a hand across her stomach: the corset and other clothing are gone. High above her is a ceiling of sand-colored stone. She looks to the right: here too there is coarse stone, not walls but rough, squared pillars, tapering slightly as they rise, supporting the heavy blocks of the structure above. The spaces between the pillars are fitted with linen curtains, thin and translucent, gently wafting in the breeze. Warm golden light pours through them, as if from a setting sun. She tilts her head back. The wall behind her is of the same tawny stone but is partly frescoed with hieroglyphs depicting a procession of creatures with human bodies and animal heads, all rendered in profile.

Sabrina lets a hand fall to the side, and rubs her fingers along whatever she lies upon. It is a block of solid stone, unmistakable in texture and rigidity, and so the place in which she has found herself is quite real, not some set designer's whimsical *papier-mâché* fantasy.

An Egyptian temple, judging by the hieroglyphs. Given the central location of the block on which she lies, it seems that she is once again laid out like a sacrifice upon an altar.

The room of her cane-induced admission could conceivably have been located in Headley Grange, but not this temple built of great blocks of stone. Even the air coming through those curtains is not temperate English air—it is too dry and too warm and too harsh: it is the air of the desert. But Sabrina observes all this in an abstracted fashion, in a meta-layer that, despite however undeniably real her surroundings may be, finds them no longer relevant to the matter at hand. She occupies a different level now: a plane of perception that is decoupled from mere sensation—a hyperstate of consciousness in which this new and unbridled perception is the only fundamental reality.

She turns the other way, to her left, and discovers that she is not alone.

There are two of them. They are both male, both dark, both naked—parodies of Nubian slaves perhaps, given the Egyptian theme. Each stands before a temple pillar and gazes at her with unhurried resignation. She rolls onto her side, propping her head on an arm raised at the elbow, and returns the gesture, surveying her company with the same long cool examination with which they contemplate her.

Her inspection soon reveals the reason for their dispassionate rectitude: they are eunuchs.

Sabrina realizes that she has been cast as a Cleopatra—or perhaps as an odalisque, a pampered concubine in some pasha's harem—and these are her attendants, unmanned and unthreatening, here to prepare her for whatever is to come. She turns onto her stomach, rests her head on crossed arms, and closes her eyes, signaling indifference.

She hears them approach and take up positions on either side of her. This is followed by the sound of a bottle or jar being opened, and then they rub their hands with whatever is inside: she is to be massaged. They apply not oil but something thicker, an unguent or balm, pungent with camphor and clove. They knead the balm into her behind, a buttock apiece in their enormous hands, slowly working in the ointment, and she soon feels a warmth—menthol perhaps—coursing through the flesh. It is a salve, she realizes, something to soothe the sting from the earlier encounter.

Soon her rear is rendered numb, feeling no remnant of the cane. Oil is drizzled between her shoulder blades and along the gully of her spine down to the small of her back, and along each leg from foot to thigh. The eunuchs take up positions at either end and begin massaging, no longer with the cautious therapeutic touch of earlier, but now with a more determined grasp, firmly working her flesh, as if to unknot it.

She has the sense of being tenderized, a carcass being prepared for consumption.

After a while they silently urge her to turn over. Again she is oiled and massaged.

Do they regret their circumstances, she wonders. Do they long for longing, to be filled with the frantic desire to be upon this body under their touch and gaze? Would they wish to ravish her with indiscriminate frenzy, like her imagined ravishment by the two satyrs at the amphitheater? Or instead, are they at ease, content to be freed from physical desire? Perhaps they are given a perception not available to those afflicted with physical yearning, able to see her body as something to be calmly appreciated rather than urgently possessed, and maybe they find this, if not necessarily preferable, at least not unwelcome.

She drifts into a deep sleep.

THIS TIME WHEN SABRINA awakens, she finds herself floating in a stream. Above her is an expanse of sky, deeply rose-hued, and dotted with clouds of a portentous dark gray. No sign of a sun, but the moon is visible, ominously close, filling an absurdly large portion of the sky, and in the firmament beyond, in exaggerated telephoto amplitude, hang the planets, red Mars and girdled Saturn. She is swiftly borne along in the luminous stream, not water but something heavier, oleaginous, supporting her weight with ease.

She is Pre-Raphaelite; she is Millais's *Ophelia*. She raises her head to see if she too is clad in a silvery gown, and discovers that she is covered in something altogether different: needles, dozens or even hundreds of them, inserted into her chest, breasts, stomach, everywhere. Each is topped with a polished metal head an eighth of an inch thick, three-quarters of an inch long, and which causes the needles, extraordinarily thin, to bend under the weight.

Acupuncture, Sabrina realizes. Despite the many piercings, she feels no pain; quite the opposite, she is sensorially alive, shockingly vibrant, abnormally alert to every subtlety of awareness.

She lowers her head back into the soft pillow of the brook and stares above at the ever-shifting sky as she floats down the stream, down the River Qi.

The stream empties into a small pond, grassy banked. Nymphs approach her, bare-breasted and waist-deep in the stream: she is no longer in the Millais; now she is in the Waterhouse, although Hylas is nowhere to be seen. The nymphs surround her and, one after another, gently pass their hands over the needles, softly brushing the weighted heads and so causing ripples of movement, like a breeze wafting across a field of ripe wheat. With each wave a flood of tiny sparks fire in Sabrina's flesh, sending out tendrils of electric heat that stream through her nerve threads and deep into her viscera. It is as if her body was woven through with a fiber-optic network into which a thousand tiny lasers were continuously discharging, sending waves of phased energy coursing through her system. Her senses were already heightened, but now too is perception: nothing can escape her—she is like a finely tuned antenna, able to distinguish the smallest of signals from deep space.

She has no awareness of time, just pure being.

The nymphs remove the needles, seven pairs of hands lightly plucking them from her flesh, and soon she is unpierced. A surge in the stream sends her onward. It swells, carrying her forward faster and faster. Now the stream is turbulent with speed, and then becomes a torrent, the restless flow bearing her ever more rapidly downstream. She suddenly plunges over the edge of a cataract, down and down, plummeting into the oblivion below.

She lands on the floor, and looks up. Before her is what she takes to be a tribunal. There are nine magistrates at a long judicial bench, raised as in a courtroom, and carved in a smooth ellipse around the point where

Sabrina now lies, naked and soaking on the floor, trying to regain her breath.

She has just been metaphorically born, she realizes—that was why the immersion had been Pre-Raphaelite: it was necessary for her to proceed from a state of innocence, from art that shunned artifice, an Eve before apples and serpents. The stream had been an ablution, a ritual cleansing prior to her examination. Now she is to be judged.

The magistrates who are to judge her are all female, as far as she can tell, and they are dressed not in judicial robes but the costumes of the Venetian *Carnevale*, highly colorful and wildly varied but for their masks: all these are identical, all the same expressionless white porcelain.

Sabrina stands, still dripping, and faces the tribunal. The magistrates are arranged in various postures, carefully posed and theatrically lit, forming a dramatic *tableau vivant,* presumably as a prelude to whatever is to follow.

One wears a brocaded maroon top, elaborated embroidered in gold thread and finished with a bright sun pendant, black gloves and a tricorn hat with a black veil—she leans casually against the wall while carefully observing Sabrina; another has adopted a coyer pose, all in white but for the delicate black lace fan with which she conceals her face below the eyes; a third wears a doublet whose puffed sleeves are ornately patterned, and with a long white plume of fabric draping down from her hat—she stands legs apart and arms crossed, a pugnacious pose; a fourth is in silver and black, and has arrayed herself languidly along the bench, one leg curled beneath her; another in a skirt with huge orange pleats and a ruff of Elizabethan magnitude sits on the arm of a chair while her neighbor, wearing a cloak of purple velvet, and a turban from which emerge long stalks supporting a variety of shining globes, perhaps representing the celestial spheres, leans forward with hands on the bench, gazing at Sabrina as if in accusation; the chief magistrate, standing in stately dignity in the middle, is the only one to display any flesh, wearing flowing classical robes, and crowned with a golden diadem.

Each of the magistrates has held in hand or sitting on the bench before them an object—one a flute; another a scroll; a third a lyre; a fourth a laurel wreath—and it is the presence of these items that spurs Sabrina's memory: they are the ancient Muses.

The chief magistrate sits, apparently the signal to begin, and then the one on the far left breaks the silence.

"Question, the first: What is the prime quality?"

"Courage," Sabrina immediately answers. She does not know where this answer came from, but come it did, and with perfect lucidity.

Now the magistrate on the far right speaks.

"Question, the second: Of what art thou formed?"

"Force and fire. Language. Yearning. Esperance. Time." Sabrina is alarmed by her response, which seems to have emerged without conscious thought. She does not even know what it means.

Now the second from the left addresses Sabrina; they are taking turns, and from their positions presumably from junior to senior.

"Question, the third: What is the condition caused by thee?"

"Deep light."

"Question, the fourth: What is thy agony?"

"Stupidity."

"Question, the fifth: For what dost thou hunger?"

"Clarity."

"Question, the sixth: When shalt thou be revealed?"

"In extremis."

"Question, the seventh: What is thy purpose?"

"Deliverance."

"Question, the eighth: To whom art thou in thrall?"

Sabrina answers without hesitation.

> *"Orchestral Satan, weeping many a rood*
> *Tears such as angels weep."*

A long silence follows Sabrina's last answer—perhaps, like her, they are trying to figure out where it might have come from. Finally, the chief magistrate rises, holding in her left arm a large book and in her right hand a writing tablet, perhaps with which to record the verdict. She does not immediately ask her question, perhaps wishing to reassess it after Sabrina's strange answer to the preceding one.

"Question, the ninth," she says. "Art thou to sunder thy bond with this Satan?"

This is the first of the questions that Sabrina has had to consider before responding, but the answer comes to her readily enough.

"There can be no sundering," she says, "where there has never been reconciliation."

# Fifth Circle

Erato

SABRINA ARRIVES AT the Ashmolean promptly at 11:00 A.M., uncomfortably aware of her lack of shame in entering an institution whose stolen property is currently sitting in her pocket. The appointment was made entirely by email, and she is surprised to discover that Dr. Jackson Nyley of the Egyptology department, who she imagined would be a tweedy gentleman of advancing years and receding hairline, someone having little patience with frivolous inquiries from young females, is in fact a Yorkshire woman about Sabrina's own age, with a broad lilting accent and a thick mass of unkempt hair, blond bordering on red, and wearing a fair and freckled expression of open good humor—a complexion less suited to a career in Egyptology would be hard to imagine, Sabrina thinks, other than albino.

Nyley offers a warm smile and welcoming handshake in greeting, perhaps as relieved as Sabrina to find that the other was not as she had imagined.

"Please call me Jackie."

"And I'm Sabrina."

Nyley leads her from the Museum's reception area through a security door into the staff quarters, where they go into a small conference room.

"I'm too junior to warrant my own office," she explains.

They soon get down to business, and Sabrina pulls from her bag a drawing of one of the hieroglyphs that had been on the back wall of the

Egyptian temple at Headley Grange—if it was Headley Grange—something that while lying on the stone altar she had memorized for later reference.

"This is what I wanted to ask you about. I tried the Sackler, but couldn't figure out a way to efficiently look it up—how do you enter a hieroglyph into a library catalog search?"

"There are lists of hieroglyphs compiled during the golden age of Egyptology; Gardiner's, which is organized by similarity; and Möller's, organized by historical period, but there are over a thousand hieroglyphs: it would be hard to do a useful translation without technical training. Plus, so much depends on context and period."

Sabrina passes the drawing across the desk, adding unnecessarily, "I'm not a very good draughtswoman."

Nyley studies it for a moment in silence. "I take it this was not meant to be a mouse," she says, pointing to the middle figure.

"Rather more a lion, I thought. Does any of it make sense?"

"Oh yes, it's quite straightforward enough. Where did you see it?"

"In a dream."

Nyley looks up in surprise but, seeing that Sabrina has no intention of explaining herself, resumes her study of the drawing.

"Did you forget anything?" she asks.

"Like what?"

"Maybe there was an oval, encircling them all?"

"As a matter of fact, there was: it was what made me focus on these particular hieroglyphs in the first place, that they were all grouped together. What is it?"

"It's called a cartouche."

"Is it significant?"

"Yes. It means that the hieroglyphs inside represent the name of a person, an important one, usually a pharaoh."

"Is that what this is, the name of a pharaoh?"

"It is." She stands. "Why don't we go into the exhibition hall?"

Nyley leads Sabrina back the way they came and then into the museum's Egyptian galleries, where she stops before a case containing a single object: a large black stone with the top broken off at an angle, and etched with a combination of hieroglyphs and alphabetic characters.

"The Rosetta Stone," Nyley announces. "Or, to be precise, the Ashmolean's reproduction of the Rosetta Stone—the original is in the British Museum. Are you familiar with it?"

"Only that it allowed hieroglyphs to first be deciphered, I think."

"Yes, exactly. It has three versions of the same text, a decree. The hieroglyphs are on top, with demotic Egyptian below, and Greek below that." Nyley takes a key from her pocket and unlocks the case, so that there is nothing between them and the exhibit. "Now see this?"

She points to the top left of the stone, where there is a cartouche, roughly carved, but recognizable as the same as in Sabrina's drawing.

"Who is it?"

"Ptolemy, one of the many Ptolemys, a dynasty that began with Ptolemy Soter—literally, Ptolemy the Savior, a general under Alexander—and whose last of the line was Cleopatra. In this case, it signifies Ptolemy V Epiphanes. The hieroglyphs are a phonetic translation of the Greek *Ptolemaios*, which is this part down here." She points to a section in the lower part of the stone: *ΠΤΟΛΕΜΑΙΟΣ*. "The square in your drawing, which is actually a stool or a stand, is the letter *P*, and this below it, which represents a loaf of bread, is the letter *T*."

"Hieroglyphs are read right-to-left?"

"Either way, left-to-right or right-to-left: the direction is determined by which way the figures face. But always top-to-bottom, hence the stand before the loaf. The lasso is *O*, the lion *L*, the altar *M*. A single reed is *I*; the two of them together represent an *I*-like diphthong, the last vowel sound in the Greek original. And the final symbol, a fold of cloth, represents the letter *S*: *Ptolemaios* in Greek; *Ptolemy* in English. This decree is from the year 196 B.C., when he had been pharaoh for nine years."

"Is there any special significance to Ptolemy V?"

"In the history of Egypt, not particularly. But there is certainly a special significance in the history of Egyptology: it was this cartouche that was the key to deciphering the Rosetta Stone. The stone was discovered by the French in 1799 during Napoleon's invasion, but Nelson destroyed the French fleet at the Battle of the Nile after which, unable to resupply, the expedition was doomed. The Rosetta Stone was taken by the English after they defeated the French and sent to the British Museum. Deciphering the Egyptian text, both demotic and hieroglyphic, proved very difficult—they are not straight translations but paraphrases, and little progress was made. Then, in about 1818, Thomas Young, a learned physician who was also the foreign secretary of the Royal Society, made a crucial finding: he realized that the cartouche represented a proper noun, using phonetic values. Champollion went on to famously finish the translation, but it was Young's deciphering of Ptolemy's cartouche that was the critical breakthrough."

"You said the Rosetta stone was a decree?"

"Yes."

"What does it say?"

"That from now on he, Ptolemy, was to be worshipped as a god."

THAT AFTERNOON, in the quiet of her rooms at Caiaphas, Sabrina makes a new entry in her journal.

> *The performances have entered a new phase: this past weekend's was the first to have taken place away from Temple Slaughter Preceptory, and the first to have involved physical force. The question is whether to continue, and since it still remains uncomfortable to sit my inclination is to say no. I have the rest of the week to make up my mind, one way or the other.*

*There is also no question of it all being just a dream: that cane was obviously real—I bear the welts to prove it—and for a short while I could still faintly make out some of the acupuncture marks. I must have been immersed in water: my hair was knotted in the way it is after drying without having being combed out. But there were dreamlike aspects: rushing down a cataract and landing on the floor of the trail chamber could not have been literally true—even at the time I realized this, but I also knew that, however I might have arrived, the fact that I was on the floor naked and soaking was entirely real.*

*How did they get me back to Caiaphas? Presumably through the Dean's Garden; there is no way they could have carried me unconscious past the porters' lodge without a fuss being raised.*

*Insatiate? Yes, I suppose so, but isn't desire a thousand times preferable to self-satisfied complacency? Who is it who says that they have had enough of what life has to offer? A saint, a hermit, a suicide? Or maybe it is simpler than that: perhaps 'satiated' would serve as a fair definition of 'bourgeois.' Better insatiate than the dull decrepitude of suburban docility.*

*But insatiate for what? Or is it non-specific: not an unquenchability for a particular thing but a general condition, an inability to be satisfied with the status quo, an endless yearning for something more, something better? It had seemed self-evidently the right response at the time of its utterance, yet now I find the precision has withered, like a dream drifting away after waking. The drug, no doubt.*

*The signing in blood was rather obvious: can't the Devil be more original?*

*Harder to explain is:*

> Orchestral Satan, weeping many a rood
> Tears such as angels weep.

*The quotation is from James Joyce's* Ulysses, *and is a corrupted concatenation of two well-separated lines of 'Paradise Lost': "Lay floating many a rood, in bulk as huge" (line 196 of Book I, 1674 edition) and "Tears, such as Angels weep, burst forth: at last" (line 620 of Book I, 1674 edition). A rood is a quarter acre, invoked to convey Satan's large size (the word has a second meaning: a crucifix hanging above the entrance to a chancel). The original Milton I might have heard recited by Bronaryre that night in the Dean's Garden, although I have no conscious recollection of it. I did* Finnegan's Wake *at school, but not* Ulysses*—I've never read a line of* Ulysses *in my life: how could I have said this?*

*The Muses have no judicial role in the ancient mythology, just inspirational and, occasionally, palliative (via forgetfulness). They are associated with water (the springs of Helicon) and are sometimes characterized as water nymphs. Hesiod has them as being the daughters of Zeus and Mnemosyne (memory), but in typical Greek fashion other writers have different genealogies.*

*The chief magistrate's book, tablet, and golden diadem identify her as Calliope—epic poetry—and there are precedents for this ranking: both Hesiod and Ovid characterize her as the chief Muse. She is also the only Muse with notable offspring: Orpheus, source of that dark underworld cult within the ancient world that gave rise to the Dionysian Mysteries.*

*Calliope is the only Muse to be named in the 'Divine Comedy,' where Dante encounters the Muses in Purgatory and seeks their aid in helping his poem arise from Hell (Courtney Langdon, sim. pub. Cambridge, Harvard University Press & London, Oxford University Press, 1920):*

> Ma qui la morta Poesì resurga,
> o sante Muse, poi che vostro sono;
> e qui Calliopè alquanto surga,
> seguitando il mio canto con quel suono

> *But here let Poetry arise from death,*
> *since, holy Muses, yours I am; and let*
> *Calliopë, here somewhat higher soaring,*
> *with those sweet tones accompany my song*

*Given my role as the Devil's amanuensis, there is an obvious parallel here: I am cast as Calliope to Bronaryre's Dante.*

*The temple is a dead end, at least so far. There are a surprising number of Egyptian temples in England—they were popular in the Nineteenth Century as follies in the grounds of the great estates—but none that I found photographs of resembles the one in the... I don't even know what to call it: fantasy?—no, there was nothing allegorical about that caning: I will stick with that same noncommittal term I have been using until now: 'masque,' something in which the lines between truth and fiction are accommodatingly nebulous.*

*The pharaonic cartouche must have a meaning—nothing in Bronaryre's masques happens without a purpose—but I have yet to nail it down. The cartouche, being the breakthrough to the deciphering of hieroglyphs, could be said to represent a key to knowledge that was previously hidden—the forbidden apple in an Egyptological Paradise—and would fit in with his mission of exciting men's minds with more desire to know.*

*On the other hand, perhaps he was just proclaiming himself a deity, and inviting me to worship him.*

IT IS NOT UNTIL late in the evening that Sabrina realizes she has left one lead unpursued: Led Zeppelin. Now that she again has a wireless connection she does some basic research.

The band was infamous in its heyday, especially when touring—the Hilton hotel chain banned them from their properties worldwide. But whereas other rock groups of the era would cultivate a reputation, knowing that notoriety would help record sales, Led Zeppelin were the opposite: highly private, shunning the press, surrounded by impenetrable security, and so unwilling to engage with anyone outside their entourage that they had their own airliner, a big Boeing emblazoned with the band's name.

Their origin story was distinctive, too: not the usual many years of weary toil before being noticed by a record company executive: instead, Jimmy Page formed the band, paid for studio time from his own pocket, and then presented the master tapes of what was to be their first album to the president of Atlantic Records in New York, insisting that he would retain full artistic control, even to the album covers, and that whereas all their other rock bands were on the Elektra label, Led Zeppelin albums would instead be released on the prestigious Atlantic label, reserved for their biggest acts: Aretha Franklin, Ray Charles, John Coltrane and the like.

The president of Atlantic Records agreed and all of a sudden, with the breakup of the Beatles, Led Zeppelin became the biggest band in the world. They played Carnegie Hall in New York, The Royal Albert Hall in London, the Jazz Festival in Newport. Soon they broke the Beatles' record for the biggest ever attendance at a single-act concert. Yet the more Page rose in fame the more remote and reclusive he became. He was already dabbling with the occult: some copies of the third album had Crowley's Thelemic injunctions *Do what thou wilt* and *So mote it be* etched into the run-off area, that mostly blank space where the needle turns in toward the spindle.

Then came the fourth album, the one recorded at Headley Grange. Page, always secretive, became extreme: not only would the album be untitled, it would also be anonymous: the band's name does not appear on the cover. This inscrutability was to be absolute: he even forbade the printing of the serial number on the spine. The Atlantic executives pleaded with Page, warning him that it would be a disaster, but he was adamant, and so in late 1971 the fourth album was released with the strangest cover in the history of recorded music: a dreary project block in the background—what the English call 'council flats'—and in the foreground a collapsed wall with peeling wallpaper, bearing a picture of an old man bent with the weight of a bundle of sticks upon his back.

That album became one of the biggest selling of all time, and remains a best seller half a century after its release, each succeeding generation discovering it anew. The Headley Grange sessions that produced it became the stuff of legend.

Page was by now fully immersed in the occult. He adopted an esoteric symbol—roughly "Zoso"—that was first revealed on the interior of the fourth album's sleeve, and which subsequently appeared on his amplifiers, his guitar cases, his clothing. He refused to reveal the meaning. He underwrote a book store and printing press devoted to publishing the classics of necromancy. He became a noted collector of occult paraphernalia. He began to wear 'dragon suits' on stage. He was accused of hiding dark subliminal messages on the records, of hosting ritualistic orgies of underage girls, of outright sorcery.

And then Sabrina finds a startling connection: in 1970, Jimmy Page bought Boleskine House, that same house on the shores of Loch Ness that Aleister Crowley had once owned: the same Aleister Crowley who, apparently resurrected, had been seen arguing with Scaglietti on the night of the Justice's death.

Sabrina looks up Boleskine House. It is a Grade B listed building, which is to say that it is protected as part of British heritage from alteration or demolition. After a quarter century of ownership Page sold it, and the house is currently held by a non-profit foundation whose stated purpose, carrying on the tradition of the house's two famous former owners, is research into the occult.

There is no detail about the foundation on the public web, but in Britain such institutions are required to register for tax purposes, and the details of those registrations are available via a service. Sabrina logs into her Bodleian account, accesses the service, and soon has the details.

It turns out that the foundation is entirely funded by Pendle Hill Investments.

TRAINS FROM OXFORD arrive in London at Paddington Station, but the train to Edinburgh leaves from King's Cross, and so Sabrina, being too unfamiliar with the tube to trust that she can make the tight connection, is forced to take a cab across London in morning rush hour traffic. She runs down the platform at King's Cross, pulling the hastily packed bag behind her, and finds her seat with just minutes to spare.

The train, operated by London North Eastern Railway, arrives in Edinburgh at lunchtime. Sabrina would like to have had an opportunity to explore the city, but all she sees of Edinburgh is Waverley Station, and twenty minutes later she leaves on a ScotRail train bound for Inverness, the capital of the Highlands.

By the time the city comes into view the skies have clouded over, and Moray Firth is a cold gray expanse. It begins to rain as the train pulls into the station, which will no doubt mean a struggle to find a cab, and Sabrina is feeling ever more foolish for having undertaken this impulsive journey north.

She exits the station building and pauses under the portico, examining the square. A clock above her chimes briefly: it is exactly 5:00 P.M. A statue of some Highland warrior stands in the center of the square, and on the asphalt are several parking spots marked TAXI, shiny in the rain, and all conspicuously unoccupied. There is a scattering of other vehicles, but none of them with a light on top.

Sabrina is about to press on when a vehicle enters the square. It is not a cab, it is a Rolls-Royce, obviously an old one, very large, claret-colored, and with a huge upright grille sporting a winged Spirit of Ecstasy radiator cap. The car glides over the pavement and curls around the square, driving in the wrong direction, but at a leisurely, unconcerned pace. The Rolls comes to a dignified halt right in front of her, at the red-painted curb that is clearly signposted *No Standing at Anytime*.

A man gets out without shutting down the engine. He is bulky, wears a bowler hat, a heavy overcoat with an Astrakhan collar, and a look of deep self-importance. No umbrella; he seems unaware of the rain, as if the heavens would not dare dampen him. He turns to Sabrina, doffs his bowler with a slight bow, and says in a deep voice, "Dr. Lancaster, I presume."

"Mr. Crowley," she replies, for there is no mistaking that big shaved head and oddly pointed ears.

Crowley nods in acknowledgment, returns to the Rolls, and opens the rear door in invitation.

Sabrina spends a moment considering the wisdom of accepting a ride from this very strange stranger, but then supposes that it is ridiculous to go to the seashore and then hesitate to swim. She steps over to the door, but pauses before getting in the back.

"I take it that I am expected?"

Crowley seems slightly affronted by the question, perhaps at being questioned at all. He leans in very close, his big face just inches from hers, his dark eyes boring into her. Sabrina resists the urge to retreat, or show any other sign of backing down.

"I have been expecting you for a hundred years," he says, in that big ringing voice.

"But how did you know that I would be here now? Arriving on this particular train?"

"I know everything, madam," Crowley states definitively. He pauses before proceeding, perhaps daring her to question this grand pronouncement, before leaning even closer. "I know you better than you know yourself. I know thy very soul."

There is not much that can be said to that, Sabrina thinks. She steps inside and Crowley closes the door behind her. He puts her bag into the trunk and then gets back in behind the steering wheel, a mighty piece of equipment fit for maneuvering a battleship. Soon the big car is underway.

Sabrina clears her throat in preparation to ask where they are going, but before she can put the question a glass partition suddenly slides up, separating the chauffeur from the passenger compartment. It comes to a halt with a faintly pneumatic thunk.

Mr. Crowley is not feeling chatty, it seems—perhaps understandable for someone who expired the best part of a century ago.

Sabrina gazes about the rear cabin: there are chrome fittings and leather straps and a forest's worth of burled walnut. She decides to sit back and enjoy the ride as the Rolls glides through the streets of Inverness, feeling a little like a fairy princess, notwithstanding that the chauffeur is a member of the undead. The rear compartment is very large, making Sabrina think of the big dresses of a bygone era: in this vehicle, a debutante could be confident of arriving at her coming-out ball with her gown uncrushed. The compartment is so large that the floor is fitted with footrests that flip open, giving the occupants something on which to brace themselves during braking in pre-seatbelt days. The forward bulkhead is fitted with fold-down tables made of the ubiquitous burled walnut, highly varnished. Open one up and a mirror is revealed, she discovers, perfectly angled, allowing one to check makeup before arriving at the party.

They leave Inverness, more a town than a true city, and are soon floating down a country road running by a long, narrow body of water: Loch Ness. Beyond it are heather-strewn Highland hills, cold and wet, shrouded in mist.

They have been traveling for about an hour, Sabrina guesses, when Crowley slows and turns into a long drive leading up a steep hill. They proceed past a graveyard and several outbuildings until arriving at the main house, situated at the top of the rise.

Boleskine House is built in the Highland style: spare whitewashed walls; roof steeped to slough off snow; treeless exposure, maybe to ensure an uninterrupted view of the Loch, or perhaps to provide minimal cover for the approach of marauding clans.

The Rolls circles around to the other side where there is a courtyard, and comes to a halt by the entrance. Crowley gets out and opens the door to the rear compartment. He offers no welcome. Sabrina disembarks and follows him wordlessly to the front door, determined to match his reticence.

The front hall of Boleskine House is an ornate passageway running through pillared arches across the house to the wings on either side. The walls are covered in worked gilt paneling, the ceiling is pressed tin, and the only furniture is a table on which Crowley tosses his overcoat and bowler.

There is no butler, but on her hands and knees on the floor is a cleaning woman. She looks up at their arrival, and Sabrina realizes that, despite the bucket and cloth with which she is washing the floor, she is not a cleaning woman after all: she is no older than Sabrina, her hair is neatly coifed, and she is dressed not for cleaning but a cocktail party: short black dress, stiletto-heeled shoes, and around her neck is a string of pearls.

Crowley notices Sabrina's look of surprise. "She misbehaved," he states, in what he apparently believes to be an explanation, "and I was compelled to confiscate her mop."

Crowley leads Sabrina into the center of the hall. He pauses, his eyes gazing along the passageway to the right.

"Do not go to the western wing at any time, no matter what you may see or hear."

He leads her in the opposite direction, to the left, until coming to a halt at the door of a bedroom.

"You may bathe and dress. We will dine at the setting of Venus. You will find all that is needed here. Clothing, everything. Wear it all, and add nothing of your own: the items have been selected to ensure Thelemic harmony, and the proper practice of tonight's ceremony requires that there be a perfect balance." He turns and walks back down the passageway.

"What time does Venus set?" Sabrina asks his retreating back.

Crowley stops and slowly turns, his face bearing the same scowl as at the train station: a man displeased at the impertinence of being questioned.

"As I said, you will find all that you need in your room."

SABRINA CLOSES THE bedroom door. There is no lock. She opens the closet and finds in there a dress. The material is Thai silk, thick, woven in a complex pattern of burnished bronze and glossy black, lustrous to the eye and pleasing to the touch. The dress is long and form-fitting, but there are slits at the sides to allow walking at something other than a shuffle. On the floor beneath are sandals, brass-colored to pick up the bronze in the dress.

She goes to the dressing table. On top is a makeup set, *circa* 1925: silver-backed brush and matching hand mirror; a leather-bound manicure set; a black glass perfume bottle from whose top dangles a small bulb pump covered in embroidered cloth and finished with a tassel, intended for spraying; various unguents and creams; a single lipstick; a powder bowl complete with puff; eye shadow; nail lacquer; and lastly a squat little crystal jar whose content when the silver cap is removed is revealed to be an extraordinarily fine black powder: kohl, she realizes—basically soot—a substance whose function was to be mascara in the days before mascara.

No laudanum; she is unsure if this is disappointing or not.

Sabrina opens the top drawer. There is an abundance of bronze jewelry: earrings and bracelets, rings and armbands. The largest is a pendant in the form of an Egyptian ankh with a crescent moon, studded with what might be diamonds but are probably just glass crystals.

The second drawer contains a thick book, soft-covered in blue. She pulls it out, expecting something esoteric, perhaps one of Crowley's own works, but the title is *Nautical Almanac*, and it turns out to contain navigational tables.

The third and last drawer is empty. Nowhere, it seems, is there to be found any underwear.

Sabrina locates the bathroom. There is a large claw-footed, roll-top tub located in the middle of the room, with industrial-looking piping and faucets. The toilet is an ancient affair, the cast-iron cistern mounted high above and activated by a pull chain. The walls are covered in mosaic tiles depicting scenes that on closer inspection remind her of Pompeii, specifically the brothel, another place that the nuns had seemed to enjoy.

Sabrina fills the tub and then sits back in it with the *Nautical Almanac*. As she leafs through the book she sees very little that is specifically nautical. Instead, the tables are mostly astronomical: they specify position data for the sun, moon, stars, and planets. Sabrina realizes that this must be how she is expected to determine the setting of Venus. The introduction explains the nautical reference: the volume was intended for mariners in the days when navigation at sea was done by the stars. The data are normalized into Greenwich Mean Time, which means that the only correction she needs to convert to British Summer Time is to add an hour for daylight savings. She goes to the pages for today's date and locates Venus. There are hourly listings for 'Greenwich

Hour Angle,' which according to the glossary is the number of degrees west from Greenwich above which the planet is at the corresponding time. Since the journey to Inverness was basically north, she makes the assumption that she is at 0° longitude, and that Venus would therefore presumably set when its Greenwich Hour Angle is 90°. Sabrina interpolates between hours and determines that the planet will set at about 9:35 P.M., giving her sufficient time for a long warming soak.

AFTER DRESSING, Sabrina examines herself in the mirror, a freestanding, full-length piece of furniture, hinged to allow it to be set at the correct angle. None of the items of makeup would have been her choice: the powder is too dark, the lipstick and eye shadow an odd bronze shade, and the kohl has turned her into a ghoul. The dress is cut too low and the bodice is too tight, even on her slender frame. The accouterments included a tortoise-shell fillet, and so she has her hair up, providing a blank canvas of uninterrupted flesh from earlobes to sternum serving as a base for much of the jewelry. Bronze is the theme: there are two enormous earrings of multistory bronze fringes, ever wider, like a Babylonian ziggurat. Her upper arms are wrapped in stylized bronze serpents. She has bronze bangles on her wrists that rattle annoyingly whenever she moves; perhaps these are intended to announce her arrival, or to ensure that she does not go sneaking into the off-limits western wing. Dominating the display is the ornament suspended between her breasts, a crescent moon two inches across and four inches high, almost enveloping the pendant ankh hanging from the upper point of the crescent. The stones sparkle with a brilliance that makes Sabrina wonder if they are not real diamonds after all.

AT PRECISELY 9:35 P.M., SABRINA enters the main salon. It is furnished less in the Highland style than in the Oriental: low divans, richly cushioned; a Persian rug; glass cabinets displaying dusty artifacts that look like cast-offs from Tutankhamun's tomb; and a large ottoman upholstered in buttoned green leather on which Crowley sits cross-legged, eyes closed and arms extended to his knees, apparently in a posture of meditation. Any hesitation about the oddness of her attire is instantly dispelled: he is wearing a large turban, what might be a caftan or just odd pajamas, toe-curled oriental slippers, and a bandolier from which hangs a scabbard sheathing what appears to be a broad-bladed scimitar.

His eyes open at her bangle-rattling arrival.

"What is the longitude of Boleskine House?" he asks.

"I assumed zero degrees."

"You have assumed incorrectly. We are approximately four and a half degrees west of Greenwich, and since every degree represents four minutes of time, you have arrived eighteen minutes early."

"Sorry to have interrupted your meditation."

"I wasn't meditating; meditation is a pretension of feeble-minded ponces. I was communing with Ra-Hoor-Khuit."

"Who is Ra-Hoor-Khuit?"

"The Crowned and Conquering Child; a war god."

"Egyptian?"

"All the good ones are." Crowley unfurls himself from the ottoman, surprisingly supple for such a large man.

"Speaking of the supernatural, you died in 1947."

"Yes, I know—I was there at the time."

"Yet here you are."

"I have been, as you can plainly see, resurrected."

"Resurrected?"

"Quite common in Egypt, and of course hardly unheard of in Western culture, given that preposterous religion at the center of it. Now, since we have eighteen minutes to spare, let us use it profitably. I propose to show you the secret tunnel."

There is indeed a secret tunnel, accessed via the cellar. Another subterranean passageway—Sabrina wonders at how her life lately has suddenly become strangely chthonic. Crowley lights a candle and continues talking as he leads Sabrina through the narrow tunnel, as claustrophobic as had been the Templar ruins of her dream. She does not know in which direction they are heading, but senses that it is sloping downward.

"I met Ra-Hoor-Khuit in 1901," Crowley says. "I was in Egypt, on a honeymoon with my wife, Rose Edith Kelly. She, like you, was a skeptic; and she was, as you will be, brought to understanding. We spent a night in the central chamber of the Great Pyramid of Giza, the Pyramid of Cheops. The chamber is located deep in the interior and is reached by a long steep passageway, very much like this one, so low that one cannot stand up straight.

"Eventually, we reached the great interior chamber, a large room. There were no furnishings or fittings other than a single sarcophagus, open and empty. One can sense above the crushing weight of all that stone. The original aim had merely been to visit the place, to tread in the footsteps of Napoleon as it were, but as soon as we entered that chamber I felt that it was a deeply spiritual place. I dismissed the guide, and we stayed there that night."

Crowley stops and turns, the light from the candle held at waist level illuminating his face from below, an effect that Sabrina finds rather gruesome.

"We disrobed. Her flesh was cream incarnate; I, a lapping leopard. We made love, again and again, impossibly and in every way possible."

"I think I saw the illustrated version in the bathroom."

"When you have proved that God is merely a name for the sex instinct, it appears to me not far to the perception that the sex instinct is God." Crowley turns and resumes leading her through the long tunnel.

Eventually, they come to an iron gate. Crowley takes a set of keys from his bandolier and unlocks it. They emerge into what Sabrina sees is that same graveyard they passed on the way in. The sun has dipped behind the hills, and in the gloaming the place has a soft and subdued feel, fitting for a burial ground. The loch lies beyond, the surface mirror flat apart from an occasional flutter, like a shiver running across the flanks of a racehorse.

The tombstones are old and lichen-covered, many lying at odd angles as the soil beneath them has subsided, perhaps brought on by the gradual rotting away of those whose places they mark. Or maybe, Sabrina thinks, they have been resurrected, too.

They walk apart among the tombstones for a few minutes in silence, broken by Sabrina.

"Why is there a graveyard on your property?"

"It used to be a church graveyard. Boleskine House is built on the site of an old Thirteenth-Century kirk that burned to the ground, killing the entire congregation. It was never rebuilt: there had always been a great deal of magic in the area; the ministers had to continually relay bones to rest due to a local warlock, who was in the habit of raising the dead."

"I can see how that would be a nuisance."

"Come, I'll show you the mortuary."

The mortuary is a stone building, surprisingly large, as big as a large house.

"How high was the death rate, that they needed so much room?"

"It was because bodies were brought here and kept under guard for a period of time before burial, until they had decomposed to the point where they would be of no use to body-snatchers. That's the original purpose of the tunnel we just came through: it was intended to allow the warden to secretly alert the authorities, should grave-robbers be spotted."

A wisp of smoke emerges from the chimney.

"What's it used for now?"

"It's where I keep my coven."

"Your coven?"

"Witches. Come and have a look."

They enter the mortuary, whose inside is a startling contrast to the building's bleak exterior: it is a place of plush sofas and fabrics, elegant satinwood furniture in the Art Nouveau style, embers in the fireplace glowing peacefully. No steaming cauldrons, no stuffed owls, no dolls with pins poking through them.

"Where are the witches?"

Crowley pulls out a pocket watch. "Sitting around the dining table in harkening and obedient silence, I hope—they are not permitted to speak when in the main house, unless first spoken to. Let us go join them."

THE WITCHES ARE AS Crowley had hoped, sitting in silence around the dining table, and among them is the one Sabrina had mistaken for a cleaning woman. They are all about her age, perhaps a little younger. They are dressed in evening wear that looks to date from the early Edwardian era—from the evidence of their clothes and furnishings, and the makeup in her own room, Sabrina concludes that Crowley is recreating the time when he was in the full flush of manhood, back when he was still alive.

"My calling is to be the vessel through which the true Law is revealed," Crowley declares. "and every Messiah needs his apostles."

There are nine of them, and Sabrina wonders if this is deliberate, intended to echo the nine circles of Dante's *Inferno*. Despite being Crowley's disciples there is nothing docile or submissive in their postures; indeed the opposite: they look like an intelligent group, and Sabrina thinks that they probably have lively discussions when back in the mortuary, out of Crowley's earshot. They inspect Sabrina with frank and good-natured interest; she can almost read the eyes of one of them, saying, "Yes, he's rather ridiculous, but kind-hearted at core; you mustn't mind us humoring him."

No doubt there would normally be four on either side with one at the end, but tonight five have been squeezed onto one side to make room for Sabrina. Crowley introduces them, starting on Sabrina's left and moving counterclockwise around the table.

"Meretseger, a Cobra Goddess, Sentinel of the Necropolis."

Meretseger winces at the introduction, but smiles in welcome.

"Baast, a Cat Goddess, Holder of Secrets."

The Cat Goddess is open and friendly; Sabrina would have taken her for more of a dog person.

"Anath, a Warrior Goddess, Instigator of War. Nekhebit, a Vulture Goddess, Protector of the Pharaoh. Pakhet, a Panther Goddess, Agent of Vengeance. Tefnut, a Lion Goddess, Bringer of Water."

Tefnut is the one whose mop had been confiscated, and Sabrina wonders if being the 'Bringer of Water' has condemned her to be the one who always has to scrub the floor.

"Hedjedjet, a Scorpion Goddess, Conveyor of the Dead. Hathor, a Sun Goddess, Eye of Ra. Nuit, a Cow Goddess, Guardian of the Cosmos."

Sabrina supposes that being given responsibility for the entire cosmos is some measure of recompense for the indignity of being labeled a Cow Goddess.

"It is Nuit who revealed to me the first part of *The Book of the Law*. These are of course not their given names; they have adopted titles from the Egyptian pantheon on taking up their necromantic novitiate, deities whose powers they seek to successfully channel. The training for the occult practices requires the sustained discipline of both body and spirit, much like that in a nunnery, and thus they do not speak: think of them as a silent order. However, tonight, in honor of your visit, this rule has been relaxed."

The first to speak is Hedjedjet, Conveyor of the Dead. "I'm on kitchen duty tonight, so right now I'm the conveyor of dead vegetables: would you like some parsnip soup?"

Sabrina replies that she would, and realizes that she has not eaten since before boarding the train at King's Cross, and she is famished.

The place explodes in a sudden frenzy: Hedjedjet leaves for the kitchen; Nekhebit fetches soup bowls from a sideboard; Meretseger goes from place setting to place setting distributing bread rolls from a basket; Hathor fills wine glasses from a decanter.

The 'witches,' Sabrina realizes, are actually domestic staff.

Hedjedjet returns with a large china tureen. Soup is served, and the meal gets underway. The witches are apparently as hungry as Sabrina—they are all skinny; Crowley obviously starves them—and it is not until the edge of hunger has been blunted that conversation gets properly underway.

"You've got good legs," Tefnut tells Sabrina. "I could see them when you arrived while I was cleaning the floor. I wanted to run my hands over your calves, but it might have alarmed you. May I do so later?"

Before Sabrina can respond to this strange request, Anath interrupts—as might be expected from the Instigator of War.

"Do you have any books?" she asks. "Anything but sorcery."

"Two," Sabrina replies. "One fiction and the other non-fiction; neither in any way occult. I'll give them to you before I go."

"How long are you staying?"

"I go back tomorrow."

This is met with general disappointment and seems to spur them to ask more questions now.

"Where do you live?"

"Are you a witch, too?"

"Do you believe in the Loch Ness monster?"

"What do you do for a living?"

"Are you Elect?"

"How are the Red Sox doing?"—Baast is evidently a fellow American.

Sabrina does her best to respond while asking some questions of her own—How long have you been here? What made you come? How did you find out about Boleskine House to begin with? The answers are a strange mixture—three months; to find sanctuary for my kind; in a transcendental vision—but are enough to make it clear that they are not kept here under any duress or compulsion. Quite the opposite: they seem to have a sense of privilege, of being special, something that the unanswerable *Are you Elect?* had hinted at, for it is evident in their quiet confidence that these young women share a sense of being Elect themselves, whatever 'Elect' might mean.

As for Crowley, he is presumably insane but gives no hint of being dangerously so, of being berserk, and while she would never characterize him as harmless there is nothing blatantly salacious or prurient in the arrangements.

The meal continues through shepherd's pie, well made although a little bland, but Hedjedjet's creative impulses expired before dessert, which is a simple dish of tinned peaches and fresh cream.

Crowley utters not a single word during the entire meal.

AFTER DINNER, THE witches clear away the table and do the washing up. Sabrina goes to her room, returning with the books she brought along for the journey. It is her habit when traveling to take two books, one fiction—this time a Dorothy L. Sayers mystery she had purchased in the hope of becoming better acquainted with Oxonianisms—and the other non-fiction—on this occasion Tolinski's *Light & Shade*, an account of the music of Led Zeppelin, which she had finished on the train while listening to the songs it discussed on headphones. She leaves the books on the table in the hall where they cannot be missed, and makes a mental note to stop at the bookstore at the railroad station before beginning the journey back south.

When Sabrina returns to the main salon she finds that Crowley has changed clothes: he is now wearing regular pants and shoes, a collared white shirt with a bow tie, and a smoking jacket. He would almost appear normal were it not for the headgear: the turban is gone, replaced by a large triangular hat, worn sideways, and with a single big eye painted in the middle.

He again sits cross-legged on the ottoman, and ignores Sabrina while reading a book from whose cover she can see is one of his own. By the evidence of his expression, he finds the author agreeable.

The witches gradually rejoin them. Nuit and Nekhebit light candles and switch off the floor lamps. Anath moves an armchair to the center of the room and places it directly facing Crowley; Sabrina is reminded of a witness stand. Anath turns to Sabrina and offers her the chair; Sabrina realizes that it is she who is to be placed on trial. Hedjedjet mixes a scotch and soda at the sideboard, a reward for herself after having prepared the meal, Sabrina thinks, but then she walks over and places it on a side table by the armchair—in this star chamber, at least the accused is made comfortable. Tefnut kneels on the carpet beside Sabrina and begins stroking her calves.

Crowley puts aside his book and scrutinizes Sabrina with intensity, as if she were the Devil herself.

"I will ask you a series of questions," he says, "the answers to which may rend the fabric of existence."

"I have a condition."

Crowley is not pleased with this response. "A *condition*?"

"If you may question me, then I may question you."

"Me?"

"Yes, and you must faithfully undertake to answer my questions honestly and frankly, as I undertake to answer yours."

Crowley considers this for a moment. "I consent," he says at last.

"Thank you."

"Consider well, but do not dwell. Answer without thought, without guile, without wit. Answer from your core being. We begin."

"As you wish."

"What is your true name?"

An easy one, Sabrina thinks, but then she realizes that perhaps it is not so easy after all: she does not know her 'true' name, nor even if she was ever given one. The *Lancaster* part she has always assumed was derived from the county name—Pennsylvania, not England—the location of the convent where she was a foundling—part Defoe's *Moll Flanders*, part Fielding's *Tom Jones*—discovered abandoned in a basket upon the chapel altar: presumably the result of an unintended pregnancy in the Amish community, a matter of deep shame in their primitive Old Testament ways. Her first name has always puzzled her: why would the nuns not have chosen something Biblical. They never bothered giving her a middle name.

"I don't know my true name," she admits, "nor if I have ever had one."

Crowley was not expecting this response, and a ripple of surprise spreads through the witches. He leans forward slightly, as if inspecting an interesting oddity.

"Describe your moral qualities," he says.

Technically not a question, Sabrina thinks, but if she is to have his cooperation later she cannot raise objections now.

"Clear-eyed," she says after a moment. "I see things as they are."

Again she senses a heightening of interest—perhaps it was predetermined that they would do this, no matter what the answers.

"What is the color of your visions?"

Interesting that he would assume she was subject to visions, she thinks, but at least this time the answer requires no thought. "Red," she answers, "the color of drying blood."

The reaction to this is beyond interest: Hedjedjet gasps in astonishment, and Anath's eyes fill with tears. Crowley remains composed though, as if however surprising her answers may seem, he had suspected all along.

"I will state ten names. You will choose he that characterizes your visions." He says them slowly, giving her time to consider each one. "Amenhotep, Mandulis, Serapis, Nefertum, Petbe, Horus, Anubis, Khesfu, Heneb, Apesh."

"Horus," she answers, because it sounds like *horror*.

There is a long pause following her response, but Sabrina cannot tell if it is of surprise or disappointment in her answer.

"Choose the figure in this room that is he."

At first Sabrina thinks that he means from among himself and the witches, but then realizes that she is to choose from the artifacts on display. She stands and goes to a cabinet. There are several figures, variously between six and eighteen inches high, carved in the round, facing forward with one leg bent in the traditional Egyptian way, some with animal rather than human heads. Half are female, which she instantly dismisses, and the others are too calm and composed to be good candidates for representing chaos. One figure is different from the rest: a scribe, seated rather than standing and, unlike the others, which were of undecorated stone, this figure has been painted, the flesh is a dark color that seems appropriate for someone living in a land of sun and desert. But the scribe is too fat and jolly, she thinks, not right at all. Her eyes move up to the next shelf: more statuettes, and behind them, mounted in a frame, a scrap of what is presumably papyrus. It depicts a figure, drawn side-on, marching forward. His head is that of a bird of prey, watchful and threatening. He wears only a short tunic. The exposed flesh is a vibrant, rust-hued red.

"This one," she says, without needing to inspect the rest. She returns to her seat with all eyes upon her, and she knows that, with this response at least, she hit a bull's-eye. He pulls a drawing from inside the front cover of his book and lays it before her. It depicts a series of hieroglyphs, this time in their encasing cartouche, that Sabrina immediately recognizes.

"I will list five pharaonic names. You will tell me which name is represented by this cartouche. They are Cheops, Ramses, Hatshepsut, Ptolemy, Thutmose."

"Ptolemy."

This response causes Crowley to pause, but it is not clear whether because it is correct or the rapidity with which she answered.

Crowley again opens his book, this time to the back cover, and extracts a handful of what look like oversized postcards. He lays these out slowly, like a fortune-teller dealing the Tarot, in an arc facing Sabrina. They are not postcards: they depict not scenes but symbols.

"Choose," Crowley commands.

There are six of them: an elongated eight drawn on its side—the mathematical sign representing infinity; a pentagram—traditional icon of the occult and so an obvious candidate; a Mobius strip—suggesting endlessness, Sabrina supposes; a depiction of a pyramid whose top is an all-seeing eye, something that could have been copied straight from the U.S. one-dollar bill; a mandala-like square within a circle surrounded by what might be alchemical symbols; and lastly a unicursal hexagram with a pentacle at its center—the pattern she first saw etched onto the cuff link she was attaching to Bronaryre's shirt, then as a relic in the Freemasons' Museum, and lastly inlaid into the lid of the wooden box containing the pen with which she had consigned her soul to the Devil.

She points wordlessly to the hexagram.

A long stillness follows. The witches stare mostly open-mouthed, and the only movement is Anath, whose eyes have been brimming since the third question, and who now weeps in silence. Crowley glowers unblinkingly at Sabrina, but eventually it is he who is the first to move, picking up the postcard with the hexagram.

"The odds of choosing this symbol were one-in-six," he says, "and the name of Ptolemy one-in-five and Horus, bringer of enlightenment, one-in-ten. There are twenty-four artifacts in the vitrine, and so for those four questions alone, the cumulative chances of you getting them all right were one-in-seven thousand, two hundred. As for the odds of the other questions, they are not readily quantifiable, but certainly much longer. Even were we to count them the same, the total odds come to less than one-in-a-million; the true figure probably a tiny fraction of that."

"Which means?"

Crowley puts aside the postcards and looks back up at Sabrina.

"Thou art—" But he seems unable to complete the thought, and Sabrina decides to take advantage of this rare chink in Crowley's confidant self-possession.

"May I ask my questions now?"

"As thou wilt."

"This past winter you attended a recital at the home of Justice Mariano Scaglietti, on the night he died."

"Yes."

"How did you know him?"

"Our paths crossed from time to time. We shared certain interests."

"What interests?"

"He was given unto the Revealing, but was unprepared. From that point his demise was inevitable."

'Are you saying that you helped bring about his death?"

"Yes."

"How?"

"By incantation."

"By incantation?"

"A hex, madam, a spell. I pulled him aside that evening and cast a spell upon him."

Sabrina sighs in frustration.

"Did he know what you were doing?"

"Of course." No wonder Scaglietti had a heart attack, Sabrina thinks, after having had this overbearing creature place a hex on him.

"And what was the Revealing?" she asks.

"The crystallization of divine ecstasy," Crowley says, as if it were obvious.

"Ah." Any line of inquiry with Crowley will inevitably lead to occult gibberish, Sabrina realizes, a sure way of avoiding answering hard questions, and all the more effective because Crowley apparently believes what he is saying. Nevertheless, she has an admission that Crowley—or this person that looks like and calls himself Crowley—was present at Netherly the night the Justice died, plus an explanation for Scaglietti's anxious behavior that night. Crowley interrupts her thoughts.

"The time has come for the next step on your journey," he announces.

"Which is?'

"A direct demonstration, which Nekhebit has agreed to perform."

Nekhebit is a redheaded girl, as tall as Sabrina but more solidly built, giving her a distinct physical presence, and from whose accent Sabrina has already guessed must be local. She wears the shortest of the dresses tonight, a Jazz Age flapper's outfit that when she sits bares the thigh above the top of her stockings, exposing a suspender belt whose little satin tags she is in the habit of absently fingering.

Crowley vacates the ottoman and Nekhebit takes his place, sitting with legs entwined in the lotus position—probably the reason she chose the short dress. The other witches adjust their seating to best view the coming spectacle. Crowley stands in the corner, arms crossed and leaning lightly on the wall in a relaxed attitude, a place from which he can observe not just Nekhebit's performance but also Sabrina's reaction to it.

Nekhebit folds her hands in her lap and closes her eyes.

Nothing happens for about a minute. No one speaks, and Sabrina is wondering if she is the only one thinking that there is remarkably little going on in this performance, but then, very slowly, Nekhebit levitates.

She rises about a foot above the ottoman, and then holds the position.

Crowley walks over to Sabrina and whispers in her ear, "Nekhebit is new to this, and will not be able to hold it for long. I invite you to inspect closely, to satisfy yourself that there are no hidden wires or the like, but be quick."

Sabrina removes her shoes and stands. She steps over to the ottoman quietly, so as not to disturb Nekhebit's concentration. She sweeps her arm slowly above Nekhebit's head and then again beneath her body, but these only confirm what Sabrina can already see: Nekhebit is moving slightly, almost vibrating, not the movement of someone being either pulled from above or pushed from below; it is the quivering motion of someone who is hovering.

"*Quod erat demonstrandum*," Crowley says.

Indeed it has been demonstrated, Sabrina thinks: Nekhebit is genuinely levitating—and that, she realizes, changes everything.

# Sixth Circle

# Polyhymnia

SABRINA MAKES HER WAY across the park toward the large neo-Gothic edifice lying on the other side. The skies cleared yesterday during her journey southward from Scotland, and the new morning is one that Colonel Swindon would think suitable for shooting down Heinkels and Dorniers: the old building's sandstone glows warmly in the brilliant summer sunshine. It is not her final destination, but the only way to enter the Pitt Rivers is via the Museum of Natural History.

Wilkins's research laboratory is located in the Pitt Rivers, the University of Oxford's archeological museum. Sabrina weaves her way through the wondrous main hall, a cavernous Victorian-era structure the size of Paddington Station and crowded with cabinet after cabinet of anthropological curiosities: South Seas' tikis brought back by Captain Cook, intrepid discoverer of Hawaii; Mexican dance masks, hideously malevolent; a fully armed and armored Japanese warlord, rendered with amazing realism, looking ready to leap out and massacre unwary visitors. At the far end she finds a set of iron steps leading up to the mezzanines, and on the second of these, situated between a Papuan war club and a Polynesian star chart, she locates a door marked:

*University of Oxford*
*School of Anthropology and Museum Ethnography*
*Laboratory B*

Sabrina presses the buzzer.

THE LAB IS small but very modern and amazingly clean—in an old iron-framed industrial-era building like the Pitt Rivers Sabrina had imagined something more Mary Shelleyish: bubbling beakers and smoking retorts. Roger Wilkins wears a white lab coat over a sports shirt and jeans: no clerical collar today. He gives her a quick tour, mostly of small appliances—the centrifuge, incubator, and scanning electron microscope she more or less understands, but items like the quad-workflow chromatograph and high-resolution mass spectrometer are a mystery to her. Wilkins is alone in the lab—maybe he arranged it that way following her call, or perhaps it is to be expected on a Saturday morning out of term, but in any case she is pleased because it will allow her to speak plainly.

"Two days ago I saw a woman levitate," she says. "It was no trick with mirrors or holograms: she was perfectly substantial—quite solidly built, in fact—and I was allowed to go and inspect for myself, close up, while she was doing it."

Wilkins looks at her for a long moment before speaking. "Should I call the Vatican and have them send out a miracle verification team?"

"She was a witch."

"Ah, there goes the Vatican idea."

Sabrina details the incident in what she hopes is an objective and scientific manner, but leaves out irrelevancies, such as her host having been that same Aleister Crowley who died in 1947. Wilkins asks an occasional question, but mostly just listens. From his expression when she finishes Sabrina can tell that he does not believe a word of it, and is uncomfortable in having been told the story in the first place, but he keeps his tone carefully neutral.

"You said there was something you wanted analyzed?"

She opens her bag, takes out the Temperley, and points to the bloodstain on the hem.

"This," she says. "I believe it's dried blood."

"You didn't mention any spilling of blood in this levitation experience."

"There wasn't. This comes from another… incident."

"Another incident?"

"They're related. The findings on one will bear on the other."

Wilkins would obviously like to ask more, but he has the admirable quality of keeping his curiosity in check. "Okay, but I still don't know exactly what analysis you're looking for."

"Firstly, I would like to know whether or not the blood is human."

"That's pretty simple to do. What else?"

"If the blood is human, I would like to know if it's mine."

"You don't know that already?"

"No."

"To know if it were yours, I would need a sample to compare it against."

"Yes, I figured as much." Sabrina pulls out a second item from her bag, a box cutter. She holds up a finger and slides out the blade. "Got a bowl?"

"I CAN'T FIND the Temperley," Polly says. "It was here the other day."

"I took it to be cleaned," Sabrina lies.

"I could have done that, miss."

"I took it to a specialist in Oxford; it had a stain"—more truthful now.

Polly huffily continues sorting through the wardrobe, coat hangers clashing loudly, unmollified. Her task is to choose something for dining *en plein air*: the return of the fair weather has continued into Saturday, and so instead of a formal dinner inside the evening meal is to be a cold supper taken on the terrace, preceded by an afternoon scavenger hunt organized for the girls, already underway. The theme of the latter is a combination of vexillological and lexicological: the items hidden through the estate for them to find are naval signal flags, and at any stage a participant may take her findings and hoist a signal of a single word from the staff mounted atop the tower. The flags have the same point value as tiles in a game of Scrabble, plus a bonus two points for every component flag, to encourage length. Whoever has the highest score will be excused from communal domestic chores for the following week.

There is a sound from outside, like yacht halyards clanking in a breeze, something Sabrina has already learned indicates that a new hoist is being hauled aloft. She goes out onto her terrace and for the first time is able to read it without having to consult the table—the underlying aim of the exercise is being achieved: to teach flag recognition in preparation for the future when in some distant part of the world the *United States* will raise a signal while lying at anchor, sending a silent message to all her people ashore.

The hoist is Q-U-E-B-E-C, same as the first flag's name, and would have been worth a hefty thirty-one points had Katy Telford remembered that proper nouns do not count in Scrabble.

Sabrina goes back inside. An envelope has been slipped under her door, familiar heavyweight ecru. This time the marbleized lining is a combination of lemon and olive, the colors of a Mediterranean summer, suitable for this fine weather. The note inside suggests the top of the bell tower as a location for evening cocktails.

Polly emerges from the dressing room. She has made a selection and lays it out on the bed for Sabrina to inspect: a cocktail dress made of see-through black chiffon embroidered with a few small flower motifs as an inadequate gesture toward modesty. At least it has improved Polly's mood.

Sabrina nods in acceptance, knowing that she can always change her mind later, when her maid has returned to the farm for the evening milking. Meanwhile, she has to keep her occupied.

"But what about shoes?" she asks, sending Polly eagerly scurrying back into the dressing room, and allowing Sabrina to resume her seat at the desk and finish updating her journal.

*How did they know I was going to Scotland? I myself did not know until making the connection between Jimmy Page and Aleister Crowley. It was late at night when I did so, and I discussed my plan with no one. The next morning I booked the tickets and left right away.*

*There are three possibilities:*

1. *Bronaryre has access to my credit card account, through which I booked the tickets*
2. *They are somehow tracking me through my phone*
3. *The porters' lodge (I mentioned that I would be gone for a few days when I left)*

*From now on I will not carry my phone; I will pay with cash, and tell the porters nothing.*

*The Boleskine House performance might have been impromptu, but the setup was not: there is no possibility of gathering the Crowley impersonator and other actors, and then getting them all up to the Highlands in time, along with the costumes and props, even if they had known I was going there the moment I did. Crowley had to have been already in residence—his artifacts, his clothes, his claret-colored Rolls-Royce—and the witches, too; those living arrangements could not have been made in just a few hours, nor was their familiarity with the place faked: Crowley and the witches were already at Boleskine House, living there, before I had even heard of the place.*

*Crowley's account of having placed a hex on Scaglietti is easily dismissible, or at least it was, until I saw Nekhebit levitating above the ottoman. I must guard against credulity—Ravenscroft warned me that his client could be uncommonly persuasive—but perhaps an investigative team from the Vatican is not so absurd after all.*

THE ENTRY AT the base of the bell tower is an imposing Romanesque arch, large enough for a horse cart to pass through. Inside is a broad space with a beaten earth floor: an undercroft, Sabrina supposes. She takes a set of solid stone stairs leading up to a series of lofts, probably used for grain storage in the original design, well aired and clear of any potential flooding. The steps thereafter are made of wood, steep and without a handrail. Sabrina continues the ascent, keeping close to the walls, and hoping that Bronaryre has preceded her to clear any cobwebs. Sabrina arrives at a small platform, very narrow, built between the bulk of the water tank on one side and the clock face on the other, the mechanicals of which look old enough to be original, and seem too simple to power something so grand on the other side.

Finally, she arrives at the top of the campanile, where there is not a single bell but a peal of three, and as she passes by them the large one in the center suddenly swings into action, emitting an enormous clang that echoes loudly in the narrow chamber. Sabrina presses her hands over her ears and continues quickly upward as the bell continues to toll behind her, as if to declare the irredeemable loss of each passing moment.

Seven rings in total: at least she is on time.

Sabrina emerges onto the top of the tower. There is a small folding table plus two matching chairs. The table bears not just cocktail gear but also a varnished wooden box.

Bronaryre is standing by the far corner, holding an apparatus to his eye and staring skyward through it. At the sound of her arrival he lowers the device and takes from the table a tiny jeweler's screwdriver, which he uses to make an adjustment to what Sabrina sees is a small mirror projecting from an arm of the instrument.

"What is it?'

"A sextant: a mechanism for measuring the heavens."

"Keeping tabs on the competition?"

"I'm just calibrating it right now. You need a true horizon to do it properly, and this is the best place on the estate to see it clearly."

I cannot recall the last time I saw anything clearly, Sabrina thinks, but she does not articulate the thought. Bronaryre opens the wooden box and places the sextant carefully inside. The interior has been fitted to hold it exactly.

"When we go to sea there will be classes in celestial navigation: my contribution to the academic enterprise."

"Why?"

"As a practical exercise in spherical trigonometry." He picks up a lemon and idly tosses it up and down as he talks. "Celestial navigation is still taught at Annapolis so that one day should the satellites no longer be available then they will still have the ability to determine their position at sea—no one can as yet shoot down the stars. One needs to use reduction tables and a *Nautical Almanac* to turn star sights into position data—a complicated process—but nevertheless a useful skill in uncertain times."

"I recently had occasion to become acquainted with the *Nautical Almanac*, in relation to the setting of Venus. That was shortly before I witnessed a witch levitate."

"Which witches will tend to do." That same ebony-handled knife has suddenly appeared in his hand, as quick as a magic trick. He snaps it open and slices the lemon. "You can join in the celestial navigation classes, if you like, but be aware that it will involve some levitating of your own, by which I mean getting up before dawn, during that brief interval when both the stars and the horizon are visible."

"I could probably manage that, providing that I'm not stupefied by opium from the night before."

Bronaryre mixes gin and tonics—apparently his standard outdoors-in-summer cocktail—and passes a glass to Sabrina. When they are sitting back after having taken the first sip, he resumes his tale without preamble.

"I told you that I left England in 1666, after the Great Fire. I did not return until 1683. During that absence, and despite many travails, I did not age. I never became ill. Such injuries as I sustained healed at an abnormal rate. In short, I came to understand both my situation, and the need to disguise that situation from my fellow man. On reaching the Continent I assumed a new name, Jack Kincaid, the first of many changes in identity that I have adopted over the years."

"Where did you go?"

"Around the world. I began in Paris, and made my way slowly through Europe—I lived two years in Venice alone—and then onward to the Levant and Egypt. I took a trading caravan to Persia, thence India. A Portuguese caravel took me from Goa to Rangoon in Burma. Thence Batavia, modern Djakarta, and throughout Southeast Asia before taking another caravel, this time to Macau. A Chinese junk carried me to Manila, a Spanish galleon to Acapulco. I traveled through Central and

South America for a couple of years before sailing for Boston. Then the Azores and the Iberian Peninsula before crossing to North Africa. Eventually, I returned to England from Tangier."

"What did you do?"

"You mean occupations? Often I was a seaman: I usually earned my passage on those many sea voyages. For a while I was a pirate, preying on Dutch ships sailing between the western end of the Malacca Strait and the Andaman Islands; later, in Macau, I became a colonial official whose responsibilities included the suppression of piracy. I was a soldier-of-fortune for a time, and fought in the defense of newly acquired Bombay against the Mughal Empire. For a year in Burma I was a Buddhist monk. In Boston, I professed at Harvard."

"So the Devil is a Harvard man—Yale had it right all along."

"My first ever employment, in Paris, was as a *plongeur* at La Tour d'Argent—like Orwell, in Paris I washed dishes. I met there an Englishman, Sir Cecil Hawkins, who was on a pilgrimage to Rome and, after learning that I had been up at Oxford and was capable of behaving like a gentleman, engaged me as his private secretary for the journey. Ostensibly he was writing a travelogue about his pilgrimage, but Hawkins spent less time inspecting the sights or making religious observances than in devouring food: he was amazingly fat, and it soon became clear that his primary motive for the enterprise was gastronomic. We made our way leisurely southward via Geneva, Lyons, Provence, with my employer availing himself of the local culinary delights at every stop: *raclette vercouline* and *fondue à la genevoise*; *quenelles de brochet* and *l'andouille campagnarde*; *ratatouille niçoise* and *bouillabaisse marseillaise*. We crossed into Italy via the same route that Napoleon was to take a hundred years later, and dallied in Alba, where Hawkins found the white truffles particularly to his taste. In Genoa there were reports of the plague; we hurried away, despite the excellence of Ligurian *pesto*. Eventually, we arrived in Rome and took rooms on the Via del Corso. There, in the capital of Christendom, Hawkins indulged himself in the sin of gluttony without restraint: I hardly ever saw the fellow in the evenings, so long were his meals. Then one night I was out over the other side of the Tiber, by the Castello di Sant'Angelo, when I saw Hawkins crossing the square. I was about to hail him when I realized that he was proceeding with more purpose than was his habit, indeed faster than I thought him capable: it was the walk of a man late for an appointment, an appointment with someone more important than himself. I watched him cross the square to a small door sunk into the ramparts of the Castello. He knocked, waited a moment, and then knocked again, but in a deliberate fashion: a knock not merely seeking entry, but of someone tapping out a code. The door opened, and he disappeared inside.

"I took a seat in a tavern with a view of that door, and waited. Three hours later, he emerged. I followed him, but eventually it became apparent that he was just heading back to our rooms. I caught up with him on the doorstep, told him frankly what I had seen, and asked what was going on. 'Not out here,' he said. 'You'll get us both killed.'

"Once we were safely inside, and after he had thoroughly searched our lodgings to be certain there was no possibility of being overheard, he told me the story. You might be aware that since the time of that war-mongering pope, Julius II, there has been, and remains today, an elevated passageway connecting the Castello di Sant'Angelo with the Vatican—the Passetto di Borgo—completely enclosed and through which the pope may be brought for safekeeping in times of peril: it was what allowed Cellini, among others, to successfully defend Clement VII against the Imperial assault in 1527.

"In short, the gluttonous Englishman on a Continental debauch was just a front to conceal Hawkins's real purpose in coming to Rome, which was to negotiate with the papal Curia, specifically with that cunning old Jesuit, Cardinal Rospigliosi, who was the Secretary of State when we arrived in Rome, and became Pope Clement IX while we were there. Hawkins always entered via the Castello di Sant'Angelo to avoid any possibility of being seen coming and going into the Vatican directly.

"He told me that he was negotiating an arrangement on behalf of 'an esteemed countryman of ours, whom I shall not name.' But it was obvious on whose behalf Hawkins would have been acting: the king's younger brother, James, Duke of York, a man whose Catholic sympathies were well known, despite his then outward adherence to the Anglican rite.

"At the time, the Duke of York was held in high regard due to his command of the navy, which had acquitted itself well against the Dutch—including the capture of their American colony of New Amsterdam, renamed New *York* in the Duke's honor—and also for his role in coordinating the efforts to halt the Great Fire before it had consumed all of London. His inclination toward the Church of Rome could be overlooked, given that primogeniture was the path to power, for his older brother Charles was still young and could confidently be expected to have a son. As it turned out, that never happened, and on his death his brother James did become king, precipitating the second revolution in the same century to depose a Stuart monarch."

"What sort of arrangement was Hawkins negotiating?"

"James's conversion to Catholicism, an act for which he—James—expected to be well compensated. It would have been couched in more diplomatic language: an arrangement to facilitate the return of York, and perhaps with him all of England, to the true faith. But the real purpose was clear: if York was to become Catholic and declare for the Roman church, then he wanted something in return."

"What happened?"

"Hawkins was successful: James formally converted to Catholicism in 1668, although it took him another ten years to publicly admit it."

"How much was he paid?"

"The answer to that question is a secret which to this day remains buried somewhere deep within the Vatican vaults. Whatever it was, it was substantial: Hawkins, who of course had no intention of conveying the money to York without a good deal of it sticking to his own fingers, became a very wealthy man. A small fraction of the transaction came to me, as a consideration for my circumspection: suddenly, for the first time in my life, I was not poor. Moreover, to help ensure that I kept my silence, I was offered a new position, in the employ of that same government that had imprisoned me in the Tower."

"As what?"

"As a spy. Hawkins soon completed his mission, and was to return to England; I, for my own reasons, would be remaining abroad. I was asked to report back whatever might be of interest to the reigning power, especially anything to do with the intentions of foreign governments. I was given to understand that I would be well remunerated for such information, and indeed I was, as I discovered when eventually I returned to England, many years later. Hawkins and I bid each other adieu; I never saw the man again."

"So you became an English spy?"

"Yes, but the trouble with being a spy is that you can never publicly admit it, which means that you need some other occupation to act as a cover. I was still in Rome, wondering what that occupation might be, when I was introduced to a Mr. Ezekiel Finnick of Kingston upon Hull. Mr. Finnick was, somewhat reluctantly, taking his wife and their three daughters on the Grand Tour. Finnick referred to himself as having been a 'projector,' which in those days meant investor. What he had invested in, I was to learn, was political cronyism: in return for a number of well-placed bribes, he was assigned land that had previously been held in common, but which was now being enclosed. He sold it back off, and kept the difference. With pockets full, he assumed squirish airs and, as a suitable adornment to his imagined new status, married a woman two decades junior in age and several steps senior in social standing. But she was a widow with three undowried teenage daughters in an unforgiving age: she had had no choice but to marry a fellow for whom she felt no affection."

"How awful."

"Indeed, she thought so, too. Finnick spoke no Italian, had no intention of learning any, and frankly despised the locals. Nor did he have any Latin, which was then the *lingua franca* of the educated classes. He engaged me to escort the party, and it was my job to deal with anyone who had the temerity not to speak English, and also to arrange their continuing travels—Finnick didn't know Verona from Vesuvius, and told me that 'the one good thing those otherwise wasted Oxford years might have equipped you for would be arranging a suitable itinerary.'

"By the time we reached Venice, the unhappy nature of the Finnick *ménage* had become apparent to me. I took a palazzo for them on the Grand Canal, and then promptly threw him out of the former and into the latter. The last I saw of Finnick, esquire, was him struggling not to drown as I explained that I had put a price of a hundred *scudi* on his head, and that bands of *bravi* were already out scouting the city, hoping to claim the reward. I wished him *bon voyage*, and closed the shutters."

Sabrina laughs out loud: she had not imagined that the Devil could be a knight in shining armor.

"What happened to the widow and her daughters?"

"They managed to conceal their sorrow over the sudden departure of Finnick, although not their mirth at the mode of his exit. He had carried with him a good deal of traveling money, of which I had relieved him before his defenestration, and it was enough for the women to last a year at least. But I had reckoned without their own resourcefulness.

"I should say that Mrs. Finnick's first husband, a Captain Thomas, had been a cavalryman in the New Model Army and a thoroughgoing devotee of the Puritan cause. He was killed in 'Fifty-two during the Cromwellian conquest of Ireland. She had married him at a tender age, in the manner of the time, and given birth to her three daughters in rapid succession before his untimely death. She, Caroline, was thirty-four. The three daughters—Amity, Prudence, and Charity—were seventeen, sixteen, and fifteen. Perhaps it was the Italian air, or the Venetian republic's easygoing reputation, or maybe just a reaction against their Puritan background, but something made all four of them suddenly bloom in what was a wholly unpredictable way. The palazzo soon became a gathering spot for a certain section of society: part salon, part literary association, part sybaritic bacchanalia.

"The format was evening *soirées*. Admittance was highly sought but very limited, and it was understood that an invitation would unlikely be forthcoming without a suitable douceur having been arranged beforehand. There would always be chamber music, typically a string quartet—Vivaldi's father, an accomplished violinist, was often among the players. Food, of course: a splendid feast with an abundance of wine, and then dancing afterward for those so inclined. But above all, there was fine conversation, the sort of conversation never too serious but also never simply frivolous, conversation in which intelligence and wit were valued in equal measure. Masks—already a feature of the festivities in Venice during *Carnevale*—were normally worn, and the anonymity that they provided no doubt helped the freedom of expression for which those evenings at the palazzo became famous. The hostesses would dress, according to their inclination on the evening, in fabulous ball gowns, frequently rather less, occasionally just undergarments, or from time to time nothing at all apart from mask and heels. This acted as an encouragement to the other female guests—typically in a majority and who, after having disembarked from their gondolas and upon removing their capes, would often be revealed to be in similar states of undress.

"Caroline Finnick was a practically minded woman, and she ensured that although her charms and those of her daughters were made available generously, they were not free—however, an exception was made for talent, and many an impecunious artist or writer was admitted to these lavish spectacles. Soon the Finnick women were quite wealthy, and it was clear that their financial futures, previously so precarious, were now fully secured. But more than that, they were content: independence from male dominance, from being told what to do, from expectations of how they should and should not behave, had made them exceedingly happy, even joyous—that palazzo was filled with light and laughter from dawn till dusk."

Bronaryre stands to refill their glasses. When he returns, Sabrina takes from her pocket the Oxford Crown and slides it across the table.

"I believe this is yours."

It is an impetuous gesture, and one that she suspects she will regret, but she does it just the same.

Bronaryre picks up the coin.

"So not all good deeds go unrewarded," he says. "A first for me, surely."

"I have a feeling that Caroline Finnick and her daughters would have wanted you to have it."

"You mustn't imagine that I was being entirely altruistic: the arrangement also suited me, in my new role as an English spy. At that time Venice was one of those cities that seems to invite intrigue, like a Constantinople or a Hong Kong: an international marketplace for not just goods, but also information. Many of the possessors of those secrets would end up in the Finnick's salon: in short, my work as a spy was fruitful. So it was that I remained there for two years."

"What made you leave?"

"You will recall that my fundamental purpose was to excite men's minds with more desire to know. To that end, I had necessarily to acquire knowledge myself. Already while in Paris I had attended meetings of the group that had first gathered around de Montmor, and which during my stay in the city was to flower, under the patronage of Colbert, into the French *Académie des sciences*. It was in their new quarters at the Biblioteque Royale that I first met Christiaan Huygens, and it was there that Roberval introduced me, by proxy, to Pierre de Fermat: regrettably, the man himself had died the previous year, but I would not have been able to meet him in person anyway, for he rarely ventured far from his native Toulouse.

"My studies continued in Italy: in Milan, I scoured the Ambrosiana; in Venice, the Marciana; in Rome, the Angelica, the Vallicelliana, and the library of what was then the *Collegium Divi Thomae*, a Dominican theological college in that same Convent of Santa Maria Sopra Minerva in which Galileo was tried and condemned, and which today is the superb Biblioteca Casanatense. I spent a month studying at the abbey at Monte Cassino. In Bologna—a city remarkable for its fertility of thought at the time—I met the young Corelli, already composing; Cassini and Malpighi in their prime; and Riccioli, the aged Jesuit astronomer who discovered the first double star; in Florence, Viviani, who had been a pupil of the great Torricelli, kept me entertained with algebraic equations and stories of his master; in Venice, I assisted Longhena in designing the library at the monastery on San Giorgio Maggiore, contributed to the *Giornale veneto de' letterati*, and first got a taste of politics by supporting Morosini during his trial following the fall of Candia to the Turks.

"Wherever I went I sought out and attended sessions of the local learned societies: the Accademia degli Ardenti in Bologna; the Accademia degli Affumicati in Ragusa; the Accademia degli Invaghiti in Mantua; the Accademia dei Ricovrati in Padua; the Accademia del Cimento in Florence; what was to become the Accademia Cosmografica degli Argonauti in Venice; and in Rome those remnants of the Accademia dei Lincei—the lynx-eyed—who had not been frightened into submission by Galileo's fate. I won't say that I had my fill of Italy—Italy is inexhaustible—but I had certainly drunk deeply, and the time had come to move on. Besides, working with all those charts of a newly revealed world at the budding Cosmografica had filled me with wanderlust.

"After many years and many adventures, I arrived in Tangier. Tangier has undergone innumerable changes of occupation and ownership over its long history. Strange to say, when I arrived there it was under the control of the English, having come to Charles II as part of the dowry of his wife, Catherine of Braganza. The Moroccans were having none of this, and Tangier was increasingly difficult to defend against them. Eventually, it was decided to evacuate. I was among the evacuees. The evacuation was performed under the nominal command of Lord Dartmouth, but the man who actually ran it was another fellow."

"Who?"

"Samuel Pepys."

"Pepys? You mean the diarist?"

"The same."

"I can't imagine him ever leaving London. What happened? Did he run out of women to chase?"

"The diary ceased in 1669, and by 1683 his amorous days were behind him. You must remember that, in addition to being a frank chronicler of his age, Pepys was also a renowned administrator: he was the chief civilian in the Admiralty and shares credit with York for having made the English fleet the professional service that it had become. He was also a learned man, enough to become president of the Royal Society. You see why in those days I still retained high hopes for the human race, when such men could be, able in so many fields: administration; arms; amours; authorship; academia—today, such men do not exist.

"In Tangier, he and I struck up a friendship, despite the apparent disparity in our ages. What brought us together was mathematics—he was enough of a mathematician to have had a theorem named after him, and in 1673 he had established the Royal Mathematical School. He was eager to hear what I had learned on the subject while abroad—or so it seemed—and we spent many hours together in discussion. One night we walked across the souk to the eastern end of the Medina—the old city—near where the New City of the French now stands, far from the Kasbah, the administrative center on the other side, where the English garrison was concentrated. Few foreigners ventured out to where we had come, but Pepys claimed there was a place with good food there, and indeed there was, although we were the only non-Moors in the place. As we dined, Pepys talked, mostly about his favorite subject: himself. At one point, he idly remarked that as a young boy he had witnessed the execution of Charles I at Whitehall Palace. I then did what I had never done before."

"What?"

"I made a mistake. I said, 'Why, so was I.' This was obviously impossible, given my apparent age, and I attempted to make it appear that I had been joking, but I could tell that he had perceived I was not. He demanded that I tell him the truth, and I—fool that I knew I was as I spoke—did so. I told him everything, at the end of which he stopped eating and stared at me for a long time in silence. Then he said something wholly unexpected. He said, 'Yes, we thought as much all along.'

"Now it was my turn to demand an explanation. Unbeknown to me, it seemed that Pepys had had full access to the reports I had been sending from around the world for all those years, including the assessment of conditions in Tangier that had helped lead the government to order the evacuation. He claimed that from those reports he suspected there was more to their author than they knew, which is why he had engineered a position for himself administering the evacuation. On arriving in Tangier and finding that I was not the man of middle age that I should have been, he said that he knew. 'Knew what?' I asked. 'I knew that *you* were the one my master sought.'

"The man he referred to as 'his master' was Richard Montagu, the first Earl of Sandwich, a distant cousin, now dead. It was he who had first found a position for Pepys in the Admiralty. Montagu, it turns out, was a descendant of a long line of Montagus going all the way back to

Drogo of Montagu, listed in the Domesday Book. Among those many Montagus was a Pierre de Montagu, who had been the Master of the Knights Templar in England from 1218 to 1232, and the Montagus remained prominent in the order until the Templars were suppressed.

"In France, where it began, that suppression had been frankly an excuse for Philip IV to erase his debts to the order, and to enrich himself with their property, which he claimed as rightfully his since there could be no concept of a legitimate heir for the organization."

"Escheatment," Sabrina says, "the legal principle that when there is no direct claim to an estate, the government takes the estate for itself."

"Quite so. The brutality of the suppression in France was in inverse proportion to its justice—many Templars, including the Grand Master Jacques de Molay, were burned alive. In England, it was quite different. For a time Edward II simply refused to act against the Templars, but when at Philip's prodding Clement V issued a papal bull in 1312, formally ordering their suppression, he felt he had no choice. The Templars were disbanded, and their property was distributed in various ways. Much of it was transferred to the Hospitallers, and some of the Templars themselves entered service as Hospitaller knights. An exception was the English Master, William de la More, who was imprisoned in the Tower until his death, purportedly because he would not make the necessary obeisances to be released, but in reality it was for another reason.

"The Templars could do nothing to protect their preceptories or other properties but they were the international bankers of their day, and so also possessed a large amount of portable wealth: gold and silver plate, jewels, coins, precious stones, and the like. The portable wealth disappeared, as portable wealth always does when governments become confiscatory—Gresham's Law—and de la More was kept imprisoned because he would not reveal what had become of it. For various reasons, Edward suspected that it was hidden in Hertfordshire, and arrested a number of Templars there, but the treasure was never found. In the Eighteenth Century, a cave system was discovered at Royston, Hertfordshire, which from the carvings was Templar, and it was assumed that was where the treasure must have once been held, four hundred years previously.

"That assumption was wrong. With the Master of their order imprisoned in the Tower, the Montagus took the initiative: it was they who hid the treasure, and it was not in Hertfordshire."

"You discovered it?"

"No. It was, after a solemn ceremony, given under my care."

"Do you still have it?"

"In the original, a few items only. But the entire treasure still exists, many times multiplied, and in a very different form."

It takes Sabrina a moment to figure it out. "Pendle Hill Investments."

"Yes, plus various other entities and holdings around the world—I have been careful to not place all my eggs in one basket."

"But what happened?"

"I returned to England with Pepys. You can imagine my curiosity, but after that night in Tangier he refused to tell me anything further, warning me that I must be patient. We landed at Hastings on a moonless night, and I was taken by a carriage with the blinds drawn to I knew not where. When at last the journey ended I was hooded and taken in charge by unknown hands. Pepys remained in the carriage. I was guided into a building.

"My hood was removed, revealing that I was in a fortification of some kind, candle-lit, and with the floor scattered with rushes. There were three maidens in the room, bare of foot, dressed in simple white linens, and staring at me as I stared back at them. In the center of the room was a large wooden tub, big enough for laundry, although it turned out that the thing to be laundered was me: the maidens moved forward in silence, and then stripped and bathed me. I was shaved and dressed: a shirt of the same fine white linen as their robes; black breeches of heavy cavalry-grade twill; boots of fine Cordovan leather, highly polished and which fit as if having been custom-made for me. Then I was blindfolded and led across what felt like a field and down a winding stone staircase into what I could tell by the echo was some kind of cellar. My escort left me. I stood still for what seemed a very long time, until a deep voice commanded me to remove my blindfold. I did so.

"I was in a groin-vaulted underground space, perhaps a cistern, or a crypt. It was lit by flaming torches mounted on the walls. It was large, built in the form of a central nave flanked by aisles, and with pillars supporting the vaults. The thing was constructed of stone, deeply carved with what I later came to know was Templar imagery. There was no furniture but dozens of chests, many of them open, revealing treasure within. Facing me were three men, dressed in the white tunics with red crosses of Templar Knights. All three were armed with broadswords and daggers. The one standing in the middle had his sword drawn, but it was resting point downward in front of him; the others had their weapons sheathed. All three were very old, and I knew none of them. They introduced themselves as the keepers of that which surrounded them, which I understood to be the treasure.

"They questioned me for a long period, mostly to establish whether I was really as old as I had admitted to Pepys. When they were convinced of that, the interrogation changed to my knowledge of the sciences, especially mathematics. Whoever they were, the men were well informed: the questions they put to me demonstrated that they were acquainted with the latest advances of the day, some that had only been discussed in the academies and which were not yet published: Leibnitz's infinitesimal differential method; Jacob Bernoulli's calculation of the mathematical constant we now know as *e*; they were even familiar with the term *centripetal force*, which Newton had only recently coined, and was something he had communicated in written form only by private letter, to Edmond Halley.

Finally, I was asked, 'What is thy purpose?' I assumed that such an open question was meant to throw me, but of course I knew the answer without thinking: *to excite men's minds with more desire to know.* Whatever response they had been expecting, this was obviously a satisfactory reply, and the three of them looked at each other meaningfully, apparently silently signaling their mutual consent to the next phase of the ceremony.

"The three men faced me again. The one in the center, standing slightly forward of the other two and presumably their leader, laid out the matter plainly: they were the last of the Templars in England, he declared, and for all they knew the last Templars anywhere. In the early Fourteenth Century, when Edward II finally decided to suppress the order and seize their wealth, three Templar knights had banded together to conceal the treasure until the time came when the order could emerge from hiding. They created a procedure for transmitting the responsibility of safeguarding that treasure through the generations, father to son or sometimes grandson, counting on the bond of blood to help guarantee loyalty. But kinship alone was not sufficient: each candidate would be assessed, and the agreement of all three current guardians to the candidate's worthiness was required for his election into the order. When one of the guardians died, the other two would enlist the oldest of those they had selected as replacements. There would be no expansion in numbers, just three at a time, the better to keep the secret until the time was ripe for the Templar order to be reestablished.

"That time never came. Indeed, the very opposite occurred: from their perspective things got progressively worse. First of all was the suppression itself: clearly unjust and motivated by the most ignoble of purposes. Further, they could not reconcile their order's betrayal with the fact that the betrayal had been agreed to by the head of a church that purported to be a force for universal good, divinely sanctioned, and to which they had pledged their lives.

"Then there was the failure of the Crusades: this was seen as not just a military disaster, but a spiritual one as well: how could Providence have allowed it to happen? Not only had the church abandoned them, so too, it seemed, had their God. Then, in 1348, came the Black Death. By the time it abated, the bubonic plague had wiped out two-thirds of the European population: God had not only abandoned his people; he smote them in his fury.

"Meanwhile, God's house on earth, the Roman church, was no longer Roman: the papacy, utterly corrupt, moved to Avignon, and had become a puppet of the French princes. This Babylonian Captivity was soon followed by the Schism: suddenly there were two popes, and then three, all of them braying like donkeys that they were the legitimate heirs to the keys of Saint Peter. Then, in 1453, the Ottomans took Constantinople, and the center of Christianity in the east fell into infidel hands. And in 1517 came the final straw: the Reformation, the fracturing of the church into a thousand tiny fragments, all of them asserting that they were the one true faith, and all eager to murder each other over the subtleties of transubstantiation, or the legitimacy of baptism, or the nature of the Trinity. In short, the Templar Guardians had lost faith in faith itself.

"But in the interim there arose a new calling, not to faith, but to reason. It had been seeded by the Scholastics, had flowered in the Renaissance, and now suddenly burst forth into the new learning. The high prophet was Francis Bacon, and his great summoning of men to the banner of rationality, the *Novum Organum*, was the new Bible. To this end, they had aligned themselves with certain groups in Oxford, especially those who went on to form the Royal Society. This included Boyle, and it was he who had alerted them to my existence: it seems that Milton was not the only man who had seen through me, and it was they who had engaged Hawkins to recruit me: my spying was merely a convenient means of keeping tabs on where I was and what I was up to—the person I was spying on was actually myself. Pepys was not the first sent to check on me; Halley had been asked to do so when returning from his 1677 Saint Helena expedition to observe the transit of Mercury, but he missed me.

"The sudden flowering of science in the late Seventeenth Century was what they had been waiting for, the Templar Guardians told me: an opportunity to deploy their treasure to support the new movement—all they needed was the right person to manage it and, since God had betrayed them, the Devil was their man.

"The initiation was straightforward: I was asked three questions: Do you solemnly pledge yourself to nobility of purpose? Do you solemnly pledge yourself to freedom from superstition? Do you solemnly pledge yourself to the enlightenment of mankind? To each of these I answered, 'I do solemnly so pledge.'

"The pact was sealed, and the gravity of the occasion emphasized, by their next act. The knight in the center said, 'And to you we now do solemnly pledge our eternal silence.' He raised his broadsword, and with a single mighty swoop, decapitated the man to his left. He repeated the action with the man to his right. Neither of his companions so much as flinched. He then rested his bloodied sword upside down, hilt jammed into a gap between the flagstones and the point of the blade toward his chest. He gave me a last long stare, as if urging me to honor my pledges as they were honoring theirs, before taking his dagger from its sheath and driving it deep into his stomach. Then he cast himself, Cato-like, upon his sword. He knew well what he was doing, for the blade pierced his heart, and he died mercifully fast.

"I had seen much in my travels, and the Devil is hardly squeamish, but even so I remained frozen on the spot for I know not how long, taking in the carnage before me. Eventually, I stepped forward and carefully withdrew the bloodied dagger from the knight's stomach—I did not know what awaited me above, but thought it best to be armed. It was a fine weapon, with a jewel-encrusted hilt and a Damascened blade that likely came back with the Templar knights from the Crusades, Damascus steel being at the time the strongest and sharpest in the world. The blade was engraved with a long scroll woven through with roses, and bearing a motto."

"What did the motto say?"

"Why don't you read it for yourself?" He passes her the knife he used to slice the lemon.

"You mean this is the same knife?"

"It is the same blade. I had it reworked into something more readily concealable."

Sabrina inspects the knife. The gleaming metal has been forged with swirling bands, 'Damascening,' she supposes, reminiscent of the marbleizing on Bronaryre's notepaper, or the shimmering finish of the *United States*' magnesium-bronze propellers. The engraving is very fine and difficult to read—perhaps centuries of polishing was gradually wearing it away—but by holding it at an angle Sabrina is able to make it out.

"*Floreat Lux Voluptarius*," she says.

"Let voluptuous enlightenment bloom. A fine sentiment, well put, and I adopted the motto as my own."

Sabrina continues to study the blade with fascination, an artifact that would have had a starring role at the Pitt Rivers.

"What happened next?"

"The pool of blood on the floor grew steadily, but before it reached me I walked away: I had just been summoned to reason, and a man of reason does not permit the needless ruin of a good new pair of Cordovan leather boots. I climbed back up the stone staircase—not spiral but helical, something that I was to reflect upon many years later, as if the builders of that place had guessed at the structure that is the true secret of life: neither gods nor demons, but strands of DNA.

"In order to achieve any particular outcome, two things are necessary: the mind to do it and the means to do it. The period from the moment that Cromwell gave me this coin until the end of my travels in Tangier had prepared my mind for the task ahead; now, all of a sudden, I had the means, too. As I emerged from the bloody crypt into the breaking dawn, I realized that my destiny was now fully determined."

DINNER ON THE TERRACE that night is a jolly affair. There is a medieval theme: mighty joints of roast meat and whole roast fowl served on big butchers' boards, accompanied by crusty loaves of peasant bread, and washed down with pewter tankards of ale hand-drawn from wooden casks. Minstrels sing madrigals and play merry tunes on lutes and fifes, while a troupe of jesters mingles among the diners, teasing here and there, setting riddles, performing acrobatics, reciting poems and doing mime, all exceedingly bawdy. Many of the girls have dressed in period costume, and play along enthusiastically.

The party moves down to the parterre after finishing the feast, lying out across the lawn while digesting the meal. Meanwhile, the sounding chamber has been opened. Some of the girls have used their summer vacation to form a choir specializing in Elizabethan music, perhaps because of the Caiaphas connection, and tonight they give their maiden performance. They wear not the traditional choristers' cassocks and surplices but instead rich silk robes shot through with metallic thread, and lace ruffs stiffly starched, presumably in honor of their college's founder. The choir assembles in the sounding chamber from which they chant the music of the era, unaccompanied and surprisingly well: mostly Tallis and Byrd, but other pieces too, including a song by another Campion, named Thomas, contemporaneous with Edmund, but this one having had the pleasant fortune not to be drawn and quartered by good Queen Bess.

The sounding chamber is well named: the music echoes loudly across the grounds, and Sabrina lies back on the soft green sward while listening to it, gazing up at the heavens. The stars seem especially bright tonight, blazingly brilliant, perhaps because the moon has waned to just a slender crescent, and so does not obliterate them. An occasional dark shape—an owl or a bat—swoops by across the sky above her.

SABRINA AWAKENS WITH A start on Sunday morning. She has the sense of not having dreamed, notwithstanding consuming the contents of the laudanum bottle before going to bed last night, and she cannot help feeling disappointed, having drifted into sleep with an expectation of visiting underground vaults in her slumbers, filled with hidden treasure and headless Templars.

She gets out of bed and goes out onto the terrace. The pheasant is out and about already, ever colorful, proudly strutting the rounds of his domain at the edge of the parterre, like a highly decorated general inspecting his fortifications. There is no clock in the room. With the lack of a wireless signal, Sabrina has fallen into the habit of ignoring her phone and judging the passage of time by sky alone. The sunlight slants across the top of the woods: it is still early, but she does not feel the usual shiver of naked flesh suddenly meeting cold air: already it is muggy, heralding something once rare in England, before global warming: a genuinely hot day. The sky is high and pale, a cirrus-streaked pink—*red in the morning, sailor take warning.*

SABRINA IS THE FIRST down to breakfast, but is soon joined by Penelope de Vere, who after greeting Sabrina goes to the sideboard and begins loading her plate. She wears heavy jeans tucked into sturdy boots, despite the warmth of the coming day.

"Going hiking?" Sabrina asks.

Penelope pauses from food gathering and slowly bends to look under the table at Sabrina's legs, bare and sandal-shod.

"Aren't you joining us today?"

"Joining you where?"

"Beating the bounds, of course."

"What's beating the bounds?"

Penelope is briefly bemused, but then realizes the reason for Sabrina's ignorance. "Ah, you didn't arrive until Saturday afternoon, so you don't know."

"Know what?'

"Wait, I'll tell you." Penelope finishes loading her plate and is soon seated opposite Sabrina, leaning forward, eating and talking eagerly and simultaneously in a manner that Sabrina thinks would have appalled her deportment teacher back at St. John's Wood.

"Beating the bounds is an old English tradition," she explains. "One day every year the village folk would gather, particularly the youngsters, and walk out in procession around the boundaries of their town or parish. In the days before accurate maps and surveys it was how the knowledge of what was theirs and what was not was passed down from generation to generation. The whole thing was festive, a day off from normal labor. That's what we're going to do today: beat the bounds of the preceptory, although of course Bronaryre has turned it into a competition."

"How?"

"Apparently there are sixteen boundary markers, in the form of large stone dragons, hidden away in the woods surrounding the estate."

"I think I've seen one."

"Then you've got a head start. They're all located along points of an imaginary compass rose, where the house is at the center. There are ordnance maps and compasses on the bureau in the hall. Bronaryre says that a quarter-ounce gold coin—a guinea—has been placed in the mouth of each dragon, and whoever finds one gets to keep it. He told us that gold was once the accepted measure of money, and that currency used to be backed by gold: the so-called 'gold standard.' Nixon took the U.S. off the gold standard in 1971, meaning that now money is worth only what everyone pretends it's worth—one of Nixon's many mistakes, according to Bronaryre: when this happened wealth no longer needed to be generated by productivity; governments could simply print money instead—and the global economy became what he calls a giant Ponzi scheme."

"He has an interesting way of teaching economics—via orienteering."

"So much better than in a classroom. Afterward, we'll have a picnic by the river and go swimming—I hope you're going to join us."

"I'll see how the day goes."

## The Unreal City

BEATING THE BOUNDS gets underway at 10:00 A.M., noisily. Sabrina watches the teams from her terrace, boisterous groups of girls eagerly fanning out in various directions across the parterre. The day is as hot and humid as the early morning had promised, but she has her doubts about the picnic: already, thunderheads are forming in the far distance, over the Vale of Evesham. But the day is too warm to stay indoors: she puts a book in a bag, takes a map and compass from the main hall, grabs an umbrella from the stand by the front door, and heads out of the house toward the high slopes of pathless wood to the north-east: difficult country, and a direction that the girls had avoided.

Her progress is slow. Sabrina has kept to a simple cotton shirt with shorts and sandals, and so has to tread carefully through the bracken and detritus of the forest floor. The umbrella, a solid wood-strutted apparatus from the days when things were built to last, does excellent duty as a walking stick. But the slope steepens as she heads further into the wood, and eventually she hits an escarpment, maybe thirty feet high, forming a broad semicircle before her. She has no choice but to double back or climb.

Sabrina leaves the umbrella hanging on a branch, more a hindrance than a help now, slings the bag across her shoulder, and begins climbing, using trunks and roots for handholds, digging her feet into the soil to gain purchase. However high she gets there always seems to be further to go, but at last the slope reduces and then flattens as she reaches the top of the bluff.

On the other side is a deep gully, thickly wooded and wonderfully verdant—it will be messy going, but she is so dirty by now that it makes no difference. She plunges forward down the slope.

The first change she notices is in the atmosphere: gone is the dappled warmth of earlier, replaced by a cool dark gloom, and Sabrina wonders if this area, separated by the escarpment from the surrounding land, has its own microclimate. She continues deeper into the wood.

The flora is different here, too: no longer the deciduous trees and flowering shrubs found elsewhere on the estate, but instead a canopy composed of conifers and vaguely palm-like trees that she cannot identify. The forest floor is covered with ferns and horsetails springing from a sea of moss and liverwort. And everywhere there are fungi: huge mushrooms growing like shelves from the tree trunks, or on the ground as large spheres, or the traditional stalk and cap, some with their tops upturned to display their gills, as if tipping their hats in passing; and what are presumably poisonous toadstools, prominent and temptingly colorful. There is a Linnaean name for such flora—vegetation that reproduces by spore rather than seed—but Sabrina cannot recall it. The smell is deeply earthen and peaty; it smells of slow decay. The wood feels ancient, Cretaceous or Jurassic, something from a past epoch.

There is also a complete absence of bird song, disquieting in an English wood in summer. A large toad, sitting atop a rock like a malignant Bodhisattva, unblinkingly observes Sabrina's approach, as if contemplating a quick tongue-lashing as she passes.

She recalls the Linnaean classification: 'cryptogams'—*crypto* meaning hidden: appropriate, Sabrina thinks, for this secret, lost world.

She takes out the ordnance survey and identifies from the closely grouped contours what must have been the escarpment. The boundary of the estate is about half a mile east of her. She sets out in that direction, using the compass and feeling like an explorer, a Walter Raleigh pushing through the strange flora of a new world in search of El Dorado. Thirty minutes later, Sabrina discovers how apt the metaphor was: she suddenly comes upon a boundary marker, a vine-swathed stone dragon standing fifteen feet high, identical to the one she had encountered when first entering the estate, and in whose ancient mouth she discovers, after mounting the great stone base, a glistening golden guinea.

The coin is dated 1666, but is as shiny as if it had been freshly minted. No wonder gold has always been so valued, Sabrina thinks: in a world of continuous deterioration, an entropic world in which everything tends to decrepitude, even the planet itself, gold is the one thing that never rusts, never tarnishes, never ages. A constant, like Bernoulli's *e*.

The coin is not the only item that has been left for the girls to find. Sitting on the stone base beneath the dragon is a plastic sandwich box. Presumably, it is intended as sustenance for youthful appetites caught out in the woods and far from food, but when Sabrina opens it she finds inside not sandwiches but a single small cupcake.

Next to the cake is a label: *Pounds, Shillings & Pence Cake.* She turns the label over and finds on the other side a terse, *Alice-in-Wonderland*-like instruction: *EAT ME!* The label is made of brown cardboard, the same as the one tied to her laudanum bottle, and Sabrina briefly wonders if this cake has been left for the girls or her alone. But no one had known that she would come this way—she had not known herself—and once she set out it would have been impossible for anyone to have overtaken her unseen.

She puts aside the label and examines the cake. Sabrina is familiar with *pound* cake, but has never heard of *pound, shilling & pence* cake—presumably an English treat, given that it is named for English currency. It seems to be made of plain cake, moist and buttery. The top is uniced but the center has been cut away in an inverted cone—a conic section—

and the gap filled with thick whipped cream before the cone was replaced, now an inch or so elevated.

She eats the cupcake. The cake itself is rather bland but the filling is extremely rich, not simple cream but some egg-and-cream custard-like mixture, and heavily flavored: vanilla certainly; perhaps cardamom; something else that she cannot name.

The cake was small but it feels heavy in her stomach, and Sabrina decides to read while digesting it. She takes a seat, settling herself comfortably with a mound of moss for a cushion and the base of the sculpture as a backrest.

Her knees are very dirty, she observes.

Sabrina takes the book from her bag, an annotated version of 'The Waste Land' that she pulled from the library shelves the previous evening. She soon comes upon the simple phrase that had been burbling about in her head ever since Bronaryre had first used it, unattributed, to characterize the London of his youth: *Unreal City*. Eliot's own annotation points to Baudelaire:

> *Fourmillante cité, cité pleine des rêves,*
> *Où le spectre en plein jour raccroche le passant*

The editor's annotation covers three pages, quoting Baudelaire's entire poem, 'Les sept vieillards'—the seven aged men—in both the original and an English translation, but the latter has been rendered to preserve meter and rhyme, and Sabrina prefers her own nearer-transliteration:

> *Swarming city, city bursting with dreams,*
> *Where in broad daylight ghosts grab at passers-by*

Both Bronaryre and Eliot had meant London; presumably Baudelaire meant Paris. Sabrina thinks of the Unreal City as Oxford—swarming, certainly, with students and tourists, and what better candidate for a city full of dreams than the city of dreaming spires.

Bronaryre has provided the ghosts, one way or another.

Or perhaps it should be New York, swarming with sky-reaching dreams.

She feels very acute; sensory.

*En plein jour*. Clear, *clair*.

She enters a fugue state, not of listless disassociation—that solipsistic sea of conceptual slop, whether opium-induced or otherwise—but its very opposite: a sudden superb clarity of vision, or clarity of understanding, as if all uncertainty had been swept aside, leaving only the relevant, only the truly real. And connectedness, almost Machiavellian in its exactitude, in knowing precisely the disposition of all effects that would result from any particular action. She could instantly count every filament of a feather, were one to float down in front of her; discern the innermost desires of anyone who might speak to her, no matter how cunning or duplicitous they might be; know at once the outcome of any chess game from the very first move, and the character of he who made it. Her mind is pure, crystalline, pristine—an instrument surgical in its precision. At this moment, she thinks, she could achieve anything.

She laughs but it is not her own laugh; it is deep and echoing, the dragon's perhaps.

Drool drips down upon her: yes, certainly the dragon then.

There is a sudden sound of stone grinding on stone. Sabrina looks up. The dragon is moving. Loose dirt falls from him. She stands and steps back instinctively, not in fright but in wonder; she cannot take her eyes from the spectacle. He carefully flexes his legs and jaw, as if arising from a long slumber. When he stretches his wings the vines encasing them snap away.

His eyes open, and his stern gaze falls instantly upon her.

They stare at each other for a long time in silence, both equally astonished by the presence of the other.

"My name is Sabrina Lancaster," she says at length. "How do you do?"

The dragon looks at her disapprovingly.

"*Latine loqueris*?" it asks. Remarkable enough that there should be a dragon; more remarkable still that it asks her if she speaks Latin.

"*Ego loquerer,*" she hesitantly replies, and somewhere far in the back of her mind she can hear Sister Aloysius reprimanding her for having lapsed into an imperfect subjunctive when a present indicative was called for. "*Si loqueris lente,*" she adds, a plea for it to speak slowly.

The creature gazes at her with evident dissatisfaction. "Thy Latin is an abomination painful to mine ear," it says. "I must scrabble for words in thine own vulgar tongue—so be it." It sighs, deeply incommoded by her poor conjugations. "Sabrina of Lancaster, thou art come at last."

"You were expecting me?"

"These centuries past."

"Are you sure you have the right person?"

"Thou art the one. The sentinels alerted me."

"What sentinels?"

"Thou didst observe the toad, didst thou not? A slimy fat slovenly creature, to be sure, foul of both habit and abode, but hardly to be mistaken. Plus that wretch the pheasant, conceited coxcomb that he is. And the harrier; she is no fool: it was she who first marked thou for whom thou art."

"They're your sentinels?"

"They are the Sentinels of the Godcaster, of whom I am one of the sixteen Guardians."

"Who is the Godcaster?"

"He that invites men to cast aside their prejudices, and look truth in the eye."

The dragon ponderously makes its way down from the stone base, clawed feet slipping a little, using its boney wings as crutches to avoid falling.

"How is it that stone is brought to life?" Sabrina asks.

"First asketh how is it that life was turned to stone."

"You were once alive?"

"Aye. The warlock Mordred of Malmesbury petrified me at the command of Hugues de Payens."

"When was that?"

"When de Payens visited England, *anno Domini* 1128."

"You've been petrified for nine hundred years?"

"Yes, except for those occasions when my services have been required, as now. So it will be again: I will return to stone once thou hast been marked."

"Marked?"

"Remove thy chemise."

"Why?"

"Thou shalt be marked at the base of thy wing, if wingèd thou wast."

Sabrina reluctantly unbuttons her shirt and takes it off, carefully laying it on the soft moss.

"Thy cuirass, too."

"Cuirass?"

"Thy chest armor," the dragon explains, sounding very put upon. "Maid, have thy no French, either?"

She does not bother arguing the point.

"Dispose thyself against the base, face to the stone, exposing thy back as for a flogging."

"A flogging?"

"Surely thou hast been flogged before?"

"No."

The dragon looks doubtful but does not pursue the matter. In its forefoot it carries what had been hidden before, or perhaps Sabrina had just missed it, small compared to its great bulk: a slender iron bar two feet long and patterned at the tip. The dragon holds it up, breathes fire upon it, and soon the iron is glowing red hot. Sabrina understands now: she is to be branded.

"Arrange thyself, cruciform in posture."

It is just a dream, Sabrina says to herself, and she turns to the big stone base. The top is at chest level. She reaches her arms out straight along the ledge, and presses firmly against the cold stone, not wanting to flinch.

The dragon approaches; its breath blows down from above, smelling of sulfur and molten metal. She feels on her back not the branding iron but something the opposite, just as bracing but ice-cold. It takes her a moment to realize that it is a dragon claw. It hooks around her long hair and gathers it across her left shoulder, so as to leave her back bare.

Another surge of roaring flame—the iron being briefly reheated—and then the thing is planted firmly onto the flesh of her right shoulder blade. It might only be a dream, but the pain is as searing as if it were real, excruciating, beyond pain she has ever felt. It is mercifully brief, however, and once the iron is removed it soon subsides into a harsh ache.

Sabrina subsides too, sliding into unconsciousness at the base of the pedestal.

SABRINA OPENS HER EYES. The sky is bursting with black cloud above her, and she has been awakened by the beginnings of what is evidently to be a downpour—perhaps it was those first drops that she had mistaken for drool. But the dream lingering in her mind is not that of the dragon; it is the dream of the Unreal City, and the sense that accompanied it of having achieved, for a moment at least, perfect lucidity. Sabrina realizes with alarm that the dream is leaving her, and she closes her eyes to concentrate, ignoring the increasingly heavy beat of raindrops upon the leaves, willing herself to remember, trying to take an imprint of that instant of wonderful clarity upon her waking mind. But she cannot get her consciousness to cooperate, and it slips away, leaving only the echo of a moment when understanding had seemed to touch perfection.

She gets up, disappointed, and turns to face the boundary marker. The dragon is as she first saw it, and the enveloping vines are intact: yes, just a dream after all.

Whom did she imagine was the 'Godcaster,' she wonders. Bronaryre? But Bronaryre travels frequently, and often lives abroad: these fifteen-foot-high stone dragons can hardly go with him. Perhaps the Godcaster is something inhabiting Bronaryre's cellar.

Then she realizes that she is topless, and instantly recalls having being branded. She reaches back to her right should blade. There is no mark or scarring, although she does feel a dull throb beneath the flesh, presumably due to having lain awkwardly upon a rock or root while asleep, and no doubt the source of the branding vision—that dream she remembers vividly.

Sabrina's clothing lies bundled at the base of the dragon sculpture. She took them off to use as a pillow, she sees, and the act had entered into her hallucination.

The sky above opens up. She quickly tucks the Eliot and underwear into her bag, throws on her shirt with just a single button to secure it for now, and hurriedly begins what is certain to be a wet and muddy walk back to the manor.

I am an Eve cast from Paradise, she thinks as she treks along, a Paradise that was one not of laborless bounty, but of absolute clarity of thought.

# Seventh Circle

Euterpe

SABRINA ARRIVES BACK AT the preceptory to Ronson's startled gaze, expressing what she supposes is disapproval of her drenched and muddy state—not until returning to her room and looking in the mirror does she discover that the thin fabric of the soaked shirt currently clinging to her chest has become perfectly transparent. She showers and changes, and then heads back downstairs to the library, quietly, so as to avoid the butler.

The Oxford English Dictionary knows nothing of pounds, shillings, and pence *cake*, but contains extensive entries on pounds, shillings, and pence as currency, including the fact that, before decimalization, they were often expressed in prices as '£.s.d.' The abbreviation is derived from the Latin *librae, solidi, denarii*, a Roman *denarius* being a small silver coin weighing 4.5 grams, and with 72 of them equal in weight to a *libra pondo*, a Roman pound. When gold replaced silver in the late Empire, the new coin of one seventy-second of a pound weight was called a *solidus*.

The '£' in '£.s.d.' is thus simply a stylized letter *L*, and so the fictional *pounds, shillings & pence cake* was in fact *LSD* cake. Now Sabrina knows what the strange taste in the custard mixture must have been: not an exotic spice but the well-known psychedelic hallucinogen, and so the vivid phantasmagoria with the dragon is explained.

At Temple Slaughter Preceptory, one must read all labels carefully, at multiple levels of meaning.

Ronson enters the room. "Will you be dining this evening, ma'am?" he asks the floor. "Mr. Bronaryre has left the estate, and the young ladies have elected to have pizzas delivered."

"Just sandwiches brought up to my room will be fine," she says.

"Certainly, ma'am. And dessert?"

"Anything but cake."

THERE ARE TWO HANDWRITTEN envelopes in Sabrina's pidge when she returns to Caiaphas on Monday. The first bears a winged-crown-and-wolf-head crest that she immediately recognizes; the second is oversized and unfamiliar to her. She takes them to a seat in a sunny corner of the second quad to read, thinking that this old-fashioned preference for epistolary communication over telephone and texting is another quality of Oxford life that she likes. She opens the envelope with the Campion Hall crest. It contains a short note.

*Watson (for so shall I address you on this occasion),*

*According to the canon, it is axiomatic that when one has eliminated all other possibilities, then whatever remains, however improbable, must be the truth.*

*I draw three items to your attention:*

1. *The levitee sat in the lotus position*
2. *The room was lit by candles*
3. *The curious case of what your jewelry was not on that night*

*The lab work should be completed tomorrow. If convenient, I propose that we meet in Caiaphas Chapel after Wednesday Evensong, where I will brief you on the results. If you have not solved the mystery on your own, I shall enlighten you then.*

*S. Holmes, (S.J.)*

Sabrina wonders if the nomination of Caiaphas as a meeting place is because his Jesuit colleagues would frown on Wilkins receiving a female guest at Campion Hall. She puts the letter aside and opens the second envelope. Inside is a folded card made from thick, high-quality stock. The front cover is printed with an architectural drawing of an ornate gated arch, gaudily Baroque, rendered in elevation, the paper bearing a patina of age, perhaps a facsimile from the original blueprints. She opens the card and a pop-up version of the arch appears, now in three dimensions. It is not composed of the stamped and pressed cardboard of a mass-manufactured greeting card, but is instead made of rice paper, so delicate as to be almost transparent, and upon which the architectural renderings of the arch have been carefully traced.

Whoever made this card is wonderfully skilled at origami, she thinks, and also has a lot of time on their hands.

*Soirée de Jeux*, someone has written on the card—game night. Elegant cursive script: a feminine hand, Sabrina thinks, too flowery to be Bronaryre's. Dress is given as *Black Tie*, with an emphatic addendum: *Masks a must!* The date is for Saturday evening, at 10:00 P.M.

There is no address, just an enigmatic instruction: *Enter via the York Watergate*.

She looks up 'York Watergate.' It is located on London's Victoria Embankment, and is apparently the last surviving piece of what was once a York House. The Watergate served as a landing point for those arriving by boat, before construction in the Nineteenth Century of the big civil engineering project that resulted in the Embankment, and which so narrowed the Thames that the York Watergate is now stranded a hundred yards inland from the river it once gave onto.

York House had a long history, and was at one stage the London seat of the Bishops of York—hence the name. For a time it had been the residence of Francis Bacon, not in his historical role as the champion of the new scientific method but in his official capacity as Keeper of the Great Seal. The Watergate itself was built in 1626, when the reckless first Duke of Buckingham had occupied the house. Today it seems that the Watergate no longer leads anywhere: it stands isolated and alone in the Embankment Gardens.

Among a catalog of nearby features is listed *The Benjamin Franklin House*, which seems a strange thing for a London landmark, and when Sabrina looks it up she is surprised to learn that Benjamin Franklin (whom Sabrina had last encountered on Bronaryre's doorstep in New York) had spent sixteen of the prime years of his life residing in London, living around the corner from the York Watergate at 36 Craven Street.

Sabrina looks again at the card. No RSVP, but nor would there be, she reasons, for an anonymous gathering at an unknown location.

CAIAPHAS COLLEGE CHAPEL conducts Evensong on Wednesdays, perhaps so as not to compete with the same service at New College and Christ Church, both held on Thursdays. Sabrina had imagined there would be sparse attendance out of term, but the chapel is again full, and she has to wait fifteen minutes after completion of the service for it finally to empty, and Wilkins to come down from the gallery.

From the look of concern on his face, she can tell that he is the bearer of bad news.

"Are you well?" he asks her, without greeting.

"Yes, and you?"

"Are you sure? Not feeling a bit off-color, not quite yourself, anything like that?"

"No, I'm fine. Why?"

"I'm very relieved to hear it," he says. "According to your blood work, you should be near death."

"What?"

"My colleague analyzed your blood sample, and reported extraordinarily high BCR and T-cell counts."

"BCR?"

"B-cell receptors: antigens, basically. She says that it's the blood of someone who is experiencing an elevated immune response, someone under attack from a severe infection, perhaps bacterial, more likely viral.

Sabrina takes a seat at the end of the pew. "Clearly, that's not the case. I genuinely feel fine. I was even caught outside in a thunderstorm on Sunday, and became thoroughly soaked, but felt no ill effects from it."

"Not even a sniffle?"

"Nothing, I've always been lucky that way. Are you sure your colleague didn't test the wrong sample?"

"She's a very careful researcher. However, given the reality, I suppose we have to admit the possibility of a mistake."

"And she's qualified?"

"Yes, very. Well, perhaps not *very* very."

"Not *very* very?"

"What I mean is, she has all the necessary training and equipment. There is one small thing, though."

"What?"

"She works on mice."

"Mice? No wonder the results are ridiculous."

"No, they're like humans. What I mean is, she works with mouse models, which is to say mice that have been genetically engineered to exhibit some trait of interest in human studies."

"What's she working on now?"

"Obesity."

"So, fat mice."

"Yes. They're quite grotesque, actually."

Sabina sits back, relieved. "I think we may safely discount the near-death hypothesis."

"Perhaps you should get a blood test anyway, just to be safe."

"Through your NHS? Sorry, but I've heard the horror stories: I don't have the time to struggle with that."

"What about a private doctor? I could ask around for a referral."

Sabrina is about to agree when she realizes that she has no need of a referral: she already has a doctor—Dorothy Aran, who had examined Sabrina for her residency permit. It would mean taking the train into London, but that would have the added benefit of deciding what to do about the mysterious invitation for Saturday night: if she were already in town for a medical appointment, then it would make sense to stay for the weekend and see what the strange business with the Watergate is all about.

"I have a doctor," she tells him. "I'll schedule an appointment."

"I'm glad to hear it," Wilkins says. He settles into a pew across the aisle and removes from his satchel the Temperley, which he returns to Sabrina.

"Well?" she asks.

"The blood isn't yours. It isn't even human; it's avian. Chicken, presumably. What happened—did you attend a voodoo ritual?"

"It was pheasant, not chicken."

"A posh voodoo ritual?"

"They'd been hung. I must have brushed the hem against the floor underneath."

Sabrina expects Wilkins to quiz her further, probably beginning with the fact that pheasants are out of season, but he changes subject instead.

"So, Watson, have you solved the mystery of the levitating witch?"

"I have not," Sabrina admits, relieved at not having to provide any further explanation.

"Why did she not fly around the room, I wonder? And why no broomstick, in the traditional manner?"

"I see that you intend to drag this out, just like the real Holmes."

"The *real* Holmes?"

"Good point: I'm obviously having trouble telling fact from fiction these days."

"Did you consider the three items I raised?"

"Of course, but frankly I failed to see their relevance. I tell you, I passed my hand above and below her, and there was nothing but air: she was levitating. It would have made no difference if there were candles or not, or whatever jewelry I was wearing."

"I agree with you."

"You agree?"

"But what of the lotus position?"

"What about it?"

"Why not just sit normally?'

“I guess she just chose to sit that way. Maybe she was meditating in order to levitate in the first place—she did seem to be concentrating very hard while doing it. And earlier in the evening the host was sitting on it the same way himself, cross-legged. It was an ottoman—Oriental—that’s just the way they sit on it.”

“But they’re not quite the same, are they? The lotus position is rather more than merely cross-legged.”

“Okay, he was not sitting in the full lotus position: he was probably too solidly built to manage it.”

“But according to you, this Nefertiti was solidly built, too.”

“Nekhebit. Yes, she was, but no so much in the legs.”

“Hefty, but with skinny legs?”

“They weren’t precisely skinny, but I would say slender. And she was young, too: limber enough to manage a full lotus. Does it matter?”

“It is of the utmost importance, Watson. And what of the candles?”

“If you’re going to suggest that the low light from the candles was to help disguise some trick, then I have to say that I doubt it: there must have been a dozen of them at least, and they were large—there was plenty of light.”

“I quite agree with you, Watson—the purpose of the candles was not to disguise a trick; it was something else entirely. And finally, the jewelry: did you reach a conclusion?”

“It all seemed handmade, and I had the sense that they were artifacts, presumably ancient Egyptian, but not so valuable: just bronze, no gold or precious stones. I assume they were part of the general Egypto-deity theme.”

“They probably *were* artifacts, and although Egyptian-themed not necessarily genuinely ancient Egyptian. But certainly they would have predated 1751.”

“What happened in 1751?”

“The discovery of nickel. Nickel is an interesting metal, with very important qualities: it is strong, ductile, and resists corrosion.”

“And so?”

“And so, ever since its discovery it has been widely used in the making of metal alloys. Nickel makes strong and long-lasting coins like your American five-cent coin, for example, which is named for the metal. Nickel is an essential component in stainless steel. Also, it is broadly used in the fabrication of precious metal jewelry. You probably know that it is unusual for gold or silver jewelry to be made of pure gold, or pure silver: those metals by themselves are too soft and, in the case of silver, too easily tarnished. Usually, they are alloys, and sometimes those alloys contain nickel. That was why you were given the jewelry to wear that night, and why that jewelry had to predate the use of nickel."

"Why?"

"Because nickel is ferromagnetic."

Sabrina suddenly sees where Wilkins is heading.

"You're suggesting that it was a trick somehow done with magnets?"

"I am. Since there was no physical apparatus lifting her, as you proved, then there is only one remaining option which, however improbable, must be the truth: it could only have been an electromagnetic force. I imagine that she had a series of permanent magnets secured in a harness around her chest, and that's the reason why this slender-legged woman seemed solidly built."

"They would have had to be very large magnets."

"Or heavily magnetized. Or perhaps not even traditional iron magnets. There are other materials that are ferromagnetic. A form of carbon has recently been discovered that exhibits ferromagnetic properties, so new that it doesn't even have a name yet: *U-carbon*, one collaborator calls it, meaning *unusual* carbon; the principal researcher has named it *Adamantia*, after 'Adamant', the so-called unbreakable lodestone for which the alchemists searched in vain. And the lotus position is explained: having one's torso lifted by electromagnets is fine, but how to make it appear that the legs also levitate? If you've ever worked out on gymnastic bars where you try to maintain your legs at an angle, you'll know how very difficult this is. But if you tie your legs together in a knot, which is essentially what the lotus position does, then it becomes possible to hold them for a while. Not easy, mind you—even that would be difficult to sustain, hence what appeared to you as her extreme concentration, and also no doubt why your magician-host urged you to get on with checking for wires and such, because he knew how hard it would be for the girl to keep it up."

It all fits, Sabrina realizes. "And the candles?"

"The magnets in a vest are just half the trick. The other half would be an electromagnet, or more likely a series of them, the polarity reversed to produce the opposing force—same as in those maglev trains and such. They might have been in the ottoman, or perhaps under the floor. Did the room have a cellar?"

"Yes."

"Wherever they were, they would have consumed a lot of power—probably as much current as the wiring could support. Maybe there was a battery pile hidden away to supplement it." In the western wing, Sabrina immediately thinks, which explains why she was warned not to go down there. "In any case, if there were electric lights they would no doubt have dimmed as soon as the trick began, hence the necessity of candles."

Sabrina is silent for a time, reviewing the theory, but she can find no obvious flaws: rationality has been restored. She returns to her rooms at Caiaphas and updates her journal.

*The levitation trick seems very simple now that Wilkins has explained the possibility of electromagnets: I should have thought of it myself. But amid the relief when he told me, I felt a small twinge of disappointment—how wonderful it would have been to have witnessed something genuinely supernatural.*

*I have re-examined the Banque Savoie-Didier check: what I initially took to be a St. George's cross is really a* croix pattée*, widening slightly at the ends of the arms and, being red on a white background, is thus a symbol of the Knights Templar. The bank was founded in 1321: nine years after Pope Clement V issued the bull* Vox in excelso*, suppressing the order. In England, the Templars hid their portable wealth in a crypt; in France, my guess is that it was smuggled into the Swiss cantons, and the keepers of the treasure put it to work by practicing the* *profession in which they were already skilled—no wonder Banque Savoie-Didier ended up as Bronaryre's bankers.*

*And so to Hugues de Payens, at whose command the dragon in my dream believed himself petrified. He was a real person: it was he who founded, along with Bernard de Clairvaux, the Order of the Knights Templar, and he was their first Grand Master. De Payens did indeed visit England in 1128. All this was unknown to me—how did these facts enter into my hallucination?*

*I asked the girls, but none of them found any cupcakes, psychopharmaceutical or otherwise, at the other boundary markers. How could Bronaryre have known I would go to that particular one?—I was not carrying my phone (not that it would have had a signal anyway) and told no one which way I was heading, although the general direction could conceivably have been observed from the house.*

*Perhaps a drone was used to track me. That same drone could have delivered the cupcake, just before I arrived.*

*None of this explains why Bronaryre bothers in the first place—why the masques? It cannot be a bribe to write a favorable book: being caned and branded are not bribes; they are anti-bribes. Instruction of some kind? An obscure form of diabolical catechism? An underworld initiation rite? A trial?*

*Yet the masques remain not unwelcome, however outrageous they have become—there is a weight to them, a gravitas, a deeper meaning that I am sure is present beneath the surface, but the nature of which I cannot quite plumb. As with Bach: something fully felt but impossible to explain. Part of it is a sense of intellectual heft: Bronaryre may be many things, but I am certain that he is neither trivial nor a fool.*

*Perhaps the answer will be found at the York Watergate—although nothing named York bodes well for a Lancaster.*

SABRINA TAKES AN EARLY TRAIN to London on Friday morning, arriving at Paddington with plenty of time to spare before her doctor's appointment. She strolls along the Serpentine and then on into Green Park and Saint James's, thinking how pleasant it is to have a country ramble in the middle of a great metropolis, same as Central Park. She arrives at Trafalgar Square just as at the other end of Whitehall Big Ben begins to toll ten o'clock, opening time for the great museums.

The nearby National Gallery is too grand for her limited time, but the adjoining and more modest National Portrait Gallery is just the right size, and soon Sabrina is inside and putting faces to famous names: the profligate Edward de Vere, to whom Penelope de Vere believes herself unrelated despite what her father might say, supposed author of Shakespeare's plays and looking every bit a man with a secret; Pepys, an intelligent face, a sheet of music in his hand and looking slightly annoyed at being distracted from it by the painter; and the rogue George Villiers, that same first Duke of Buckingham who had built the York Watergate of her coming assignation, just two years before he was stabbed to death by a disgruntled soldier, to the general approval of all England—one look at that self-satisfied face, she thinks, and you knew he had it coming.

After her appointment, Sabrina makes her way south from Dr. Aran's Harley Street offices, through Hanover Square, and finally to Bruton Street in Mayfair, the location of the Temperley boutique. With her own Temperley at the cleaners to remove the blood stain—thankfully not her own—she needs something to wear tomorrow night. The woman at the shop quizzes her about the event and, on learning that it is a mysterious masked *Soirée de Jeux* to which Sabrina has received an anonymous invitation, enthusiastically begins selecting candidate gowns. The final choice—ornately embroidered organza over a sheer and frankly translucent chiffon sheath—is even less modest than her other Temperley.

Sabrina's penultimate stop is a store in Covent Garden specializing in Venetian carnival accouterments, where she purchases a Colombina mask—just a lace half-mask around the eyes, leaving the mouth uncovered and so allowing for the consumption of champagne—cream-colored and crystal-accented, a mask that will at least go well with the dress.

Her last stop is the Embankment Gardens, where she soon locates the York Watergate: a big stone structure fifteen feet high and twenty feet across. It is essentially two arches back-to-back—one facing the garden, the other the footpath and steps leading up to Buckingham Street—and the space between them is enclosed, intended to provide protection from the elements while waiting for the boat to arrive. There are iron gates on both sides, both locked shut.

Neither side leads to anywhere in particular. It has been selected only as a meeting point, she realizes, and it is an isolated one: the garden would be deserted at night, and there would be no traffic on nearby Buckingham Street, which comes to a dead end at the Watergate.

Perhaps this is a deliberate choice, she thinks, the better to do whatever is to be done here unobserved.

The one thing in the Watergate's favor is that it is only a short stroll from the Savoy. Sabrina turns in that direction and heads back to the hotel.

LONDON HAS MANY RAILROAD STATIONS—*railway* stations, Sabrina is starting to think of them, as she becomes accustomed to the English patois: Paddington, with which she is well familiar by now; King's Cross, from where she took the train to Scotland; plus Waterloo, Blackfriars, Euston, Fenchurch Street, Marylebone. This Saturday morning she is on the platform of another one she has not been to before: Liverpool Street, the station from which trains depart for Cambridge.

The journey only takes forty minutes, and Sabrina soon disembarks. The 'other place' is not a large city, considerably smaller than Oxford, but the train station is located at the extreme south-eastern end, about as far away from her destination as possible, and Sabrina takes a long walk north toward the center of town along the absurdly named Hills Road—this is flat fen country, and there is not a hill in sight, apart from Gog and Magog looming far astern—then west past Peterhouse and St. Catharine's until crossing the Cam via the Mathematical Bridge. She strolls along the Backs, past the lovely green fields belonging to King's and Trinity, the former's famous chapel rising in dignified splendor on the other side.

Sabrina finally arrives at her destination: Magdalen, the only one of the old Cambridge colleges located on the west bank of the river.

Pepys was an alumnus of this Cantabrigian Magdalen, she has learned, and his personal library—at the time one of the finest in the land—was bequeathed to the college on his death in 1703. A grand neo-classical structure was built to house it. Pepys was an avid bibliophile, and his library includes an important collection of incunabula and medieval manuscripts. He was also a keen musician, as the painting in the National Portrait Gallery had suggested, and his library includes thousands of madrigals and ballads that would otherwise have been lost.

The library is quaint in the sense that not only are most documents undigitized, there is not even an online catalog: hence the necessity for this trip north. Sabrina presents her academic credentials at the front desk and senses the librarian's faint shiver of reserve at registering that this visitor is an Oxford fellow, but sufficiently puts aside her prejudices to help Sabrina with the items that she has come to see: not the invaluable incunabula, nor the medieval music, nor even the famous diary, but something much more prosaic: naval records.

Sabrina soon has the documents arrayed before her on a reading table. She discovers that Pepys began a second diary during the Tangier expedition to record the evacuation, this one in plain script rather than coded shorthand. He did not like Tangier, 'nothing but vice in the whole place of all sorts, for swearing, cursing, drinking and whoring'—a verdict not without a hypocritical taint to it, Sabrina thinks, considering the contents of the first diary. It is not Pepys's opinions that she wants, it is facts—she puts aside the diary, and moves on to a sheaf of documents. It takes her an hour of researching to get a result, but Pepys was a meticulous administrator and her persistence is rewarded: she locates among the manuscripts a manifest listing the names of all those who accompanied Pepys on his return to England from Tangier.

Sabrina carefully transcribes the list into her notebook before leaving the library and returning to London. There is no mention of a

Jack Kincaid, the name Bronaryre had taken on leaving England, nor that of Aubrey Greystoke, the identity he assumed on his return—let the Devil explain that, she thinks.

## A Game of Chess

A LIGHT RAIN BEGINS TO fall on Saturday evening, and Sabrina accepts the doorman's offer of an umbrella as she leaves the Savoy. She walks through the Embankment Gardens, poorly lit and emptied of other people by the inclement weather. To her right is the city, near yet in the dank darkness seemingly isolated, as if a neighboring galaxy. To her left lies the rushing river, unnaturally compressed by the landfill on which she now walks, a seething black torrent. The loom of London illuminates a low layer of sopping scud overhead, weighing down on the city, threatening to crush it.

The York Watergate comes into view—a gate named for her family's ancient enemies, were she truly a Lancaster.

It is unlit, the iron gates are closed, and there is not a soul in sight. Sabrina is not displeased, as this gives her an excuse to turn around and head back to the warmth of her room at the Savoy, but then a figure appears.

He emerges from the shadows at the side, little more than a silhouette. He is facing her, she thinks, watching her approach. His features are indistinct, but from the streetlight behind he appears to be wearing a very large raincoat, what the English call a *mac*. But as she nears the Watergate she sees that it is not a mackintosh but a robe, like monk's robes, complete with a large hood pulled up over his head, perhaps as protection from the weather, or maybe to disguise his identity.

Sabrina comes to a halt ten feet away. She stands facing him in silence: the fact of the evening wear and mask should be explanation enough for her presence. His eyes are in shadow, but she can sense him staring back at her. At last he moves, opening the iron gate in invitation. Sabrina takes a deep breath, and steps into the structure. He swings the gate closed, removes a key from somewhere inside his robes, and locks it—she is now effectively imprisoned, locked inside this isolated cell on the Victoria Embankment.

But then she is immediately paroled: he unlocks the gate on the other side, steps out, and holds it open for her to follow. She does so and he locks the gate behind them, completing the formal but surely unnecessary entrance ceremony. He leads her a short distance away before stopping and turning to face her. He puts a hand into his robes and emerges with a weapon, which he holds aloft for Sabrina to see. It is a big iron hook, like a butcher's hook.

He bends a knee and begins working the hook into what she sees is a manhole cover, and all at once Sabrina understands: wherever he is taking her, they are to go there via the sewers.

He enters the black hole first, his robes billowing with a breeze coming up from beneath. Sabrina can hear the sound of rushing water below. A minute later a faint yellow light appears, and soon her guide reemerges head-and-shoulders above the pavement. He makes a single gesture with a black-gloved hand: an imperative downward thrust with an index figure, instructing her to descend.

He disappears back down the hole. To descend a ladder in an evening gown and high heels is not practicable. She takes off the latter and rebuckles their ankle straps, forming a loop with which to dangle them in the crook of her left elbow, along with the wrist strap of her evening purse. She then hitches up her dress and secures it in the only way possible, by biting down on a mouthful of hem, and uncomfortably aware that this has left her naked below the navel, apart from the one skimpy piece of underwear that she is wearing this evening, more a gesture than an actual garment.

Sabrina backs down the manhole, carefully to begin with, but quickly becoming more confident, and she soon reaches the bottom. If her companion has any reaction to witnessing her descent he does not show it, instead heading straight back up the ladder to replace the cover. Meanwhile, Sabrina looks around.

She is standing on a small brick landing set into the side of the tunnel. The only source of light is an oil lantern hanging from a hook. The sewer itself is a large circular or perhaps elliptical channel, tall enough to accommodate a man, and constructed of what look like dark glistening tiles, but which Sabrina supposes are more likely the sides of small bricks like those she is standing on, the ubiquitous building material of the Victorian age, and the glossy effect is merely due to seeping damp.

There is water washing by, several feet deep, the flow no doubt swollen by the rain. A small flat wooden boat with a pole, like a miniature punt, is secured by a line to a rusted iron ringbolt sunk into the landing. The smell is close and dank, but not particularly malodorous: presumably the real sewerage must go to a treatment plant, and this is just rainwater runoff.

Her guide comes back down the ladder. As he descends she briefly catches a glimpse of his boots—knee-high, black and highly polished, but rather old, the leather bearing the creases of many years of use. No zipper or elasticized sides: the sort of boots that are difficult to get on and off.

He has brought her umbrella down with him, which she had abandoned above. He hauls the boat in close and gestures for her to board. She does so, and then he transfers the lantern to a little mast at the bow before boarding himself, standing behind the athwartships bench on which she now sits, and then casts off.

They get underway. A hand reaches around from behind her left shoulder and taps the umbrella lying by her side: he is telling her to open it. She does so, and soon discovers the reason why: the ceiling sometimes drips. They make their way slowly, pushing against the current, a parody of punting on the Cherwell, parasol open against the sun. But the main image that comes to her mind is not of that gentle Oxford pastime, but something quite different: this sewer is the River Acheron, she thinks, and behind her this robed Charon is ferrying her to some version of Tartarus.

They come to a junction, and then another and another, all anonymous but her guide is familiar with the route and chooses the way without hesitation. She wonders how many other women have been transported on this strange journey from the York Watergate. The only sign of life is an occasional rat: mostly they flee, but one chooses to swim alongside them for a time, as if in a macabre caricature of a dolphin dancing in the bow wave of a ship.

After twenty minutes they come alongside another landing, larger than the first, and here instead of a ladder there is a set of stone stairs leading upward. As her companion secures the boat Sabrina extracts a penny from her purse, not a modern one but an older bronze version that she had been given in change, and which she had retained for its pleasing size and heft. She steps from the boat and pays for her passage. Charon accepts his due without comment, and Sabrina begins her ascent: technically the wrong direction for Tartarus, she realizes, but no analogy is perfect.

The door at the top of the stairs opens into a vestibule, with a set of stairs leading further up on the far side. There is music coming from somewhere above, and the faint murmur of a gathering. There is a door to the right with a large roundel mounted on it, depicting the head of a woman carved in relief in white against a blue background, like an oversized cameo brooch. Sabrina steps across and opens it, revealing a ladies' restroom, the first section of which is a space fitted with dainty sofas and mirrored makeup tables. Sabrina deposits the umbrella in a stand, sits to put on her shoes, and makes a final check that her mask is properly in place.

She leaves the restroom and resumes the ascent. At the top of the first landing there is a window giving onto the street, or more exactly giving onto a small cutting sunk below the street, leaving the sidewalk at eye level, like the bottom floor in a New York City brownstone. She takes the next flight up, which brings her to what must be the main hall.

The floor is flagged in marble, the walls are two curved and pillared expanses stretching around from the big windows flanking the front door. On the far side is another staircase, this one very grand and imposing in marble with broad balustrades, splitting at the landing before doubling back and continuing up to the next floor. It is less the entrance to a house than a palace.

Seven individuals are present in the hall. Two are guests, both wearing masks and apparently having just arrived: a man in evening wear and his companion, an elegant creature shedding her cloak to reveal a royal blue evening dress, backless, and with the front so narrowly cut from the halter neck as to be effectively sideless, too: the curve of her breast is visible.

The other three women in the room are less clothed. Two of them are naked, apart from masks and high heels, both atop a circular table situated in the middle of the hall where a bowl of flowers might normally be placed. One of them is on her hands and knees, rhythmically undulating from head to hips, the other is perched on the edge, arms outstretched behind to support her weight, dangling legs playfully kicking back and forth, frankly inspecting the new arrivals. Their masks are identical, round and gilt-covered, expressionless. They are a welcoming exhibit, Sabrina realizes, a live sculpture to amuse new arrivals.

The third woman, bare-breasted, holds a tray bearing glasses of champagne.

Sabrina feels less self-conscious about her own outfit now.

The final two are male: a butler, greeting the new arrivals, and a footman, accepting the lady's cloak. Her companion takes only one glass from the tray, which he hands to the woman. They commence their ascent of the stairs, but the woman leads and the man trails dutifully behind, holding her evening bag: they are not a couple, Sabrina realizes; he is her attendant.

Sabrina steps forward, and is greeted by the butler.

"Welcome, madam. Would you care for champagne?"

"Yes, please."

The footman fetches the glass while the butler explains the layout.

"The first floor is entirely open this evening. Diversions and amusements have been arranged there, and it will provide the best vantage point for the main show. The second-floor rooms are also at guests' disposal. When you choose to make your departure, we have chauffeured cars waiting to take you wherever you may wish."

Sabrina takes the stairs up to what the butler referred to as the first floor. It turns out to be a broad mezzanine giving onto the space below, which is a wide area checkered in black and white, probably intended as a ballroom in the original design. The mezzanine stretches around all four sides, with salons leading off it. The ceiling high above is a sky-colored dome set with white figures representing the zodiac, carved or molded in low relief. A large crystal chandelier hangs from the center.

The mezzanine is occupied by a mixture of guests, attendants, and entertainers. At the far end of the space is an alcove with a raised platform, where musicians would have performed when dances were held in the ballroom below. It is occupied by musicians now, a quartet, all women, all in black evening wear that contrives with long leg slits and transparent panels to be more revealing than would be found in Carnegie Hall. They play a difficult Debussy piece with obvious technical skill: they were not chosen for their looks alone.

Sabrina slowly circumnavigates the mezzanine while sipping her champagne. It appears to be genuinely a game night: poker is underway at one table, and for high stakes, as one woman has already lost her gown, and is down to mask and underwear alone, but since this last includes a garter belt and stockings she is not as yet penurious, and is laughingly calling for another hand; at another table, six people are playing a board game along the lines of Clue, but with seduction rather than murder as the theme, and the house they now occupy is represented on the playing board. Sabrina watches as a turn is played: a man in a paisley cummerbund accuses Miss Scarlet, who is indeed wearing red. It turns out that his guess is correct, and they retire to the room in question—the conservatory—apparently to reenact the crime.

Interspersed with the guests are performers. A petit young acrobat performs with a large metal ring mounted on a broad base—Sabrina watches her for a time as she shifts with slow and dignified precision from one contorted position to another, displaying not just strength but also balance and flexibility. In one pose she holds herself chest down, and then brings her legs back completely over her body, coming to a halt with ankles by either cheek and toes meeting under her chin.

In the far corner, a woman sits atop a rocking horse, moving back and forward in time with the music. She is naked but for boots and spurs, and her breasts undulate in pendulous rhythm with the rocking; she is evidently enjoying the ride. In the other corner an Oriental woman, also naked, has been heavily bound and hangs suspended from the ceiling by the same rope that was used to tie her. A brocaded silk tag hangs from a single pierced nipple—it is an *omamori*, a Shinto amulet of brocaded silk more often hung by Japanese women from a handbag or iPhone. She is fabulously tattooed, wears an expressionless Ko mask, and slowly twists with passing shifts in the air current, like a living Calder mobile.

The guests themselves are entertainment: one woman sits astride a man, slurping oysters from the half-shell and then feeding them to her companion with her tongue. Further down two women sit straight-backed on a sofa, deep in conversation. Behind the first a man stands, bending down and nuzzling her neck, while behind the second another man, perhaps prevented from nuzzling by his full-face mask, has slipped a hand beneath her backless gown. None of this interrupts the women's conversation—they are discussing the appalling behavior of a mutual acquaintance, evidently one of the lesser European princesses. The first woman sometimes flicks a hand by her ear, distractedly, as if shooing away a vaguely perceived fly and not interrupting the conversation, but this does nothing to discourage the nuzzling.

Moving between them are attendants with trays of champagne or hors d'oeuvres, bare-breasted like the one downstairs, but Sabrina notices something that she had missed before: the back of her underwear is printed with a phrase in French: *lèche-moi*—lick me. She leans on the railing a moment to observe others in passing, and finds that their bottoms have been inscribed with a variety of expressions, all equally emphatic: *touche-moi*—touch me; *attache-moi*—tie me up; plus a *mange-moi*, an *aime-moi*, and a *fesse-moi*—the familiar form no doubt appropriate for a request to be spanked, she thinks, even when not having been invited to use the *tutoiement*.

Sabrina nears the completion of her circumnavigation. She comes to an extraordinarily striking woman, maskless, about her own age, arrayed on a red velvet sofa. She is dressed in a body-hugging black evening gown with a deep *V*-cut, and elbow-length satin gloves. Her hair is long and wavy, so glossily black as to have a dark blue luster, framing a face of quiet beauty and serene calm. Her skin is extremely pale, contrasting startlingly with her hair and clothing. The only points of color are her lipstick and the soles of her high-heels, both a matching bright vermillion. She looks, Sabrina thinks, like the antimatter partner of a Raphael Madonna.

She has a snake draped around her neck, a large one whose multicolored scales form a complex geometric pattern, and the snake is alive.

There is a deck of Tarot cards laid out on the low table in front of her, but as Sabrina passes the woman lifts her head from their contemplation and catches Sabrina's eye.

"Would you like to know your destiny?" she asks.

Not a guest but a performer, Sabrina realizes, a fortune-teller.

"To be perfectly honest, no, I would not."

"Very wise. But your past, that I can see you would like to know."

"How could I not already know it?"

"You are an orphan, I assume." The woman smiles at Sabrina's expression of surprise and pats the space beside her. "Why don't you take a seat by me?"

Sabrina accepts the invitation and sits on the sofa.

"Have you been briefed on all the guests," she asks, "or just me?"

"It is you yourself who does the briefing—your speech, your expression, even your posture."

"And from that you can tell that I am an orphan?"

"Yes. I watched you circle the room just now: while you observed, you *were* observed—I observed you."

An attendant comes by with more champagne. Sabrina takes a fresh glass and turns to the fortune-teller.

"Very well, what is my past?"

"I'm trying to determine that now."

"Don't you need the cards?"

"They help to perceive only what is to come."

The fortune-teller takes Sabrina's hand in hers and then closes her eyes, as if to concentrate. This continues for about a minute, the only movement a faint furrowing of the woman's brow, before she again opens her eyes. She stares at Sabrina, saying nothing. Sabrina supposes that this is a dramatic pause before the revelation of her origins, no doubt so generalized as to be effectively meaningless.

"Well?"

"Nothing."

"Nothing?"

"Nothing at all."

"Honesty is an admirable quality, but perhaps something of a drawback in your profession."

"My profession?"

"Fortune-teller." But this just makes the other woman laugh, something that sufficiently disturbs the snake for it to leave her neck and curl into her lap.

"I'm an oracle," she says. "Specifically, a Pythian oracle."

The presence of the snake is now explained.

"I'm not sure of the difference," Sabrina admits.

"A fortune-teller is—assuming not an outright charlatan—someone who claims to be able to foresee events."

"Isn't that what an oracle does, too?"

"No. The function of an oracle is to guide certain people toward the fulfillment of their destiny. I am not allowed to make things up, and nor do I claim any special knowledge of future events, other than what is already implicit in their destiny."

"Implicit in their destiny?"

"Like the ides of March: prescient, of course, but it didn't take a genius auspex to work out that Caesar's life was in danger."

"So what is my destiny?"

"I thought you didn't want to know."

"I've changed my mind."

The oracle hesitates for a moment, as if deciding whether or not to refuse. Eventually she gathers the deck in front of her into a pack, but instead of dealing the cards puts them aside. She reaches into a bag and takes from it a box containing another deck, older than the first, very worn, and passes them to Sabrina.

"This deck contains only the major arcana and royal minor arcana. Choose some cards without looking at what they are. The number of cards is entirely up to you: it can be just one, or it can be the entire deck. When you've chosen, place them on the table, face down. Shuffle them around as you would mahjong tiles, making sure they are well mixed. It is important that at the end every card overlap another, even if only a little, but do not gather them all together again neatly, just leave them as they are when you're done."

Sabrina selects nine cards from the deck and follows the instructions. When she has finished, the oracle spends a long time looking at their backs, perhaps to determine the order, before carefully separating them, still face down. She forms three rows: four cards top and bottom, and just a single card in the middle row. Six of the cards are oriented vertically as normal, but three are on their sides.

The oracle slowly turns the cards face-up in order, left-to-right and top-to-bottom, but saving the middle card for last. Their faces are finely drawn and richly painted in vibrant colors, like the illuminated manuscripts of the medieval past. Each is numbered with a Roman numeral at the top, and its name in Gothic script at the base.

The first row is The High Priestess, rendered in deep lapis lazuli robes with a gilt crescent moon at her feet; The Star, depicting a naked woman at a pool with a brilliant star above; The Queen of Staves, fabulously robed, but this card is upside down; and lastly, on its side, The Chariot, a winged figure in a chariot drawn by two sphinxes.

The bottom row is The Magician on its side, The Tower inverted, The Devil, and Death.

The final card, the one in the middle, is The Fool, also on its side.

The oracle clicks her tongue in annoyance when turning over this last card. "He renders the bottom row, which is your ultimate destiny, unreadable. All I can tell you is what is revealed on the top row, which is your path."

"What is it?"

"You will undergo a fire sermon."

"Did you say 'fire sermon'?"

"Yes."

"What's a fire sermon?"

"I don't know. Don't you?"

"No."

The oracle gazes back down at the cards before her and stares at them for a minute in hierophantic contemplation.

"Celestial fire," she says at last. "You will be immersed in a celestial fire, but it will not harm you. Instead, it will be revelatory: it will guide you to your ultimate destiny. More than that I can't say." She taps The Fool, a juggling figure standing on one foot, smiling stupidly. "This character ruins the rest."

But Sabrina can tell that she is using the fact of The Fool to conceal the meaning.

"I thought you said that you were not allowed to lie to me."

The oracle looks at her for a long moment before responding. "It is not untrue that the fallen Fool confuses things: I genuinely cannot make them out. But I can see that the disposition of the cards is extremely… unfortunate."

"Unfortunate?"

"I am sorry to say that a great tragedy awaits you."

"You mean death?"

The comment makes the woman shake her head. "No at all," she says, "I suspect that death could seem preferable in comparison. All I can tell you is that, whatever it is, it is coming soon. It is deeply malevolent, and it is coming specifically for you."

Before Sabrina can reply, a footman approaches. "Madam, the game is about to begin," he announces. "You may wish to take a position from which to observe it."

SABRINA LEANS ON the broad marble balustrade, a fresh glass of champagne in hand, and gazes down at the ballroom below. The checkerboard pattern of the floor has been arranged with pieces, turning it into a playing board: it is to be a game of chess.

The pieces are living women. The pawns are all petite, carefully matched for size and with identical bobbed haircuts or perhaps wigs in blond or brunette, and each wearing a silken sash of either black or white to further signify to which side they belong. They are barefoot and wear no clothing apart from the sashes, but are armed with what might be pikes or halberds, the weapons standing higher than themselves.

Those in the back row are all taller than the pawns, becoming taller the closer they are to the center, as in a real chess set. The rooks are arrayed in ersatz biker outfits—heavy boots, peaked caps, leather corsets—and they carry chrome-link chains as their weapons. The knights wear a variation on riding pinks, conventionally attired at the extremities—top hats and hunting boots—but without breeches, and shirtless beneath their jackets; for them, the weapon is a riding crop. The bishops are distinguished by miters, embroidered cloaks of translucent material secured at the collar, and are equipped with shepherd's crooks. The kings are crowned and robed, holding scepters as their symbols of office, but otherwise unarmed. The queens are configured as elaborate creatures, as much witches as royalty, and carry wands as their weapons—they might have been modeled on the Queen of Staves.

At each end is a throne on a dais, raised to give a good view over the playing area. A large board representing the game hangs from the mezzanine across from Sabrina, and below it stands a footman with a long pole to move the symbols. An usher comes to the center of the chessboard and announces the contestants.

"M'Lords and Ladies, playing White, Asclepius of Delphi."

A man enters and goes to the throne at the White end. He sits back and crosses his legs. Sabrina does not recognize him—he is masked—but she recognizes his shoes: not black like all the other men in evening wear, but a deep, rich oxblood: the same shoes that she had last glimpsed when strung up in Headley Grange, about to be caned.

He is escorted by a woman in classic robes, draped to reveal a single breast, and bearing a snake-entwined staff—the second live snake Sabrina has encountered tonight. She is unmasked and has a look of calm intelligence, an expression strangely reserved amid this Grand Guignol phantasmagoria.

She takes her place by the side of the throne, and the usher makes a second announcement.

"M'Lords and Ladies, playing Black, Hecate of Thrace."

A woman enters, whom Sabrina immediately recognizes: the woman in the royal blue gown who arrived just ahead of her. She is attended by her companion of earlier, who now trails an animal on a leash. It is the size of a terrier, solidly built and quite fierce-looking, a wolverine perhaps, and Sabrina can tell from its sudden alert movement that it has become aware of the snake. Hecate seats herself on the throne at the other end, briefly surveys the board, then raises an imperious hand. A footman scurries forward with a glass of something too dark to be champagne. She accepts it without looking at the man, used to being waited on.

The game gets underway with Asclepius signaling over the usher and quietly giving him instructions. The usher announces the move, 'Pawn to Queen's Bishop Four," and the pawn in front of the White Queen's bishop moves two spaces forward. Hecate of Thrace immediately summons the usher and counters with pawn to King Three, so that viewed from above the game has already assumed a clockwise momentum after just one move, with each side advancing on its left wing. The footman with the pole struggles to keep up. So it continues until the first capture, in the eighth move, performed by the same White pawn that had opened the game. On announcement of the move the object of the attack, a Black pawn, leaves the board. The White piece occupies the vacated spot. Black immediately counterattacks, taking the offending pawn with a knight, and again the piece leaves the board.

The game proceeds briskly, and from the occasional glance of the players at a point beneath her Sabrina assumes that there is a turn-clock mounted somewhere underneath, out of sight from where she stands.

As pieces are eliminated from the board they reappear on the mezzanine, mingling with guests and wistfully gazing out over the game from which they have been eliminated, like a group of wandering Banquo's ghosts.

Their opening lines established, and a few pieces having been exchanged, White's queen suddenly comes marauding out beyond the pawn chain, a move which brings a quiet gasp of surprise among the audience, apparently having anticipated a more conservative game. Black underestimates the threat, firming up the queenside defenses with just a countermoving pawn, rather than bringing over the heavy artillery. The end game comes when Black, although numerically equal, allows her remaining knight to become pinned down, while White's bishop controls the center of the board, allowing his queen and her companions to relentlessly hunt down the Black king. Black, seeing that the situation is hopeless, concedes.

The audience applauds warmly; Sabrina, too, found the contest genuinely engaging. Hecate of Thrace stands and bows in defeat to Asclepius, who acknowledges her good grace with a salute. The pair leave their thrones, the remainder of the ballroom empties, and the chandelier dims to a soft diffused light.

Sabrina takes a fresh glass of champagne and for the first time in an hour the board no longer holds her attention. Various performances resume. A midget ringmaster sets up a mini-circus, with two extraordinarily tall and slender women taking the role of performing animals, perfectly naked apart from high heels and headgear, doing tricks like standing on their hind legs and pawing at the air while the ringmaster cracks his little whip.

A White pawn stands near Sabrina, and another walks past, similar enough to be a twin. Soon a third comes by, this one Black, but apart from the different hair color—presumably a wig—she is a dead ringer for the first two. Sabrina begins a second circumnavigation of the mezzanine, this time paying close attention to the chess pieces scattered among the guests.

She returns to the spot from which she began, her glass now empty. The pieces are not absolutely identical: one Black knight had a small scar on her left cheek that was not shared by the other knights, and of the dozen or so pawns she came upon, just one had a mole on her right breast. But these differences are acquired differences, due to accident or circumstance, and the fact of these random additions seems only to make the underlying reality more vivid: all the pieces of a particular type are not just alike but identical, genetically identical. Twins or quadruplets, it could be argued, in the case of the superior pieces—something vaguely credible—but sixteen duplicate pawns are beyond the bounds of the possible. The identical pieces are not the result of a bizarre set of multiple births, Sabrina realizes. They can only be the result of human cloning.

One of the clones approaches her, the Black knight with the scar, naked now but for top hat, boots, and riding crop. The top hat is veiled: a gesture of modesty that serves to highlight the lack of it elsewhere. She comes to a halt in front of Sabrina and gently takes her hand.

"Please come with me."

Sabrina allows herself to be led by the Black knight along the mezzanine and then into a salon. At one end a man and two women are sitting together on a velvet sofa, engaged in conversation, but Sabrina's companion leads her to the other end, which has been configured as a photographic studio: a large-format professional camera sits atop an adjustable tripod, and a twelve-foot-wide roll of paper is mounted on the wall, with a fresh section rolled out as a backdrop. The paper is softly mottled, something frequent in fashion photography, but Sabrina assumes it is not an accident that the coloring is a mixture of those same Rothko reds and grays with which she has become so familiar.

Sabrina submits to being photographed, her only prop the champagne glass. She is vaguely aware that there must have been more in the glass than just the wine—she can feel the effect of whatever it is flowing through her; maybe this is pounds-shillings-and-pence champagne.

Soon, at the knight's suggestion, she discards the Temperley, but retains her mask and high heels.

The shoot continues. The conversation at the other end of the room has ceased.

Another woman joins Sabrina, the rocking horse rider from earlier. In addition to boots and spurs, she is now equipped with a shining brass syringe. She sits should-to-shoulder with Sabrina, places Sabrina's left arm between her breasts, and presses down tightly to produce a vein at the elbow. She holds the hypodermic inverted and pushes upon the plunger until a little stream of liquid spurts out.

"What is it?" Sabrina asks.

"Cream," is the reply.

Rocking Horse Woman injects her. The Black knight continues to snap away without pause.

When the syringe is removed a little bubble of blood emerges. Rocking Horse Woman puts her lips to Sabrina's ear and whispers, "Fresh out of Band-Aids." She then leans down and licks the blood away.

Sabrina's memory is less clear from then on, but she knows that together they had continued the shoot. At one point someone else took over the photography, and the Black knight joined them. She remembers thinking that the champagne was very good. She remembers the oxblood shoes appearing at some point. She also remembers thinking *What a long way I have come since receiving that letter with its foreign stamp and red wax seal.*

# Eighth Circle

Clio

SABRINA SITS ON A PARK BENCH by the garden rail in Berkeley Square, inspecting the building across the street. The large windows are uncurtained, and she recognizes the sweeping marble staircase on the other side, confirming her guess: this was the site of last night's *Soirée de Jeux*.

Sabrina had been exhausted when leaving the previous evening—more likely early morning, but she had lost all sense of time, even of existing in time. The square had been ill-lit. On the short journey from the front portico to the waiting Rolls-Royce—this one modern and lacking the dignified charm of Crowley's fifty-year-old Phantom V—she had a vague impression of a square with a gated garden in the middle. But London is full of such squares, and she would have had little chance of identifying this particular one had it not been that, soon after leaving, she saw through the car's darkened windows a shop with a brightly lit sign that she recognized: Temperley.

Temperley has only one boutique in London, she discovered, indeed in all the world, the same one that she had visited Friday, located on Bruton Street in Mayfair, less than a hundred yards from Berkeley Square.

After arriving in the square this Sunday morning, Sabrina quickly located the elegant Georgian building that she suspected was the site of last night's extravagant debauch. The map identifies it as Cavendish House.

She looks up Cavendish House: it is a Palladian mansion built in 1793 by William Taylor Cavendish after he returned from the Americas, having made a fortune from what was variously reported to be sugar or tobacco or slaves, and was designed by the renowned Scottish architect Robert Adam, who died the year before it was finished and so never saw the completed house.

A feature of the mansion, not part of the original plan, is a distinctive Jasperware frieze, commissioned from Josiah Wedgwood by Cavendish, and depicting a Parthenon-like procession in which the figures are philosophers and scientists from antiquity through to the then-current age, escorted by naked nymphs and naiads in what at the time was considered scandalously public nudity, and ending at what is nominally a ceremony before the Altar of Enlightenment, but which the wits of town labeled *The Great Blue and White Orgy*.

The scandal was not limited to the frieze: the place acquired a reputation for being a favorite rendezvous of the fast set of the age: frequent visitors included Mary Wollstonecraft—radical free-thinker, author of *A Vindication of the Rights of Women*, and mother of Mary Shelley—and Samuel Taylor Coleridge, already brilliant and already insane. Jeremy Bentham condemned Cavendish House as 'a fiendish lair fit only for the dissolute of spirit, a den of the depraved, a haunt for those on their way to the necropolis via the paths of heedless and wanton dissipation.' He recommended that for the moral health of the nation it be razed 'rather than permit this monument to turpitude to persist.'

Cavendish House had certainly lived up to its reputation last night, Sabrina thinks.

Ownership is now under an unnamed private equity group, and the building's use is listed uninformatively as 'private.'

In the thirty minutes that she sits observing the house, no one enters or leaves by the front door, but for all she knows there is a service entrance around the back, out of sight from where she now sits, where the caterers and florists are coming and going, cleaning up from the previous evening.

Sabrina returns her gaze to the frieze, and finds that her time at the National Portrait Gallery was not wasted: she recognizes some of the figures: Isaac Newton, long-faced and very serious, and who probably would have been identifiable by the place of honor accorded him, still supreme more than a century after publication of the *Principia Mathematica*; Francis Bacon, pointy-bearded and proudly bearing the insignia of his government office, Keeper of the Great Seal; and the distinctively prognathic Flamsteed, holding a telescope to help further identify him has the famous Astronomer Royal.

There are many supporting maidens, mostly unclad—she can see how this pagan paean to philosophy might have aroused comment.

She removes the band-aid from the crook of her left arm, revealing the puncture mark and bruising resulting from her visit to Dr. Aran's office, where a nurse had taken her blood, not very skillfully. Next to it is the second puncture mark, fresher than the first, that she had discovered after waking this morning, and which had caused her a few moments of anxious confusion before remembering how it got there. No bruising around this one: Rocking Horse Woman was a skilled practitioner with a hypodermic syringe.

There is a third puncture mark, this one not in a vein but in her right shoulder, vaguely throbbing. She has no recollection of receiving that one at all.

TEMPLE SLAUGHTER PRECEPTORY has nothing so mundane as a swimming pool, but there is a water garden, a little collection of fountains and ponds surrounding a small willow-fringed lake. The garden is walled, and on a bright and cloudless Saturday in which the temperature is forecast to hit the thirties—about ninety degrees Fahrenheit; unnatural in England—it is declared off-limits to estate staff, allowing the girls to frolic and sunbathe *au naturel*, not that the presence of any males would have inhibited them, Sabrina thinks, for they are a generally blithe and carefree bunch.

She removes her own bathing suit, too, not wishing to be perceived as prudish, and works on acquiring a tan-line-free bronzing in preparation for the upcoming voyage to the South Seas.

Sabrina feels healthier in the sun. The week-old bruising on her arm has almost faded, although both puncture marks are still faintly visible. The third, in her shoulder, has disappeared completely. The results of the blood test were negative: there was nothing abnormal, and Wilkins's colleague had obviously gotten her analysis wrong.

She spends the afternoon reading and dozing, interrupted by an occasional cooling dip in the water, which with all the naked women in it resembles the *Hylas and the Nymphs* that Mortimer Pence had so admired.

SABRINA HAS NOT SEEN BRONARYRE since before the *soirée*, but as she walks down the long parade heading from the water garden back to the house, she sees that the E-Type has reappeared in its usual parking spot.

She stops at the library on the way upstairs. Among the oversized art books she finds two volumes that were not there before: one she half-expected, the other is an astonishing discovery.

The one she half-expected is titled *Cavendish House Dishabille*, bound in green Morocco and this time with no pretense of aging—the cover is completely unmarked and still smells of freshly applied neatsfoot oil. At least she is not the only subject in the volume, although she is indeed extremely dishabille. As photography it is first-rate, dramatically saturated coloration and with deep *chiaroscuro* shadowing, vivid pictures of vivid scenes, a volume that gives the viewer a sense of having stumbled into an aristocratic, expensive, and deeply debauched bacchanal—a privileged world without limit or bound, profoundly voluptuous and completely unbridled.

Bronaryre's world, she realizes—the world of actions without consequences, of unfettered indulgence, something only conceivable with an imaginative mind and an unconstrained bank account.

For most of the photographs she is either facing the camera or side-on, but in one she has her back to the lens, with her head twisted over her shoulder, gazing back at the photographer. She is standing perched on platform stilettos, exaggeratedly long-legged, astride her companion who sits entwined about her shins. The skin of Sabrina's back is rendered in a metallic copper glow, shadowed to show the musculature, and with every vertebra discernable.

Also discernable is a mark on her right shoulder blade, and since she is looking over her right shoulder it forms a natural focus of the shot. It appears at exactly the place that she imagined she was branded in her LSD-fueled dragon-fired delirium. The mark falls in the shadow of her shoulder blade and so it is hard to make out the pattern clearly, but it could be a unicursal hexagram.

The second volume she has seen before, and destroyed: *The Wonders of the Windrush*. It is the same book that she had tossed into the fire in her room, the very same copy: she recognizes the mottling on the front cover, among other things. She had watched it burn, yet here it undeniably is, miraculously arisen.

She does not bother taking them upstairs to burn this time, given the phoenix-like reappearance of the *Wonders*, and anyway in *Cavendish House Dishabille* the one article of clothing that she never lost was her mask.

When she returns to her room she finds that an envelope has been pushed under the door. The marbling this time is white and black, recalling the chess game. The note inside suggests the hedge maze as the location for evening cocktails.

There is a dress laid out on the bed, simple white linen with blue piping, and for once Sabrina agrees with Polly's selection. She goes to the desk and, having had a week to recover her objectivity, makes the first entry since the *soirée*.

> *Bronaryre has cloned human beings for use as playing pieces—as evil goes, that's not too bad: a nice combination of frivolous indifference to ethical standards and simple self-absorbed depravity. Announcing his achievement to the world by serving them up unclad for a chess game demonstrated a real showman's touch, I think—just the right amount of swaggering audacity.*

*The* soirée *was like the after-party following a runway show: one needs to flaunt the right people, and the crowd at Cavendish House had hit the mark: dissipation incarnate. A bravura performance; his best masque yet. How will he top this?*

*I looked up Asclepius: he is the Greek god of health and healing. He was the son of Apollo and born in the Temple of Apollo, that same temple of which the Pythian Oracle was the high priestess. The staff with entwined snake—a python, of course—was indeed his symbol and, augmented with the wings of Hermes, remains the emblem of the medical profession today.*

*Two deities from the Temple of Apollo at the same party: clearly, I am meant to 'know myself.' Actually, I have no understanding at all, and very little memory of the evening once that photo session began.*

*Hecate of Thrace is a witch-goddess. The animal with her was a polecat, Hecate's traditional companion—not a true cat but a carnivorous mammal related to badgers and otters.*

*How reckless I have become! I am a slave to an addiction, but not to laudanum or LSD or whatever it was the woman injected me with that night (warm blissful repose; one becomes like a living artwork, a Bonnard or Matisse). I am addicted to the masques themselves: I do not want them to stop.*

*I rechecked the Liberty-print dress. The thread securing the two waist buttons appears to be slightly different than the others, not quite the same shade, and hand-stitched. Is it part of a trick, designed to make me believe that a dream that had been somehow induced was real? Or am I becoming paranoid, imagining conspiracies that do not exist? Maybe, in a delirium, I resewed those buttons myself, wishing the dreams to be real—why did I think to recheck the buttons in the first place? It is possible, although I have no sense of it, that I am going mad.*

*I will cast aside self-doubt for now, and focus on the main threat: Bronaryre. He will expect a reaction to Cavendish House: outrage, resentment, condemnation, etc.—I will not give him that satisfaction. Instead, I will pin him to the lie with my passenger manifest from the evacuation of Tangier.*

## Unburying the Dead

IT TAKES SABRINA twenty minutes of dead ends and double backs to complete the hedge maze, the center of which turns out to be a small circle of lush lawn surrounded by a gravel border. In the middle is a statue, life-sized, but in contrast to the Olympian marbles of the Long Garden this figure is emphatically ungodlike: it is of a rotund, middle-aged man, wrapped in heavy robes to preserve his dignity or perhaps just as protection against the English damp.

By the statue are a garden table and chairs. On top of the table is the usual tray with cocktail gear, plus a small wooden case, open, with a pair of polished instruments inside, like a barometer and thermometer set. Bronaryre is standing over the open case, concentrating intently, apparently taking measurements. He is not aware of Sabrina's arrival, and so she remains silent, allowing him to complete his readings undisturbed, but then he is the first to speak.

"You solved the maze," he says, without lifting his gaze from the instruments.

"More easily than some other puzzles I have been set lately. Did you choose it as a metaphor?"

"I chose it because of the company. Our stone friend here plays a role in tonight's story."

He records a reading in a small notebook and then notes the time on his wristwatch.

"What are those instruments?'

"Ship's chronometers, which is to say they are robust and highly accurate clocks, intended for marine use. It was instruments such as these that first fulfilled the sixteenth of Boyle's twenty-four wishes: *The practicable and certain way of finding longitudes.* Mechanical chronometers like these are no longer made—one gets longitude from a satellite now. This pair was manufactured in 1873, by the firm of Frodsham."

She comes beside him and looks down at the two chronometers. Their faces were probably originally white but have aged into ivory, and bear the maker's name in elegant black lettering: CHA$^{S}$ FRODSHAM N$^{o}$ 84 STRAND. There are two anchor-and-crown shields, the first reading BY APPOINTMENT TO THE QUEEN—presumably Victoria—and the second reading GOLD MEDAL OF HONOUR PARIS EX$^{N}$ 1855. The outer dial measures hours and minutes. There is a separate inner dial for seconds, and above that a third dial whose purpose eludes her.

"What's this one for?"

"A rewind indicator. Fully wound, the chronometer will run for fifty-six hours, but you can see that here it recommends rewinding with twenty-four to run." He points to where the word *WIND* is printed in minute capitals; she had thought it was wind with a short *i*, and wondered what the breeze could have to do with horological measurement. "They must never be allowed to run down at sea, since there is nothing to reset them by, hence the existence of the indicator."

The chronometers are fixed in frames of concentric metal rings, set to pivot at different angles.

"Why are they mounted on these rings?"

"They're called gimbals. They are intended to allow the instrument to remain steady in a heaving ship."

"Why two chronometers?"

"Redundancy: if one fails you always have the other."

"Are you repairing them?"

"No, just measuring. No mechanical chronometer can keep perfect time, but the error rate can be measured, and that's what I'm recording." He consults his notes. "The one on the left gains a second every six days. The one on the right loses a second every ten days."

He puts away the notebook and begins mixing cocktails.

"I've come across some interesting instances of identical things recently," Sabrina says. "Not just inanimate objects, like these chronometers, but people, too."

She does not expect a direct response, but Bronaryre surprises her.

"Unremarkable, really. Since Dolly, it was just a matter of time."

"Dolly?"

"A sheep that was cloned, back in 1996. Just a small step from there to humans."

"But surely illegal?"

"Highly illegal, I expect." He hands her a glass—gin and tonic as usual, welcome on a warm day like this. "But there are higher laws than those of men."

"Those of God?"

"I hope you are not going to expect me to share in that superstition."

"A strange sentiment to come from the Devil."

"The difference is that I am real, as you can plainly see. The other is a myth, something to comfort the simple of mind and faint of heart. The higher law I speak of is the Law of Inevitability."

"What's the Law of Inevitability?"

"If something can be, then it inevitably will be. This is a universal truth, from the terrible—after the secrets of the atom were revealed, the hydrogen bomb was inevitable—to the trivial—after Pablo Picasso, Jeff Koons passing off a vacuum cleaner as a piece of art was inevitable. One might call it a *double entendre* pun on the vacuity of post-Modernism, but Koons doesn't think that deeply."

"If cloning is unremarkable, then why the big performance at Cavendish House?"

"Did you not enjoy the evening?"

"It was certainly engaging. As for enjoyable: I have to say that the part I most *enjoyed* was the chess game. But I still don't see why such a big performance was necessary."

"Preparation."

"Preparation for what?"

"Preparation for tonight, for a start."

"What's happening tonight?"

"Tonight you will see something that really is remarkable."

Bronaryre gestures for Sabrina to take a seat, then sits himself and puts his glass on the table. "As I told you, I returned to England in 1683."

"What was your name then?"

"Aubrey Greystoke."

"When did you take up the new identity?"

"Right away, after having received the Templar fortune."

"And you were Jack Kincaid until then?"

"Yes, I was." *There*, Sabrina thinks, *I have caught you out*, but then Bronaryre adds, "Except for the voyage back to England, of course."

"What do you mean?"

"You must remember that Jack Kincaid was an English spy, not to mention a one-time pirate. If we had been taken prize by the Spanish I would no doubt have been hanged as one or the other—perhaps twice, knowing the vengeful Spanish—and so Pepys arranged to have me listed on the ship's manifest under a false identity."

"As whom?"

"Thomas Wainwright, merchant of Bristol."

Sabrina hopes that her face does not reveal her shock—she recalls transcribing the exact words *Thos. Wainwright, merch. of Bristol* from Pepys's records.

She did not take her phone with her to Cambridge, paid for the train fare in cash, and since she was staying at the Savoy there was no college porter to witness her departure: he cannot have known that she had checked the original records—but then she recalls his familiarity with the hotel's doorman. Bronaryre takes up his account.

"That return to England marked the end of my becoming, of the first forty years of my life: the point at which a man arrives at his full maturity—his apogee, if you will. Ordinarily, the rest is downhill. For me, it was *status quo*. I had studied much, and in my travels I had experienced more than most men would in a dozen lifetimes: in short, I was fit for purpose. And now, with the Templar fortune, I was also extremely wealthy—I had not only the necessary knowledge to excite men's minds with more desire to know, I also had the means.

"Several things happened in rapid succession. In Europe, the Sun King was casting the continent in shadow, his boundless ambition metastasizing into war, seemingly continuous and everywhere. In 1685, Louis further inflamed the situation by revoking the Edict of Nantes: intolerance was given royal sanction by the most powerful man alive. In that same year Charles II died, and James became king—England once again had a Catholic monarch, one who intended to impose his religion by decree, and political chaos reigned. But in 1687 *Principia Mathematica* was published: chaos might have reigned on earth, but order had been brought to the heavens; then late in the following year James was deposed in that bloodless coup known to history as the Glorious Revolution. William and Mary came to the throne, and it was understood that from then on, in England at least, thought would be left free.

"I will compress the following century into just a minute or two. I pursued my purposes steadily, and used my fortune and judgment to lubricate the paths of illumination. I found it prudent to keep a low profile, but complete withdrawal from society was impossible—I had to keep up with the affairs of men to effectively achieve my objectives, and so I fell in with the leading lights of the age.

"In England in the first quarter of the Eighteenth Century, that meant the circle of Bolingbroke, and I was on familiar terms with his friend, Harley, and his enemy, Walpole. I knew both Alexander Pope and Jonathan Swift well—one of them a hunchbacked midget who happened to be a glorious poet, the other a gloomy Anglican clergyman who happened to be an unapologetic atheist. They were the strangest pair imaginable, and yet two of the most clear-thinking men in that Augustan age known for clear-thinking men. Misanthropes, both of them, but writers of the highest order—the two qualities often seem to go together.

"In 1726, a new member joined our circle. He was a Frenchman who had been a political prisoner in the Bastille. He had escaped and subsequently gone into exile in England. His name was François-Marie Arouet—although all the world knows him by the sobriquet he adopted: Voltaire.

"I was already due for a change in identity, and my two-year acquaintance with Voltaire convinced me to leave England and return to Paris. So it was that I had a front-row seat for the greatest of all events in Western history, greater even than the Industrial Revolution: that giant intellectual leap which germinated in England but came to full flower in France, what we now call the Enlightenment.

"I moved freely between Paris and London. In the latter, I became a member of the Hellfire Club, founded in part by John Montagu, the Fourth Earl of Sandwich, great-great-grandson of that same Edward Montagu who had been patron to Pepys and spymaster to me. It was nominally a secret society, but a secret poorly kept, and the members had a reputation for licentiousness and debauchery, not totally unearned: the club's motto was *Fais ce que tu voudrais*—Do what thou wilt. But its aims were primarily sociopolitical: firmly in the Whig camp, disdaining church and crown, and above all championing freedom of thought and action. The Prince of Wales was a member, to the mortification of the King and the Tories.

"In Paris, I moved in the circle of the *philosophes*, in particular the *Encyclopédistes*: Diderot and d'Alembert, d'Holbach and Turgot. I need not give you a history lesson: freedom of intellect burst forth in the hothouse that was the Paris of the time but, by the Law of Inevitability, so too did the freedom to be stupid. With the storming of the Bastille in 1789, it seemed that reason was to be victorious. By the September Massacres in 1792, it was clear that stupidity would carry the day. The democratically conceived Assembly was replaced by a frankly totalitarian Convention. Louis XVI was executed in January 1793: I witnessed the beheading of a second king, one-hundred and forty-four years after the first. Robespierre became dictator in all but name. France fell into chaos, and the Reign of Terror became inevitable. In short, my work was a failure—I abandoned France and returned to England. Chaos invites its antithesis, and the French got it in spades with Napoleon, but by then I was long gone."

"Returning to England as William Taylor Cavendish, supposedly coming back from somewhere in the Americas, having made a fortune?"

"Yes, it was a convenient time for another change in identity."

"I like the house you built on Berkeley Square."

"Robert Adam was the architect—a gifted man; he was the Wren of his time."

"But the frieze was your idea?"

"Indeed, it was. I have made it a habit to declare my purposes openly, twice by way of a frieze, and Josiah Wedgwood's brilliant new Jasperware was the perfect medium in which to do it the second time. I aimed to depict a ceremony celebrating not capricious gods that must be appeased, but eager men thirsty for knowledge. It was what had been happening in Paris, before the Revolution ran out of control, and I wanted to convey that sense to London."

"I can report firsthand that the Bacchanalian spirit lives on in Cavendish House."

"At this point I should tell you that in my time in Paris the most profound of the Enlightenment figures that I met was not a Frenchman, nor even English. He was an American; in fact he was America's minister to France, the man who arranged the critical alliance with which the English were defeated and the United States came into being."

"Who?"

He nods toward the statue. "Him."

Sabrina is about to look for an identifying plaque when she realizes that she recognizes the figure: it is a statue of Benjamin Franklin.

"Would you like to meet him?" Bronaryre asks.

"I think I already did, very briefly, on the threshold of your apartment in New York."

"Indeed, and a second time, although you were not aware of it." Sabrina shifts her gaze from the statue to Bronaryre, inviting him to explain. "I told you of my return from Tangier, in the company of Pepys," he says, "and how on arrival I was taken into an underground vault where the treasure of the Templars lay hidden."

"Yes."

"You never asked me where that underground vault was."

"You said you were taken there in a carriage with the windows curtained, and a hood was placed over your head before you got out."

"I did not know where it was at the time I was taken there, but remember how it ended: the treasure was given unto my care, and I emerged unmolested from the vault—of course, I made sure to understand its location."

"Where was it?"

In response, he stamps a foot upon the ground. Sabrina looks down.

"You mean that it's below us?"

"It is. And how natural that the Templars should have hidden their treasure somewhere near one of their former preceptories—now abandoned—accessed via what was at the time a narrow cleft in a small rise, heavily wooded and overgrown. The first thing I did was to buy all the surrounding land, and then begin building the mansion over the preceptory ruins. A mansion needs grounds, and I made sure to fully conceal the entrance to the vault with a hedge maze: something that ensured no one could ever approach directly or, given the gravel paths, noiselessly. Plus there would never be a chance of anyone, whether by accident or some spy, catching from a distance the sudden disappearance of someone down into the vault. You see how a hedge maze is the ideal camouflage, for what is the purpose of a maze but to disorient and conceal?"

"Something you practice with and without hedges, I would say."

Bronaryre stands. "Are you ready?"

"For what, exactly?"

"For the dinner of the dead."

THE STATUE OF BENJAMIN FRANKLIN, which with its base Sabrina guesses must weigh as much as a small car, swings aside, revealing a stone stairway leading down.

"Counterweights," Bronaryre says in answer to her look of surprise at the ease with which he opened it. "Go ahead. I will close the entrance."

She begins her descent.

There are no lights, and as Sabrina twists downward away from daylight she is soon enshrouded in gloom. The stairway is helical, as in Bronaryre's tale, with the hollow core occupied by several hanging chains, large enough to support ships' anchors. These start to slowly move, in opposite directions, their deep rhythmic clanking echoing in the enclosed stone chamber of the stairwell. The end of the ascending chain passes by Sabrina on its journey, and there is a lead weight suspended by a shackle from the final link, like an oversized plumb bob, fat and pendulous: the counterbalancing avoirdupois, she realizes, moving upward as above her Bronaryre returns the statue to its position concealing the entrance. This has the effect of eliminating what little light was filtering down from above, and for a moment Sabrina has to stop, unable to see.

Her eyes gradually adjust. The darkness is not total: there is a glimmer of illumination from below, and Sabrina haltingly advances toward it. The light gradually becomes brighter, and soon she can continue without having to feel her way. From the flickering she can guess the source: flame—and for a moment Sabrina is acutely aware of the supposed identity of her companion above, and the nature of his abode below.

The stairs go deeper than she had imagined from Bronaryre's story; she loses count of the turns, loses her sense of orientation completely. Despite the approach toward fire she feels the temperature drop.

The end of the twisting stairway comes into view at last, and Sabrina pauses to allow Bronaryre time to catch up. But he does not catch up, nor does she hear from above the footsteps that would be audible if he were following her. This causes Sabrina to review their earlier conversation, and she realizes that Bronaryre never explicitly stated that he was joining her: he must have instead stayed on the surface and closed the entrance behind her—an entrance secured by a statue that would weigh a ton, and even if there was a mechanism to release it she would have little hope of finding the thing in the dark. She is effectively trapped down here; she is entombed.

Sabrina wonders what awaits her below. The dinner of the dead, Bronaryre said—if in a tomb presumably something to do with crypts or sarcophagi, perhaps those of the same Templar guardians who had given him charge of the treasure centuries earlier. There is no choice but to go forward, and she continues down the remaining steps.

Sabrina emerges into a broad underground space.

It is vaulted, similar in feel to a tube station, but here instead of glazed tiles the material is plain stone—ironstone, she can tell, from its Rothko coloration. The space is perhaps fifty feet wide and half again as long. Two rows of pillars support the vaults, and flaming torches have been fitted into sconces mounted on the walls, their illumination supplemented by large candles in wrought iron holders. There is a long refectory table situated in the center of the space, laden with food. It is made of thick rough-hewn timber, blackened with age—she can imagine that once Knights Templar sat around this table, swilling ale from pewter goblets while swapping tales of Jerusalem and Acre.

The people surrounding it now, nine in total, are not knights, although the gentlemen have stood in courtly response to Sabrina's arrival.

She recognizes the man nearest her, dressed much as when she first met him: favoring hose and breeches instead of trousers; a long black coat over a brocaded vest and linen shirt; collar secured with a broad floppy bow tie. He steps forward in hesitant welcome, and makes a small bow of greeting.

"You arrive amongst us like a glorious apparition, my dear, a spirit sent from above to enlighten the gloom of our purgatorial interment."

"It's very nice to see you again, Mr. Franklin. I recall our brief acquaintance in New York City with pleasure, but Bronaryre tells me that we have met a second time."

"Indeed, that is true: it is I who was your Charon, ferrying you through the Stygian sewers of central London."

"That was very kind of you."

"Not at all, the pleasure was all mine, and I thank you for the shiny penny, which now occupies pride of place on my little mantlepiece. Now, please allow me to make introductions."

He indicates the young black woman sitting on his left, who now stands.

"Miss Josephine Baker, of St. Louis, Missouri."

The woman steps forward, hand outstretched. Her hair is close-cropped and plastered down with a little kiss curl across her forehead.

She wears a fringed flapper's dress from the Roaring Twenties, very short, revealing her long dancer's legs to advantage. She is smiling broadly.

"I haven't been to St. Louis in ages," she says, shaking Sabrina's hand. "I live in France, now. I hope you'll come and visit me."

"I would love to," Sabrina responds, meaning it, for she takes an instant liking to Baker.

The next introduction is to a man who was seated across from Franklin, taller and gaunter, and whose dowdy tweeds and dour manner are in striking contrast to the vivacious Baker. He wears a toothbrush mustache, little round granny spectacles, and beneath them an eye-patch over his left orb. He comes forward, transferring a cigarette holder to his left hand to free up the right, which he hesitantly offers to Sabrina.

"James Joyce," he says awkwardly. "Sorry."

"I've read *Finnegans Wake* three times," she says, meaning to encourage him.

"Then I'm triply sorry," Joyce responds. His spectacles are rose-colored, Sabrina sees, in contrast to his prose. He retires back to his place without further comment.

Franklin resumes introductions. The fourth person reminds Sabrina of her students, young and full of life.

"It is traditionally considered a *faux pas* to seat writers together at a dinner party," Franklin says, "but tonight we have made an exception. May I introduce Mrs. Mary Shelley, *née* Wollstonecraft."

Mary Shelly makes a curtsey in greeting.

"One volume does not a writer make," she says, "and so very slender in comparison to Mr. Joyce's great works."

Sabrina recognizes the next dinner guest instantly: it is Miles Davis, the pre-funk version of the first great quintet days, a period when he dressed in conservative Brooks Brothers suits while shattering the bounds of music. He picks up a trumpet from the floor beside his chair and raises it in greeting.

"I hope you'll play later," Sabrina says.

"Cool, yeah, if these cats dig it," he responds, in his characteristic hoarse whisper.

Franklin continues introductions. "One may chance multiple writers at a single gathering, but never more than one philosopher: ours tonight is Ayn Rand."

"Most philosophers are just looters of other people's ideas," Rand says, "and therefore one is by definition sufficient." She is a short woman, dark-haired and retaining a trace of Russian accent from the land of her birth. Bronaryre had quoted her that evening in the *pied-à-terre*, Sabrina recalls, when they were gazing out over Manhattan: *Ayn Rand says that when the lights go out in New York City, civilization will be at an end*—at the time she had thought the use of the present tense peculiar, probably a grammatical error: now she sees that it had been both deliberate and correct.

Rand focuses her intense gaze on Sabrina. "I am told that you are Dagny Taggart made manifest. Is that so?"

"Hardly," Sabrina says. "Who could be?"

"Good answer," Rand says, nodding with approval.

The man across from Davis is dressed in military uniform. Sabrina is a little alarmed to see an Iron Cross at his collar, and swastika-carrying eagles emblazoned on his jacket.

"Rommel," he says, with a curt bow of his head and a click of his heels. "*Enchanté, madame*."

Next to him is a blond bombshell sitting back languidly in her seat, dressed in a form-fitting sequined gown, blue smoke snaking up from a cigarette in one hand, with a Martini held in the other. She has been observing the others with hooded eyes and a look of world-weary ennui.

"Of course our penultimate guest requires no introduction," Franklin says carefully, "for all the world knows the greatest of film stars."

"You're right," Sabrina says, following Franklin's lead. "Who would not instantly recognize Marlene Dietrich?"

Dietrich casts a cool glance of appraisal over Sabrina, then utters a single elongated *Daarrrling* by way of acknowledgment. Sabrina senses Franklin's relief—clearly Dietrich can be difficult, and has to be coddled. He turns toward the last person, standing at the far end of the table.

"And I believe you are already acquainted with tonight's final guest," he says.

"Indeed I am. Pleased to see you again, Mr. Crowley."

"And how enraptured I am to see you, madam. You are blooming, I find. Your complexion is like cream, and I am a lapping leo—"

"I trust all the girls are well?"

"They are. They received the musical recordings that you sent, and thank you for them." Since the Led Zeppelin book she had left for the girls would not make much sense without the music, Sabrina had ordered copies of all nine studio albums to be delivered to Boleskine House—vinyl, since the only music player she had seen there was an old phonograph in their living quarters. "The Victrola has been spinning ceaselessly ever since," Crowley continues, "and the music appears to drive them into a sort of ecstatic frenzy: they dance lasciviously, like crazed Maenads. I believe the music has a hypnotic effect, somewhat akin to the trance music of Morocco—that is, to Gnawa—as I believe William S. Burroughs has noted, but more fevered and chaotic. Near naked and writhing crazily: they look quite ready to tear Orpheus to pieces; I've taken to avoiding the mortuary."

"Mortuary?" Dietrich asks.

"Where they live, madam. They are witches."

Dietrich's eyes open fully for the first time tonight.

Sabrina looks around at the nine of them, all looking back at her, awaiting her reaction.

"I am amazed," she admits, a comment which draws smiles from her dinner companions—they must have been concerned that she would be angry, or frightened, or perhaps just call their bluffs. Franklin pulls out the chair at the head of the table for her. She sits, and the others follow suit.

"There are no scullery facilities down here," Franklin explains, "and so I'm afraid that it's just a simple cold supper tonight. I believe that we should take what we wish, and pass the dishes along."

The 'simple cold supper' turns out to be a feast. The soup is a vichyssoise, and a bowl of freshly cut chives follows its anticlockwise journey around the table. Smoked salmon with dill sauce is the primary appetizer, plus a mound of oysters and shrimp on ice, from which Franklin in particular takes freely. Mary Shelley favors the pickled herring. A cold saddle of pink-rare roast beef forms the centerpiece, with abundant horseradish cream in lieu of gravy, and accompanied by glazed, herb-encrusted roasted vegetables, plus a ham, sliced directly off the bone, served with sharp, bright-yellow mustard, and cold pork pie. There are decanters of wine and pitchers of ale, plus a jug of iced gin for Dietrich. No water: the dead are not abstemious drinkers.

Sabrina notices that Joyce, who is sitting to her right, eats with more relish than his slender frame would suggest. Joyce catches her observing him. He briefly stops eating and leans toward her conspiratorially.

"I have known poverty," he whispers, smiling ruefully, "and poverty's bosom companion is hunger." Then, with his good eye, he winks.

Rommel is more restrained: he seems to need nothing but rough pieces of bread torn from a crusty loaf and a large slice of cheese, plus an occasional pickled onion, all washed down with beer in true German fashion. The Iron Cross at his neck, Sabrina realizes, is a form of cross patty.

Dietrich dines mostly on olives from the bottom of her Martinis.

Since Joyce is so engrossed in his food Sabrina converses mostly with her companion to the left, Franklin.

"I'm surprised to see you on this side of the Atlantic," she says. "Among the enemy, so to speak."

"You may be surprised to learn that I lived a good deal of my first life in London, sixteen years in total. Before the War of Independence, I was a colonial representative at the court of St. James. I lived in Craven Street, just a stone's throw from the York Watergate and now, in my second life, I have a little townhouse in nearby Northumberland Street, so it was very convenient to ferry you about the other night."

"You are in your second life?"

"Certainly. The first ended when I died in Philadelphia, in 1790."

"So you are an actor, not Benjamin Franklin?"

"As it happens, I am both. You see, my old place in Craven Street still stands and, if you'll forgive the immodesty of my mentioning it, the house has been turned into a museum dedicated to me. So from time to time I dress up in my old duds and drop by to tell a few stories, or give a little talk, especially when there are school visits—I suppose that does indeed make me an actor. Besides, I like visiting the old place: they've kept it much as it was when I lived there."

"When *you* lived there?"

"My dear, I don't blame you for being skeptical—a healthy skepticism is the first requirement of a sound mind. But as to whether or not I am really Benjamin Franklin, I can assure you that I am."

"How can that be, if you died in 1790?"

"It is entirely due to the museum on Craven Street."

"The museum preserved you?"

"In a manner of speaking, yes. You see, when in my first life I left London for the last time, it was something of a furtive departure. It was March of 1775, and revolt was in the air—indeed, when I landed back in America the battles of Lexington and Concord had already taken place: the great struggle had begun. While I was still here in London I had been arguing the cause of the colonies to anyone who would listen, even before the Privy Council, but this had made me many enemies, including the Solicitor General, the highest magistrate in the realm. It seemed that I was about to be arrested, and so my departure was necessarily rushed."

"What has this to do with Craven Street?"

"In my haste, I left my second-best blue coat behind. That coat was packed away, along with some of my other belongings, by my housekeeper's daughter for the day when I would return. I never did, and these items subsequently passed down through her family. When the museum opened, her descendants donated my old things to it."

"What was so special about your second-best blue coat?"

"I'm embarrassed to say, but there was dander on the collar—mine."

Sabrina suddenly makes the connection. "Your DNA?"

"Precisely, my dear. I have been resurrected."

Joyce pauses from his rush to ingest food. "I think that's not quite true, Franklin. To be sure, we've been reborn, but we have no original memory of our first lives." He puts down his fork and addresses Sabrina directly. "I was reborn of a dried drop of blood found on a sheet of paper from the first draft of *The Dubliners*. I am told that I am me, and certainly I look the part, even feel the part, but I have no memory of actually writing *The Dubliners*, or of anything else in my so-called first life. Naturally, I have thoroughly researched that first life, and I suppose I have internalized the details, made them if not actual memories, then near-memories—we all do, having no true first-hand experience of ourselves. But to say that we have been resurrected goes too far, I think. We have not been resurrected; we have been reincarnated."

"I bow, sir, to your superior subtlety in the English language," Franklin concedes amiably. "Reincarnated it is."

"But how did your second lives begin?" Sabrina asks them. "How did you grow up?"

"For my part, I have no recollection," Joyce says. "I just came into consciousness of myself, much as you see me before you now. I had language, including my Irish accent. I also spoke French and Italian, as I did in my first life. I even knew my name, and was aware that I was the author of *Ulysses*. But I didn't remember writing it; had no memory of Nora, either."

"Nora."

"Nora Barnacle, my wife."

"I speak English," Rommel says from down the table. "In my first life I did not, although I had always wanted to, so that I could read that stuff Guderian was always on about: the Englishman Liddell Hart's treatises on armored warfare—most of them were never translated."

"Guderian?"

"A fellow field marshal, in my first life. He and I conquered France together."

"If he was from your first life, how could you have known he was always on about it?"

"I assume that I must have been told, same as Joyce was told about *Ulysses*."

"I think it's true of all of us," Mary Shelley says. "I knew I had been married to Shelley, even knew of that dreadful night with Byron on the shores of Lake Geneva, but I had no actual memory of either. Ironic, is it not, that I should have ended up in the same situation as my own fictional creation?"

"I could play the trumpet," Miles Davis says. "I even had the nip."

"The nip?'

He points to the top of his upper lip. "A small callus, right here, that trumpeters get. So, whatever those cats were doing before they reset my memory, they taught me to play the horn—real tight, too. That's not something comes from just genes, man; that requires practice."

"Were you all together?"

"No, we were not," Dietrich says, her first significant utterance of the evening. "I came to consciousness in a suite at the Adlon, just like the good old days."

"The Adlon?"

"A hotel, in Berlin. *The* hotel, darling, even before the war. I've lived there ever since: fully staffed, fully paid for—I must say that I've rather taken to the role of being Bronaryre's kept woman."

"Do you know who Bronaryre purports to be?"

"Darling, the Devil and I were always well acquainted."

"And I have much the same arrangement," Ayn Rand says, "but in Los Angeles: I have a house in the Hollywood Hills, and staff who take care of everything—although in my case, given my views on individual responsibility, I am less comfortable with these arrangements than is *Fräulein* Dietrich."

"How long ago did this happen?"

"Just a few months ago."

Sabrina looks around the table inquiringly, and receives nods of agreement: all nine of them apparently came into existence, or at least their conscious existence, only recently.

"December," Rommel says. "Twelfth of December. I began a campaign log immediately, out of old habit."

"I was December, too," Baker says. "Even the south of France is cold in winter, and one of my first impressions was wishing that it was spring instead."

"The winter for me as well," Joyce says. "It snowed."

"When did you first meet each other?"

"Early spring, at a dinner party in Bronaryre's New York apartment."

"The night on which I encountered you on his doorstep," Franklin adds. "We had all become acquainted with him individually beforehand, but that was the first and only time we met each other, until tonight."

Sabrina realizes that this must have been why Bronaryre seemed so distracted the night she first met him—he had bigger things on his mind: the first gathering of his resurrections.

"Do you know why you? I mean, how it was that you were chosen?"

"I have given this matter much consideration," Franklin says, "but I think that courteous reserve would prevent my colleagues from responding. Some of the choices I think are too obvious to require any explanation: if you were going to start reincarnating people, you would naturally wish to begin with those at the top of their fields, and thus Mr. Davis, Mr. Joyce, and *Fräulein* Dietrich are to my sense self-evident. The Devil is a clear-eyed creature, and so Miss Rand's forthright Objectivist philosophy would naturally appeal to him. The Field Marshal is famous for not only his supreme competence and uncommon bravery on the battlefield—what general today would willingly endanger himself by personally reconnoitering behind enemy lines?—but also his sense of honor, celebrated by the soldiers of both sides—what general today, if finding himself in danger behind enemy lines, would stop to aid wounded soldiers of the other side? And the Field Marshal tried to bring down Hitler, which cost him his life—this alone would endear him to the Devil, who is opposed to all forms of absolutism (other than his own). Miss Baker has a rare combination of three qualities that I believe Bronaryre holds in high regard: courage, talent, and resolution: jazz dancer, opera diva, movie star, French resistance fighter, civil rights leader, and adopter of orphans on a truly heroic scale. As for Mrs. Shelley, her seminal work *Frankenstein* is of course the very essence of his project, as you have now been made aware. And Mr. Crowley, having reputedly been the wickedest man in England, is a perfectly logical choice for the Devil to make. As for myself, I suppose that I am something of a Jack-of-all-trades, and he no doubt wanted a generalist to round it out, so to speak."

"Your modesty does you no credit, sir," Sabrina says with a smile. "You are, apart from anything else, a father to the greatest experiment in freedom in human history. But tell me, how did you get back here from New York?"

"An aircraft. A private one. An amazing conveyance: had such a thing existed in 1775 I would not have missed Lexington and Concord."

Sabrina turns to Dietrich. "And you?'

"The same, darling—I would have preferred a train; such a more thrilling way to travel: one never knows who one may bump into."

"All this, just for interesting guests at dinner parties?"

"I suppose it proves a point," Franklin says. "Bronaryre's equivalent of my kite-flying."

"But to whom does he demonstrate? Does he show you to other people?"

None of them immediately answer, instead looking at each other, as if to invite a contradiction before someone offers the response they all instinctively know to be true.

"No, we have been presented to no one else, except to each other, and Bronaryre himself."

"And now to you, too." Mary Shelley reminds her.

"He wouldn't be doing something like this just for my benefit," Sabrina says. "This had to have been underway long before he knew that I existed, before I was even born."

"I think you're right," Baker says. "He's got something else in mind for us. The problem is, we don't know what it is."

The sudden clanking of the heavy chains momentarily silences the dinner guests.

"That's your signal," Franklin whispers. "We are to remain here until you leave: no one will come for us until you are gone."

Sabrina stands and says her farewells to each of these strange facsimiles—reincarnations, as Joyce would have it. Baker scribbles her address on a scrap of paper and passes it to Sabrina, renewing her invitation to visit.

"My place is in Cap d'Antibes, right up by the *phare*—the lighthouse. It's a mid-century modernist house—Claude Parent was the architect, designed in the style he termed *spatio-dynamisme*—the top floor is basically a big glass box looking out over the Mediterranean, a wonderful place."

"I hope I can come. Maybe I can persuade Bronaryre to send the SS *United States* that way, although he seems determined to head straight for the South Pacific."

Sabrina takes a candle and begins the slow climb back up the helical stone stairway, carefully guarding the flame, for it will be dark above by now. Eventually she emerges into a clear crisp evening, with the stars splayed brightly across the heavens. The moon hangs low in the northeast, waxing gibbous, reminding her that it will soon be a lunar month since that night in the amphitheater, when last it was full—how much has happened in the interim, and how different she feels. She is a changeling, in this case the faeries having achieved the substitution not in infancy but in the middle of adult life.

She makes her way slowly down the long gravel drive back to the house, thinking about the man who made her dinner companions. She does not know if he is a monster or a madman or a miracle worker. Maybe he is merely a clever magus, fooling her all along with well-trained and well-made-up actors. But, whatever the answer, it cannot all be just for the sake of a monumental pantomime: Bronaryre is up to something, something big, something far beyond her, and when Scaglietti figured out what it was it cost him his life.

Sabrina approaches the house, ready to confront Bronaryre right away, but as she nears the entrance she sees that the E-Type is missing from its usual spot. She goes to her room instead, where before retiring she makes a single terse entry in her journal.

*Bronaryre resurrects the dead. It is not the Devil he is playing; it is God.*

# Ninth Circle

Urania

SABRINA STANDS ON THE STOA, gazing out at her surroundings. What was once Greenwich Hospital lies arrayed over broad swathes of green grass on the banks of the River Thames, several miles downriver from Tower Bridge. It was never really a hospital, Sabrina has discovered, but more a nursing home for sailors invalided out of naval service. She marvels at the generous public mentality that would conceive of a palace for such a purpose, akin to Les Invalides in Paris: what a contrast to the grim, mold-laden facilities of a modern VA—mankind might have advanced technology-wise, she thinks, but in much else the human race has regressed, and here before her is the evidence.

Greenwich Hospital was turned into a naval academy at one stage—it is officially known today as the Old Royal Naval College—and then some of it was leased to the University of Greenwich with the rest drifting into that pallid state of public indifference known as a museum—presumably the fact that it was Wren-designed saved it from outright destruction. But now—for a short time at least, it is once again a living, working congeries of buildings, buzzing with activity as it hosts the guest of honor currently lying docked at the wharf: the SS *United States*.

Bronaryre, who she has not seen since the night he entombed her for the dinner of the dead, has taken over the entire establishment, and the dormitories are occupied by the students and staff who are soon to embark, among them Sabrina. Everyone dines together in the Grand

Hall, a great frescoed and gilded space that must have astonished its original inhabitants, used to salt pork and hardtack consumed on a heaving deck between cannons and hammocks. She wonders if they missed the weevils.

Many of the girls are out on the lawns, full of high spirits, playing impromptu games or capering about in laughing groups, enjoying this last piece of *terra firma* before beginning what is to be a long period at sea. Sabrina sees a familiar figure walking along the porch toward her: Captain Dunning.

He spies her and comes over, saluting in greeting. His uniform is impressive, and his sleeve bears four gold stripes.

"Doctor Lancaster, a pleasure to see you again."

"Good morning, Captain. I hope that you had an agreeable voyage across the Atlantic."

"Ah, headwinds the whole way."

"Surely not a problem for a ship driven by steam?"

"No, but it meant that we were always running against the sea—we got held up with last-minute items in Virginia, and so I had to crack on: it made for an uncomfortable crossing, and some of our bow paint was scoured away. I've got a team on a pontoon now, touching it up before we leave: she needs to look her best for what will formally be her maiden voyage."

They turn toward the ship, gleaming in the sunshine.

"I think she looks magnificent," Sabrina says, meaning it. "I've never been to sea; I'm looking forward to it."

"We'll see if you're still saying that forty-eight hours from now: there's a bit of a sou'westerly blow forecast for our passage down-Channel." For sailors the weather is something always to be gauged warily, Sabrina realizes, never taken for granted, and certainly never trusted.

"I read that Nelson himself was habitually seasick when beginning a new voyage, but he never complained—I hope that I may show similar fortitude."

Dunning laughs at the comparison and bids her a good day. As he continues walking down toward his ship Sabrina is joined by a breathless pair of girls, Penelope de Vere and Katy Telford.

"We need an eleventh for cricket," Penelope exclaims. The students have been divided into two watches, Starboard and Larboard, and it seems that the sides decided to take advantage of their last day ashore to play a game impossible at sea, but Penelope and Katy's Starboards have come up a player short.

"I've never played cricket," Sabrina protests.

"Neither have I," says Katy. "At least, not real cricket. It's just for fun."

Sabrina agrees, and spends the rest of the day in happy confusion on the cricket field, alternating between positions variously identified with obscure and vaguely obscene names like 'fly slip' and 'square leg' and 'silly mid-on.' Her time at bat is brief, a single broad swipe that completely misses the ball and results in the sticks behind her—the 'wicket,' they call it, although bafflingly this term is also applied to the flat ground in front of her on which the ball is bounced—being suddenly smashed all askew, apparently an undesirable event, and which results in her being ordered back to the dugout. However, in the field she manages to amaze everyone, including herself, by catching a ball bare-handed, resulting in an out.

It seems that the game is mainly an excuse to enjoy being outside, and several long breaks are taken, firstly for fresh lemonade, then for a lunch comprising cheese-and-chutney sandwiches, and lastly for tea and scones served with strawberry jam and Devonshire cream, something that sufficiently fills the girls that they decide to 'draw stumps,' and spend the remainder of the afternoon dozing under the trees instead.

It is six o'clock by the time Sabrina returns to her rooms, situated in the old hospital's Queen Anne Court. She finds that two envelopes have been pushed under her door.

The first is a large Savoy Hotel envelope, typewritten, but inside is a second envelope addressed in the distinctive handwriting with which she is well familiar by now. The marbleizing this time has been done in shades of blue, the colors of the uninterrupted sea and sky to come. It contains an invitation to join Bronaryre for cocktails in the Octagonal Room of the Old Royal Observatory, a building located up on a hill overlooking Wren's great hospital.

Something about the note strikes her as ominous—maybe the oddly remote tone, or perhaps just the lack of variance in coloration—and without quite knowing why she has the sense that this will be the last such invitation that she will receive.

The second note has a plain envelope, and has been hastily scrawled on a scrap of paper.

*Watson, can't find you anywhere. Urgent we meet. I'll be in the usual place—come at once.*

*Holmes*

From the handwriting and Holmes reference, the author can only be Roger Wilkins. Sabrina puzzles for a moment over the phrase *usual place*. Except for the one occasion that she visited his laboratory, the only place she has ever met with Wilkins is in the chapel at Caiaphas College—but given that she is in London he cannot mean that he is waiting for her in Oxford. She consults a map of the Greenwich Hospital grounds.

There is a chapel. It is located in the Queen Mary Court.

THE CHAPEL AT GREENWICH HOSPITAL is a splendid, soaring space, richly ornamented, on a par with the college chapels of Oxford. The ceiling is frescoed with circular coffering in gold and Prussian blue. Two long balconies run beneath the clerestory windows on either side, a carved wooden pulpit with a little curved staircase stands before the chancel, and at the far end is the altar. Sabrina strolls down between the pews. There are several people in the chapel—visitors rather than worshippers; some are taking pictures—but none of them is Roger Wilkins.

She comes to a halt at the other end of the chapel by a semicircular altar rail, fitted at the base with kneeling cushions upholstered in navy-blue velvet. There is a door to the right of the altar, perhaps leading to a sacristy, but when she tries the handle Sabrina finds it locked. She turns around and leans back against the door, pensively gazing down at her shoes while thinking through what else Wilkins might have meant by *the usual place*.

She looks up and finds inspiration. At the other end of the chapel, directly above the portal through which she entered, there is a third balcony, much smaller than the other two. Above it are banks of organ pipes.

Sabrina walks quickly back to the main portal, which is flanked by two wooden doors. The first one is unlocked and reveals a set of stairs leading up. At the top is a landing, with another door leading off it. Sabrina ignores the *No Entry* sign and steps through onto the third balcony.

Roger Wilkins is sitting on the floor with his back against the organ. By his side is a battered leather briefcase. He scrambles to his feet.

"There you are at last," he says. "Are you well?"

"Perfectly. And you?"

"My colleague says that it's not possible that you are well, and she is certain she made no mistake with your blood sample."

"What do you mean?"

"You've been infected with a pathogen, something flu-like, although she wasn't able to fully sequence it. You genuinely have no symptoms?"

"I just spent the day playing cricket. Would someone unwell do that?"

"Strange that someone would do it at all, well or not."

"I'm sorry to disappoint your colleague, but I'm in robust good health."

"I told her that you would be. That's when she gave me this." Wilkins rummages through his briefcase, soon emerging with a small plastic-wrapped disposable syringe. "She wants another sample, this time taken with something more sterile than a box cutter."

Sabrina is inclined to refuse, but since Wilkins and his colleague have gone to so much trouble on her behalf she decides against it and rolls up her sleeve instead. Wilkins undoes a little foil pouch and uses the disinfecting gauze it contains to wipe the crook of Sabrina's left arm. He suddenly stops.

"What have you been doing?"

"What do you mean?"

"Puncture marks."

"I told you, I visited my doctor in London, and she took a sample."

"How many?"

"Just one." All too late, Sabrina realizes that she should have lied.

"Then why are there two puncture marks?"

Sabrina sighs in annoyance. "That's from something else."

"Something else?"

"Yes, something else."

"Would you care to tell me what that something else is?"

It occurs to Sabrina that as a Jesuit, famous for turning blind eyes to venial peccadilloes, Wilkins could use some extra training.

"Someone injected me."

"Someone?"

"A naked woman on a rocking horse," she admits.

It takes a while for Wilkins to process this answer before responding. "How did she manage it, while moving back and forth?"

"She got off the horse first."

"Ah. And with what did she inject you?"

"I was told *cream*."

"Cream? Does that have a vernacular meaning?"

"No idea."

"Are you a drug addict?"

"Would I admit it if I was?"

"No, I suppose not."

"Then why don't you just go ahead and take your sample?"

Wilkins looks unsatisfied with her response but takes the sample, in silence. He carefully caps the syringe, then pulls out a pair of scissors.

"What are they for?"

"My colleague wants a lock of hair, too."

"Why?"

"Baseline DNA: it will help distinguish what is you from what is foreign."

Sabrina undoes her hair, which had been gathered into a bun for the cricket, and holds out a hank for him to clip. Wilkins cuts several strands, a few inches above the ends. He mutters to himself as he carefully deposits them into a cellophane envelope.

"*Perceptio Corporis et Sanguinis tui, Domine Iesu Christe, non mihi proveniat in iudicium et condemnationem.*"

"What?"

"I was thinking that it's rather like Communion, isn't it—blood and body? I was reciting the part of the Latin liturgy that the priest utters before himself partaking of the Eucharist: *May the receiving of your Body and Blood, Lord Jesus Christ, not bring me to judgment and condemnation*. That's from the Pauline version, not Tridentine."

How different his mind is to hers, Sabrina thinks, how alien. He packs the envelope and syringe into his briefcase.

"How long will it take?" she asks.

"Just a few days."

"We'll be at sea, but there's still phone service so you can call or text me."

"I don't have your number."

Sabrina suddenly realizes that what she had assumed was a charming Oxford habit of epistolary communication was, at least in Wilkins's case, more likely the result of having had no other way to contact her. She gives him her number, but instead of entering it directly into his phone he writes it down in a notebook bulging with scraps of paper and held shut with an elastic band—something that makes her think he probably does favor pen and ink after all.

## The Fire Sermon

SABRINA WALKS INTO THE COURTYARD of the Old Royal Observatory, where she passes in a single step from the eastern hemisphere to the western hemisphere as she crosses the Prime Meridian—longitude 0°—marked by a metal rail embedded into the cobblestones. She enters Flamsteed House and soon locates the Octagonal Room.

Her first impression is of space. The room is not especially large, but outsize windows and an exceptionally high ceiling—necessitated by its role as an observatory—give the impression of an airy, light-filled limitlessness. There are a surprising number of clocks in the room, some fitted into the walls, others freestanding in their cases, but all with very long pendula: another reason for the room's height, she supposes.

Bronaryre is sitting on a chair while gazing through a polished brass telescope, as big as a naval gun and conveying a sense of heft, but poised seemingly weightlessly on a slender frame. Usually when she joins him for cocktails he is the first to speak, but today it is Sabrina who begins their conversation.

"Do you have any concerns about raising the dead in order to throw interesting dinner parties?"

Bronaryre responds distractedly, without taking his eye from the telescope.

"Concerns? Like what?"

"Ethical."

"I am the Prince of Darkness," he says. "Ethics is not my strong suit."

"I see from your note that you're back at the Savoy—I hope they had your room available."

"They did," he says. "I've been staying there since that occasion I last saw you, overseeing the arrangements for setting forth on the maiden voyage." Bronaryre turns at last from the telescope and looks at Sabrina directly. "Do you know where you are?"

"Literally or figuratively?"

"Literally."

"I am in the Octagonal Room at the Old Royal Observatory, Greenwich—one of the many places in England which you seem to be able to commandeer on a whim."

"A fat checkbook opens many doors. This room was designed by that ubiquitous wonder we know as Christopher Wren. He was a gifted architect, but with exteriors: one thinks immediately of St. Paul's, although many claim that the hospital down the slope from us, where you are now staying, is his grandest achievement. Personally, I find grandeur an uncompelling argument for worth; of all his buildings, I take most pleasure in the elegant simplicity and delicate spire of St. Vedast in Foster Lane, a church whose little courtyard is the most peaceful place to sit in all of London.

"Wren was not known for interiors, but in this room I think one feels the supreme expression of his genius. It is, most importantly, immensely practical for the purpose: form without function is merely a frill: Bartolo Mascarello's 'rouge on the cheeks of a clown.' But more than that, this interior conveys the sensibility behind it: of reason, of rationality, of an ordered and uncluttered mind. Above all, this room excites men's minds with more desire to know. It was commissioned by Charles II in 1674: if I'd realized he was planning it I may never have left England. I knew him, you know?"

"Charles II?"

"Wren."

"No, you never told me."

"He was the Savilian Professor of Astronomy when I was up, long before he ever designed a building—perhaps that's why this room is so perfect: he deeply understood the purpose. I attended his lectures while at Oxford. Also, he was the founding president of the Royal Society, and so I remained acquainted with him through Boyle. I was surprised when he turned his hand to architecture: I worshipped at the altar of mathematics in those days, and did not yet realize that great architecture is mathematics in corporeal form. That was back in my youth, when I was still becoming, and therefore still subject to error. Now, I am like the pope: perfectly infallible."

Bronaryre puts his hand on the telescope. "In 1677, Flamsteed observed the transits of Sirius at this window, through an instrument not too dissimilar to this one, and from those observations established the fundamental principle that the earth spins isochronously: that is, it revolves at precisely the same rate at all times—an important finding, otherwise celestial navigation would be impossible."

He stands and moves to a small side table, where cocktail gear is laid out, and begins mixing. There is no tonic water by the familiar bottle of Physic Gin tonight; instead, there is an unlabeled decanter containing a clear, faintly orange-colored liquid.

"No gin and tonics tonight?"

"No, something different."

"What is it?"

"It has no name."

"What's in it."

"Cactus."

"Cactus?"

"Juice, not flesh."

"Like tequila, or mezcal?"

"Yes, something like those."

He finishes mixing, hands her a glass, and then does something unusual: he offers a toast.

"To the completion of our sessions together."

"Completion?"

"Yes, tonight's will be our last."

"But we've only gone as far as 1794, when you returned to England and built Cavendish House."

"The rest is just history: the Industrial Revolution, which gave men the means to free themselves from labor, but which they used to kill each other *en masse*; the rise of the great democracies, which gave men the means to shape their own destinies, but which they used to create nonsense dogmas anew; the technological revolution, which gave men the means to rid themselves of untruths, but which they used to perpetrate fresh lies no more believable than those that had preceded them."

Sabrina leaves a pause after this indictment, delivered not bitterly, but as a series of simple and objective facts. "But what about you personally?"

"I remained in England for a while. The original manor at Temple Slaughter had burned down while I was away in France. I had it rebuilt, better than before, and the result is what you see today. But I was spending much time in London, and so I built Cavendish House as both a showcase for the Palladian architecture and a meeting place for the Hellfire Club.

"I had already become involved with James Watt's new invention, the steam engine. You must realize how revolutionary it was: until then, almost all work was done by human labor, and the extreme limit of physical force that could be practically brought to bear on any single task was that of a team of oxen: indeed, so important were such animals that a city is named for them, at the point where they could safely ford the River Isis. But the possibilities of the steam engine seemed immense, boundless, and one could cheerfully foresee a new world in which men, now relieved of their burden of labor, would have leisure to think. I imagined that this might lead, if not to outright wisdom, then at least to a shedding of idiocies; instead, men used their leisure to invent new idiocies; today in their leisure they watch television, which is idiocy prefabricated.

"I encouraged the development of the steam engine with Templar money, carefully concealed, of course—I was a silent backer, via Matthew Boulton. Early in the next century I repeated the exercise with those twin progeny of Watt's invention, the locomotive and the steamship. The Templar fortune was thus multiplied many times over, but gradually I grew weary of Victorian England—prim hypocrisy is not to my taste—and after the American Civil War I spent most of my time in the United States, and so it has been ever since. But I move from place to place, as mood and circumstance dictate. I maintain many homes around the world: three in Italy alone—Venice, Lake Como, Positano; in France, I have an apartment in Paris and a villa on Cap d'Antibes. You've seen my *pied-à-terre* in New York; I also have a residence in South Beach, another in the Hollywood Hills, a third on the Big Isle in Hawaii. There is a remote island in Phang Nga Bay, off the Andaman Sea, on which I maintain a traditional Thai house, made of teak wood, open and airy. There are no roads, no electricity, and just one village on the other side of the island, where the people who look after the place while I'm away live."

"Passchendaele?"

Bronaryre smiles ruefully. "A low point for me, the war representing as it did the failure of all that I had tried to build until then. I decided to experience this failure for myself, became an officer in the Black Watch, and was given a taste of mustard gas for my trouble. Afterward, I favored democracy, not from any great respect for the rule of the mob—I frankly have little regard for the *demos*—but from the very practical consideration that all other forms of government inevitably lead to war: whether rule by king, or prince, or emperor, or Führer, or Duce, or Secretary-General of the Communist Party, these governments usually result in the person in power wanting to inscribe his name in the history books with other people's blood. Only rule by the many prevents this: the mob may be foolish, but they know whose blood it is that will be shed—theirs—and they avoid needless conflict: you know that in the entire history of the human race, no two genuine democracies have ever gone to war with each other: proof of my proposition, I think, given the inherent belligerence of men.

"Meanwhile, I devoted myself to science, trusting that better knowledge, better health, better education, and better life would lead to better people. Of course, it was not to be: the people remained the same; the only thing that improved was their means of doing harm. And so now you know almost everything."

"I feel that I know very little."

"There is only one last thing that you do not know, and you will learn it this evening. The thing that you will learn is the relation between what is measurable and what is not: that is, the resolution of the philosophical problem of incommensurability. It was what the men who built this place were trying to achieve: they wished both to gaze upon the infinite, by definition unmeasurable, and yet also to solidly establish their place within that infinite, hence the great concern with position, as evidenced by the establishment here of the Prime Meridian, and also with time, as evidenced by the fact that we still measure the passage of that unknowable dimension with reference to Greenwich Mean Time. The great number of clocks in this room reflects that concern, and their acute understanding of it: for instance, that clock by you measures not normal time but *sidereal* time—star time—which is a small fraction shorter than our earthbound time, since the earth's passage along its own orbit is irrelevant to the stars: a subtle but significant astronomical distinction.

"One may therefore think of the Old Royal Observatory as an origin point. Humankind has always sought this, a fixed place from which to derive things, whether derivation of position in time and space, as in this room, or derivation of other fundamental truths—an *umbilicus conscientia.* The ancient Greeks placed an origin point in a cleft at Delphi; Virgil placed his at the mouth of Vesuvius; the alchemists in an imagined philosopher's stone, as enshrined by their acrostic motto 'vitriol': *visita interiora terrae rectificando invenies occultum lapidem*—visit the interior of the Earth; by rectification thou shalt find the hidden stone. Alfred North Whitehead and Bertrand Russell saw as their origin point the concepts of singularity and set theory (and it famously took them 360 pages to then advance to one plus one equals two).

"Let us now stipulate the Octagonal Room as being the ground zero of Western consciousness, the origin marker, the point from which all else will be measured. And note how different an observatory is to those earlier attempts: previously, men looked inward toward the bowels of the earth to find enlightenment, that is, to find me—quite literally in Dante's case. But here in this room the opposite is true; here men looked not inwardly but outwardly, as far into space and as far back in time as they could—here, they sought enlightenment in the cosmos. A suitable place, is it not, for you to complete your own enlightenment?"

"How is that to be done?"

"I will open a wormhole into deep spacetime, and you will travel along it."

"Really?"

"Speak no more. Sit."

Bronaryre gestures toward the chair on which he was sitting earlier, angled back so that the sitter is almost lying down, presumably custom-built to make looking up through the telescope more comfortable. He takes Sabrina's empty glass as she walks over.

"Sit back and relax. The wormhole, despite being a macro-passage into deep space, will exhibit certain quantum characteristics: that is, characteristics from the world of fundamental particles under which standard physics breaks down. For example, you will experience both spin and chirality, meaning twist in an asymmetric manner, which you may think of as left-handedness and right-handedness. You will be both bound and unbound, and both symmetry and supersymmetry will break: do not be alarmed when this happens. You yourself will be a factor in the system, and so it is not possible to describe what will happen in literal terms. However, I can describe it mathematically—in terms of combinatorial topography—with great precision: you will be transformed into a localized nonlinear photonic wave function of a type called a soliton. Time-reversal symmetry will be broken by propagation along a suitable periodic medium—in this case, Flamsteed's telescope, acting as a waveguide. This will enable your waveform to remain topologically protected while at the same time inheriting other topologies: in this case, those of the cosmos. Together, you and the cosmos will form an integrable wave system, for which there will be nonlinear PDEs—

"PDEs?"

"Partial differential equations—there will be nonlinear partial differential equations possessing an infinite number of symmetries. These will be precisely solvable, and the solutions will manifest as your passage through the wormhole. You will become a linear edge wave with nontrivial topological invariants. The system will be characterized by infinite conservation laws, and so although your state may shift you will be preserved under all circumstances. The propagation through the waveguide will be both cyclical and helical, describable by a discrete nonlinear Schrödinger equation in two spatial dimensions, and with periodic coefficients in the propagation variable: in other words, you will journey. Further, the system will exhibit the integer quantum Hall effect: you will experience quantized leaps—meaning sudden jumps from one state to another—and the states will be integral, which is to say, coherent and meaningful, not just flow alone.

"You may close your eyes if you wish—you will not fall asleep. The cocktail contained Mescaline, an extract from the peyote cactus, and it will help calm you."

Sabrina is too unsurprised to react: she is used to being drugged by the Devil by now.

"The journey's prime motor will use the phenomenon of entanglement: Einstein's so-called spooky action at a distance. That entanglement will allow the instantaneous crossing of spacetime barriers: it is faster than the speed of light because all boundary conditions are broken, and the concept of the speed of light no longer has relevance. Breathe normally, and allow it to run its course—no harm will come to you."

Sabrina can hear him take a seat close behind her, like a psychoanalyst by a patient on the couch.

"I think I mentioned that at one time, while living in Burma, I became a Buddhist monk. It was there that I learned how to open the wormhole. The wormhole is formed by the words of the Buddha. We begin.

*All things, O monks, are on fire. And what, O monks, are all these things which are on fire?*

*The eye, O monks, is on fire; forms are on fire; eye-consciousness is on fire; impressions received by the eye are on*

> *fire, and whatever sensation, pleasant, unpleasant, or indifferent, originates in dependence on impressions received by the eye, that also is on fire.*
>
> *And with what are these on fire?*
>
> *With the fire of passion, say I, with the fire of hatred, with the fire of infatuation; with birth, old age, death, sorrow, lamentation, misery, grief, and despair are they on fire.*"

The soothing tone, the slow cadence, the many fire repetitions: Sabrina wonders if he is attempting to hypnotize her.

> "*The ear is on fire, sounds are on fire; the nose is on fire, odors are on fire; the tongue is on fire, tastes are on fire; the body is on fire, things tangible are on fire; the mind is on fire, ideas are on fire; mind consciousness is on fire, impressions received by the mind are on fire, and whatever sensation, pleasant, unpleasant, or indifferent, originates in dependence on impressions received by the mind, that also is on fire.*
>
> *And with what are these on fire?*
>
> *With the fire of passion, say I, with the fire of hatred, with the fire of infatuation; with birth, old age, death, sorrow, lamentation, misery, grief, and despair are they on fire.*"

A pause. Sabrina is gently drifting, as if afloat, like Millais's *Ophelia*, washing down a cool River Windrush.

> "*Perceiving this, O monks, the learned and noble disciple conceives an aversion for the eye, conceives an aversion for forms, conceives an aversion for eye-consciousness, conceives an aversion for impressions received by the eye, and whatever sensation, pleasant, unpleasant, or indifferent, originates in dependence on impressions received by the eye, for that he conceives an aversion.*
>
> *He conceives an aversion for the ear, conceives an aversion for sounds. He conceives an aversion for the tongue, conceives an*

> *aversion for the body, conceives an aversion for things, and whatever sensation, pleasant, unpleasant, or indifferent, originates in dependence on impressions received by the mind, for that he also conceives an aversion.*"

Bronaryre's soft patter continues, but she registers only portions of it now. Beneath her, the earth heaves.

> "*And in conceiving this aversion he becomes divested of passion, and by the absence of passion he becomes free, and when he is free he becomes aware that he is free, and that he is no more for this world.*
>
> *And whosoever shall take a lamp unto themselves, and a refuge unto themselves, shall betake themselves no external refuge, but hold fast to the Truth as their lamp, they shall reach the very topmost height. But they must be anxious to learn.*"

The earth shrugs again, and this time Sabrina shunts forward into the telescope, and then through it.

Momentary darkness, and suddenly she blasts into space like a rifle shot. Ah, she thinks, Flamsteed's telescope not merely observes the heavens, it accesses them as well—it is a great gun after all. The tube must have rifling, for she is spinning wildly, spiraling into space like a well-thrown football.

The spinning gradually slows and then stops, allowing for perception. She is weightless, space-floating, slowly tumbling away through the galactic emptiness. She is naked and pale in the silver starlight. Her long hair swirls about her. Her trajectory is upward, still rising higher above the planet below. She looks down and sees there not familiar blue-white Earth but something else, dark in its core and Rothko red at the event horizon: it is a black hole, with the mass of a thousand-million suns.

Sabrina is inside a vortex, a whirlpool of slowly spinning energy wrapping around her, vast and silent and invisible, like water swirling down some cosmic-scale drain. But she revolves in the opposite direction, twisting ever upward, although she cannot be sure which of them is really moving, she or the vortex, or both. Below her, the matter-devouring black hole, supermassive, engulfs whole galaxies, but it recedes as she moves up and up, always higher. The vortex envelops her, miles wide, unhurried but inevitable, while she floats weightless through the galactic maelstrom.

The vortex is a helix, Sabrina realizes: she has been swaddled in strands of cosmological DNA. It carries various items that gently swirl past and then disappear deep into the black hole below, a celestial Charybdis carrying objects down into their oblivion, but which leaves her untouched.

A kite flies nearby, whirling through the eddies although there is no atmosphere to support it, alive with an aurora of buzzing bright-pastel neon light, weaving about her like a curious bird before drifting away.

A tropical island floats by, turquoise sea-ed. It circles about her for a few minutes on its long spiral downward, and Sabrina sees bare-breasted maidens dancing on the distant shore. Bronaryre's E-Type races by, revving in silence, and then King Charles I, mounted on an elaborately caparisoned horse, holding himself with kingly dignity, and carrying his severed head under his left arm.

Sabrina continues to drift and twirl in a cosmic delirium, tumbling weightless borne, slowly plummeting through the cataclysm.

A battleship comes spiraling down, its sides rust-streaked from a long period at sea. It smells of brine and coal and hot metal and rot. Its guns are brass and the hull all Nora Barnacled. It revolves around her as it approaches, and mermaids swim in and out of an imaginary bow wave, long-tressed with algal locks, tempting sailors; tempting death by water.

*Who is the third who walks always beside you?*

The council Tridentine triumvirate Trinitarian convenes. A d-d-determination is made.

The rocking horse rider swirls past, pitching to and fro in pendulous slow motion. She holds forth a broadsword, gleaming with galactic light. She gazes upon Sabrina and points the sword long-armed behind her, where the ranks of the condemned sluggishly march, drudgingly and downcast.

A body of men. The blood of man.

Behold this, the sword sings out to her, and thou shalt be free.

*A young man of Oxford, a tad in a pinch*
*Went down to the plodge to check on his pidge*
*His battels were due*
*Unpayable, he knew*
*But better be poor than in bloody Cambridge*

A gleaming golden rocket appears, blunt-nosed and smooth-sided, dildomorphically resplendent. She mounts it, legs astride the mighty frame, and reaches behind to twist the knob. Ignition commences, deep and bone-shakingly resonant, and then the thrusters burst into life, swelling with power and flinging them forward. Faster and faster, beyond the speed of light, beyond any limit at all. The turbulent stars spin and swirl all about. Cosmic waves crash in, washing against them, and the rocket pitches and dips beneath her. Sabrina grips tightly with her knees. Her hair flows behind, strands of spectral silver streaming for miles into the abyss. She is wraith-like, her naked skin as translucent as rice paper. She sees the veins beneath, dark red, why are they not blue? She straightens her back and lifts her chin to the void, a pink-nippled space-hussar upon a goldenrod steed, blue-blooded of mind and red-blooded of body, streaming, streaming.

Sabrina is sheathed in unguents of hemlock and mandrake. She has been anointed, but by whom? She tastes of belladonna, but who is it that tastes her? She can feel the tongue upon her flesh. Who is it that consumes her? The desert air is hot and dry; she can barely stand upon the sand. The wheat-colored dunes wave unwavering in the still desert sea. Her unguents melt and she feels them flow down her neck into the vales of her collar bones, down her ribs, down the gully of her spine. He licks at them; she is cyanic-blooded; he is dying.

She comes to a door.

*Take a face from the ancient gallery!*

She takes a face from the ancient gallery. It is a porcelain face that will go with her porcelain skin. It is the face of no expression and no acknowledgment. It is smooth but see, look more closely, there are fine cracks! Am I not to age, as thou ageth? See the cracks! See them! See them!

The door opens into a garden of red roses—Lancastrian roses. It is the garden of a dragon, but he is asleep or perhaps of stone, not a real dragon at all. Sabrina sneaks by him, tiptoeing to the brook, softly burbling away. She bathes. She sees that her blood is violet now: at once both red and blue. A knife appears—*Is this a dagger I see before me*? She incises a fingertip to taste her blood: her blood tastes of—

It cannot be said of what her blood tastes.

The bed of the stream is comprised of small rounded stones. This is the lair of Naiads, who lure men to water. This is the place where kings come to conduct their ablutions, before they are to be beheaded. This is the constellation Pleiades, where one may hide among one's sisters.

The drowned clutch at her as they float past. She slices away their hands, slices off their arms, but still they cling. They are gray of body, and red of blood.

Jennet Devize appears standing upon the bank. She wears a small girl's smock. Beside her sits the dog called Ball. They stare down at Sabrina, Devize with a sly smirk, the dog with calculating cunning. Sabrina stands, and water pours in torrents from her body, flows and flows in an endless deluge; how is it, she wonders, that I am so wet. She gazes down at the water gushing from her, and when she looks back up Devize is gone, and only the dog called Ball remains.

"Rise," the dog commands.

Sabrina rises above the stream, floating in the air. She holds her arms outstretched, cruciform. Still the water flows in torrents from her flesh.

"*Corpus Domini nostri,*" Ball says, "*custodiat animam meam in vitam œternam*."

The sky begins to open above them.

"Bleed," the dog commands.

She bleeds.

"*Sanguis Domini nostri,*" Ball says, "*custodiat animam meam in vitam œternam*. Amen"

The dog genuflects, and Sabrina ascends through the sky hole. A bell begins to toll, very deeply, doom-tellingly, proclaiming an end to all destinies.

Far away, two stars collide. There is a sudden bright point of yellow light, a supernova, but it quickly expands into a billowing ball of fire, hydrogen fire, fire of fusion, growing ever larger. It soon swells to engulf the surrounding stars, but still does not stop. The fireball inflates ever faster, consuming everything in its path: planets, stars, nebulae, galaxies. A great front of ballooning fire approaches her at the speed of light; unstoppable, immutable, irresistible. It comes rushing past Sabrina, sounding like a thousand freight trains, overwhelming everything, a massive wave of fusion fire, a billion suns simultaneously exploding.

All at once, it retreats. It has consumed everything that is consumable. It shrinks and shrinks, losing luminosity, growing ever smaller and darker. At last it stops, infinitesimal in size, a tiny speck of dust perched upon the point of a pin.

It contains all the matter and all the energy in the universe—everything except Sabrina, and the pin.

She picks up the pin, carefully folds the universe into her handkerchief, and tucks it safely away in the pocket of her pinafore.

## Apologia

THE DEPARTURE of the SS *United States* from Greenwich is a ceremonious affair, with a podium and seats arrayed on the lawn, an area set aside for press and another for photographers. Lord Batten, the Chancellor of Oxford University, arrives in ermine robes and is escorted by beadles bearing on their shoulders mighty silver maces. There are speeches and a blessing, and when finally the *United States* quits the dock a brass band plays 'Auld Lang Syne.' Firefighting tugboats lead the ship downriver while spraying plumes of water from their upturned hoses. Spectators line the shore; they wave and cheer as she passes by.

There is no sign of Bronaryre.

When they leave the estuary the clouds thicken and the wind whips up, and after rounding the Downs to transit Dover Strait the ship's deck begins to heave. The passage through the Channel is as rough as Dunning predicted, but Sabrina quickly finds her sea legs, and by the time they clear Ushant the next day, the skies have begun to brighten again.

Soon land has been left far astern, and the ship settles into a routine that is a strange mixture of the easygoing life at an Oxford college and the strict discipline of a naval officers' academy.

Each weekday begins at 5:30 A.M. with a morning run—three times around the Main Deck, equal to a mile—followed by a swim: the ship comes to a stop and the girls descend by scrambling nets from the bow and then swim the length of the vessel before taking an accommodation ladder astern back up to the deck. A boat is lowered in case anyone gets into difficulties, and on the bridge wing a crewman with a rifle stands duty as shark guard. If the sea is running too high, a lap across the saltwater pool is substituted.

Penelope de Vere, Katy Telford, and Sesuna—who have become fast friends and emerged as leaders of the student body—take to doing their morning swim naked, apparently as a challenge to the cold sea breeze and bracing chill of the ocean—a habit that makes the duty of shark guard popular among the crew.

After their morning dip the girls shower and change, and must also clean their cabins—the scouts do not perform this duty, as at a regular college—and so by the time they breakfast they have already been up and active for over an hour. During the week they wear uniforms that are patterned on those of British naval officers: long-sleeved white shirt and black tie, and black gabardine trousers for cooler climes, but as they move south toward the Equator this changes to tropical whites: shorts and open-necked shirts.

Classes are more relaxed, sometimes lectures but mostly tutorials. Sabrina finds that teaching is more demanding than she had anticipated, but perhaps more rewarding, too.

Late afternoon is given over to sports and games, or theatrical and musical pursuits, or classes unrelated to academic disciplines—Glamis's weapons training is well attended, and so too, less predictably, is nautical ropework, conducted by an amused ship's bosun. In Bronaryre's absence, it is Dunning who conducts the celestial navigation classes, extraordinarily popular, since the taking of morning stars excuses the participant from the swim, but there are only ten sextants, and all of the slots are quickly taken. Wednesday dinners are formal with subfusc as the dress code; Saturday nights are black-tie.

In the evenings Sabrina updates her journal.

*The Latin that the dog called Ball recited in the star journey:*

> *Corpus Domini nostri custodiat animam meam in vitam æternam*

*is an abridged line of the Latin liturgy (trans.: May the body of our Lord Jesus Christ preserve my soul unto life everlasting; Ball omits 'Jesus Christ'), as is the second line:*

> *Sanguis Domini nostri custodiat animam meam in vitam æternam*

*(trans.: May the blood of our Lord Jesus Christ preserve my soul unto life everlasting; again Ball omits 'Jesus Christ'). Both are from the Tridentine form of the mass, as recommended by the Counterreformationist Council of Trent (Roman Tridentium) and promulgated in 1570. It was the Roman Catholic standard until replaced by Pope Paul VI in 1969. Wilkins's earlier Eucharistic reference was from this later 'Pauline' version, but the fact that in my vision the language is Tridentine suggests that the orphanage in which I was raised must have kept to the older form of the mass* (Usus Antiquior) *despite the pope's proclamation—otherwise, how could I have dreamt it?*

*How much of Bronaryre's absence is attributable to an unwillingness to be confronted after that strange evening at the Old Royal Observatory? None, I suspect: the Devil does not fear the wrath of a woman, however vexed she may be, nor that of a perplexed wraith, as then I was. Even after I awoke—naked on the observatory roof, as if deposited there by the cosmos at the conclusion of the star journey—lying beneath the celestial canopy whose acquaintance it seemed to me that I had just made, I still felt that strange disassociative spectral apartness of the dream; I continue to feel it now.*

*A combination of mescaline and mesmerizing fire sermon? Maybe, if it were only a mental state, but I fear that it is more. My flesh is transforming. I knew it that night, I think, after staring up at those stars for who knows how long, uncaring of the cold, when I had eventually sat up and checked for damage. Nothing broken or even bruised, despite what must have been an awkward ascent to the roof, but I could see right away that my skin had changed: very pale—almost luminescent in the moonlight—and the texture as well: it felt like fabric instead of skin, like fine silk tautly drawn, tight but thin, something easily pierced.*

*So it remains. I overdress for the climate and wear makeup. I avoid the senior common room; I dine in my cabin. I can sense the inquiring looks following me—too pale, too thin, is she unwell? I would join the girls for the morning swim, but I dare not be seen in a swimsuit.*

*Besides, the brand on my right shoulder blade has reappeared—it is a unicursal hexagram, as I suspected. And I smell; I smell like a burning matchstick: I smell of fire and brimstone.*

*I never recovered from that night, struggling down from the roof and searching without success for my clothing—except for the shoes, and those I found only because I had taken them off to negotiate the cobblestones of the observatory's courtyard, and then placed them out of the way in a corner of the Octagonal*

*Room—Bronaryre, or whoever removed my clothing, missed them. But he, or they, left a garment for me over the back of the chair in which I had sat gazing through the telescope: a pinafore, not the Braithwaite & Slether nightdress of the encounter with Mortimer Pence—*Daguerriste de la nature*—but a real pinafore, an apron of the type Alice wore over her dress in Wonderland.*

*In the pocket, wrapped in a dainty lace handkerchief, I found a pin; I have it still. Presumably that part of the star journey was suggested under hypnosis (maybe all of it was) and the pinafore prop was left as a reminder. But of what? Perhaps Pendle Hill, the trials having been precipitated by the attempted purchase of a pin.*

*Then the ridiculous return to my rooms at the Old Naval College, wearing high heels and a frilly wisp of clothing, like some pornographic version of a French maid—thankfully too late for anyone to be about. It was not until I was inside and in front of a mirror that I saw the full extent of the transformation: the tan had disappeared; my skin had turned into something unnaturally pallid, to the point of translucency; my hair had turned fair, as if sun-bleached; my eyes had subtly changed, too, the color paler, cooler, and perhaps the look behind them as well. I am becoming a Botticelli.*

*My dreams appall me.*

*The Fire Sermon was not a journey into outer space; it was a voyage into the dreadful sublime.*

*Is Bronaryre the Devil? At what point does a forgery so equate to the real thing that to draw a distinction is no longer meaningful?*

IT IS THE *United States*' maiden voyage after many years of having lain idle, and not everything goes smoothly: they spend several hours adrift with the engines stopped due to an overheating shaft bearing; the satellite service fails completely, apparently because of a faulty relay in the antenna, leaving them without telephone or internet service; and one morning they wake to find that there is no hot water, and so the girls are given a reprieve from their morning swim.

Sabrina soon discovers a favorite place on the ship: the signals deck. It is a small platform atop a compartment built above the bridge, accessible only by an external ladder, and intended to be the place from which flag signals are hoisted. It is never occupied; she thinks of it as her own secret spot. There are two large flag bins on either side, carefully arranged from Alpha (divided vertically; navy blue and white) to Zulu (quartered diagonally; yellow, blue, red, and black), plus long tapering numbered pennants.

Raised on a halyard overhead is the Explorers Club flag, flapping away at the yardarm day and night in all weathers—how pale it will be by the time we return, Sabrina thinks: we are both of us losing our color.

There is always wind at sea, she learns, even in times of rare calm the ship's passage creates an artificial breeze, and so most people favor the large open decks aft, where the intervening superstructure creates a windbreak. The signals deck is always blustery, but Sabrina likes the fresh smell of the sea and occasional waft of salty spray. She leans on the forward rail and gazes out over the ever-restless ocean, with its endless variations in color and mood, pierced by the *United States*' mighty prow, relentlessly plunging onward.

Since the evening in the Octagonal Room, Sabrina has heard nothing of Bronaryre—as far as she can tell he did not even attend the departure ceremonies, but this is in keeping with his principle that the Devil should keep a low profile. Although the satellite service is down the HF radio is still functional, allowing for transmission and reception of the ship's operational traffic with her agents, and one day Dunning announces that a signal has been received establishing a South Pacific rendezvous where Bronaryre will join them. He will bring with him two important items: the spare relay needed to fix the satellite antenna; and an aircraft: he will arrive by seaplane, of a type designed to be based on a ship, with folding wings, and it will remain with the *United States*—the ship will hoist it aboard and stow it in the hanger with the helicopter.

The days quickly pile on top of one another, and soon turn into weeks. The weather warms pleasantly, and then becomes sweltering with frequent thunderstorms, signaling their arrival in the tropics. The sea breeze all but ceases when they enter the doldrums. It had been expected that they would transit the Panama Canal, but the ship's agents report delays there and so Dunning, with the inexhaustible power of nuclear reactors on tap, opts to go the long way around, via Cape Horn, to be certain of making his rendezvous.

All they see of South America is a distant tip of land as they pass by Brazil, and the seemingly uninhabited desolation of Patagonia as they approach the Cape.

At the end of Michaelmas Term, ten weeks after having set sail, they finally make rendezvous, about 350 miles south-southwest of Tahiti.

The plane arrives, high-winged, twin-engined, and with a big, boat-shaped belly. It makes several orbits of the ship, perhaps to establish wind direction by inspecting the ship's flags, and Sabrina hopes that aboard it Bronaryre or someone else is taking photographs of the *United States*, resplendent on a tropical aquamarine sea.

The seaplane makes its landing. A boat has been lowered for the passengers to disembark, before the longer work of hoisting the aircraft aboard gets underway. Only three people emerge, two of them aircrew, judging from their uniform. The third is not Bronaryre; it is his lawyer, Thomas Ravenscroft. He has a satchel slung across his shoulder, carries a suitcase plus several packages, and struggles clumsily in the passage from aircraft to boat, and then again from boat to accommodation ladder.

He is greeted by the welcoming committee at the top of the ladder, but then spies Sabrina, who is standing separate from the rest. After a moment he excuses himself and approaches.

"A pleasure to see you again, Dr. Lancaster."

"And you too, Mr. Ravenscroft. I hope that you had a pleasant flight."

"I was not made for flying, as I think I may have mentioned, but it was tolerable enough. I imagine that you are surprised to see me?"

"I am. I expected Bronaryre."

"I regret that Mr. Bronaryre is otherwise engaged, but he did entrust me with three items that are for you." He opens his satchel and withdraws an envelope and a wooden box the size of a cigarette case. The box is highly polished and the lid has been inlaid with that same unicursal hexagram that she first saw on Bronaryre's cuff link, and has lately appeared on her shoulder blade.

"Here are two of the items," he says, proffering the box and envelope. "The third is a set of documents, still on the aircraft, and which I will have sent to your cabin when it has been brought on board."

She takes the two items and begins to open the envelope, but he gently places a halting hand on her arm. "In your stateroom would be better, may I suggest." Sabrina feels her heart sink; it is the sort of thing that is only said when the news is bad. "Please rejoin us when you're ready, but you must not feel rushed to do so. Take your time." He turns back to the others, but she can see that they have already picked up on the changed mood, and their faces betray concern.

Sabrina retreats to her stateroom, where she opens the envelope, marbleized as usual, but this time in deep reds and dark grays: Rothko colors. The letter it contains is a long one, covering many sheets of notepaper.

There is a newspaper clipping attached. It is from the *New York Times*, the headline rendered in large print common in the tabloid press, but rare for the Old Gray Lady: *Epidemics Sweep the World.*

The story is brief, sending readers to other stories in the inner pages for detail, but what has happened is plain enough: all of a sudden, a disease has swept through the world, or perhaps multiple diseases. Unlike a normal epidemic, it seems to have occurred everywhere all at once. Extraordinarily virulent. Health systems overwhelmed. Society collapsing. Millions dead; millions more dying.

She checks the date: ten days after they sailed.

Now she understands why they did not transit the Panama Canal, and have not touched land in nearly three months. They have escaped it, and that seems unlikely to have been a coincidence.

Sabrina puts aside the clipping and picks up Bronaryre's letter.

*Lancaster,*

*By now you will have guessed what I have done: I have unleashed the Apocalypse—still harbor any doubts as to my identity?*

*Why? you ask.*

*In the middle of the last century, when it became clear—through Watson and Crick and others—that humanity was approaching an understanding of the basis of life, I saw the risk at once: what happens if people crack the code for how to be like me, that is, to live forever? I immediately devoted the bulk of the Templar fortune to getting ahead of the game in decrypting this new diploid-helical cipher—something of a natural challenge to my mathematical bent. I hope from my various demonstrations that you will agree it was money well spent.*

*Firstly, to address my own idiosyncrasies. DNA, as you will perhaps recall from your school days, is a series of just four nucleotides, usually labeled C, G, A, and T from their bases (they also have a sugar and a phosphate group). They do not act by themselves, but sequences of bases form genes, and genes are the fundamental encoding elements. To use a blueprint analogy, think of nucleotides as the possible markings on an architectural rendering of, say, an ancient Greek temple. The markings by themselves do not mean much—a line here, a curve there—but put them together in the correct sequence and you end up with a discrete architectural component: a column, a capital, an architrave, a pediment. These are the fundamental architectural elements, in the same way that genes are the fundamental encoding elements. Assemble these architectural elements in a particular way, and you get the Parthenon. Assemble these encoding elements in a particular way, and you get me.*

*In my* DNA, *there are one thousand, five hundred and ninety-seven genes that are unique, about 5% of the total genome. They are not found in any* DNA *other than mine.*

*These unique genes—unique nucleotide clusters, to be more precise—either individually or in combination encode for many of my peculiarities: the rapid regeneration from wounds, for example, or the hyper-efficient immune system. The processes leading to my longevity primarily involve stem cells and telomeres.*

*My stem cells are, due to a process mediated by the acid α-ketoglutarate, as pluripotent now as when I was a child: that is, they remain undifferentiated until needed, standing by ready to replace a damaged cell of any tissue type—heart, skin, bone, teeth, anything.*

*Telomeres are strands of repeated nucleotides at the ends of chromosomes, and their function is to signal termination of the replication process, essential to cell regeneration. The problem is that in each replication some fraction of the telomere itself is lost: the tails get truncated. When this occurs the terminations of succeeding replications are less well signaled, and as a result mutations can occur. On every replication, a little more fidelity to the original is lost. Think of it as continuously taking photocopies of the previous photocopy: each one is a little less clean, leading to gradual degeneration: this is a central cause of aging. But not with me: the telomeres capping my chromosomes are fully preserved (in fact, they* are *shortened, but then immediately rebuilt via a reverse transcription) and so each replication is not so much a photocopy of a photocopy, but more like a digital copy—that is, precisely the same as the original, every time.*

*Hence, I do not age.*

*That covers the genetics, but not the epigenetics. Returning to the architectural analogy, let's say that the blueprint has an entablature composed in the Vitruvian manner: an architrave at the base with a frieze on top of it, a cornice above that, and then the whole thing capped by a pediment. But suppose the builder decides to ignore the frieze, and instead puts the cornice directly on top of the architrave, with nothing intervening. In the same way, gene expression—that is, what actually gets built—is mediated by epigenetic processes: methylation, adenylation, acetylation, and many others, even microbes. The phenotype—the person that is created—is thus a combination of two things: the genotype—DNA, which lays out what is possible—and these multifaceted epigenetic processes, which choose what becomes actual from what is possible. Control those, and you control life.*

*I know how to control them.*

*As to the old argument of nature versus nurture: having mastered the first, could I also regulate the second? This is the function of Headley Grange, and I think that the results speak for themselves.*

*Franklin was the first, and you have seen for yourself what a marvelous success he is. Crowley came next—maybe not the wisest choice, but he certainly rose to the occasion when you suddenly took yourself up to Scotland, and I believe he is a man who can be relied upon under stress: nothing shakes him. Perhaps this is a benefit of lunacy; in any case, humanity without insanity would be like a gin and tonic without a slice of lemon: not quite the thing. You have met most of the others, although I think you may have missed identifying Lewis Carroll—his real name was Charles Dodgson, and it was he who at the amphitheater that night delivered the lecture on the Fibonacci sequence. I think I mentioned in the Dean's Garden that the author of* Alice in Wonderland *was a mathematics don at Christ Church.*

*By the way, you were on the mark with the dinner guest comment: that is precisely how I chose whom to resurrect, imagining those whose company I would find most agreeable as dining companions—as long as I could locate a DNA sample, of course, which ruled out luminaries like Cleopatra or Tamburlaine or Du Fu, the great T'ang dynasty poet—all three of whom I would have resurrected had it been possible. Usually, these DNA samples were obtained from clothing or an old hairbrush and the like—the Ashmolean is not the only museum from which I have filched.*

*You were also correct about the chess game: in a beautiful house brimming with beautiful people, it* was *the most beautiful thing of all: a replay of Bobby Fischer versus Boris Spassky in Reykjavik, 1972, Game 6, sometimes considered the greatest game ever. Fischer began with the Queen's Gambit Declined, something that must have astonished Spassky, it being an opening that Fischer had only ever played twice in competitive chess, and one that he publicly disparaged. Spassky fell back on his trusted Tartakower Defense, with which he had never lost, having always been able to force at least a draw. Fischer demolished him in 41 moves, with such astonishing economy and elegance that when the crowd stood to applaud Fischer at the end of the game, Spassky joined them.*

*You see why I have expended so much effort to avert the self-destruction of humankind—a species that can create such abstract beauty from a simple checkered board and a few playing pieces is worth preserving, is it not?*

*A question for you, Lancaster: when did human civilization reach its apogee?*

*I propose 1776 as a suitable candidate for that honor. The Enlightenment was at its height, and the horrors of the French Revolution were yet to come. In that year, two seminal works were published: Adam Smith's* Wealth of Nations, *doing for economics what Newton had done for physics: explaining what had until then seemed inexplicable: in his case, the unaccountable gyrations of the common weal; and Gibbon published* The Decline and Fall of the Roman Empire*: from that moment, mankind was no longer simply subject to the whims of history; he had been made aware that it was in his power to bend history to his will. These works promised a brighter future, but across the Atlantic men had already taken history into their own hands and were building the world anew. The 'Declaration of Independence' is not only the greatest publication in that* annus mirabilis *of great publications, but of all time: the ultimate statement of human purpose:* life, liberty, and the pursuit of happiness*—who but a genius or a madman could have come up with something so simple in words, but so noble in purpose and majestic in scope?*

*There was a short time, in the early 1990s, when I thought that 1776 might be eclipsed. The Soviet Union collapsed, and overnight Russia became vigorous, outward-looking, and free. Tiananmen Square had failed, but it was clear that the Chinese people were desperate for their freedom, and the collapse of the totalitarian state there had seemed to be only a matter of time. Meanwhile, the Western democracies had clearly carried the day, and it appeared self-evident that liberty would reign henceforth. 'The end of history,' it was bruited about at the time.*

*What happened? I will not attempt to answer why, but I think I can address how. By definition, democracies can only succeed when there is at the core of the population a critical mass of sober, clear-eyed citizens: people capable of looking beyond their own immediate self-interest; people with a sense of something greater than themselves. But what happens if instead the majority are a malignant, slovenly-minded rabble—petty, irrational, weak of spirit, and lacking in character? This is why democracy failed in so many countries that recently became free. It is also why it is beginning to fail in the West. If the critical mass collapses, then it follows that incompetence will rise to power, and today the Western democracies have indeed largely devolved into asynetocracies—that is, government by the foolish and fatuous. Worse is to come: it is an axiom of history that when government becomes incompetent, malevolence soon replaces it. What was it that caused the democracies to fall below critical mass? Was it the deterioration in education, producing graduates who are functionally illiterate and all but innumerate; or the media, vomiting forth a never-ending diet of predigested pap, fit only for consumption by the intellectually toothless; or the general malaise of societies in which the individual, weakened by dependency, looks to the state instead of himself?*

*In nature, stupidity is a capital crime, swiftly punished. In society, it has become a state that is immune to consequence, and flourishes.*

*The result is a world in which the shallow and thoughtless dominate, through the sheer weight of numbers. And what numbers! In 1649, when Charles I was beheaded, the world population was 500 million. In 1793, when Louis XVI was beheaded, the world population had doubled: that took a century and a half. The next 500 million took less than a century. Now, it takes less than a decade. The world population will hit 10,000 million in the blink of an eye: a 2,000% increase since I have existed. But the earth has stayed the same size.*

*When Malthus first identified the issue—geometric increase in population, but only arithmetic increase in the food supply, he did not know that mechanization would allow for much broader cultivation and so, for a while, food production could keep pace. However, the arable land has now run out, and Malthus's time has come. Indeed, the world is running out of not just land but water, too, and raw materials, and trees, and even air: the planet is choking on human effluvium. Mankind is killing the earth, and everything on it, including himself.*

*How much worse will it be when people can live for four hundred years? The technology to do so is within reach, as I have demonstrated. It is only a matter of time before someone outside of my power comes upon it—they are already on the brink—and then we are doomed. Who is it that when given the choice between a natural span and immortality will, in the interests of the greater good, put up their hands and say, 'Not me'? And who, in an age when it will soon be possible to manipulate the DNA of the unborn to fabulous advantage, will raise their hands and say, 'Not my children'?*

*No one. Thus, I have chosen to say it for them.*

*We are entering a new age—the age of programmable DNA—a change that will be as profound as the shift from hunting to agriculture, or agriculture to industry, and something for which humanity is not just unprepared but also manifestly unsuited—it is a fundamental truth that populations who cannot govern themselves competently in the present are simply unfit to face the challenges of the future.*

*A culling was called for. I have packed a series of papers documenting the details separately, so that there will be a complete scientific record. Here, I give you just the bare facts.*

*The biological agents were derived from four viruses and one bacterium. They are all based on known pathogens—Ebola, SARS, yellow fever, smallpox, and* Bacillus anthracis, *which causes anthrax—but with many mutations that collectively increase both their contagiousness and lethality, and also render current treatments ineffective. The vectors will be the global parcel delivery services: FedEx, UPS, TNT, and the like. Commercial lists of names and addresses are widely available—this is how you end up receiving catalogs from companies that you have never heard of. Tens of thousands of parcels will simultaneously be sent around the world, each with a free 'introductory' gift inside, suitable to the interests of the recipient. These presents will also contain minute amounts of pathogens in nurturing media—like minuscule Petri dishes, too small to be noticeable—that will preserve them until they reach their new hosts.*

*Five distinct new epidemics, arising all over the world, all at once. No prophylaxis; no cure. The global medical system will be overwhelmed within a week.*

*Vaccines were developed alongside the pathogens. It would take years for these to be developed again from the start, too late to make a difference. Everyone on board the SS* United States *has received the combined shot—Dr. Aran inoculated you in London, many months ago. One reason to send you all so far into the South Seas was to keep the ship away from civilization, in case there was an attempt to distribute the vaccine. By the time you read this letter it will be too late, and the choice has been taken out of your hands.*

*The mortality rate will be close to 100%—it will be an extinction event. The global population will fall far below the 500 million that it was in 1649, probably to just some thousands of survivors, frightened and alone. But the air will no longer be polluted, water will no longer be poisoned, rain will no longer be acidified, ozone will no longer be depleted—the fields will lie fallow, the forests will grow, the oceans will cool, the aquifers will replenish, the ice-caps will recover, the weather will stabilize, the planet will survive.*

*Which brings us to the ultimate fate of that pernicious and brilliant species,* Homo sapiens. *I did not unleash the Apocalypse without first ensuring civilization's survival: what better way to do this than gather the best and brightest young minds onto a ship, completely self-contained and with an inexhaustible fuel supply? Better yet, configured as a floating university, so as to ensure that as far as possible the collective knowledge gained by mankind over painful millennia of human existence is not lost, and that a new Dark Age has not been brought forth.*

*Who gets a second chance? Is this not everyone's secret dream, an opportunity to do it all again from the beginning, but knowing what they now know—imagining being returned to youth, but with the wisdom of age. This is what I am offering the human race: the ultimate dream: a second chance at existence.*

*I have bandied about the term 'forever' a little too freely here. Nature abhors not a vacuum, but immutability. Biological processes can be made resilient, but not unchangeable—in short, I am aging. I first noticed this thirty years ago, just a few signs to start with, but unmistakable: given that I had stared at precisely the same reflection when shaving every morning for centuries, even the slightest change was obvious. I would guess that biologically I am now in my mid-thirties, not the ageless twenty-five that I had always been. I expect that this process will accelerate, hence the need to act.*

*Which brings me to you.*

*I see from your Oxford faculty documentation that you state your birthday as March 26—I presume that when those nuns plucked you from their chapel altar they called the authorities and a medical examination was made, which would have included an assessment of your age—about a week—and so a birth certificate was issued with a best guess as to date. They guessed incorrectly: it was March 25.*

*You were born of a woman, but she was not your mother. You have no mother, nor father either. Your* DNA *was created in a lab, by me.*

*A critical technique that the scientific community has not yet achieved—apart from some initial experiments with yeast—is building* DNA *from scratch. 'Genetic Engineering' in current scientific parlance means getting a piece of existing* DNA*, and then editing it. This is why such a fuss, including a Nobel, was made for* CRISPR*-Cas9: it enabled more efficient editing. But I have little need for such tools: I have been building* DNA *myself, from scratch, for many years. Again, Franklin was the first: I needed a sample of his* DNA *not to clone—the sample was unclonable, in any case—but to sequence, so that I would know exactly what to build. By the time it came to you, I had the procedure down pat. I threw in what seemed to be best, from whatever source. That includes me: all one thousand, five hundred, and ninety-seven nucleotide clusters that were unique to me are now in your* DNA.

*Have you never wondered at yourself? At why you are so different? So healthy? So serious? So self-contained? At why you seem not to age? I had those two photographic volumes printed*—The Wonders of the Windrush *and* Cavendish House Dishabille—*so that the evidence of your persistent youth (among other things) would be laid plainly before you—did you really not see?*

*This is why the girls take so naturally to you: subconsciously, they perceive you as being one of their own.*

*The violet eyes were a whim. My own dark gray disturbs people, and I chose not to encumber you with them.*

*After you were born, I took your fingerprints as a means of positively identifying you in the future and had you deposited on the convent altar. I left you nothing but a name. You never asked me what name I was first given. According to Colonel Hendrick's note, it was Lancaster, Ishmael Lancaster. It was I, not you, who was given a surname from their place of birth. Your surname comes not from the county in which you were found abandoned; your surname is Lancaster because I so named you. It was printed on a card pinned to your basket.*

*As to your first name, I wanted to ensure that the nuns did not burden you, as I had been burdened, with an Old Testament moniker. I chose Sabrina because it is the Roman name for the River Severn, which rises in the Cambrian Mountains, a little south of Lancaster. Sabrina was the daughter of the legendary King Locrine by his mistress Estrildis. In her fury, Locrine's wife, Guendolen, slew him and had Sabrina thrown into the river, which from that time was called Sabrina. The first verse that I ever read of my guardian Milton's poetry sang of her rescue.*

> The water Nymphs that in the bottom plaid,
> Held up their pearled wrists and took her in,
> Bearing her straight to aged Nereus Hall,
> Who piteous of her woes, rear'd her lank head,
> And gave her to his daughters to imbathe
> In nectar'd lavers strew'd with Asphodil,
> And through the porch and inlet of each sense
> Dropt in Ambrosial Oils till she reviv'd,
> And underwent a quick immortal change
> Made Goddess of the River; still she retains

*There, now you have a family, of sorts: the Devil, and a water nymph. (You do exhibit a fondness for brooks and streams, I have observed.)*

*It was not some sort of cruel experiment, Lancaster. From the moment I discovered that I was not immortal, but merely extremely long-lived, it became clear that I would need a successor: someone biologically capable of an objectivity unmarred by the press of time. I could control genotype, and even phenotype, but what of character—how would I know that the woman you grew into would be fit for the purpose?*

*There was only one way to do so: by ordeal—that is, to make a trial of your life so that you could prove yourself, Arthurian-like, by quest. I therefore conferred upon you every possible disadvantage: no family, no wealth, no connections, no prospects, nothing. All you had was yourself.*

*You overcame everything, and became courageous and true.*

*The time came to initiate contact with you. You were too intelligent not to be suspicious were I suddenly to enter into your life, and so I decided instead to engineer your entry into mine. I cultivated an acquaintance with Justice Scaglietti for that purpose, and I hoped that it would be he who suggested that you might like to teach at the new floating university I was founding.*

*I underestimated him: he saw me for who I was, and divined my true intentions. For such a sharp-minded jurist he was a strangely superstitious man, given to religion and seeing the Devil's hand in everything—he just happened to be right on this occasion. Strange to say, I did not kill him—he died of a heart attack before I could do so. But that turned out, quite serendipitously, to be the perfect introduction: you hunted me down. The rest you know.*

*And so now you see the purpose behind the book you have been writing. It is not an apologia to mankind—I don't give a fig for the opinions of men. That was just a convenient excuse; the actual intention was to pass on the tribal lore, in a tribe of just two. Beating the intellectual bounds of Hell, so to speak. Think of it as an instruction manual.*

*The journey you began when you first walked through that rough green door in the Dean's Garden was not just one of preparation, but also edification and, preposterous as this might sound, purification. It was necessary that when you arrived at this moment you be metaphorically washed and penitent—a mental equivalent of cleansing and anointing, and dressing in simple robes of undyed linen, ready to meet your fate. This meant an undoing of what came before, of the ordinary bounded world, so that you might face the future fully unbridled, open in mind and spirit—forgive the occasional clumsiness in method.*

*I was not totally reckless with the liberties I took with you: there was a doctor at hand during some of the more hazardous passages, particularly where we could not be certain of your reaction to the pharmaceutical cocktails to which you were subjected—he was usually out of sight, but you might remember him from Cavendish House where he was cast as Asclepius—the original doctor, I suppose. (That was the only occasion he saw fit to intervene and, although it turned out that you were not in any difficulty, he gave you a Vitamin B12 shot for good order).*

*So here you are. Shall I characterize you, as you emerge from the Stygian mire into which I have plunged you these past months? A partial list:*

- *Preternatural calm (how matter-of-factly you dealt with my various creatures, conjured into passing existence in that otherworld lying beyond the perception of the dull)*
- *Resolute determination, served rare*
- *Decisiveness (you almost wrong-footed me with the sudden trip to Scotland, although we had intended that you should go there at some stage)*
- *Discrimination—how swiftly you discard the peripheral, and cut to the core*
- *Intensity of concentration—having cut to the core, you bring to bear upon it a focused combination of curiosity, judgment, and intellect: this would have been valuable enough in the practice of law, but will be of the utmost necessity in the great task that now lies before you*
- *Keen supra-conscious perception—intuition, if you prefer*
- *Plain hard work—I wondered at your pointed questions about my identity when returning from Tangier, and it was not until we found your signature on the sign-in sheet at the Pepys Library that I figured it out: you must have gone there for the passenger manifests*
- *Courage (I should have listed this first, of course—without it, all the others are meaningless)*

*There may be some survivors from the global epidemics that I have unleashed, but they will be isolated and unprepared: likely they will quickly die out, either naturally in the course of time or, more likely given that they are human, they will perish in savagery.*

*I have established various outposts around the world, peopled by handfuls of the Elect, inoculated against the storm. The Boleskine House contingent you have already met. Those I resurrected live with people they imagine are their staff in a scattering of locations across the globe—Ravenscroft has the details. But they are all just fail-safes against catastrophe at sea.*

*There is a sealed laboratory on board that has all you will need: the complete apparatus and methodology for creating* DNA *to order, should you choose that route; a highly selective and cryogenically maintained sperm bank if not. (You must not look to the crew: we restricted recruitment to the childless, for the obvious reason that it would be best if those on board had a minimal personal stake in what was to occur, but also because it made it more likely that we would find a genetic impairment of fertility. This was an eligibility requirement, although of course not one that we revealed; in any case, all males on board have microdeletions in the* AFZ *gene of the type associated with infertility: humanity's second opportunity could not be left to chance.)*

*Money has no meaning anymore; the only value is in utility, and in that laboratory is the most valuable utility of all: the ability to create life.*

*The* SS United States *is now the Noah's Ark of human civilization. Ravenscroft will brief those who must be briefed—he is doing so now as you read this letter, if at last he has learned to follow my instructions. You must realize that I have long planned for this moment, and selected accordingly. Dunning will remain the captain of the ship, the Master will continue to manage the girls, and you can be sure that Glamis will act swiftly and decisively against any physical threat that might arise. But they all know who is in charge now: the only one among them with the long view necessary to ensure that, this time around, humanity gets it right.*

*To you, Lancaster, I thus give dominion over humankind.*

*What will you do, I wonder? Your dinner guests from the other evening were some of the finest people from the past: perhaps you will consider gathering them into a privy council to assist your rule. Franklin has firsthand experience in founding a great nation, and I'm sure Rand and Rommel would make formidable advisors. Joyce would be an excellent propaganda minister: he would confuse everyone. And I know that Baker—who possesses a rare combination of keen judgment and kindly disposition, the stuff of a first-rate chief of staff—was hoping you might make Cap d'Antibes your capital (although Temple Slaughter Preceptory is yours, if you can tolerate the English climate).*

*Me, you will never see or hear from again.*

*I must now close. As such things go, Lincoln knew better than Pericles: keep it brief.*

*I would wish you good luck, but we both know that luck is just another superstition. Instead, I return to you the object that you returned to me, the only possession that I have ever truly valued, as a token of my... I find this last sentence is one that I cannot satisfactorily complete.*

*May you end your* narratio diabolicae *better than I close this* donatio dominatum.

*Bronaryre*

Sabrina opens the box. Inside, sitting in black velvet lining shaped to accommodate it, is the Oxford Crown. She removes the coin and holds it close, gently rubbing the thing while trying to calm her whirling emotions.

She must clear her mind. She composes herself, and then rereads the letter, this time more soberly and technically, in the way that a well-trained lawyer would when reviewing an opposing witness's deposition: closely, critically, and checking the facts. She researches the more obscure references, to be certain that she has the meaning clear.

Finally, she puts the letter aside. She needs to order her thoughts, and takes up her journal to do so.

> *"This is why such a fuss…was made for CRISPR-Cas9: it enabled more efficient editing."*

*CRISPR stands for 'Clustered Regularly Interspaced Short Palindromic Repeats,' which are used to efficiently identify the location for a DNA edit. Cas9, 'CRISPR-associated protein 9,' is the enzyme used to perform the cut.*

> *"all one thousand, five hundred and ninety-seven nucleotide clusters that were unique to me"*

*1,597 is the seventeenth number in the Fibonacci sequence (starting with zero), and the ninth that is prime. Is he just making this up?*

> *"By the way, you never asked me what name I was born with. It was Lancaster, Ishmael Lancaster"*

*An echo of "Call me Ishmael," the famous first line from Melville's* Moby Dick*? (with Bronaryre as the obsessed-to-madness Ahab?)*

> *"I took your fingerprints as a means of positively identifying you in the future"*

*This must have been why there was an electronic handprint reader in the lobby of Bronaryre's building in New York.*

> *"Sabrina was the daughter of the legendary King Locrine by his mistress Estrildis. In her fury Locrine's wife, Guendolen, slew him and had Sabrina thrown into the river"*

*The tale is recounted by Geoffrey of Monmouth, the Twelfth-Century popularizer of the Arthurian legend. (Bronaryre uses the term 'Arthurian-like' later in the letter: the notion of a great quest was obviously on his mind.)*

> *"The first verse of my guardian Milton's poetry that I ever learned sang of her rescue"*

*A rare case of imprecision by the Devil: the passage he quotes is not from a poem, but from a masque he (Milton) wrote when just 26 years of age, and performed for Lord Bracly at Ludlow Castle on Michaelmas, 1634. The masque is untitled, but is commonly referred to as 'Comus,' from the name of the seducer and necromancer who deceives the main character, lures her into his pleasure palace, and tests her virtue—presumably a deliberate parallel to what Bronaryre has done with me.*

> *"And gave her to his daughters to imbathe*
> *In nectar'd lavers strew'd with Asphodil,"*

*The flower Asphodil, or Asphodel, is associated in mythology with Persephone, abducted by Hades into the underworld where, according to Homer, it grows in the haunt of the dead. Again a clear parallel: I saw this flower in the Long Garden, after my own descent into the cellar of Temple Slaughter Preceptory.*

> *"I must now close. As such things go, Lincoln knew better than Pericles: keep it brief."*

*Presumably, Bronaryre is comparing Lincoln's 'Gettysburg Address,' just 271 words long, with Pericles' 'Funeral Oration,' which, in the original Greek as related by Thucydides, is 1,908 words long. Both were delivered at mass burials for victims of a great war that was still in progress—the American Civil War between the states and the Peloponnesian War between Athens and Sparta—and both were articulations, after staggering losses, of the larger purpose for which the war was being waged. Bronaryre apparently sees his letter to me as serving a similar purpose: certainly, if what he writes is to be believed, the losses have been stunning. At around 5,000 words, his* donatio dominus—*gift of sovereignty—far exceeds both Lincoln and Pericles.* Narratio diabolicae—*demonic tale—is meant to be the apologia, I think, but it could also refer to the larger project: i.e., the rejuvenation of humankind.*

> *"Who is it who, when given the choice between a natural span and immortality, will in the interests of the greater good put up their hands and say, 'Not me.'?"*

*This might be why Bronaryre introduced me to 'Boyle's Wish List' of twenty-four things that could one day be made possible through science—he is saying that if even so thoughtful and selfless a man as Boyle, who turned his back on wealth in the pursuit of knowledge, would put 'The Prolongation of Life' at the top of the list, then what hope is there that the unthinking masses would accept foregoing it?*

*Now I know what Bronaryre meant by his obscure remark to Colonel Swinton that his pheasant were poised to 'inherit the earth': the animal kingdom will no doubt make a comeback, with the chief predator now eliminated.*

*The predisposition for mechanical things was not just an aesthetic choice: the E-Type, the Breguet, the fountain pen, the Frodsham chronometers—Bronaryre was preparing for a post-electronic, post-disposable era: a world without batteries and without silicon chips; a world in which when things fail they are not replaced but repaired.*

*The sextant, too: he was readying for a future when navigation by satnav would no longer be possible. And pen and paper: no more electronic communication.*

*What were the 'among other things' that I was meant to see in those photographs? The 'desire to know'?—or perhaps the desire to desire, without restraint (insatiate).*

*Also explained is the no-expense-spared attitude: money is soon to be—probably already is—worthless: this is why he had characterized the Caiaphas endowment as easy generosity.*

*Ravenscroft's strange insistence on the wharf in Philadelphia about going back to the beginning: so he had known even then that his client's real intention with the* United States *was to use it as a modern-day Noah's Ark.*

*On the whole, the letter feels less diabolical than soteriological: the theme is not so much damnation as salvation. I think Bronaryre is confusing identities: he is not Mephistophelian here; he is Messianic. Maybe he was suggesting this from the very first moment I met him when, to allow me to secure his cuff links, he assumed the posture of the crucified Christ. And perhaps again in the Ptolemaic hieroglyph, with himself cast at Ptolemy Soter—'Savior.'*

*Bronaryre said that I would understand it all, and I think that now perhaps I do. In the end the whole thing was simple: it was an invocation of the Doctrine of Necessity on a monumental scale. Bronaryre has committed the second greatest crime possible—the destruction of humanity—in order to prevent the greatest crime possible—the destruction of the entire planet, and every living thing on it.*

*It is exactly as Bronaryre warned me: for him, the end always justifies the means.*

Sabrina's phone, set to recharge in the expectation that service would soon be restored with the arrival of the spare relay, suddenly makes a sound, a tone indicating that a new text has been received—its first activity in months. The message is from Wilkins, an old one sent soon after they had sailed, and now at last delivered, presumably by an orbiting satellite unaffected by the affairs of earthbound men. The text is short and to the point:

*We analyzed your* DNA. *Who are you? What are you?*

Sabrina puts away the phone and closes her journal. She washes her face and brushes her hair. Her eyes are still puffy and red, but she must face the future and leaves her stateroom.

It is dusk; she must have spent many hours with Bronaryre's letter. She goes up to the signals deck, intending to get some fresh air before conferring with the others, but as she climbs the last ladderway she finds that it is already occupied by three people: Captain Dunning, Professor Pearson, Captain Glamis—they must have chosen it as the best place to talk with no chance of being overheard.

It is evident that Ravenscroft has delivered his news. They stand facing her in silence, and she wonders what has stunned them more: the wiping out of the human race, or to have learned that she is all but immortal. Glamis is the first to speak.

"So the Devil exists, and he's an eco-terrorist."

"So it would seem."

Dunning clears his throat.

"At the moment we are steaming slow ahead in lazy eights, basically maintaining our position here until we have a destination."

The captain's eyes are on Sabrina, and it is clear that he is not making a statement but asking a question.

"Hawaii," she says. "The Big Isle. We can resupply there: there'll be food in the fields and plantations, even if…" But Dunning is already nodding in understanding, without requiring her to complete the sentence. "Plus there are the observatories on Mauna Kea: they might have telecommunications equipment that we can use. Most satellites should still be operational; maybe we can connect with them and survey the state of the planet without having to circumnavigate it."

"I'll see to it now." Dunning leaves for the bridge, touching his cap in salute.

"And the girls?" Pearson asks.

"They must be told. We should have a general assembly first thing tomorrow, right after breakfast."

"And to which unfortunate soul does the duty of telling them fall?"

"I'll do it."

"I can't say that I'm not relieved. I'm not sure that I could get through it myself." Pearson is the most shaken; perhaps the others are still in shock; she excuses herself, leaving Sabrina alone with Glamis.

Glamis is less unsettled than the other two, a loner by nature and inured to adversity by training.

"We'll need to do a threat assessment. Aerial survey, as soon as we're in range, then a reconnaissance team sent ashore by helicopter before the ship approaches."

"And a plan to help survivors, if we find them."

"Yes, of course," he says, but Sabrina can tell that helping survivors will not be high on his priorities.

He walks over, delivering a soft punch to her shoulder in passing, and goes down the ladder. "Now you can have your wee deck back to yourself," he says before disappearing.

Sabrina takes a seat on a locker and leans back against a flag bin. She pulls from the pocket of her pea jacket Bronaryre's letter and reads it again, this time not in ignorant trepidation, as on the first occasion, nor in forensic exactitude, as on the second, but now in a way she never expected to do with any communication from that reserved and brooding creature.

After reading it for the third time, Sabrina carefully refolds the letter and returns it to her pocket. She finds that her reappraisal has confirmed the thought that had been sitting unacknowledged at the back of her mind since first reading the letter, something crowded out at the time by the larger considerations of the enormity of the crime that has been committed, and the tumultuous task that now lies ahead. What she finds astonishes her: it is the realization that she is loved.

She moves to the forward railing and leans on it while gazing out thoughtfully at the sea ahead. Above her the Explorers Club flag flaps loudly, a sign that the breeze has picked up: Dunning must have already increased speed. From the fading sunlight to her left she can tell that they are now heading north, toward the Hawaiian Islands.

Sabrina has never been loved before, not genuinely loved. Some of the nuns had held a maternal affection for her, and more lately there had been any number of hormonal young men all cow-eyed, even to the point of declaring their undying devotion, on such a slender basis as to have made her wonder if they were quite sane, but she has never mistaken these as anything other than passing fancies, full of hot air.

This, however, is the real thing.

Loved she may be, but the nature of it eludes her.

Not parental love, despite the fact that much of her DNA, and probably most of the interesting parts, are hers and Bronaryre's alone. Nor is it romantic love: Bronaryre is certainly a Romantic figure, but there is nothing of the small-*r* romantic about him: he is too singular for something so trite, so commonplace. Nor is it a meeting of minds: she might have graduated *summa cum laude*, but intellectually she knows that he crushes her.

In the absence of anything better, she decides to label it *strange love* for now.

Sabrina considers their new destination. The reasons she gave the others for choosing the Big Isle were true enough, but far from complete. She believes that she will find Bronaryre there.

The first clue came back when the voyage began: she had tried to find the Frodsham chronometers in those initial days at sea, knowing that they would need rewinding and anxious to ensure that they were being properly attended to in Bronaryre's absence, but neither Dunning nor the navigation officer knew anything about them. Then there were the sextants: all ten are stored not in wooden boxes but in plastic cases molded to fit them, and they are modern versions made of gray-enameled metal, not the black-powdered brass of Bronaryre's instrument. She had assumed that, since there was no evidence of his sextant in the chartroom, it must instead have been stowed in what would be Bronaryre's private quarters. But as the weeks passed and she became more familiar with the ship, Sabrina realized that there were no such quarters: all of the staterooms were taken, and the palatial owner's suite that she had imagined must be located somewhere did not exist.

Bronaryre never intended to join the *United States*. He must therefore have had another use for his chronometers and sextant, and what could that be but to navigate a vessel of his own. A sailing yacht, she assumes: no one could be certain about fuel anymore, but the wind is always available. And why would Bronaryre need a yacht, unless he intended to take refuge on an island? He had once told her that, among his residences around the world, he had a place on the Big Isle, and it does not escape her that the Big Isle is a *paradise* complete with an active *volcano*—that twin allusion to Milton and Dante would surely have appealed to Bronaryre.

Now that the ship has gathered way the big bow has begun plowing into the waves, sending occasional sprays of seawater sweeping across the fo'c'sle, and suddenly a large one gusts up as far as the flag deck, flecking her with briny spindrift. The feel of it rouses Sabrina from her reverie.

## A Revelation and a Requiem

SABRINA RETURNS TO HER STATEROOM and opens the library's digital catalog. She pulls up a publication that she has never before consulted without compulsion, and never at all in adulthood: the Bible. But this is a very specific Bible: an exact facsimile of the Bodleian's rare first edition of Taverner's 1539 translation, Bronaryre's favored version.

She opens the Taverner to the Book of Revelation, and the initial section upon which her eyes fall seems to be a very strange verse to find in so patriarchal a work:

> *And to the woman were gyven two wynges of a great egle, that she myght flee into the wyldernes, in to her place, where she is nourysshed for a tyme, tymes, and halfe a tyme, from the presence of the serpent.*

Sabrina spends a few moments reflecting on this enigmatic passage that she has incidentally happened upon—surely opposite in sense to the intended meaning: the Bible would hardly countenance a 'nourishing' Satan. She pulls up the authorized King James Version and comparing the verse finds that the translation is handled differently in the later work, making it clear that it is not Satan doing the nourishing—no wonder Bronaryre prefers the Taverner. Sabrina supposes that perhaps she too has been nourished for a time (and times, and half a time; perhaps nine times in all)—certainly she is no longer the same person that she was, or believed herself to be, when first encountering the Serpent, slithering about in his fashionable Manhattan lair.

It is nine months since she met Bronaryre, Sabrina calculates—another nine: the usual period of human gestation, although she has been reborn in a way that no Bible-reader would ever condone. Under this Satan's tutelage she has undergone a metamorphosis—and, however bizarre the process, can she resent something to which she has admitted becoming addicted?

She has been transfigured. Ought she to be grateful?—she cannot say.

Sabrina returns to the Taverner and soon locates the verse she sought, the one beginning with that strange and emphatic statement from the 'Sancta Civitas' oratorio:

*And I saw an angel standing in the sun.*

She reads through to the end of the chapter. The Gothic lettering is hard to decipher, and made more difficult still by the many alphabetic curiosities—the indiscriminate suffixing of an *e*, the frequent substitution of *y* for *i*, and, especially confusing, sometimes *f* for *s*, despite there also being a normal *s*-character, so that the *flesh of horses* is rendered as *fleffhe of horfes*. But there is no mistaking the particular item that she somehow knew she would find in this brief passage: the supreme fate of Satan. *The beeft was taken* according to the Taverner, and *caste in to a ponde of fyre burnyng with brymftone*.

Sabrina sits back in thought.

She knows what that *strange love* is now, at least in part: it is the same peculiar relationship that Bronaryre had witnessed as a young child when watching Charles on the gallows, quietly conversing. It is the peculiar bond, quite brief but intensely intimate, that exists between a man and his executioner.

This is why Bronaryre chose Hawaii, she realizes, with its active volcanoes providing plentiful ponds of burning fire. He knows that she will figure it out eventually. He is probably already there, patiently waiting for her to show up. He knows that she will find him in the end, and then—like the avenging Furies of the mythological past—she will inflict upon him the fate that he must recognize is his undeniable due, and ultimate destiny.

## *Typographical Note*

*The fleuron used for section demarcation on pages 116, 225, 320, 445, 493 & 511 (& for convenience shown again here, enlarged) is taken from the arabesque border on the first page of the First Edition of Milton's 'Paradise Lost' (1667), printed by Samuel Simmons, whose place of business was listed as 'next door to the Golden Lion in Aldersgate Street.'*

*Not much is known about Simmons. He was likely a son or relative of Matthew Simmons, who had been an official printer for Cromwell's Government, someone with whom Milton would have dealt in his role of Secretary of Foreign Tongues, and who in 1649 had printed Milton's* Eikonoklastes.

*According to David Masson's foreword to an 1877 facsimile reproduction of the First Edition, Samuel produced "a very carefully printed book. It may rank, I think, as the best-looking book of Milton's printed in his life-time—superior both in compositor's work and in press-work to any of his pamphlets, and certainly superior to any other volume of his in verse form."*

Lightning Source UK Ltd.
Milton Keynes UK
UKHW010322080223
416649UK00015B/618/J